BY THE SAME AUTHOR.

(Leisure-Hour Series.)

JOSEPH NOIREL'S REVENGE. Translated by WM. F. WEST, A.M.

COUNT KOSTIA. Translated by O. D. ASHLEY.

PROSPER RANDOCE. Translated by CARL BENSON. *(In preparation.)*

LEISURE HOUR SERIES.

COUNT KOSTIA

A NOVEL

Translated from the French

OF

VICTOR CHERBULIEZ

BY

O. D. ASHLEY

NEW YORK
HOLT & WILLIAMS
1873

Poole & Maclauchlan,
printers and bookbinders,
205–213 *East 12th St., New York.*

COUNT KOSTIA.

CHAPTER I.

At the beginning of the summer of 1850 a Russian nobleman, Count Kostia Petrovitch Leminof, had the misfortune to lose his wife suddenly, and in the flower of her beauty. She was his junior by twelve years. This cruel loss, for which he was totally unprepared, threw him into a state of profound melancholy; and some months later, seeking to mitigate his grief by the distractions of travel, he left his domains near Moscow, never intending to return. Accompanied by his twin children, ten years of age, a priest who had served them as tutor and a serf named Ivan, he repaired to Odessa, and then took passage on a merchant ship for Martinique. Disembarking at St. Pierre, he took lodgings in a remote part of the suburbs. The profound solitude which reigned there did not at first bring the consolation he had sought. It was not enough that he had left his native country, he would have changed the planet itself; and he complained that nature everywhere was too much alike. No locality seemed to him sufficiently a stranger to his experience, and in the deserted places, where the desperate restlessness of his heart impelled him, he imagined the reappearance of the obtrusive witnesses of his past joys, and of the misfortune by which they were suddenly terminated.

He had lived a year in Martinique when the yellow fever carried off one of his children. By a singular reaction in his vigorous temperament, it was about this time that his sombre melancholy gave way to a bitter and sarcastic gayety, more in harmony with his nature. From his early youth he had had a taste for jocularity, a mocking turn of spirit, seasoned by that ironical grace of manner peculiar to the great Moscovite nobleman, and resulting from the constant habit of trifling with men and events. His recovery did not, however, restore the agreeable manners which in former times had distinguished him in his intercourse with the world. Suffering had brought him a leaven of misanthropy, which he did not take the trouble of disguising; his voice had lost its caressing notes and had become rude and abrupt; his actions were brusque, and his smile scornful. Sometimes his bearing gave evidence of a haughty will which, tyrannized over by events, sought to avenge itself upon mankind.

Terrible, however, as he sometimes was to those who surrounded him, Count Kostia was yet a civilized devil. So, after a stay of three years under tropical skies, he began to sigh for old Europe, and one fine day saw him disembark upon the quays of Lisbon. He crossed Portugal, Spain, the south of France and Switzerland. At Basle, he learned that on the borders of the Rhine, between Coblentz and Bonn, in a situation quite isolated, an old castle was for sale. To this place he hurried and bought the antique walls and the lands which belonged to them, without discussing the price and without making a detailed examination of the property. The bargain concluded, he made some hasty and indispensable repairs on one of the buildings which composed a part of his dilapidated manor, and which claimed the imposing name of the fortress of Geierfels, and at once installed himself therein, hoping to pass the rest of his life in peaceable and studious seclusion.

Count Kostia was gifted with a quick and ready intellect, which he had strengthened by study. He had always been passionately fond of historical research, but above everything, he knew and wished to know, only that which the English call "the matter of fact." He professed a cold scorn for generalities, and heartily abandoned them to "dreamers;" he laughed at all abstract theories and at the ingenuous minds which take them seriously. He held that all system was but logical infatuation; that the only pardonable follies were those which were frankly avowed; and that only a pedant could clothe his imagination in geometrical theories. In general, pedantry to his eyes was the least excusable of vices; he understood it to be the pretension of tracing back phenomena to first causes, "as if," said he, "there were any 'first causes,' or chance admitted of calculation!" This did not prevent him however from expending much logic to demonstrate that there was no such thing as logic, either in nature or in man.

These are inconsistencies, for which skeptics never dream of reproaching themselves; they pass their lives in reasoning against reason. In short, Count Kostia respected nothing but facts, and believed that, properly viewed, there was nothing else, and that the universe, considered as an entirety, was but a collection of contradictory accidents.

A member of the Historical and Antiquarian Society of Moscow, he had once published important memoirs upon Sclavonic antiquities and upon some of the disputed questions in the history of the Lower Empire. Hardly was he installed at Geierfels, before he occupied himself in fitting up his library, but a few volumes of which he had carried to Martinique. He at once ordered from Moscow most of the books he had left, and also sent large orders to German bookstores. When his "seraglio," as he called it, was nearly complete, he again became absorbed in study, and particularly in that of the Greek historians of the Byzantine Empire, of whose collective works he had the good fortune to possess the

Louvre edition in thirty-six volumes folio; and he soon formed the ambitious project of writing a complete history of that Empire from Constantine the Great to the taking of Constantinople. So absorbed did he become in this great design, that he scarcely ate or drank; but the further he advanced in his researches the more he became dismayed by the magnitude of the enterprise, and he conceived the idea of procuring an intelligent assistant, upon whom he could shift a part of the task. As he proposed to write his voluminous work in French, it was in France this living instrument which he needed must be sought, and he therefore broached the project to Dr. Lerins, one of his old acquaintances in Paris. "For nearly three years," he wrote to the Doctor, "I have dwelt in a veritable owl's nest, and I should be much obliged to you if you would procure for me a young night bird, who could endure life two or three years in such an ugly hole without dying of *ennui.* Understand me, I must have a secretary who is not contented with writing a fine hand and knowing French a little better than I do: I wish him to be a consummate philologist, and a hellenist of the first order,—one of those men who ought to be met with in Paris,—born to belong to the Institute, but so dependent upon circumstances as to make that position impossible. If you succeed in finding this priceless being, I will give him the best room in my castle and a salary of twelve thousand francs. I stipulate that he shall not be a fool. As to character, I say nothing about it; he will do me the favor to have such as will suit me."

M. Lerins was intimate with a young man from Lorraine named Gilbert Saville, a savant of great merit, who had left Nancy several years before to seek his fortune in Paris. At the age of twenty-seven he had presented, in a competition opened by the Academy of Inscriptions, an essay on the Etruscan language, which took the prize and was unanimously declared a master-piece of sagacious erudition. He had hoped for some time that this first success, which had gained him renown among learned men, would aid him in obtaining some lucrative position and rescue him from the precarious situation in which he found himself. Nothing resulted from it. His merits compelled esteem; the charm of his frank and courteous manner won him universal good will; his friends were numerous; he was well received and caressed; he even obtained, without seeking it, the *entrée* to more than one *salon*, where he met men of standing who could be useful to him and assure him a successful future. All this however amounted to nothing, and no position was offered. What worked most to his prejudice, was an independence of opinion and character which was a part of his nature. Only to look at him was to know that such a man could not be tied down, and the only language which this able philologist could not learn was the jargon of society. Add to this that Gilbert had a speculative, dreamy temperament and the pride and indolence which are its accessories. To bestir himself and to importune were torture to him. A promise made to him could be forgotten with impunity, for he was not the man to revive it; and besides, as he never complained himself, no one was disposed to complain for him. In short, among those who had been desirous of protecting and advancing him, it was said: "what need has he of our assistance? such remarkable talent will make its own way." Others thought, without expressing it: "Let us be guarded, this is another Letronne,—once 'foot in the stirrup,' God only knows where he will stop." Others said and thought: "This young man is charming,—he is so discreet,—not like such and such a person." All those cited as not "discreet," were provided for.

The difficulties of his life had rendered Gilbert serious and reflective, but they had neither hardened his heart nor quenched his imagination. He was too wise to revolt against his fate, but determined to be superior to it. "Thou art all thou canst be," said he to himself; "but do not flatter thyself that thou hast reached the measure of my aspirations."

Gilbert was a singular character. When he had suffered some vexation, some mortification; when he had seen some cherished hope frustrated; when a door nearly opened was rudely closed upon him, he would leave his habitual occupation a few hours and go off to botanize in the environs of Paris. This enabled him to forget everything.

After having read M. Leminof's letter, Dr. Lerins went in search of Gilbert. He described Count Kostia to him according to his remote recollections, but he asked him, before deciding, to weigh the matter deliberately. After quitting his young friend he muttered to himself—

"After all, I hope he will refuse. He would be too much of a prize for that *boyard*. Of his very Muscovite face, I remember only an enormous pair of eyebrows,—the loftiest and bushiest I ever saw, and perhaps there is nothing more of him! There are men who are all in the eyebrows! What a contrast to our dear Gilbert?—that mixture of strength and gentleness, which is his alone; that noble head and expansive forehead; those large blue eyes in which so much kindly curiosity expresses itself; that air of self-possessed gravity, often enlivened by a fresh and youthful smile which harmonizes with his frank look; that voice, pure, clear and musical, which gives a heart accent even to the discussion of things purely intellectual. What could Count Kostia do with all this? I do not deny that he can be amiable and fascinating when he pleases; but the claw is always beneath. Indeed, to give Gilbert to him would be like throwing a pearl between the paws of a leopard."

Thus reasoned Dr. Lerins,—but two hours later Gilbert received a letter which decided him to leave at once for Geierfels. It was addressed to him by one of the guardians of the Imperial library, and announced that a vacant place in the department of manuscripts had just been given to one of his competitors, less deserving than himself, but apparently born under a luckier star. The last lines were as follows: "Do not be discouraged, you have a marshal's staff in your knapsack. A man of your stamp has an assured future."

"They will say that until my dying day," said Gilbert to himself, shaking his head, and without further delay he ran to M. Lerins. The doctor tried to shake his resolution,—then finding it was trouble wasted, he ended by saying, "My dear Gilbert, as you seem to be decided, permit me to give you a little advice. This grand Muscovite lord, with whom you are going to live socially in a savage retreat, I have the honor of being acquainted with, and I think I know him by heart. I beg of you not to be captivated by the graces of his mind, or by the fascination of his manners, and for God's sake don't grow to love this man; don't give him an hundred thousandth part of your heart; it would only be so much thrown away, and afterwards you would have the mortification of finding that you had been duped. In this connection, you may justly say, that if he gives his secretary a salary of twelve thousand francs, it is because he expects a great deal of him. It will be an 'eye for an eye, a tooth for a tooth;' besides, you remember this passage from his letter: 'I will trust that the young night bird will do me the favor of having such a character as will suit me.' So, Count Kostia will demand of you twelve thousand francs' worth of self-abnegation. Are you well stocked? That amount must be on hand! For Heaven's sake be consistent, and having accepted the contract, don't dispute with the hope of getting an abatement. Such quibblings would amount to nothing, and your dignity would suffer. Such is my second piece of advice; and now for the third, for it is always well to put method into one's reasoning. This gracious *boyard* has renounced all faith; he is the king of skeptics, and I assure you that Russian skepticism attains most incredible dimensions. This man has no belief, and I even doubt if he has opinions. Do not let him suspect your enthusiastic disposition. He would but trifle with it. I can almost see him now pouncing upon such a prey with his wildcat claws. Let your heart feign death, my dear Gilbert, or look out for the blows of those claws. And in spite of all you say, I know that heart of yours is a sensitive plant that can't stand much."

"And now in my turn," said Madame Lerins, who had just come in in time to participate in the conversation, "my dear sir, listen to me attentively. M. Lerins imagines that Geierfels is a desert, but I don't believe anything of the kind. When M. Leminof was here, he voluntarily went into the world. I do not put much faith in his taste for seclusion. You will find that they have balls there, fêtes, riding parties, Polish ladies with their pensive airs, theatrical princesses, Muscovite beauties, white roses, necklaces, plumed hats, diamonds, adventurers, *billets doux*, songs to the guitar, and what not. My poor philosopher, what will become of you in this whirlwind? I fear that your head will be turned, and this is my advice, which is very good if not divided into three heads, like M. Lerins' sermon. Do not, my dear sir, commit the folly of throwing your heart to the world;—the world is a badly trained dog, it will not bring back the game."

"It is always so with women," cried M. Lerins shrugging his shoulders. "Their advice never has any common sense in it. Madame Lerins reasons like that admirable mother, whose son was leaving for the mines, and who placed in his trunk a prescription against sunstroke."

Gilbert could not help feeling that he had too

much advice, and that Boileau hardly spoke from experience when he said,

"Love to be counselled and not to be praised."

"If some Muscovite beauty breaks my heart," he laughingly replied to Madame Lerins, "I will carefully gather up the pieces and bring them to you. You can join them together and make me a heart almost as good as ever."

A week later he was on his way to Geierfels.

CHAPTER II.

At Cologne Gilbert embarked on board a steamboat to go up the Rhine ten or twelve leagues beyond Bonn. Towards evening, a thick fog settled down upon the river and its banks, and it became necessary to anchor during the night. This mischance rendered Gilbert melancholy, finding in it, as he did, an image of his life. He too had a current to stem, and more than once a sad and sombre fog had fallen and obscured his course.

In the morning the weather cleared; they weighed anchor, and at two o'clock in the afternoon, Gilbert disembarked at a station two leagues from Geierfels. He was in no haste to arrive, and even though "born with a ready-made consolation for anything," as Mr. Lerins sometimes reproachfully said to him, he dreaded the moment when his prison doors should close behind him, and he was disposed to enjoy yet a few hours of his dear liberty. "We are about to part," said he to himself; "let us at least take time to say farewell."

Instead of hiring a carriage to transport himself and his effects, he consigned his trunk to a porter, who engaged to forward it to him the next day, and took his way on foot, carrying under his arm a little valise, and promising himself not to hurry. An hour later he quitted the main road, and stopped to refresh himself at an humble inn situated upon a hillock covered with pine trees. Dinner was served to him under an arbor,—his repast consisted of a slice of smoked ham and an *omelette au cerfeuil*, which he washed down with a little good claret. This feast *à la Jean Jacques*, appeared to him delicious, flavored as it was by that "freedom of the inn" which was dearer to the author of the *Confessions* than even the freedom of the press.

When he had finished eating, Gilbert ordered a cup of coffee, or rather of that black beverage called coffee in Germany. He was hardly able to drink it, and he remembered with longing the delicious Mocha prepared by the hands of Madame Lerins; and this set him thinking of that amiable woman and her husband.

"It is singular," said he to himself, "that those excellent people love me so much and know me so little. All the advice which they gave me the other day was addressed to a Gilbert of their own imagination. They don't know how very rational I am. At moments it seems to me that I have already lived one life, so easily does my mind adapt itself to the exigencies of new situations."

Gilbert soon forgot Paris and Madame Lerins, and fell into a vague revery. It was one of the earliest days of May, and the trees had commenced putting on the green livery of spring. It was that sweet and solemn moment when the earth wakes from her long sleep; she gazes about her with languishing glances; through the shadows which still veil her eyes she catches confused glimpses of the sun, and recognizes in it that adored phantom of which she dreamed while sleeping; a joyous madness seizes her, and the life which gushes out of her bosom flows in waves of sap into the growing stems of flowers, and the knotty trunks of rejuvenated trees. And this sap of spring mounted also to Gilbert's heart. He was stupefied and depressed by it. A caressing breeze came like a sigh through the growing foliage of a neighboring chestnut, and a bird began to sing. It seemed to Gilbert that the song and the sigh came from the depths of his own being. In revery the heart, like an echo, repeats the great music of the universe; it becomes like the sea-shells which, when held to the ear, breathe into it the confused but majestic murmur of the ocean.

But Gilbert's revery soon took another turn. From the bank where he was sitting, he saw the Rhine, the tow-path which wound along by the side of its grayish waters, and nearer to him the great white road where, at intervals, heavy wagons and post-chaises raised clouds of dust. This dusty road soon absorbed all of his attention. It seemed to him as if it cast tender glances upon him, as if it called him and said: "Follow me; we will go together to distant countries; we will keep the same step night and day and never weary; we will traverse rivers and mountains, and every morning we will have a new horizon. Come, I wait for thee, give me thy heart. I am the faithful friend of vagabonds, I am the divine mistress of those bold and strong hearts which look upon life as an adventure."

Gilbert was not the man to dream long. He became himself again, rose to his feet, and shook off the vision. "Up to this hour I thought myself rational; but it appears I am so no longer. Forward, then,—courage, let us take our staff and on to Geierfels!"

As he entered the kitchen of the inn to pay his bill, he found the landlord there busy in bathing a child's face from which the blood streamed profusely. During this operation, the child cried, and the landlord swore. At this moment his wife came in.

"What has happened to Wilhelm?" she asked.

"What has happened?" replied he angrily. "It

happened that when Monsieur Stephane was riding on horseback on the road by the mill, this child walked before him with his pigs. Monsieur Stephane's horse snorted, and Monsieur Stephane, who could hardly hold him, said to the child: 'Now then, little idiot, do you think my horse was made to swallow the dust your pigs raise. Draw aside, drive them into the brush, and give me the road.' 'Take to the wood yourself,' answered the child, 'the path is only a few steps off.' At this Monsieur Stephane got angry, and as the child began to laugh, he rushed upon him and cut him in the face with his whip. God-a-mercy! let him come back,—this little master,—and I'll teach him how to behave himself. I mean to tie him to a tree, one of these days, and break a dozen fagots of green sticks over his back."

"Ah! take care what thou sayest, my old Peter," replied his wife with a frightened air. "If thou'dst touch the little man thou'dst get thyself into a bad business."

"Who is this Monsieur Stephane?" inquired Gilbert."

The landlord, recalled to prudence by the warning of his wife, answered dryly: "Stephane is Stephane, pryers are pryers, and sheep are put into the world to be sheared."

Thus repulsed, poor Gilbert paid five or six times its value for his frugal repast, muttering as he departed: "I don't like this Stephane; is it on his account that I've just been imposed upon? Is it my fault that he carries matters with such a high hand?"

Gilbert descended the little hill, and retook the main road; it pleased him no more, for he knew too well where it was leading him. He inquired how much further it was to Geierfels, and was told that by fast walking he would reach that place within an hour, whereupon he slackened his pace. He was certainly in no haste to get there.

The spring had always been his season of melancholy. When the trees clothed themselves with new foliage, he found it natural that his life too should put on freshness; but he looked on all its branches in vain, he saw no signs of new leaves or blossoms. It appeared to him that his life had a color of dead leaves; but nevertheless the perfume and the sounds of spring welled up from his heart, for in spite of all, that heart remained young. "And yet this is not my heart which is young," he mused as he walked on, "it is my mind. The good doctor took me for a sensitive plant; he little knows how completely I am master of my feelings. And, to tell the truth, I have no trouble in keeping them in check, as they have never assailed me at all dangerously. I shall be thirty next St. Médard, and I do not yet know, except by hearsay, what this folly is which the world calls love. It is a fairy land which I have never entered,—for my love passages at twenty are not worth mentioning, they taught me nothing. I believe, in fact, that nature, in creating me, wanted to avoid expense; she didn't fit me out anew, for I know she has lodged in my breast an old heart, worn out in service. This heart bears the scars of wounds which I never received, and it has vague recollections of passions which I do not remember ever to have felt. In my actual existence I am but an impassioned dreamer. May my spirit preserve its youth forever! Eternal truth! would that my thoughts always had wings to ascend to thee! But then, intellectual ambition is a source of suffering. Life is easy for owls, for space does not invite them; but the eagle desires to rise to the sun: should he fall with glazed eye and broken wing, and his shattered body become the plaything of the sea-foam, for one instant at least, the splendors of the empyrean would have quenched the ardent thirst of his eyes, and his glance would have emptied at a single draught the chalice of celestial light. I, Gilbert, who am not of the fraternity of eagles, have often in the distance followed their aërial flights, and more than once have felt the agonizing voluptuousness of a vertigo. These are the only adventures of my life. Ah! may I never be afraid of such glorious prostration!"

And then he added with exultation: "He alone can boast of having lived who, for one day, has held the truth,—who with pure lips has pressed this holy Eucharist,—who has felt his flesh thrill at the sacred touch, and life divine diffuse itself like a torrent through his burning veins. And yet, even that would not suffice me. I want an opportunity to do something—one single act, into which I could throw my whole soul—an act of which it could be said, 'God was in it!' an act of faith, of devotion, the remembrance of which might spread as a perfume over my life. Will this opportunity ever present itself? Alas! in the matter of heroism, fate seems to condemn me to the average allowance."

While making these reflections, Gilbert pursued his way. He was but half a league from the castle when, upon his right, a little out of his road, he perceived a pretty fountain which partly veiled a natural grotto. A path led to it, and this path had for Gilbert an irresistible attraction. He seated himself upon the margin of the fountain, resting his feet upon a mossy stone. This ought to be his last halt, for night was approaching. Under the influence of the bubbling waters, Gilbert resumed his dreamy soliloquy, but his meditations were presently interrupted by the sound of a horse's feet which clattered over the path. Raising his eyes, he saw coming towards him, mounted upon a large chestnut horse, a young man of about sixteen, whose pale thin face was relieved by an abundance of magnificent bright brown hair, which fell in curls upon his shoulders. He was small but admirably formed, and his features, although noble and regular, awakened in Gilbert more of surprise than sympathy: their expression was hard, sullen and sad, and upon this beautiful face not any of the graces of youth appeared.

The young cavalier came straight towards him, and when at a step or two from the fountain, he called out in German, with an imperious voice: "My horse is thirsty,—make room for me my good man!"

Gilbert did not stir.

"You take a very lofty tone my little friend," replied he in the same language, which he understood very well, but pronounced like the devil,—I mean like a Frenchman.

"My tall friend, how much do you charge for your lessons in etiquette?" answered the young man in the same language, imitating Gilbert's pronunciation. Then he added in French, with irreproachable purity of accent: "Come, I can't wait, move quicker," and he began cutting the air with his riding-whip.

"M. Stephane," said Gilbert, who had not forgotten the adventure of the little Wilhelm, "your whip will get you into trouble some of these days."

"Who gave you the right to know my name?" cried the young man, raising his head haughtily.

"The name is already notorious through the country," retorted Gilbert, "and you have written it in very legible characters upon the cheek of a little pig driver."

Stephane, for it was he, reddened with anger and raised his whip with a threatening air; but with a blow of his stick Gilbert sent it flying into the bottom of a ditch, twenty paces distant.

When he looked at the young man again, he repented of what he had done, for his expression was terrible to behold; his pallor became livid; all the muscles of his face contracted, and his body was agitated by convulsive movements; in vain he tried to speak, his voice died upon his lips, and reason seemed deserting him. He tore off one of his gloves, and tried to throw it in Gilbert's face, but it fell from his trembling hand. For an instant he looked with a scornful and reproachful glance at that slender hand whose weakness he cursed; then tears gushed in abundance from his eyes, he hung his head over the neck of his horse, and in a choking voice murmured:

"For the love of God, if you do not wish me to die of rage, give me back,—give me back—"

"He could not finish; but Gilbert had already run to the ditch, and having picked up the riding-whip, as well as the glove, returned them to him. Stephane, without looking at him, answered by a slight inclination of the head, but kept his eyes fixed upon the pommel of his saddle,—evidently striving to recover his self-possession. Gilbert pitying his state of mind, turned to leave; but at the moment he stooped to pick up his portmanteau and cane, the youth, with a well directed blow of his whip, struck off his hat, which rolled into the ditch, and when Gilbert, surprised and indignant, was about to throw himself upon the young traitor, he had already pushed his horse to a full gallop, and in the twinkling of an eye he reached the main road where he disappeared in a whirlwind of dust. Gilbert was much more affected by this adventure than his philosophy should have permitted. He took up his journey again with a feeling of depression, and haunted by the pale distorted face of the youth. "This excess of despair," said he to himself, "indicates a proud and passionate character; but the perfidy with which he repaid my generosity is the offspring of a soul ignoble and depraved." And striking his forehead he continued: "It just occurred to me, judging from his name, that this young man may be Count Kostia's son. Ah! what an amiable companion I shall have to cheer my captivity! M. Leminof ought to have forewarned me. It was an article which should have been included in the contract."

Gilbert felt his heart sink; he saw himself already condemned to defend his dignity incessantly against the caprices and insolence of a badly trained child, —the prospect was not attractive! Plunged in these melancholy reflections, he lost his way, having passed the place where he should have quitted the main road to ascend the steep hill of which the castle formed the crown. By good luck, he met a peasant who put him again upon the right track. The night had already fallen when he entered the court of the vast building. This great assemblage of incongruous structures appeared to him but a sombre mass whose weight was crushing him. He could only distinguish one or two projecting towers whose pointed roofs stood out in profile against the starlit sky. While seeking to make out his position, several huge dogs rushed upon him, and would have torn him to pieces if, at the noise of their barking, a tall stiff valet had not made his appearance with a lantern in hand. Gilbert having given him his name, was requested to follow him. They crossed a terrace, forced to turn aside at every step by the dogs who growled fiercely,—apparently regretting 'these amiable hosts' the supper of which they had been deprived. Following his guide Gilbert found himself upon a little winding staircase, which they ascended to the third story, where the valet, opening an arched door, introduced him into a large circular apartment where a bed with a canopy had been prepared. "This is your room," said he curtly, and having lighted two candles and placed them upon the round table, he left the room, and did not return for half an hour, when he re-appeared bearing a tray laden with a *samovar*, a venison pie and some cold fowl. Gilbert ate with a good appetite and felt great satisfaction in finding that he had any at all. "My foolish reveries," thought he, "have not spoiled my stomach at least."

Gilbert was still at the table when the valet re-entered and handed him a note from the Count, which ran thus:

"M. Leminof bids M. Gilbert Saville welcome. He will give himself the pleasure of calling upon him to-morrow morning."

"To-morrow we shall commence the serious business of life," said Gilbert to himself, as he enjoyed a cup of exquisite green tea, "and I'm very glad of it, for I don't approve of the use I make of my leisure. I have passed all this day reasoning upon myself, dissecting my mind and heart,—a most foolish pastime, beyond a doubt"—then drawing from his pocket a note book, he wrote therein these words: "Forget thyself, forget thyself, forget thyself," imitating the philosopher Kant, who being inconsolable at the loss of an old servant named Lamp, wrote in his journal: "Remember to forget Lamp."

He remained some moments standing in the embrasure of the window gazing upon the celestial vault which shone with a thousand fires, and then threw himself upon his bed. His sleep was not tranquil; Stephane appeared to him in his dreams, and at one time he thought he saw him kneeling before him, his face bathed in tears; but when he approached to console him, the child drew a poignard from his bosom and stabbed him to the heart.

Gilbert awakened with a start, and had some difficulty in getting to sleep again.

CHAPTER III.

A GREAT pleasure was in store for Gilbert at his awakening; he rose as the sun began to appear, and having dressed, hastened to the window to see what view it offered.

The rotunda which had been assigned to him for a lodging formed the entire upper story of a turret which flanked one of the angles of the castle. This turret, and a great square tower situated at the other extremity of the same front, commanded a view of the north, and from this side the rock descended perpendicularly, forming an imposing precipice of three hundred feet. When Gilbert's first glance plunged into the abyss where a bluish vapor floated, which the rising sun pierced with its golden arrows, the spectacle transported him. To have a precipice under his window, was a novelty which gave him infinite joy. The precipice was his domain, his property, and his eyes took possession of it. He could not cease gazing at the steep, wall-like rocks, the sides of which were cut by transverse belts of brush-wood and dwarf trees. It was long since he had experienced such a lively sensation, and he felt that if his heart was old, his senses were entirely new. The fact is that at this moment, Gilbert, the grave philosopher, was as happy as a child, and in listening to the solemn murmur of the Rhine, with which mingled the croaking of a raven and the shrill cries of the martins, who, with restless wings grazed the abutments of the ancient turret, he persuaded himself that the river raised its voice to salute him, that the birds were serenading him, and that all nature celebrated a fête of which he was the hero.

He could hardly tear himself from his dear window to breakfast, and he was again engaged in contemplation when M. Leminof entered the room. He did not hear him, and it was not until the Count had coughed three times that he turned his head. Perceiving the enemy, Gilbert started, but quickly recovered himself. The nervous start, however, which he had not been able to conceal, caused the Count to smile, and this smile embarrassed Gilbert. He felt that M. Leminof would regulate his conduct to him upon the impression he should receive in this first interview, and he determined to keep close watch upon himself.

Count Kostia was a man of middle age, very tall

and well made, broad shouldered, with lofty bearing, a forehead stern and haughty, a nose like the beak of a bird of prey, a head carried high and slightly backwards, large, wide open gray eyes which shot glances at once piercing and restless, an expressive face regularly cut, in which Gilbert found little to criticize except that the eyebrows were a little too bushy, and the cheek bones a little too prominent; but what did not please him was, that M. Leminof remained standing while praying him to be seated, and as Gilbert made some objections the Count cut him short by an imperious gesture and a frown.

"*Monsieur le Comte*," said Gilbert mentally, "you do not leave this room until you have been seated too!"

"My dear sir," said the Count, pacing the room with folded arms, "you have a very warm friend in Dr. Lerins. He sets a great value upon your merit; he has even been obliging enough to give me to understand that I was quite unworthy of having such a treasure of wisdom and erudition in my house. He has also expressly recommended me to treat you with the tenderest consideration; he has made me feel that I am responsible for you to the world, and that the world will hold me to a strict account. You are very fortunate, sir, in having such good friends, they are among Heaven's choicest blessings."

Gilbert made no answer but bit his lips and looked at the floor.

"M. Lerins," continued the Count, "informs me also, that you are both timid and proud, and he desires me to deal gently with you. He pretends that you are capable of suffering much without complaint. This is an accomplishment which is uncommon now-a-days. But what I regret is, that our excellent friend M. Lerins apparently considers me a sort of human wolf. I should be very unhappy if I inspired you with fear." Then, turning half round towards Gilbert: "Let us see, look at me well; have I claws at the ends of my fingers?"

Poor Gilbert inwardly cursed M. Lerins and his indiscreet zeal.

"Oh *Monsieur le Comte,*" replied he in his frankest tones and with the most tranquil air he could command, "I never suspect claws in a fellow-creature;—only when occasion makes me feel them, I cry out loudly and defend myself."

The sound of Gilbert's voice, and the expression of his face struck M. Leminof. It was his turn if not to start (he seldom started) at least to be astonished. He looked at him an instant in silence, and then resumed in a more sardonic tone:

"This is not all; M. Lerins (ah! what an admirable friend you have there!) desires also to inform me that you are, sir, what is called now-a-days, a beautiful soul. What is 'a beautiful soul?' I know nothing of the species." While thus speaking he seemed to be looking by turns for a fly on the ceiling and a pin on the floor. "I have old-fashioned ideas of everything, and I do not understand the vocabulary of my age. I know a beautiful horse very well or a beautiful woman;—but *a beautiful soul:* Do you know how to explain to me, sir, what 'this beautiful soul' is?"

Gilbert did not answer a word. He was entirely occupied in addressing to Heaven the prayer of the philosopher: "Oh my God! save me from my friends, and I will take care of my enemies." "My questions seem to you perhaps a little indiscreet," pursued M. Leminof; "but M. Lerins is responsible for them. His last letter caused me great uneasiness. He introduces you to me as an exceptionable being; it is natural that I should wish to enlighten myself, for I detest mysteries and surprises. I once heard of a little Abyssinian prince, who to testify his gratitude to the missionary who had converted him, sent to him, as a present, a large chest of scented wood. When the missionary opened the chest, he found in it a pretty living Nile crocodile.

Fancy his delight! Experiences like this teach prudence. So when our excellent friend M. Lerins sends me a present of a beautiful soul, it is natural that I should unpack it with caution, and that before I install this beautiful soul in my house, I should seek to know what is inside of it. A beautiful soul!" he repeated, in a less ironical but harsher tone, "by dint of pondering upon it, I divine to be a soul which has a passion for the trumpery of sentiment. In this case, sir, suffer me to give you a piece of advice. Madame Leminof had a great fancy for Chinese ornaments, and she filled her parlors with them. Unfortunately, I am a little brusque, and it happened more than once that I overturned her tables laden with porcelain and other gewgaws. You can judge how well she liked it! My dear sir, be prudent, shut up your Chinese ornaments carefully in your closets, and carry the keys."

"I thank you for the advice," answered Gilbert gently; "but I am distressed to see that you have received a very false idea of me. Will you permit me to describe myself as I am?"

"I have no objection," said he.

"To begin then 'I am not a beautiful soul,' I am simply a good soul, or if you like it better, an honest fellow who takes things as they come and men as they are; who prides himself upon nothing, pretends to nothing, and who cares not a straw what others think of him. I do not deny that in my early youth I was subject, like others, to what a man of wit has called 'the witchery of nonsense;' but I have recovered from it entirely. I have found in life a morose and rather brutal teacher, who has taught me the art of living by severe discipline; so whatever of the romantic was in me, has taken refuge in my brains, and my heart has become the most reasonable of all hearts. If I had the good fortune to be at the same time an artist and rich, I should take life as a play; but being neither the one nor the other, I treat it as a matter of business. Believe me, sir, life for me is simply a business a little more vexatious and complicated perhaps than some others, but I find no fault, because it is not an idyl, nor an opera. Only, as it is good to take relaxation sometimes, when I wish to rest from any great occupation which is tiring, I shut up shop and go to the play. I carry here," he added, touching his forehead, "a pretty company of puppets." The scenery is not very extensive, but my puppets are well behaved; they understand their profession very well, and play comedy and tragedy with equal success. I have but to say a word and immediately they spring out of their boxes, dress themselves, put on the rouge, the foot lamps are lighted, the curtain rises, the play begins, and I am the happiest of men."

M. Leminof paced the room no longer. He stood motionless in the embrasure of the window, and looked out upon the valley.

"I will force you to sit down yet, *Monsieur le Comte*," said Gilbert to himself.

"You pique my curiosity," at length said M. Leminof after a long silence: "will you not let me see your puppets some day?"

"Impossible," answered he; "my Punchinello, my Harlequins and my Columbines are so timid that they would never consent to brave the fire of your gaze, and, without having claws at the ends of your fingers, sir, you appear to me to have but little sympathy with the imagination of others, and at your approach my poor puppets would run the risk of a short life—they know very well that their repertoire would not be to your taste."

M. Leminof commenced his walk again, and in passing Gilbert, gave him a look at once haughty and caressing, such as a huge mastiff would cast upon a spaniel, who fearing nothing, would approach his great-toothed majesty familiarly and offer to play with him. He growls loudly, but feels no anger.

There is something in the eye of a spaniel which forces the big dogs to take their familiarity in good part.

"Ah then, sir," said the Count, "by your own avowal you are a perfect egotist. Your great aim is to live, and to live for yourself."

"It is nearly so," answered Gilbert, "only I avoid using the word, it is a little hard. Not that I was born an egotist, but I have become one. If I still possessed the heart I had at twenty, I should have brought here with me some very romantic ideas. You may well laugh, sir, but suppose I had arrived at your castle ten years ago; it would have been with a fixed intention of loving you a great deal, and of making you love me. But now, *mon Dieu!* now I know a little of the world, and I say to myself that there can be no question between us but a bargain, and that good bargains should be advantageous to both parties."

"What a terrible man you are," cried the Count with a mocking laugh. "You destroy my illusions without pity, you wound my poetical soul. In my simplicity, I imagined that we should be enamored of each other. I intended to make an intimate friend of my secretary,—the dear confidant of all my thoughts, but at the moment when I was prepared to open my arms to him, the ingrate says to me in a studied tone: 'Sir, there is nothing but the question of a bargain between us; I am the seller, you are the buyer; I sell you Greek, and you pay me cash down.' *Peste!* Monsieur, 'your beautiful soul' does not pride itself on its poetry. As an experiment, I will take you at your word. There is nothing but a bargain between us. I will make the terms and you will agree without complaint, though I am the Turk and you the Moor."

"Pardon me," answered Gilbert, "it is naturally to your interest to treat me with consideration. You may give me a great deal to do, I shall not grudge my time or trouble, but you must not overburden me.

I am not exacting, and all that I ask for is a few hours of leisure and solitude daily to enjoy my puppets in peace.

M. Leminof stopped suddenly before Gilbert, his hands resting upon his hips.

"You will sit down, you will sit down, Monsieur le Comte ;" muttered Gilbert between his teeth.

"So you are a dreamer and an egotist," said M. Leminof, looking fixedly at him. "I hope, sir, that you have the virtues of the class. I mean to say, that while wholly occupied with yourself, you are free from all indiscreet curiosity. Egotism is worth its price only when it is accompanied by a scornful indifference to others. I will explain : I do not live here absolutely alone, but I am the only one with whom I desire you to have any intimate acquaintance. The two persons who live in this house with me know nothing of Greek, and therefore need not interest you. Remember, I have the misfortune of being jealous as a tiger, and I intend that you shall be mine without any division. And as for your puppets, should you think better of it, you will find me always ready to admire them ; but you show them to no one else, you understand, to no one ! "

Count Kostia pronounced these last words with a tone so emphatic that Gilbert was surprised, and was on the point of asking some explanation ; but the stern and almost threatening look of the Count deterred him. " Your instructions, sir," answered he, " are superfluous. To finish my own portrait, I am not very expansive, and I have but little sociability in my character. To speak frankly, solitude is my element ; it is inexpressibly sweet to me. Do you wish to try me ? If so, shut me up under lock and key in this room, and provided you have a little food passed through the door to me daily, you will find me a year hence seated at this table, fresh, well and happy, unless, perhaps," he added, " I should be unexpectedly attacked with some celestial longing, in which case, I could some fine day easily fly out of the window; the loss wouldn't be very great. Finding the cage empty, you would say, 'He has grown his wings, poor fellow—much good may they do him.'"

"I don't admit that," cried the Count, "Monsieur Secretary. You please me immensely, and for fear of accident, I will have this window barred."

With these words he drew a chair towards him, and seated himself facing Gilbert, who could have clapped his hands at this propitious result. Their conversation then turned upon the Byzantine Empire and its history. The Count unfolded to Gilbert the plan of his work, and the kind of researches he expected from him. This conversation was prolonged for several hours, and M. Leminof had hardly re-entered his study, before he took his pen and wrote to M. Lerins as follows:

"My dear Doctor:—Receive my thanks for the precious subject which you have sent me. If he had been made expressly for me, he could not be more to my taste. This is precisely the implement I have been in search of; but permit me to say that if this young man pleases me, it is because he bears no resemblance to the picture you drew of him. You described one of Berquin's heroes, and I was prepared to send him back to you, for such a character would have been quite unbearable. My dear Doctor, the young men of to-day are more complex than you think; candor is not their forte; they are all very sound in arithmetic, and the most ingenuous among them is, to say the least, a Chinese in embryo. What charms me in your *candid friend* is, that he exhibits himself as a showman does his elephant. He was anxious to explain to me in detail that petty mechanism that you call his 'beautiful soul;' he has shown me the mainspring, the movement, the balance wheels, the hands and the striking apparatus. The greatest advantage in this clock is, that it goes according to directions and always indicates the hour one wants it. Besides, the young man appears to me admirably endowed; he is a consummate scholar; has good judgment and the true critical spirit. In fact I could not have met a more satisfactory man. Adieu, my dear Doctor; rely upon my gratitude, and give my humble regards to Madame Lerins, if she has not forgotten her unworthy servant,

"KOSTIA PETROVITCH LEMINOF."

CHAPTER IV.

A FORTNIGHT later, Gilbert wrote to his friends a letter conceived thus:

"Madame: — I have found here neither fêtes, cavalcades, gala days nor Muscovite beauties. What should we do, I beg to know, with these Muscovite beauties? or perhaps I ought to ask, what would they do with us? We live in the woods; our castle is an old, very old one, and in the moonlight it looks like a spectre. What I like best about it, is its long and gloomy corridors, through which the wind sweeps freely; but I assure you that I have not yet encountered there a white robe or a plumed hat. Only the other evening a bat, who had entered by a broken pane, brushed my face with his wing and almost put out my candle. This, up to the present time, has been my sole adventure. And as for you, sir, know that I am not obliged to resist the fascinations of my tyrant, for the reason that he has not taken the trouble to be fascinating. Know also that I am not bored. I am contented; I am enjoying the tranquility of mind which comes from a well defined, well regulated, and after all, very supportable position. I am no longer compelled to urge my life on before me and to show it the road; it makes its own way, and I follow it as Martin followed his ass. And then pleasures are not wanting for us,—listen! Our castle is a long series of dilapidated buildings, of which we occupy the only one habitable. I am lodged alone in a turret which commands a magnificent view, and I have a grand precipice under my window. I can say 'my turret,' 'my precipice!' Oh, my poor Parisians, you will never understand all there is in these two words: *My precipice!* 'What is it then but a precipice?' exclaimed Madame Lerins. 'It is only a great chasm.' Ah! *mon Dieu*, yes, Madame, it is 'a great chasm;' but imagine that this morning this chasm was a deep blue, and this evening at sunset it was — stay, of the color of your nasturtiums. I opened my window and put my head out to inhale the odor of this admirable precipice, for I have discovered that in the evening precipices have an odor. How shall I describe it to you? It is a perfume of rocks scorched by the sun, with which mingles a subtle aroma of dry herbs. The combination is exquisite. Standing here at my window, I saw on my right, eighty feet below, starting up from behind a clump of rhododendrons the horns and head of a white goat. You must know that on the side of the Rhine, my gulf, or my abyss, whatever you wish to call it, is flanked by a grassy eminence, up the slope of which a path winds. It was by that route that this little white-footed amazon had clambered, and she was evidently bent on mounting higher; but where was the path? She found herself at the foot of a formidable projection of rocks which I would defy the most agile chamois to scale. The poor goat was much afflicted at being stopped by this unexpected obstacle, and in her vexation thrust her horns into the bushes, then bleating she looked up at me, and I looked down at her laughing, while at intervals our heads were both turned to look at the river dashed here and there with great gorgeous streaks of gold and purple.

Now honestly, Madame, do you not envy me my window, and would you not exchange all the shopmen in the *Rue Jacob*, for my white goat?

"And now take a turn with me, I beg you, through our beautiful domain. The proud rock, of which we occupy the summit and which deserves its name of Vulture's Crag, is bounded at the north as you already know, at the west by a ravine which separates it from a range of hills higher and fantastically jagged, and following the windings of the river. This line of hills is not continuous; it is cut by narrow gorges, which open into the valley and through which the last rays of the sun reach us. The other evening there was a red sunset, and one of these gorges seemed to vomit flames; you might have supposed it the mouth of a furnace. Upon the east, from its heights and its terrace, Geierfels overlooks the Rhine, from which it is separated by the main road and a tow-path. At the south it communicates by steep paths with a vast plateau, of which it forms, as it were, the upper story, and which is clothed with a forest of beeches, and furrowed here and there with noisy streams. It is on this side only that our castle is accessible,—and here not to carriages,—even a cart could reach us but with difficulty, and all of our provisions are brought to us upon the backs of men or mules. Mountains, perpendicular rocks, turrets overhanging a precipice, grand and sombre woods, rugged paths and brooks which fall in cascades, do not all these Madame make this a very wild and very romantic retreat? On the right bank of the Rhine which stretches out under our eyes, it is another thing. Picture to yourself a landscape of infinite sweetness, a great cultivated plain, which rises by imperceptible gradation to the base of a distant chain of mountains, the undulating outlines of which are traced upon the sky in aërial indentations. Assuredly, Madame, the two banks of the Rhine are not consecrated to the same divinity. Around Geierfels, within the mysterious horror of the woods, reigns that primitive and fearful goddess of nature, whose votaries, ferocious as herself, crimson with their blood the mossy rocks, whilst round about them, delirious priestesses, with hair flying in the wind, seem to imitate in their frenzied dances, the erratic course of stars still uncertain of their orbits and the wild discord of ancient chaos. Below, on the contrary, Ceres the blonde, Ceres crowned with ripening grain, tutelary and beneficent goddess, who takes pleasure in the exhalations of the ground broken by long furrows, in the grinding sound of ploughs, in the lowing of herds, and in the song of the reapers binding their golden sheaves.

"Directly in front of the château, beyond the Rhine, a market town, with neat houses carefully whitewashed and with gardens attached, spreads itself around a little cove, like a fan. Upon the right of this great village a rustic church reflects the sun from its tinned spire; on the left, some large mills show their lazily turning wheels, and behind these mills, the church and the market town, extends the fertile plain which I have just endeavored to describe to yon, and which I cannot praise too much. Oh! charming landscape! This afternoon I was occupied in feasting my eyes upon it, when the white goat came to distract my attention, followed at a distance by a little girl whom I suspected of being very pretty; but I forgot them both in watching a steamboat passing up the river towing a flotilla of barges, covered with awnings and attended by their lighters, and a huge raft laden with timber from the Black Forest, manned by fifty or sixty boatmen, some of whom in front, and some in the rear, directed its course with vigorous strokes of the oar. Then my eyes wandered from the white waters of the river over the soft outlines of the shores, the curves of a little brook seeking its adventures in a meadow, between two rows of willows and poplars, and over the tree-shadows lengthened by the twilight, which slept peaceably upon the bosom of the fields. Here a green meadow where three brown sheep were browsing, watched by a shepherdess seated upon a large stone, while her black and white spotted cow raised herself upon the slope of a bank to nibble the tempting branches of a hedge row. By this a road ran in a hollow through which a miller passed upon a large gray horse; further on a small cottage, from the roof of which escaped a thin thread of blueish smoke, ascending in undulations to the sky. At some distance from me, a bird of prey with an immense spread of wings, soared slowly above the valley; his wings seemed motionless, and suspended in the air, he traced great curves regular and concentric. Apparently he was plunged like myself in a dreamy contemplation from which he could not tear himself, and when at times he essayed to break the spell which held him enchained, and flapping his great wings took his flight towards the sky, the victorious charm soon triumphed over his efforts, and he descended to resume his wheeling course, apparently prisoned within a magic circle, and fascinated in spite of himself by the heavenly graces of these enchanted shores.

"But what pleases me above every thing else is, that Geierfels, by its position, is a kind of acoustic focus to which all the noises of the valley incessantly ascend. This afternoon, the dull murmuring of the river, the panting respiration of the tug-boat, the vibration of a bell in a distant church tower, the song of a peasant girl washing her linen in a spring, the bleating of sheep, the *tic tac* of the mills, the tinkling bells of a long train of mules drawing a barge by a rope, the reverberating clamors of boatmen stowing casks in their boats—all these various sounds came to my ear in vibrations of surprising clearness, when suddenly a gust of wind mingled them confusedly together, and I could hear but a vague music which seemed to fall from the skies. But a moment afterwards all of these vibrating voices emerged anew from that whirlwind of confused harmony, and each, sonorous and distinct, recounted to my enraptured heart some episode in the life of man and nature. And then, when night comes, Madame, to all of these noises of the day succeed others more mysterious, more penetrating, more melancholy. Do you like the hooting of the owl, Madame? But first, I wonder if you have ever heard it. It is a cry— No, it is not a cry, it is a soft, stifled wail; a monotonous and resigned sorrow, which unbosoms itself to the moon and stars. One of these sad birds lodges within two steps of me, in the hollow of a tree, and when night comes, he amuses himself by singing a duet with the sighing wind. The Rhine plays an accompaniment, and its grave subdued voice furnishes a continuous bass, whose volume swells and falls in rhythmic waves. The other evening this concert failed; neither the wind nor the owl was in voice. The Rhine alone grumbled beneath; but it arranged a surprise for me and proved that it could make harmony of its own without other aid. Towards midnight a barge carrying a lantern on its prow had become detached from the bank and had drifted across the river, and I distinctly heard, or imagined that I heard, the wash of the waves upon the side of the boat, the bubbling of the eddy which formed under the stern, the dull sound of the oar when it dipped into the current, and still sweeter, when raised out of it the tender tears which dripped from it drop by drop. This music contrasted strongly with that I had heard the night before at the same hour. The north wind had risen during the evening, and near eleven o'clock it became furious; it filled the air with sad howlings, and increased to a rage that was inexpressible. The weathercocks creaked, the tiles ground against each other, the roof timbers trembled in their mortices, and the walls shook upon their foundations. From time to time a blast would hurl itself against my window with wild shrieks, and from my bed I imagined I could see through the panes the bloodshot eyes of a band of famished wolves. In the brief intervals when this outside tumult subsided, strange murmurs came from the interior of the castle; the wainscotting gave forth dismal creakings;—there was not a crack in the partitions, nor a fissure in the ceiling from which did not issue a sigh, or hoarse groans. Then again all this became silent, and I heard only something like a low whispering in the far off corridors, as of phantoms murmuring in the darkness as they swept the walls in their flight; then suddenly they seemed to gather up their forces, the floors trembled under their spasmodic tramping, while they clambered in confusion up the staircase which led to my room, throwing themselves over the threshold of my door and uttering indescribable lamentations.

"But enough of this, perhaps you will say; let us now talk a little of your patron: This terrible man, will you believe it, has not inspired me with the antagonism which you prophesied. But in the first place we do not live together from morning to night. The day after my arrival, he sent me a long list of difficult or mutilated passages to interpret and restore. It is a work of time, to which I devote all my afternoons. He has had some of his finest folios sent to my room, and I live in these like a rat in a Dutch cheese. It is true, I pass my mornings in his study, where we hold learned discussions which would edify the Academy of inscriptions; but to my delight, after nightfall I can dispose of myself as I choose. He has even agreed that, after seven o'clock, I may lock myself in my room, and that no human being under any pretext whatever shall come to disturb me there. This privilege M. Leminof granted to me in the most gracious manner, and you can imagine how grateful I am to him for it. I do not mean to say by this that he is an amiable man, nor that he cares to be; but he is a man of sense and wit. He understood me at once, and he means to make me serviceable to him. I am like a horse who feels that he carries a skilful rider.

" You find fault, Doctor, with his absolute lack of faith, enthusiasm or sympathy.*

" But one cannot be a Russian without paying this price. What is Russia? The hyphen between Europe and Asia. We consider ourselves very cosmopolitan, because by taxing our wits we succeed in convincing ourselves that Dante, Goethe and Shakspeare were not entirely destitute of common sense. Fine pleasantry that! In Russia more than thirty languages are spoken. In Russia they worship all the gods in the world. In Russia there are Germans, Greeks, Laps, Tchuds, Saymoïedes and Kamtschatkians. A true Russian ought to have as many souls as there are governments in his empire—he ought to decipher at sight the heart of a Mantchoo or Tchutsche; he should honor Panagia without embroiling himself with Dalaï-Lama; he should be able to acclimate himself anywhere and naturalize himself everywhere, to understand everything without becoming enthusiastic over anything.

" We Russians," said M. Leminof to me day before yesterday, " are called upon to found the unity of the human race."

" And how will you accomplish it?"

" The way is very simple; we are self-constituted missionaries of M. Scribe, and we aspire to spread him over Asia."

" And in retaliation," I asked, " will you spread the Dalaï-Lama over Europe?"

" Not at all," replied he. " Let every nation have its own Catechism. Religion divides men. The *vaudeville* unites them."

" I am mistaken: the Russians are not all to be condemned, without appeal, as skeptics and cynics. Their cosmopolitanism can become a spirit of uni-

* These last six words are expressed in French by one—*deniaisement.*

versal sympathy. I once knew in Paris a native of Moscow, an admirable man, who united to a clear and dispassionate intellect a warm and tender heart; he knew everything and despised nothing; men were no mystery to him, and he was ready to devote himself to them; he united the unbounded tolerance of a philosopher to the ardent charity of a saint. He had passed his life in studying things as they are, and he persisted in believing that faith in God explains all life's mysteries. I asked him one day what mission he assigned to Russia. He answered: 'To reconcile all by understanding all.' Utopian or not, it is better than carrying M. Scribe to the Mantchoos."

"You dislike the Russians, my dear Doctor; you have often run them down before me, and I never defended them. Now that I live in Russia, I feel obliged to answer you. You call them Kalmucks; that is eluding the question by a subterfuge. The Russians are Occidentals with the cheek-bones and imagination of Orientals. You may fear them, I will not contest that, but it is no reason why you should speak disparagingly of them. Russia has a piercing eye and fine ear; her glance extends even to Pekin, and she uses both ears in listening to what is said in Europe. You may be sure that she does not lose a word. On her part, she has many things to say to us; she only waits to make overtures to us until her voice can be heard from Constantinople to Lisbon. All that is very disquieting, but that does not prove that the Russians are not a great people. The Sclavonians are, of all nations of the earth, the most malleable, the most flexible; they are plastic clay capable of receiving all impressions, and of assuming all forms. Thus they possess by nature the talent of imitation, and the gift of assimilating foreign habits; but as this flexibility of mind is allied to an elevated character, the fortunate conjunction produces marvellous results. The mind of a Sclavonian who happens to have a mind, has more breadth than most others, without being less profound, and gives to his virtues a versatility which we give only to our vices.

"After this declaration of principles, you will be convinced forever that I adore my tyrant. Add, too, if you wish, that I also adore Monsieur, his son! Apropos, I believe I met this amiable youth upon the road the day of my arrival; since which time I have not had the privilege of seeing him. I have taken all my meals in my room; the dining-room, they tell me, has been in the hands of the plasterers. Now the repairs are completed, and we shall henceforth dine *en famille.* Ah! my good friends, if it were only you that I am to dine with to-morrow! When shall I taste that aromatic coffee again!"

CHAPTER V.

THE next day was Sunday, and for Gilbert was a day of liberty. Towards the middle of the forenoon, he went out to take a walk in the woods. He had wandered for an hour, when, turning his head, he saw coming behind him a little troop of children, decked out in strange costumes. The two oldest wore blue dresses and red mantles, and their heads were covered with felt caps encircled by bands of gilt paper in imitation of aureoles. A smaller one wore a gray dress, upon which were painted black devils and inverted torches. The last five were clothed in white; their shoulders were ornamented with long wings of rose tinted gauze, and they held in their hands sprigs of box by way of palm branches.

Gilbert slackened his pace, and when they came up with him, he recognized in the one who wore the *san-benito* the little hog drover, so maltreated by Stephane. The child, who while marching looked down complacently on the torches and the devils with which his robe was decorated, advanced towards Gilbert, and without waiting for his questions, said to him, "I am Judas Iscariot. Here is Saint Peter, and here is Saint John. The others are angels. We are all going to R——, to take part in a grand procession, that they have there every five years. If you want to see something fine, just follow us. I shall sing a solo and so will Saint Peter; the others sing in the chorus.

Upon which Judas Iscariot, Saint Peter, Saint John and the angels resumed their march, and Gilbert decided to follow them. The first houses of the village of R—— rise at the extremity of the wooded plain which extends to the south of Geierfels. In about half an hour, the little procession made its entry into the village in the midst of a considerable crowd which hastily gathered from the neighboring hamlets. Gilbert made his way along the main street, decorated with hangings and altars, and passed on to an open square planted with elms, of which the church formed one of the sides. Presently the bells sounded a grand peal; the doors of the church opened, and the procession came out. At the head marched priests, monks and laymen of both sexes, bearing wax tapers, crosses and banners. Behind them came a long train of children representing the escort of the Saviour to Calvary. One of them, a young lad of ten years, filled the rôle of Christ.

His head was crowned with thorns, and he bore upon his shoulder a large wooden cross, under the weight of which he seemed ready to sink. On either side were the two thieves, one of whom made faces, while the other, with eyes cast down and hanging head, seemed a prey to profound remorse. They were surrounded by guards armed with lances, who threatened them and insulted them by word and gesture. Then followed a little girl, whose black robe was penetrated by a poniard over the heart. This young *mater dolorosa* was escorted by the twelve

Apostles. The procession was closed by a long troop of angels, some bearing sprigs of box in their hands, and others censers, which they swung gracefully through the air. The procession made the tour of the square twice, and then stopped. The bells ceased, and an orchestra placed upon a platform discoursed soft and pathetic music: and when the prelude was finished, the chorus of angels joined in a canticle, which stirred Gilbert to the depths of his soul. A profound silence reigned in the crowd. The men clasped their hands devoutly, the women kneeled. The young choristers were grave and collected; above their bent heads floated the banners upon which figures of the saints were painted. At intervals a cloud of incense rose into the air; a gentle breeze rustled the foliage of the old elms, and the sky, clear blue and cloudless, seemed to listen eagerly to the harmony which breathed from these infantile lips, and to that other silent and deeper harmony which stirred their young hearts.

Gilbert, the philosopher, was not of that order of enfranchised spirits who, in exchanging faith for knowledge, obey an inward fatality which they deplore, but are powerless to resist. These slaves, whose chains are broken in spite of themselves, regret their former servitude, and would recover at any cost their past ingenuousness and that serene happiness with which religion blessed their childhood. What has become of those raptures which they felt at the sound of the bells calling the faithful to prayer, the perfume of the incense floating over the altar, and the radiance of the monstrance illuminating the august shade of the sanctuary? Alas! they have felt those living springs of devout emotion drying up under the glare of the light which has penetrated their souls, and they curse the implacable sun which has exhausted the streams where they were wont to quench the thirst of their eager souls. Behold them condemned to think, to reason, to discuss, to criticise, whilst they are longing to feel, to love, and to adore! Oh! desolating sterility of heart! how willingly would they give their dearly bought wisdom for a single impulse of love and devotion! These unhappy souls are like the bees that begged Heaven for a sting, but received it only on condition of giving up their invaluable proboscis by means of which they extract the honey from the flowers. Frustrated in their hopes, they wander on restless wing among the gardens of Heaven and gaze with longing eyes on the loved plants which a fatal decree has placed forever beyond the reach of their enjoyment. Sometimes in their delirium they throw themselves on one of these perfumed corollas, bruising it with their wings and piercing it with their sharp stings, but drawing none of its coveted nectar. It is not with stings that celestial bees make that divinely perfumed honey which spreads a sovereign balm over all wounds of the spirit. Gilbert had never experienced these struggles or this mental anguish; science and the cold spirit of criticism penetrating his soul, had troubled nothing there, deranged nothing; his convictions transformed themselves by a kind of slow, insensible metamorphosis, no painful crisis altering or precipitating the quiet progress. Educated by a devoted mother, he had never desired to abjure her faith; it had unconsciously grown and ripened in him, and he had always remained faithful to his early beliefs, although he interpreted them differently; and the more profound the interpretation, the dearer and more sacred did they become. Gilbert reasoned much, and always found God at the end of his reasoning. Thus it came to pass, that he had been able to taste the fruits of the tree of knowledge with impunity; the flaming sword of the angel did not appear to him; his temerity had not been punished by the pains of exile, and the flowery gardens of Eden remained open to him; he entered them at pleasure and felt himself at home.

So Gilbert looked with both eyes and listened with both ears to the young choristers. Their air of innocence and ingenuousness, their modest demeanor indicating sincere devotion, their fresh and silvery voices, their artlessness, which lent an infantine character to the ineffable joys and sorrows of the Passion, all gave him a lively pleasure and moved him deeply. He compared them in imagination to the angels in Rubens' pictures, which are neither Loves nor spirits nor living abstractions, but winged children, who without penetrating the hidden meaning of these divine mysteries, still are happy before them; they love Christ even though they cannot understand him; they seem to ask why he has not wings like themselves; they do not fathom the secret of his humanity. "Fly!" Christ says to them, "fly little birds of Heaven, for it is the nature of angels to fly: God and man walk."

At the moment when Gilbert was most absorbed in his reflections, a voice which was not unknown to him murmured in his ear these words, which made him shudder:

"You seem prodigiously interested, Monsieur, in this ridiculous comedy!"

This interruption was like discord in a beautiful harmony, and Gilbert felt exceedingly irritated by the profane intrusion. Turning his head quickly he recognized Stephane. The young man had just dismounted from his horse, which he had left in the care of his servant, and had pushed his way through the crowd, indifferent to the exclamations of the good people whose pious meditations he disturbed. Gilbert looked at him a moment severely, and then fixed his eyes on the procession, and tried, but in vain, to forget the existence of this Stephane whom he had not met before since the adventure at the fountain, and whose presence at this moment caused him an indefinable uneasiness. The reproachful look which he had cast upon the young man, far from intimidating him, served but to excite his mocking humor, and after a few seconds of silence he commenced the following soliloquy in French, speaking low, but in a voice so distinct that Gilbert, to his great regret, lost not a word of it:

"*Mon Dieu!* how ridiculous these young ones are! They really seem to take the whole thing seriously; what vulgar types! what square, bony faces. Don't their low, stupid expressions contrast oddly with their wings? Do you see that little chap twisting his mouth and rolling his eyes? His air of contrition is quite edifying. The other day he was caught stealing faggots from a neighbor . . . . And look at that other one who has lost his wings! What an unlucky accident! He is stooping to pick them up, and tucks them under his arm like a cocked hat. The idea is a happy one! But thank God, their litanies are over. It's Saint Peter's turn to sing. The little rascal has a good voice, and says his lesson well. It must have cost trouble enough to get it into his head. The schoolmaster has undoubtedly cudgelled his inspiration into him,—an infallible method it is too! But you grieve too much, my good Peter, your repentance is excessive. You have denied you master but three times, and that is hardly worth talking about. With only three dastardly acts on his conscience a man can still be an honest fellow, after a fashion. Do you know which of these actors is the only one who pleases me? It is Judas. Now that fellow's whole soul is in his part, he has just the face for his business too. I have a particular affection for this young leader. See how tenderly he ogles the leather purse he carries in his hand! It is the lady of his heart. Now he begins to sing. What is he going to say? Gracious heavens! he too is deploring his sins like the rest. Does the innumerable race of Judases know how to repent? Their treasons are deeds of prowess which they are generally proud of. I withdraw my friendship from the young traitor on the spot; his mealy tones are revolting."

For a long time Gilbert looked about him anxiously, seeking an opportunity to escape, but the crowd was so compact that it was impossible to make his way through it. He saw himself forced to remain where he was and to submit, even to the end, to Stephane's amiable soliloquy. So he pretended not to hear him, and concealed his impatience as well as he could; but his nervousness betrayed him in spite of himself, and to the great diversion of Stephane, who maliciously enjoyed his own success. Fortunately for Gilbert, when Judas had stopped singing, the procession resumed its march towards a second station at the other end of the village, and this caused a general movement among the bystanders who hedged his passage. Gilbert profited by this disorder to escape, and was soon lost in the crowd, where even Stephane's piercing eyes could not follow him.

Hastening from the village he took the road to the woods. "This Stephane is decidedly a nuisance," thought he. "Three weeks since he surprised me at a bright fountain, where I was deliciously dreaming, and put my fancies to flight, and now by his impertinent babbling he has spoiled a *fête* in which I took interest and pleasure. What is he holding in reserve for me? The most annoying part of it is, that henceforth I shall be condemned to see him daily. Even to-day, in a few hours, I shall meet him at his father's table. Presentiments do not always deceive, and at first sight I recognize in him a sworn enemy to my repose and happiness; but I shall manage to keep him at a distance. We won't distress ourselves over a trifle. What does philosophy amount to, if the happiness of a philosopher is to be at the mercy of a spoiled child!"

Thus saying, he drew from his pocket a book which he often carried in his walks: It was a volume of Goethe, containing the admirable treatise on the *metamorphosis of plants.* He began to read, often raising his head from the page to gaze at a passing cloud, or a bird fluttering from tree to tree. To this pleasant occupation he abandoned himself for nearly an hour, when he heard the neighing of a horse behind him, and turning, he saw Stephane advancing at full speed on his superb chestnut and followed at a few paces by his groom, mounted on a gray horse. Gilbert's first impulse was to dart into a path which opened at his left, and thus gain the shelter of the copse; but he did not wish to give Stephane the pleasure of imagining that he was afraid of him, and so continued on his way, his eyes riveted upon the book.

Stephane soon came up to him, and bringing his horse to a walk, thus accosted him:

"Do you know, sir, that you are not very polite? You quitted me abruptly, without taking leave. Your proceedings are singular, and you seem to be a stranger to the first principles of good breeding."

"What do you expect, my dear sir," answered Gilbert. "You were so amiable, so prepossessing the first time I had the honor of meeting you, that I was discouraged. I said to myself, that do what I would, I should always be in arrears to you."

"You are spiteful Mr. Secretary," retorted Stephane. What, have you not yet forgotten that little affair at the spring?'"

"You have taken no trouble, it seems, to make me forget it."

"It is true, I was wrong," replied he with a sneer; "wait a moment, I will dismount, go upon my knees there in the middle of the road, and say to you in a dolorous voice, 'sir, I'm grieved, heart broken, desperate,'—For what? I know not. Tell me, I pray you, sir, for what must I beg your pardon? For if I rightly remember, you commenced by raising your cane to me."

"I did not raise my cane to you," replied Gilbert,

beside himself with indignation; "I contented myself with parrying the blow which you were about to give me."

"It was not my intention to strike you," rejoined Stephane impetuously. "And besides, learn once for all, that between us things are not equal, and that even should I provoke you, you would be a wretch to raise the end of your finger against me."

"Oh! that is too much;" cried Gilbert laughing loudly. "And why so, my little friend?"

"Because—because—" stammered Stephane; and then suddenly stopped.

An expression of bitter sadness passed over his face; his brows contracted and his eyes became fixed. It was thus that terrible paroxysm had commenced which so alarmed Gilbert at their first meeting. This time, fortunately, the attack was less violent. The good Gilbert passed quickly from anger to pity; "there is a secret wound in that heart," thought he, and he was still more convinced of it when, after a long pause Stephane, recovering the use of speech, said to him in a broken voice: "I was ill the other day, I often am. People should have some consideration for invalids."

Gilbert made no answer; he feared by a hard word to exasperate this soul so passionate, and so little master of itself; but he thought that when Stephane felt ill, he had better stay in his room.

They walked on some moments in silence until, recovering from his dejection, Stephane said ironically: "You made a mistake in leaving the *fête* so soon. If you had stayed until the end, you would have heard Christ and his mother sing; you lost a charming duet."

"Let us drop that subject," interrupted Gilbert; "we could not understand each other. Yours is a kind of pleasantry for which I have but little taste."

"Pedant!" murmured Stephane turning his head, then adding with animation: "It is just because I respect religion that I do not like to see it burlesqued and parodied. Let a true angel appear and I am ready to render him homage; but I am enraged when I see great seraph's wings tied with white strings to the shoulders of wicked, boorish little thieves, liars, cowards, slaves and rascals. Their hypocritical airs do not impose on me, for I read their base natures in their eyes, and the canticles which come from their lips fill the air with impure miasmas which suffocate me. I detest," he continued with increasing vehemence, which frightened Gilbert, "I detest all affectations, all shams. I have the misfortune of being able to see through all masks, and I have discovered that all men wear masks, with the exception of some great personages, who feel themselves strong and formidable enough to allow their faces to be seen in public. There are tyrants who, whip in hand, make others adore their natural ugliness, and before whom the great masquerade bows and cringes. And that is the world!"

"These are very old words for such young lips," answered Gilbert sadly. "I suspect, my child, you are repeating a lesson you have learned."

"And what do you know of my age?" cried he angrily. "By what do you judge? Are faces clocks which mark the hours and minutes of life? Well, yes, I am but sixteen; but I have lived longer than you. I am not a library rat, and have not studied the world in duodecimos. Thank God! for the advancement of my education. He has gathered under my eyes a few specimens of the human race which have enabled me to judge of the rest, and the more experience I gain, the more I am convinced that all men are alike. On that account I scorn them all,—all without exception!"

"I thank you sincerely for myself and your groom," answered Gilbert smiling.

"Don't trouble yourself about my groom," replied Stephane, beating down with his whip the foliage which obstructed his path. "In the first place, he knows but little French; and it is useless to tell him in Russian that I despise him,—he would be none the worse for it. He is well lodged, well fed and well clothed; what matters my scorn to him? And besides, let me tell you for your guidance, that my groom is not a groom, he is my jailer. I am a prisoner under constant surveillance; these woods constitute a yard, where I can walk but twice a week, and this excellent Ivan is my keeper. Search his pockets and you will find a scourge."

Gilbert turned to examine the groom, who answered his scrutinizing look by a jovial and intelligent smile. Ivan represented the type of the Russian serf in all his original beauty. He was small, but vigorous and robust; he had a fresh complexion, cheeks full and rosy, hair of a pale yellow, large soft eyes and a long chestnut beard, in which threads of silver already mingled. It was such a face as one often sees among the lower classes of Sclavonians; indicating at once energy in action and placidity in repose.

When Gilbert had looked at him well, he said, "My dear sir, I do not believe in Ivan's scourge."

"Ah! that is like you bookworms," exclaimed Stephane with an angry gesture. "You receive all the monstrous nonsense which you find in your old books for gospel truth, and without any hesitation, while the ordinary matters of life appear to you prodigious absurdities, which you refuse to believe."

"Don't be angry. Ivan's scourge is not exactly an article of faith. One can fail to believe in it without being in danger of hell-fire. Besides, I am ready to recant my heresy; but I will confess to you that I find nothing ferocious or stern in the face of this honest servant. At all events, he is a jailer who does not keep his prisoners closely, and who sometimes gives them a relaxation beyond his orders; for the other day, it seems to me, you scoured the country without him, and really the use you make of your liberty—"

"The other day," interrupted Stephane, "I did a foolish thing. For the first time I amused myself by evading Ivan's vigilance. It was an effort that I longed to make, but it turned out badly for me. Would you like to see with your own eyes what this fine exploit cost me?"

Then pushing up the right sleeve of his black velvet blouse, he showed Gilbert a thin, delicate wrist marked by a red circle, which indicated the prolonged friction of an iron ring. Gilbert could not repress an exclamation of surprise and pity at the sight, and repented his pleasantry.

"I have been chained for a fortnight in a dungeon which I thought I should never come out of again," said Stephane, "and I indulged in a good many reflections there. Ah! you were right when you accused me of repeating a lesson I had learned. The pretty bracelet which I bear on my right arm is my thought teacher, and if I dared to repeat all that it taught me—" Then interrupting himself:

"A lie!" exclaimed he in a bitter tone, drawing his cap down over his eyes. "The truth is, that I came out of the dungeon like a lamb, flexible as a glove, and that I am capable of committing a thousand base acts to save myself the horror of returning there. I am a coward like the rest, and when I tell you that I despise all men, do not believe that I make an exception in my own favor."

And at these words he drove the spurs into his horse's flank so violently that the fiery chestnut, irritated by the rude attack, kicked and pranced. Stephane subdued him by the sole power of his haughty and menacing voice; then exciting him again, he launched him forward at full speed and amused himself by suddenly bringing him up with a jerk of the rein, and by turns making him dance and plunge; then urging him across the road he made him clear at a bound, the ditch and hedge which bordered it. After several minutes of this violent exercise, he trotted away, followed by his inseparable Ivan, leaving Gilbert to his reflections, which were not the most agreeable.

Although Gilbert was born a poet, destiny had made him a man of order and discipline; he had banished adventure and fancy from his existence, and had prescribed for himself a rule of life, observing it with almost military exactness. By dint of persistency, the habit of putting everything in its place, and of doing everything in its time, had now become a kind of second nature. The regularity of his life displayed itself in his person; all of his movements were correct and precise; from his walk, his figure, the carriage of his head, his proud calm glance, this great friend of puppets might have been taken for an adjutant-major retired before his time. Gilbert certainly considered it paramount to preserve an unalterable composure of mind; and by a severe control of himself practised without any relaxation, he had acquired a mastery over his emotions and his impressions,—so far at least as human infirmity will admit. Poverty ,which is a source of dependence, having compelled him to have intercourse with many men whose society was not agreeable to him, he had contracted the habit of coolly observing character, and of keeping full control of himself under all circumstances. Therefore he was much astonished at what had just happened. He had experienced in talking with Stephane an uneasiness, a secret trouble which had never oppressed him before. The passionate character of this young man, the rudeness of his manners, in which a free savage grace mingled, the exaggeration of his language, betraying the disorder of an ill-governed mind, the rapidity with which his impressions succeeded each other, the natural sweetness of his voice, the caressing melody of which was disturbed by loud exclamations and rude and harsh accents; his gray eyes turning nearly black and flashing fire in a paroxysm of anger or emotion; the contrast between the nobility and distinction of his face and bearing, and the arrogant scorn of proprieties in which he seemed to delight—in short, some painful mystery written upon his forehead and betrayed in his smile—all gave Gilbert much to speculate upon and troubled him profoundly. The aversion he had at first felt for Stephane had changed to pity since the poor child had shown him the red bracelet, which he called his "thought-teacher,"—but pity without sympathy is a sentiment to which one yields with reluctance. Gilbert reproached himself for taking such a lively interest in this young man who had so little merited his esteem, and more especially as with his pity mingled an indefinable terror or apprehension. In fact, he hardly knew himself; he so calm, so reasonable to be the victim of such painful presentiments! It seemed to him that Stephane was destined to exercise great influence over his fate, and to bring disorder into his life.

He seated himself at the foot of a great walnut tree which spread its knotty branches with their young reddish-brown leaves over the road.

"I am getting to be absurd," said he, "and certainly have a strong imagination. The spring sun must have affected my brain. It is hardly necessary to take so seriously all the nonsense that crowds into my head."

He re-opened the book, which he still held in his hand, and tried to read, but the image of Stephane constantly interposed between the page and his eyes. He thought he saw him, with pale face and inflamed eyes his cap on one side, and his long blonde hair falling in disorder upon his shoulders. This sphinx looked at him with a smile, at once sad and mocking, and said to him in a threatening tone: "Divine me if thou canst; thy happiness depends upon it."

Suddenly, he heard once more the sound of

horses' hoofs and Stephane re-appeared. Perceiving Gilbert, the young man stopped his horse and cried out, "Mr. Secretary, I am looking for you."

And then laughing continued:

"This is a tender avowal I have just made; for believe me, it is years since I have thought of looking for anybody; but as in your estimation I have not been very courteous, and as I pride myself on my good manners, I wish to obtain your pardon by flattering you a little."

"This is too much goodness," answered Gilbert. "Don't take the trouble. The best course you can pursue to win my esteem is to trouble yourself about me as little as possible."

"And you will do the same in regard to me?"

"Remember that matters are not equal between us. I am but an insect,—it is very easy for you to avoid me, whilst—"

"You are not talking with common sense," interrupted Stephane; "look at this green beetle crawling across the road. I see him, but he does not see me. But to drop this bantering—for it's quite out of character with me—what I like in you is your remarkable frankness, it really amuses me. By the way, be good enough to tell me what book that is which never leaves you for a moment and which you ponder over with such intensity. Do tell me," added he in a coaxing, childish tone, "what is the book that you press to your heart with so much tenderness."

Gilbert arose and handed it to him.

"'Essay on the Metamorphosis of Plants.' So, plants have the privilege of changing themselves? *Mon Dieu*, they must be happy! But they ought to tell us their secret."

Then closing the volume and returning it to Gilbert, he exclaimed:

"Happy man! you live among the plants of the field as if in your element. Are you not something of a plant yourself? I am not sure but that you have just now stopped reading to say to the primroses and anemones covering this slope, 'I am your brother!' *Mon Dieu!* I am sorry to have disturbed the charming conversation! And hold! your eyes are a little the color of the perriwinkle. That flower has a great deal of merit, it has little odor but it has no thorns. I see now why you listened with such religious feeling to the psalms of the seraphim. In your passion for plants you see them everywhere, and you involuntarily compared those wicked little rustics to your white lilies,—emblems of truth and innocence. And I, monster that I am! said to you: 'Poor innocent, you had better look a little closer at the angels, and you'll find the devil in the depths of their eyes.' Humanity is not a bed of roses and lilies, but an uncultivated and abandoned field where nettles, the deadly nightshade and hemlock flourish. Oh, how you must curse my impertinence and misanthropy!"

"Do not distress yourself, sir," answered Gilbert with a bland smile. "You exaggerate the effect of your words. I took them for what they were worth, that is to say, for the whims of a young man. I don't know what reason you may have for despising your fellow-creatures; but the intemperance of your language betrays your youth and inexperience. At your age one is apt to be positive, harsh and obstinate in his judgments, to build up his impressions with system, to dogmatize in prose and verse, and to love strong, decided colors; for then there is little shading in mind or manner. In all ages intolerance has characterized the novices; the old monks are more indulgent, they do not see the devil in the eyes of their neighbors so quickly; rather, they know that the devil himself is not so black as he is painted. Early youth is the season of chimeras, it is a law of nature; only they are rose-colored—some of them, however, turn black. Yours are a little sombre, and I am sorry for you, my child."

This little sermon and the grave and steady tone in which it was delivered, was very revolting to Stephane. He turned his head and looked at Gilbert with a scornful air, and had already prepared to leave this insupportable mentor, when a glance over the road dispersed his ill-humor, for in the distance he saw Wilhelm and his comrades returning from the *fête*.

"Come quick, my children," cried he, rising in his stirrups. "Come quick, my lambs, for I have something of the greatest importance to propose to you."

Hearing this challenge, the children raised their eyes and recognizing Stephane, they stopped and took counsel together. The somewhat brutal impudence of the young Russian had given him a bad reputation, and the little peasants would rather have turned back than encounter his morose jesting or his terrible whip.

The three apostles and the five angels, after consulting together, concluded prudently to beat a retreat, when Stephane drawing from his pocket a great leather purse, shook it in the air crying, "there is money to be gained here,—come, my dear children, you shall have all you want."

The large full purse which Stephane shook in his hand was a very tempting bait for the eight children; but his whip, which he held under his left arm, warned them to be careful. Hesitating between fear and covetousness, they stood still like the ass in the fable between his two bundles of hay; but Stephane at that moment was seized with a happy inspiration and threw his switch to the top of a neighboring tree, where it rested. This produced a magical effect, the children with one accord deciding to approach him, although with slow and hesitating steps. Wilhelm alone, remembering his recent treatment, darted into a path near by and disappeared in the bushes.

The troup of children stopped a dozen paces

from Stephane and formed in a group, the little ones hiding behind the larger. All of them fumbled nervously with the ends of their belts, and kept their heads down, awkward and ashamed, with eyes fixed upon the ground, but casting sidelong glances at the great leather purse which danced between Stephane's hands.

"You, Saint Peter," said he to them in a grave tone; "you, Saint John, and your five dear little angels of Heaven, listen to me closely. You have sung to-day very pretty songs in honor of the good Lord; he will reward you some day in the other world; but for the little pleasures people give me, I reward them at once. So every one of you shall have a bright dollar, if you will do the little thing I ask. It is only to kiss delicately and respectfully the toe of my boot. I tell you again, that this little ceremony will gain for each of you a bright dollar, and you will afterwards have the happiness of knowing that you have learned to do something which you can't do too well if you want to get on in this world."

The seven children looked at Stephane with a sheepish air and open mouths. Not one of them stirred. Their immobility, and their seven pairs of fixed round eyes directed upon him, provoked him.

"Come, my little lambs," he continued persuasively, "don't stretch your eyes in this way; they look like barn doors wide open. You should do this bravely and neatly. Ah! *mon Dieu!* you will see it done often enough, and do it yourselves again too in your lifetime. There must always be a beginning. Come on, make haste. A thaler is worth thirty-six *silbergroschen*, and a *silbergroschen* is worth ten *pfennings*, and for five *pfennings* you can buy a cake, a hot muffin, or a little man in liquorice—"

And shaking the leather purse again, he cried:

"Ah, what a pretty sound that makes! How pleasantly the click, click of these coins sounds to our ears. All music is discordant compared to that.

Nightingales and thrushes stop your concerts! we can sing better than you. I am an artist who plays your favorite air on his violin. Let us open the ball, my darlings."

The seven children seemed still uncertain. They were red with excitement, and consulted each other by looks. At last the youngest, a little blond fellow, made up his mind.

"Monsieur *has one chevron too much*," said he to his companions, which being interpreted means: "Monsieur is a little foolish with pride, his head is turned, he is crack-brained, and," added he laughingly, "after all, it's only in fun, and there is a dollar to get."

So speaking he approached Stephane deliberately, and gave his boot a loud kiss. The ice was broken; all of his companions followed his example, some with a grave and composed air, others laughing till they showed all their teeth. Stephane clapped his hands in triumph:

"Bravo! my dear friends," exclaimed he. "The business went off admirably, charmingly!"

Then drawing seven dollars from his purse, he threw them into the road with a scornful gesture:

"Now then, Messrs. Apostles and Seraphim," cried he in a thundering voice, "pick up your money quick, and scamper away as fast as your legs can carry you. Vile brood, go and tell your mothers by what a glorious exploit you won this prize!"

And while the children were moving off, he turned towards Gilbert and said, crossing his arms: "Well, my man of the perriwinkles, what do you think of it?"

Gilbert had witnessed this little scene with mingled sadness and disgust. He would have given much if only one of the children had resisted Stephane's insolent caprice; but not having this satisfaction, he tried to conceal his chagrin as best he could.

"What does it prove?" replied he dryly.

"It seems to me it proves many things, and among others this: that certain emotions are very ridiculous, and that certain mentors of my acquaintance who thrust their lessons upon others—"

He said no more, for at this moment a pebble thrown by a vigorous hand whistled by his ears, and rolled his cap in the dust. Starting, he uttered an angry cry, and striking spurs into his horse, he launched him at a gallop across the bushes. Gilbert picked up the cap, and handed it to Ivan, who said to him in bad German:

"Pardon him; the poor child is sick," and then departed hastily in pursuit of his young master.

Gilbert ran after them. When he had overtaken them, Stephane had dismounted, and stood with clenched fists before a child, who, quite out of breath from running, had thrown himself exhausted at the foot of a tree. In running he had torn many holes in his *San-benito*, and he was looking with mournful eyes at these rents, and replied only in monosyllables to all of Stephane's threats.

"You are at my mercy," said the young man to him at last. "I will forgive you if you ask my pardon on your knees."

"I won't do it," replied the child getting up. "I have no pardon to ask. You struck me with your whip, and I swore to pay you for it. I'm a good shot. I sighted your cap and I was sure I'd hit it. That makes you mad, and now we're even. But I'll promise not to throw any more stones, if you'll promise not to strike me with your whip any more."

"That is a very reasonable proposition," said Gilbert.

"I don't ask your opinion, sir," interrupted Stephane haughtily,—then turning to Ivan: "Ivan, my dear Ivan," continued he, "in this matter you ought to obey me. You know very well the Count does not love me, but he does not mean to have others insult me: it is a privilege he reserves to himself. Dismount, and make this little rascal kneel to me and ask my pardon."

Ivan shook his head.

"You struck him first," answered he; "why should he ask your pardon?"

In vain Stephane exhausted supplications and threats. The serf remained inflexible, and during this talk, Gilbert approached Wilhelm, and said to him in a low voice:

"Run away quickly, my child; but remember your promise; if you don't, you'll have to settle with me."

Stephane seeing him escape would have started in pursuit; but Gilbert barred his way.

"Ivan!" cried he wringing his hands, "drive this man out of my path!"

Ivan shook his head again.

"I don't wish to harm the young Frenchman," replied he; "he has a kind way and loves children."

Stephane's face was painfully agitated. His lips trembled. He looked with sinister eye first at Ivan, then at Gilbert. At last he said to himself in a stifled voice:

"Wretch that I am! I am as feeble as a worm, and weakness is not respected!"

Then lowering his head he approached his horse, mounted him, and pushed slowly through the copse. When he had regained the wood, looking fixedly at Gilbert:

"Mr. Secretary," said he, "my father often quotes that diplomatist who said that all men have their price; unfortunately I am not rich enough to buy you; you are worth more than a dollar; but permit me to give you some good advice. When you return to the castle, repeat to Count Kostia certain words that I have allowed to escape me to-day. It will give him infinite pleasure. Perhaps he will make you his spy-in-chief, and without asking it, he may double your salary.

The most profitable trade in the world is burning candles on the devil's shrine. You will do wonders in it, as well as others."

Upon which, with a profound bow to Gilbert, he disappeared at a full trot.

"The devil! the devil! he talks of nothing but the devil," said Gilbert to himself, taking the road to the castle. "My poor friend, you are condemned to pass some years of your life here between a tyrant who is some times amiable, and a victim who is never so at all!"

CHAPTER VI.

When Gilbert got back to the castle, M. Leminof was walking on the terrace. He perceived his secretary at some distance, and made signs to him to come and join him. They made several turns on the parapet, and while walking, Gilbert studied Stephane's father with still greater attention than he had done before. He was now most forcibly struck by his eyes, of a slightly turbid gray, whose glances, vague, unsteady, indiscernible, became at moments cold and dull as lead. Never had M. Leminof been so amiable to his secretary; he spoke to him playfully, and looked at him with an expression of charming good nature. They had conversed for a quarter of an hour when the sound of a bell gave notice that dinner was served. Count Kostia conducted Gilbert to the dining-room. It was an immense vaulted apartment, wainscoted in black oak, and lighted by three small ogive windows, looking out upon the terrace. The arches of the ceiling were covered with old apocalyptic paintings, which time had molded and scaled off. In the centre could be seen the Lamb with seven horns seated on his throne; and round about him the four-and-twenty elders clothed in white. On the lower parts of the pendentivse the paintings were so much damaged that the subjects were hardly recognizable. Here and there could be seen wings of angels, trumpets, arms which had lost their hands, busts from which the head had disappeared, crowns, stars, horses' manes, and dragons' tails. These gloomy relics sometimes formed combinations that were mysterious and ominous. It was a strange decoration for a dining-hall.

At this hour of the day, the three arched windows gave but a dull and scanty light; and more was supplied by three bronze lamps, suspended from the ceiling by iron chains; even their brilliant flames were hardly sufficient to light up the depths of this cavernous hall. Below the three lamps was spread a long table, where twenty guests might easily find room; at one of the rounded ends of this table, three covers and three morocco chairs had been arranged in a semi-circle; at the other end, a solitary cover was placed before a simple wooden stool. The Count seated himself and motioned Gilbert to place himself at his right; then unfolding his napkin, he said harshly to the great German *valet de chambre:*

"Why are not my son and father Alexis here yet? Go and find them."

Some moments after, the door opened, and Stephane appeared. He crossed the hall, his eyes downcast, and bending over the long thin hand which his father presented to him without looking at him, he touched it slightly with his lips. This mark of filial deference must have cost him much, for he was seized with that nervous trembling to which he was subject when moved by strong, emotions. Gilbert could not help saying to himself:

"My child, the seraphim and apostles are well revenged for the humiliation you inflicted upon them."

It seemed as if the young man divined Gilbert's

thoughts, for as he raised his head, he launched a ferocious glance at him; then seating himself at his father's left, he remained as motionless as a statue, his eyes fixed upon his plate. Meantime he whom they called father Alexis did not make his appearance, and the Count becoming impatient, threw his napkin brusquely upon the table, and rose to go after him; but at this same moment the door opened, and Gilbert saw a bearded face which wore an expression of anxiety and terror. Much heated and out of breath, the priest threw a scrutinizing glance upon his lord and master, and from the Count turned his eyes towards the empty stool, and looked as if he would have given his little finger to be able to reach even that uncomfortable seat without being seen.

"Father Alexis, you forget yourself in your eternal daubs!" exclaimed M. Leminof reseating himself. "You know that I dislike to wait. I profess, it is true, a passionate admiration for the burlesque master-pieces with which you are decorating the walls of my chapel; but I cannot suffer them to annoy me, and I beg you not to sacrifice again the respect you owe me to your foolish passion for those coarse paintings; if you do, I shall some fine morning bury your sublime daubings under a triple coat of whitewash."

This reprimand, pronounced in a thundering tone, produced the most unhappy effect upon father Alexis. His first movement was to raise his eyes and arms towards the arched ceiling where, as if calling the four-and-twenty elders to witness, he exclaimed:

"You hear! The profane dare call them daubs, those incomparable frescoes which will carry down the name of father Alexis to the latest posterity!"

But in the heart of the poor priest terror soon succeeded to indignation. He dropped his arms, and bending down, sunk his head between his shoulders, and tried to make himself as small as possible; much as a frightened turtle draws himself into his shell, and fears that even there he is taking up too much room.

"Well! what are these grimaces for? Do you mean to make us wait until to-morrow for your benediction?"

The Count pronounced these words in the rude tone of a corporal ordering recruits to march in double-quick time. Father Alexis made a bound as if he had received a sharp blow from a whip across his back, and in his agitation and haste to reach his stool, he struck violently against the corner of a carved sideboard; this terrible shock drew from him a cry of pain, but did not arrest his speed, and rubbing his hip, he threw himself into his place and, without giving himself time to recover breath, he mumbled in a nasal tone and in an unintelligible voice, a grace which he soon finished, and everybody having made the sign of the cross, dinner was served.

"What a strange rôle religion plays here," thought Gilbert to himself as he carried his spoon to his lips. "They would on no account dine until it had blessed the soup, and at the same time they banish it to the end of the table as a leper whose impure contact they fear."

During the first part of the repast, Gilbert's attention was concentrated on father Alexis. This priestly face excited his curiosity. At first sight it seemed impressed with a certain majesty which was heightened by the black folds of his robe, and the gold crucifix which hung upon his breast. Father Alexis had a high, open forehead; his large, strongly aquiline nose gave a manly character to his face; his black eyes, finely set, were surmounted by well-curved eyebrows, and his long grizzly beard harmonized very well with his bronzed cheeks furrowed by venerable wrinkles. Seen in repose, this face had a character of austere and imposing beauty. And if you had looked at father Alexis in his sleep, you would have taken him for a holy anchorite recently come out of the desert, or better still, for a Saint John contemplating with closed eyes from the height of his Patmos rock, the sublime visions of the Apocalypse; but as soon as the face of the good priest became animated, the charm was broken. It was but an expressive mask, flexible, at times grotesque, where were depicted the fugitive and shallow impressions of a soul gentle, innocent and easy, but not imaginative or exalted. It was then that the monk and the anchorite suddenly disappeared, and there remained but a child sixty years old, whose countenance, by turns uneasy or smiling, expressed nothing but puerile pre-occupations, or still more puerile content. This transformation was so rapid that it seemed almost like a juggler's trick. You sought St. John, but found him no more, and you were tempted to cry out, "Oh, father Alexis, what has become of you? The soul now looking out of your face is not yours." This father Alexis was an excellent man; but unfortunately, he had too decided a taste for the pleasures of the table. He could also be accused of having a strong ingredient of vanity in his character; but his self-love was so ingenuous, that the most severe judge could but pardon it. Father Alexis had succeeded in persuading himself that he was a great artist, and this conviction constituted his happiness. This much at least could be said of him, that he managed his brush and pencil with remarkable dexterity, and could execute four or five square feet of fresco painting in a few hours. The doctrines of Mount Athos, which place he had visited in his youth, had no more secrets for him; Byzantine æsthetics had passed into his flesh and bones: he knew by heart the famous "Guide to Painting," drawn up by the monk Denys and his pupil Cyril of Scio. In short, he was thoroughly acquainted with all the receipts by means of which works of genius are produced, and thus, with the aid of compasses, he painted from inspiration those good and holy men who strikingly resembled certain figures on gold back-grounds in the convents of Lavra and Iveron. But one thing brought mortification and chagrin to father Alexis,—Count Kostia Petrovitch refused to believe in his genius! But on the other hand, he was a little consoled by the fact that the good Ivan professed unreserved admiration for his works; so he loved to talk of painting and high art with this pious worshipper of his talents.

"Look, my son," he would say to him, extending the thumb, index and middle fingers of his right hand, "thou seest these three fingers: I have only to say a word to them, and from them go forth Saint Georges, Saint Michaels, Saint Nicholases, patriarchs of the old covenant, and apostles of the new, the good Lord himself and all his dear family!"

And then he would give him his hand to kiss, which duty the good serf performed with humble veneration. However, if Count Kostia had the barbarous taste to treat the illuminated works of father Alexis as daubs, he was not cruel enough to prevent him from cultivating his dearly loved art. He had even lately granted this disciple of the great Panselinos, the founder of the Byzantine school, an unexpected favor, for which the good father promised himself to be eternally grateful. One of the wings of the Castle of Geierfels enclosed a pretty and sufficiently spacious chapel, which the Count had appropriated to the services of the Greek church, and one fine day, yielding to the repeated solicitations of father Alexis, he had authorized him to cover the walls and dome with "daubs" after his own fashion. The priest commenced the work immediately. This great enterprise absorbed at least half of his thoughts; he worked many hours every day, and at night he saw in dreams great patriarchs in gold and azure, hanging over him and saying:

"Dear Alexis, we commend ourselves to thy good

care, let thy genius perpetuate our glory through the Universe."

In short, father Alexis was so charmed with his frescoes that, occupied in contemplating the white beard of a colossal Noah, painted the day before, he had not heard the sound of the dinner-bell. It is thus that our passions devour each other, and it often happens that the little ones consume the great. M. Leminof at first remained silent. Perhaps he wished to give Gilbert time to recover himself; but when the soup was removed, he broke the silence and engaged in animated conversation with his secretary. He spoke to him in the same tone of respect that he did on the terrace, but mingled with it a larger ingredient of affection than ordinarily. The caressing inflections of his voice, the kindly glances which accompanied them, the air of sympathetic interest which he manifested in questioning him the attention which he paid to his replies, all testified to the great consideration he had for Gilbert. Evidently all this was intentional, and Stephane and father Alexis might feel themselves duly notified that the new-comer was a being apart, an important personage, called to live under a *régime* of favor, a sort of prime minister, whose unobtruded power was to be dreaded. The notification was understood. Father Alexis, all occupied as he was by his plate, did not fail to stealthily cast more than one look of admiration on Gilbert. He could not remember having seen Count Kostia testify such respect to any other human being. It is true that the Count paid kindly attentions to Solon, his monkey, a charming but very badly educated animal, all of whose tricks he approved; but in the attentions which he bestowed upon the monkey, the shade of respect was less marked. Father Alexis observed this with well-founded surprise; so he looked with staring eyes at this curious animal who threatened to supplant Solon. On his part, Gilbert watched Stephane. He felt that from moment to moment a greater chasm was widening between this young man and himself; but Stephane betrayed nothing, his eyes were as mute as his lips.

The conversation at length turned upon subjects which the Count amused himself by debating every day with his secretary. They spoke of the Lower Empire, which M. Leminof regarded as the most prosperous and most glorious age of humanity. He had little fancy for Pericles, Cæsar, Augustus and Napoleon, and considered that the art of reigning had been understood by Justinian and Alexis Comménus alone. And when Gilbert protested warmly in the name of human dignity against this theory:

"Stop just there!" said the Count; "no big words, no declamation, but listen to me! These pheasants are good. See how father Alexis is regaling himself upon them. To whom do they owe this flavor which is so enchanting him? To the high wisdom of my cook, who gave them time to become tender. He has served them to us just at the right moment. A few days sooner they would have been too tough; a few days later would have been risking too much, and we should have had the worms in them. My dear sir, societies are very much like game. Their supreme moment is when they are on the point of decomposition. In their youth they have a barbarous toughness. But a certain degree of corruption, on the contrary, imperils their existence. Very well! Byzantium possessed the art of making minds gamey and arresting decomposition at that point. Unfortunately she carried the secret to the grave with her.

He further declaimed against chivalry and revolution, which he considered as two variations composed upon the same theme. "Godfrey of Bouillon," said he, "is the great grandfather of Robespierre. The one exclaimed, while brandishing his sword: 'My heart and God will it!' The other cried, looking askance at Heaven: 'Virtue the end, terror the means!' These two mottoes are the same. It is a proclamation of abstract ideas as sovereign of the universe; it is the first fool arrogating to himself the right of arranging the world according to his own fancy; it is a new and unparalleled tyranny, the tyranny of good intentions, and see what, in process of time, good intentions have made of the West!"

"A good deal can be said in answer to that," said Gilbert.

"Answer nothing, my dear Gilbert," pursued the Count, "and just let me direct your attention to the fact that chivalry, whose avowed end was to submit all human affairs to the decrees of that revolutionary tribunal called the heart, ought in consistency to manifest the greatest respect for that half of the human race whose nature represents the feebleness, caprices, and follies of sentimentality. And it did not fail in this respect. Rebellious to the lessons given it by the wisdom of the Byzantines, instead of burying woman in the shade of the harem, it placed her on a throne. And what disorders has not this absurd idolatry given birth to in society!"

"Oh!" exclaimed Gilbert, "I must protest! This is a theory to which I shall never be converted."

"Let us see, be sincere," replied Count Kostia. "We are among men, we can speak without constraint and tell these dames the truth about themselves. Forget for a moment those principles of insipid gallantry which the romance of the middle ages has bequeathed to us, and which the revolution has restored to honor. Can you deny that woman is an inferior being, incapable of consecutive thought, greedy for dramatic emotions, always in revolt against common sense, always ready to sacrifice the general interests to her passions? *Mon Dieu!* I am willing to pardon her irrationality. She is not responsible for it. A cruel fatality weighs upon her. The great misfortune is, that in the design of nature, careful for the perpetuation of the species, woman is but a means, and she cannot help considering herself an end. It reminds me of a poor greyhound, who was employed to turn a spit; she was never able to persuade herself that the roast was not for herself; every day it was a new deception, and I must add, that the roast was more than once in danger. Therefore it would be well for the roast, I mean to say society, to take precautions against the appetite for happiness possessed by this creature at once feeble and violent, and wholly incapable of understanding her true destiny. And I know of nothing better designed than the captivity of the Byzantine or Mussulman harem, to remind the daughters of Eve that they have not the right to live on their own account."

M. Leminof developed this fine system with much energy and animation. Gilbert thought such language but indifferently respectful to the memory of Mme. Leminof, and looking at Stephane, internally remarked to Count Kostia: "I want to see how your teachings impress him." But Stephane appeared to hear nothing; for a long time he had ceased eating, and with impassible face he looked fixedly at his empty plate. "What strikes me as amusing," continued M. Leminof, terminating his address, "is that women are not in the least grateful to society for the absurd consideration which it shows them. To take their word for it, they groan under an intolerable yoke. These strange creatures have such a thirst for power, that they would like to bring the sun moon and stars under subjection; and, to complete the anomaly, professed friends of progress are found to aid their pretensions. It is these same innovators who petition for the suppression of quarantines; for the enfranchisement of women and the emancipation of the plague are two questions closely allied. My dear Gilbert, you are a rational man. Join me in a toast to harems and lazarettos!"

"*Amen!*" exclaimed father Alexis, who, listening

with but one ear, had but little suspicion of the subject under discussion; but at the word *toast* he had started, for he never refused to drink a health.

His exclamation drew the Count's attention to him.

"Father Alexis is of my opinion," said he to Gilbert, "and he has his own reasons for it. Ask him to give you the history of his love affairs."

"I fear that the recital would not interest this excellent young man," timidly objected the priest.

"Change your mode of speech," answered the Count in a severe tone. "M. Gilbert Saville is not an 'excellent young man;' he is a very distinguished scholar, whose character and talents I esteem infinitely, and I mean that he shall be respected here as myself."

"My position is defined, behold me the favorite of the tyrant!" thought Gilbert. And he saw a faint and scarcely perceptible smile pass over the lips of the motionless Stephane, which seemed to signify, "I thought as much."

"Go on, good father," resumed the Count, "do not require too much urging; tell your little story, or else I must tell it my own way."

The good father hastened to comply, for it is better to give one's self a blow than receive it from some one else. He entered upon his tale with a tremulous voice, and while speaking glanced sadly from the corner of his eye at some dishes which he had but slightly attacked. I shall not here repeat the faithful exposé which he made of his conjugal misfortunes. Suffice it to say, that he had had the ill-luck to marry a very imperious and very coquettish little woman, to whom he had been more slave than husband. Father Alexis recounted his long tribulations with a candor which was revolting to Gilbert. He was indignant with M. Leminof too, for forcing the holy man to unveil thus to a stranger the secrets of his private life; but father Alexis had not the least idea in the world that he was compromising his dignity; he had not a metaphysical head, and understood nothing of abstractions; only he did not like to have any one speak of his wife, nor be forced to speak of her himself, because it recalled to him the most unhappy period of his life. He finished his story by some edifying reflections, and commenced to quote Saint Basil, when he discovered that M. Leminof was sound asleep. Considering himself absolved therefore from finishing his homily, he devoted himself to emptying the plates of figs and nuts which he had all the while kept under his eye.

A profound silence reigned in the great hall, uninterrupted except by the rhythmic sound of the good father's jaws. Stephane leaned his elbows on the table; his attitude expressive of dreamy melancholy; his head inclined and leaning against the palm of his right hand; his black tunic without any collar exposing a neck of perfect whiteness; his long silky hair falling softly upon his shoulders; the pure and delicate contour of his handsome face; his sensitive mouth, the corners curving slightly upwards, all reminded Gilbert of the portrait of Raphael painted by himself, all, except the expression, which was very different. The glances of a Sanzio are winged messengers which express in their mute language the happy contemplations of a great and inspired soul, and announce its betrothal to the eternal beauty of the universe. The expression of Stephane's face when not excited by passion was alternately that of a cold and disdainful curiosity, or the distrust of a soul seeking to conceal its true self and stealing away from the light. At this moment his gaze was fastened on the Apocalyptic pictures of the ceiling, as though he had found there the symbolic expression of his own thoughts; his eyes lingered on a dragon's head, much dilapidated by time, which made it the more hideous; he seemed to address a question to this monster; apparently he asked him the secret of his destiny.

His statue-like immobility, and the transfixed gaze, made poor Gilbert shudder; he turned his eyes from this young forehead crowned with a mysterious sadness, and let them rest on the priest, but father Alexis' air of sanctimonious resignation appeared as pitiful as the sombre weariness of Stephane. A profound melancholy filled Gilbert's heart. Nothing about him commanded his sympathies, nothing promised any companionship for his soul: at his left the stern face of a drowsy tyrant, made more sinister by sleep; opposite him a young misanthrope, for the moment lost in the clouds; at his right an old epicure who consoled himself for everything by eating figs; above his head the dragons of the Apocalypse. And then this great vaulted hall was cold, sepulchral; he felt as though he were breathing the air of a cellar; the recesses and the corners of the room were obscured by black shadows; the dark wainscottings which covered the walls had a lugubrious aspect; outside were heard ominous noises. A gale of wind had risen and uttered long bellowings like a wounded bull, to which the grating of weathercocks and the dismal cry of the owls responded.

It suddenly occurred to Gilbert that the Count was not really asleep, and that this sudden drowsiness was a ruse intended to set at liberty the enchained tongues of his guests. Gilbert fearing that Stephane, coming out of his revery, would address some rude remark to him that the watchful ear of the master might catch, decided to feign sleep too, and leaning back in his chair, closed his eyes and dropped his head upon his breast. This situation was prolonged some time, and Gilbert was already strongly tempted to forget his rôle of sleeper, when luckily father Alexis, who had just finished his last fig, breathed a long sigh. This was a sufficient pretext for the Count to awaken; he raised himself on his chair, passed his hand ever his eyes, rung for tea, and when the cups were empty, pressed Gilbert's hand cordially, and left the hall, followed by Stephane and the priest.

When Gilbert had re-entered his own room he opened the window that he might better hear the majestic roll of the river. At the same moment a voice, carried by the wind from the great square tower, cried to him:

"Monsieur the grand vizier, don't forget to burn plenty of candles to the devil! this is the advice which your most faithful subject gives you in return for the profound lessons of wisdom with which you favored his inexperience to-day!"

It was thus Gilbert learned that Stephane was his neighbor.

"It is consoling," thought he, "to know that he can't possibly come in here without wings. And," added he closing his window, "whatever happens, I did well to write to Mme. Lerins yesterday—to-day I am not so well satisfied."

CHAPTER VII.

THIS is what Gilbert wrote in his journal six weeks after his arrival at Geierfels:

A son who has towards his father the sentiments of a slave toward his master; a father who habitually shows towards his son a dislike bordering on hatred—such are the sad subjects for study that I have found here. At first I wished to persuade myself that M. Leminof was simply a cold, hard character, a skeptic by disposition, a blasé grandee, who believed it a duty to himself to openly testify his scorn for all the humbug of sentiment. He is nothing of the kind. The Count's mind is diseased, his soul tormented, his heart eaten by a secret ulcer, and he avenges its sufferings by making others suffer. Yes, the misanthrope seeks vengeance for some deadly affront which has been put upon him by man or by fate; his irony breathes anger and hatred; it conceals deep resentment which breaks out occasionally in his voice, in his look and in his unexpected and violent acts; for he is not always master of himself. At certain times the varnish of cold politeness and icy sportiveness with which he ordinarily conceals his passions, scales off suddenly and falls into dust, and his soul appears in its nakedness. During the first weeks of my residence here he controlled himself in my presence, now I have the honor of possessing his confidence, and he no longer deems it necessary to hide his face from me, nor does he try any longer to deceive me. So much is gained anyway! I even flatter myself that he feels for me all the friendliness of which he is capable. He respects my learning, he knows my inclination to be useful and even necessary to him without over-estimating my services. Besides, he probably appreciates the interested discretion of a poor devil who desires to earn his livelihood, and who therefore submits to great restraints in his speech and actions. In short, he considers me a man of good sense, with the virtues of my trade, and although he sometimes reproaches me for what he calls my metaphysical vagaries, he esteems me too much to suppose that they can exercise any influence upon my conduct. The idea as a rule of life is decidedly his *bête noire.* "Hideous monster," he says, "veritable dragon of the Apocalypse, whose offspring, deformed and repulsive like their mother, are chivalry and revolution."

Oh, my dear puppets, you must be a spectacle for my eyes alone, and a passing diversion for my mind! Be careful not to quit the stage where you acquit yourselves with so much grace. The footlights mark the frontiers of your empire. Do not attempt to leap over them to take your place among the living! My dear puppets, when the play is finished, go back to your boxes, intertwine your wires amicably, close your fine eyes, my daughters, and slumber— But what do I hear? these puppets speak or sing while sleeping! From their securely closed boxes come soft whisperings, a secret music, intoxicating, echoing vague celestial harmonies — "Gilbert, Gilbert, distrust thyself! thy puppets are not as inoffensive as Count Kostia would fain believe."

Distrust thine eyes also, Gilbert! They too are speaking. It is singular, I thought myself entirely master of my glances, but in spite of myself, they betrayed too much curiosity on one occasion. The other day while I was working with him in his study, he suddenly became dreamy and absent, his brow was like a thundercloud: he neither saw nor heard me. When he came out of his revery his eyes met mine fixed upon his face, and he saw that I was observing him too attentively.

"Come now," said he brusquely, "you remember our stipulations; we are two egotists who have made a bargain with each other. Egotists are not curious; the only thing which interests them in the mind of a fellow-creature, is in the domain of utility."

And then fearing that he had offended me, he continued in a softer tone:

"I am the least interesting soul in the world to know. My nerves are very sensitive, and let me say to you once for all, that this is the secret of all the disorders which you may observe in my poor machine."

"No, Count Kostia, this is not your secret!" I was tempted to answer. "It is not your nerves which torment you. I would wager that in despite of your cynicism and skepticism, you have once believed in something, or in some one who has broken faith with you," but I was careful not to let him suspect my conjectures. I believe he would have devoured me. The anger of this man is terrible, and he does not always spare me the sight of it. Yesterday especially, he was transported beyond himself, to such an extent that I blushed for him. Stephane had gone to ride with Ivan. The dinner-bell rang and they had not returned. The Count himself went to the entrance of the court to wait for them. His lips were pale, his voice harsh and grating, veiled by a hoarseness which always comes with his gusts of passion. When the delinquents appeared at the end of the path, he ran to them, and measured Stephane from head to foot with a glance so menacing that the child trembled in every limb; but his anger exploded itself entirely upon Ivan. The poor jailer had, however, good excuses to offer: Stephane's horse had stumbled and cut his knee, and they had been obliged to slacken their pace. The Count appeared to hear nothing. He signed to Ivan to dismount; which having done, he seized him by the collar, tore from him his whip and beat him like a dog. The unhappy serf allowed himself to be whipped without uttering a cry, without making a movement. The idea of flight or self-defence never occurred to him. Riveted to the spot, his eyes closed, he was the living image of slavery resigned to the last outrages. Indeed I believe that during this punishment I suffered more than he. My throat was parched, my blood boiled in my veins. My first impulse was to throw myself upon the Count, but I restrained myself; such a violent interference would but have aggravated the fate of Ivan. I clasped my hands and with a stifled voice cried: "Mercy! mercy!" The Count did not hear me. Then I threw myself between the executioner and his victim. Stupefied, with arm raised and immoveable, the Count stared at me with flaming eyes; little by little he became calm, and his face resumed its ordinary expression.

"Let it pass for this time," said he at last, in a hollow voice; "but in future meddle no more in my affairs!"

Then dropping the whip to the ground, he strode

away. Ivan raised his eyes to me full of tears, his glance expressed at once tenderness, gratitude and admiration. He seized my hands and covered them with kisses, after which he passed his handkerchief over his face, streaming with perspiration, foam and blood, and taking the two horses by the bridles, quietly led them to the stable. I found the Count at the table; he had recovered his good humor; he discharged several arrows of playful sarcasm at my "*heresies*" in matters of history. It was not without effort that I answered him, for at this moment he inspired me with an aversion that I could hardly conceal. But I felt bound to recognize the victory which he had gained over himself in abridging Ivan's punishment. After dinner he sent for the serf, who appeared with his forehead and hands furrowed with bloody scars, his lips bore their habitual smile, which was always a mystery to me. His master ordered him to take off his vest, turn down his shirt and kneel before him; then drawing from his pocket a vial full of some ointment whose virtues he lauded highly, he dressed the wounds of the *moujik* with his own hands. This operation finished, he said to him:

"That will amount to nothing, my son. Go and sin no more."

Upon which the serf raised himself and left the room, smiling throughout. Ivan's smile is an exotic plant which I am not acquainted with, and which only grows in Sclavonic soil, a strange smile,—real prodigy of baseness or heroism. Which is it? I am sure I cannot tell.

In spite of my trouble, I had been able to observe Stephane at the beginning of the punishment. At the first blow, a flash of triumphant joy passed over his face; but when the blood started he became horribly pale, and pressed one of his hands to his throat as if to arrest a cry of horror, and with the other he covered his eyes to shut out the sight; then not being able to contain himself, he hurried away. God be praised!

compassion had triumphed in his heart over the joy of seeing his jailer chastised. There is in this young soul, embittered as it is by long sufferings, a fund of generosity and goodness; but will it not in time lose the last vestiges of its native qualities? Three years hence will Stephane cover his eyes to avoid the sight of an enemy's punishment? Within three years will not the habit of suffering have stifled pity in his breast? To-morrow, to-morrow perhaps, will not his heart have uttered its last cry!"

"Poor Stephane! I pity this child from the bottom of my soul. He is very unhappy! not only is his life sad, but does not his imagination aggravate his misfortunes? There are secrets in his nature of which I am ignorant, and which make it inexplicable to me; but what I see of it is sufficient to make me pity him. His character is lively, variable, energetic, expansive; it needs air, light, freedom of movement. It has strength to expend, appetites for life and happiness to satisfy. This young colt wants to disport himself in the open fields, to frolic in green pastures, to drink in with open nostrils the perfumed breezes of the forest, to plunge breast deep in the silvery foam of running waters. The hurrying wind challenges him to the chase—he pants to follow it, to outrun it; his ears stand erect, his eyes flash, he attempts to bound and plunge into space. Alas! there are fetters upon his feet, a merciless tether holds him bound to one of the milestones on the road, and the master is there with menacing eye and whip in hand. Poor, poor Stephane! what close captivity is his, and what solitude! Except two walks a week in the company and under the guard of Ivan, he passes his life in the great tower alone,—absolutely alone. What does he find to do in this prison from which he goes only at the dinner hour? From the tone in which he expresses himself on books and libraries, he does not appear to have any passion for study. How does he pass the time? He keeps silent and consumes himself. It is possible to live so, and it is possible to die so!

"But why can't this poor child be deaf as well as mute? Since you have no tender words for him, Count Kostia, would that I could close his ears to the desolating lessons that you give him! Do you not see that the life he leads is enough to teach him to hate men and life, without the necessity of your interference? He knows nothing of humanity, but what he sees through the bars of his prison; and imagines that there is nothing in the world but capricious tyrants and trembling, degraded slaves. Why thus kill in his heart every germ of enthusiasm, of hope, of manly and generous faith? His mother died long ago, and he has nearly forgotten her; women are for him an unsuspected mystery; why teach him to despise them? My child, come to Gilbert, Gilbert the heartless, that Gilbert who perhaps has never loved, and he, this man of ice, will teach thee that scorn for woman is the supreme depravity in the heart of man; he will teach thee that the man is tainted to the very bone, who dares in his thought to outrage the treasures of sweet innocence or of sublime wisdom enshrined in the heart of a virgin or of a mother; he will teach thee, child, to bow before that strength which has the semblance of weakness, before that sacred weakness which is more heroic than all strength. . . . . Alas! he would refuse to hear me, and my voice would be lost in the empty air. The insolence of the triumph of tyranny is, that its victims, while cursing it, make themselves its slaves and apostles. Hear slaves talk; in vain do they hate their master, for they vie with each other in repeating his maxims.

"But six weeks have passed since I saw this young man for the first time; but a month since I began to pass a few minutes with him daily, yet I am sure that I understand the secret of his state of mind. His malady is so apparent that it requires no clairvoyant to see it, and I can define it in a word. Stephane is a noble nature, to which poetry and religion are a closed book.—Religion! Great God! it is interpreted to him by father Alexis. He sees it sitting at the lower end of the table in the person of this grotesque priest every day, devouring his affronts and the wing of a truffled fowl with the same appetite. Religion in his eyes is an affair of a few prayers, of a few genuflections, of a copper-gilded image kissed by cold and heedless lips, of a mass droned every Sunday by an old priest whose thoughts belong to the earth. Ah! doubtless Stephane sincerely believes in the holy mysteries which are wrought over the altars behind the gilded partitions of the *iconostase;* but does he know those other mysteries of consolation and hope which a living faith accomplishes in our hearts? Has he ever felt the presence of the Divinity in his life and in things that surround him? Has he ever felt his soul, beaten by the tempests of divine love, founder with joy in the ocean of eternal light? Father Alexis, father Alexis, how much evil you have done this child!

"But may not Stephane be a vicious child, whose perverse instincts a justly provoked father seeks to curb by a pitiless discipline? No, a thousand times no! It is false, it is impossible, it is only necessary to look at him to be satisfied of this. His face is often hard, cold, scornful; but it never expresses a low thought, a pollution of soul, or a precocious corruption of mind. In his quiet moods there is upon his brow a stamp of infantile purity. I was wrong in supposing that his soul had lost its youth. At least it has preserved the faculty of rejuvenating itself at intervals. There are moments when it shakes off the heavy burden of its sorrows, to breathe and to repose. In these moments Stephane appears younger than he really is. His eyes which become limpid, his delicate and transparent complexion, his smooth cheeks and even his chin, where yet not a single downy hair appears, all these indicate the child. But when the master appears, a gloom instantly spreads over his face, extinguishing all its light; his closed lips express a weight of wearines which is fearful, and one would say that, like St. John the Silent, he had not spoken for forty-eight years. Again, the master gone, his years vanish, and but fourteen remain. There is youth in the violence of his language, in his inordinate taste for hyperbole, in these overflowing torrents of words by which he relieves his oppressed heart. The other day he came into the dining-hall before his father, and finding himself alone with me, he discharged all in a breath, a volley of sharp and biting words: 'Take me for a target, without hesitation,' I inwardly said to him; 'this fencing does you good.'

"Another sign of innocence is the freshness and vividness of his impressions. In vain he tries to conceal them, he affects little things profoundly, and has not lost the faculty of living in detail, which is most conclusive testimony that a mind has not done with childhood. In short, he is not voluntarily unhappy, and however heavy the cross may be upon his young shoulders, he stoops to gather up little consolations, the slight pleasures which he meets on his way. In the prosecution of his suit against destiny, he has lost his great claim, but still pleads for the incidentals. And in this I see a proof that the energies of his being are not entirely shattered. Ah! if hope ever again diffuses in this soul a pale and flickering glimmer, winds of heaven respect the humble flame, quench not the last smoking spark of the candle! A single star shining in the blackness of the night is almost day to those who suffer. Alas! with what cruel harshness they dispute the little pleasures which remain to him. In spite of his jests over the perriwinkles, he has a taste for flowers, and had obtained from the gardener the concession of a little plot of ground to cultivate according to his fancy. The Count, it appears, had ratified this favor; but this unheard-of condescension proved to be but a refinement of cruelty. For some time, every evening after dinner, Stephane passed an hour in his little parterre; he plucked out the weeds, planted, watered, and watched with a paternal eye the growth of his favorites. Yesterday, an hour after the sanguinary castigation, while his father was dressing Ivan's wounds, he had gone out on tiptoe. Some minutes after, as I was walking upon the terrace, I saw him occupied, with absorbing gravity, in this great work of watering. I was but a few paces from him, when the gardener approached, pickaxe in hand, and, without a word, struck it violently into the middle of a tuft of verbenas which grew at one end of the plot of ground. Stephane raised himself briskly, and, believing him stupid, threw himself upon him, crying out:

"'Wretch, what are you doing there?'

"'I am doing what his excellency ordered me to,' answered the gardener.

"At this moment the Count strolled towards us, his hands in his pockets, humming an aria, and an expression of amiable good humor on his face. Stephane extended his arms towards him, but one of those looks which always petrifies him kept him silent and motionless in the middle of the pathway. He watched with wild eyes the fatal pickaxe ravage by degrees his beloved garden. In vain he tried to disguise his despair; his legs trembled and his heart throbbed violently. He fixed his large eyes upon his dear devastated treasures; two great tears escaped them and rolled slowly down his cheeks. But when the instrument of destruction approached a magnificent carnation, the finest ornament of his garden, his heart failed him, he uttered a piercing cry, and raising his hands to Heaven, ran away sobbing. The Count looked after him as he fled, and an atrocious smile passed over his lips! Ah! if this father does not hate his son, I know not what hatred is, nor how it depicts itself upon a human face. Meantime I threw myself between the carnation and the pickaxe, as an hour before between the knout and Ivan. Stephane's despair had rent my heart; I wished at any cost to preserve this flower which was so dear to him. The face of Kostia Petrovitch took all hope from me. It seemed to say:

"'You still indulge in sentiment; this is a little too much of it.'

"'This plant is beautiful,' I said to him; why destroy it?'

"'Ah! you love flowers, my dear Gilbert;' answered he, with an air of diabolical malice. 'I am truly glad of it!'

"And turning to the gardener, he added:

"'You will carefully take up all these flowers and place them in pots—they shall decorate Monsieur's room. I am delighted to have it in my power to do him this little favor.'

"Thus speaking, he rubbed his hands gleefully, and turning his back upon me, commenced humming his tune again. He was evidently satisfied with his day's work.

"And now Stephane's flowers are here under my eyes, they have become my property. Oh! if he knew it! I do not doubt that M. Leminof wishes his son to hate me; and his wish is gratified. Overwhelmed with respect and attentions, petted, praised, extolled, treated as favorite and grand vizier, how can I be otherwise than an object of scorn and aversion to this young man? But could he read my heart! what would he read there, after all? An impotent pity from which his pride would revolt. I can do nothing for him; I could not mitigate his misfortunes or pour balm into his wounds.

"Go, then, Gilbert, occupy yourself with the Byzantines! Remember your contract, Gilbert! The master of this house has made you promise not to meddle in his affairs. Translate Greek, my friend, and, in your leisure moments, amuse yourself with your puppets. Beyond that, closed eyes and sealed mouth; that must be your motto. But do you say, 'I shall become wretched in seeing this child suffer?' Well! if your useless pity proves too much of a burden, six months hence you can break your bonds, resume your liberty, and with three hundred crowns in your pocket, you can undertake that journey to Italy,—object of your secret dreams and most ardent longing. Happy man! arming yourself with the white staff of the pilgrim, you will shake the dust of Geierfels from your feet, and go far away to forget, before the façades of Venetian palaces, the dark mysteries of the old gothic castle and its wicked occupants."

CHAPTER VIII.

As Gilbert rapidly traced these last lines, the dinner-bell sounded. He descended in haste to the grand ha l. They were already at the table.

"Tell me, if you please," said Count Kostia, addressing him gayly, "what you think of our new comrade?"

Gilbert then noticed a fifth guest, whose face was not absolutely unknown to him. This newly invited individual was seated at the right of father Alexis, who seemed to relish his society but little, and was no less a personage than Solon, the favorite of the master, one of those apes which are vulgarly called "monkeys in mourning," with black hair, but with face, hands and feet of a reddish brown.

"You will not be vexed with me for inviting Solon to dine with us?" continued M. Leminof. "The poor beast has been hypochondriacal for several days, and I am glad to procure this little distraction for him. I hope it will dissipate it. I cannot bear melancholy faces; hypochondria is the fate of fools who have no mental resources."

He pronounced these last words half turning towards Stephane. The young man's face was more gloomy than ever. His eyes were swollen, and dark circles surrounded them. The indignation with which the brutal remark of his father filled him, gave him strength to recover from his dejection. He resolutely set about eating his soup, which he had not touched before, and feeling that Gilbert's eyes were fixed upon him, he raised his head quickly and darted upon him a withering glance. Gilbert thought he divined that he called him to account for his carnation, and could not help blushing,—so true is it that innocence does not suffice to secure one a clear conscience.

"Frankly, now," resumed the Count, lowering his voice, "don't you see some resemblance between the two persons who adorn the lower end of this table?"

"The resemblance does not strike me," answered Gilbert, coldly.

"Ah! *mon Dieu*, I do not mean to say that they are identical in all points. I readily grant that father Alexis uses his thumbs better; I admit, too, that he has a grain or two more of phosphorus in his brain, for you know the savants of to-day, at their own risk and peril, have discovered that the human mind is nothing but a phosphoric tinder-box."

"It is these same savants," said Gilbert, "who consider genius a nervous disorder. Much good may it do them. They are not my men."

"You treat science lightly; but answer my question seriously: do you not discover certain analogies between these two personages in black clothes and red faces?"

"My opinion, interrupted Gilbert impatiently, "is that Solon is very ugly, and that father Alexis is very handsome."

"Your answer embarrasses me," retorted the Count, "and I don't know whether I ought to thank you for the compliment you pay my priest, or be angry at the hard things you say of my monkey. One thing is certain," added he, "that my monkey and my priest,—I'm wrong,—my priest and my monkey, resemble each other in one respect: they have both a passionate appetite for truffles. You will soon see."

They were just serving a fowl with truffles. Solon devoured his portion in the twinkling of an eye, and as he was prone to coveting the property of others, he fixed his eyes, full of affectionate longing, on his neighbor's plate. Active, adroit, and watching his opportunity, he seized the moment when the priest was carrying his glass to his lips, to extend his paw, seize a truffle, and swallow it, was the work of but half a second. Beside himself with indignation, the holy man turned quickly and looked at the robber with flashing eyes. The monkey was but little affected by his anger, and to celebrate the happy success of his roguery, he capered and frisked in a ridiculous and frantic way, clinging with his fore paws to the back of his chair. The good father shook his head sadly, moved his plate further off, and returned to his eating, not, however, without watching the movements of the enemy from the corner of his eye. In vain he kept guard; in spite of his precautions,—a new attack, a new larceny—and fresh caperings of joy by the monkey. Father Alexis at last lost patience, aud the monkey received a vigorous blow full in the muzzle, which drew from him a sharp shriek; but at the same instant the priest felt two rows of teeth bury themselves in his left cheek. He could hardly repress a cry, and gave up the game, leaving Solon to gorge himself to his beard in the spoils, while he busied himself in staunching his wound, from which the blood gushed freely.

The Count affected to be ignorant of all that

passed; but there was a merry sparkle in his eyes which testified that not a detail of this tragic comedy had escaped his notice.

"You appear to distrust Solon, father," said he, seeing that the priest pushed back his chair and kept at a distance from the baboon. "You are wrong. He has very sweet manners; he is incapable of a bad action. He is only a little sad now, but in his melancholy, he observes all the rules of good breeding; which is not the case with all melancholy people," added he, throwing a look at Stephane, who, taken with a sudden access of sadness, had just leaned his elbow upon the table and made a screen of his right hand to hide his tears from his father. Gilbert felt himself near stifling, and as soon as he could, left the table. Fortunately no one followed him onto the terrace. Stephane had no more flowers to cultivate, and went to shut himself up in his high tower. On his part, father Alexis went to dress his wound; as to M. Leminof, he was displeased with the cool and, as he thought, composed air with which Gilbert had listened to his pleasantries, and he retired to his study, promising himself to give to Monsieur his secretary, whom, nevertheless, he valued very highly, that last touch of pliancy which he needed for his perfection. Count Kostia was of an age when even the strongest mind feels the necessity of occasional relaxation, and he would have been glad to have near him a pliant, agreeable companion, and enchanted could that companion have been his secretary.

Gilbert strode across the terrace, and, leaning over the parapet, gazed long and silently at the high road. "Ten months yet!" said he to himself, and contracting his brows, he turned to look at the odious castle, where destiny had cast his lot. It seemed as if the old pile wished to avenge itself for his ill humor: never had it been clothed with such a smiling aspect. A ray of the setting sun rested obliquely upon its wide roof; the bricks had the warm color of amber, the highest points were bathed in gold dust, and the gables and vanes threw out sparks. The air was balmy; the lilacs, the citron, the jasmine, and the honeysuckle intermingled their perfumes, which the almost imperceptible breath of the north wind spread in little waves to the four corners of the terrace. And these wandering perfumes mingled themselves, in passing, with other odors more delicate and more subtle; from each leaf, each petal, each blade of grass, exhaled secret aromas, mute words which the plants exchange with each other, and which revealed to Gilbert's heart the great mystery of happiness which animates the soul of things.

Intoxicated in all his senses, he congratulated himself that he was still able to relish those contemplative joys which had rendered him so happy during the first two weeks of his stay at Geierfels. He crossed the terrace to where, between an acacia elegantly trimmed and a catalpa with pale green leaves, there nestled a marble basin whose cracked edges were covered with moss and wild cresses. Limpid water filled this cup, encircled by the velvety grass of the lawn, and from its centre, on a porphyry pedestal, rose a statue yellowed and defaced by time, representing a dancing faun. An Olympian smile played about his lips. The horned god leaned forward from the height of his pedestal, gazing at his tremulous image, to which the water lilies bordering the basin formed a verdant frame. He seemed to take delight in seeing his mirth reflected in the limpid reservoir which, rippled at intervals by the straying wind, multiplied his laugh and dispersed it in every direction. At the same time, the mouth of the subterranean canal which conveyed the water to the basin, emptying itself with a slight noise, lent a voice to this soul of silent irony which the sculptor had enclosed in the marble bosom of his statue.

Gilbert, leaning his back against the trunk of the

catalpa, gazed upon this fresh and charming picture; but the mocking mirth of the fawn said nothing to his heart, and his eyes rested in preference upon a magnificent nymphæa which, upborne upon its long stem, floated dreamily on the surface of the water. Its brilliant white corolla seemed to him the symbol of the deep pure joys which enter the heart of man when God descends from heaven to dwell in it, and at moments he repeated to himself in a low voice the sacred device of Buddhism: *Eternal peace in the lotus!* As he crossed the grass-plot which surrounded the basin, his eye fell upon something which made a dark spot in this brilliant parterre. It was a little piece of uncultivated ground, a place gloomy and desolate—the poor devastated garden of Stephane. At this sight, his heart was oppressed; he hurried away and took refuge in the northern extremity of the terrace. There grew an immense weeping ash, the branches of which bending down to the ground, formed a charming arbor. In the middle of this summer house of entwined branches, a neighboring laburnum hung its grapes of yellow gold, which exhaled an exquisite odor. A circular bank surrounded the trunk of the ash, and Gilbert threw himself dejectedly upon it. He was angry with himself, when he found that the tearful face of Stephane pursued him anew. "Ah!" thought he, "this child has just had new cause for sorrow, and is probably still weeping shut up in his tower, leaning upon his table, alone, a prey to himself, without a friend to ask about his trouble, to console, to pity and to comfort him. But I cannot dry his tears. Why trouble myself about him? Plague on a useless pity which spoils my life and helps no one!

Gilbert was determined to drown his sorrows this evening in the divine harmonies of nature. To succeed the better, he called poetry to his aid, for the great poets are the eternal mediators between the soul of things and our feeble hearts of earth and clay.

He recited the distichcs where Goethe has related in a tongue worthy of Homer or Lucretius the metamorphosis of the plants. This was placed like a preamble at the beginning of the volume which he carried with him in his walks, and he had learned it by heart a few days before. The better to penetrate the sense of these admirable lines, he tried to translate them into french alexandrines, which he sometimes composed. This effort at translation soon appeared to him beyond his abilities; all the French words seemed too noisy, too brilliant or too vulgar, or too solemn to render these mute accents, these intonations veiled as if in religious mystery, by which the author of Faust intended to express the subtle sounds and even the silence of nature. We know that it is only in German poetry that we can hear the grass growing from the bosom of the earth, and the celestial spheres revolving in space.

Every language has its pedals and its peculiar registers; the Teutonic muse alone can execute these solemn airs which must be played with the soft pedal. For more than an hour Gilbert exhausted himself in vain attempts, and at last, disheartened, he contented himself with reciting aloud the poem which he despaired of translating. He uttered the first part with the fire of enthusiasm; but his voice fell as he pronounced the following passage:

"Every flower, my beloved, speaks to thee in a voice distinct and clear; every plant announces to thee plainly the eternal laws of life; but these sacred hieroglyphics of the goddess which thou decipherest upon their perfumed foreheads, thou wilt find everywhere hidden under other emblems. Let the caterpillar drag itself creeping along, and soon the light butterfly darts rapidly through the air; and let man also, with his power of self-development, follow the circle of his soul's metamorphoses. Oh! then wilt thou remember that the bond which united our spirits was first a germ from which sprang in time a sweet and charming acquaintance; friendship in its turn soon revealed its power in our hearts, until love came at last, crowning it with flowers and fruits."

At this place a light cloud of sadness passed over Gilbert's face; he felt a secret dissatisfaction at meeting in the verses of his favorite poet, a passage which he could not apply to his own experience.

"Apparently," said he to himself after some reflection, "up to this time I have not met the soul, twin sister to my own, which God destines for my love, or if I have met her, she has not given me time to recognize her. In matters of passion, I am not one of those who precipitates events. My sentiments are submissive to the law of insensible progress; they know nothing about sudden and miraculous developments. Yes, a simple acquaintance to commence with, then friendship and at last love, the caterpillar becoming a butterfly, and trying his azure wings, and the tree covering itself with flowers and fruit,—some day perhaps—in my pilgrimage to Italy —*chi lo sa?*"

Meanwhile night had come, a night like a softened and refreshed day. The radiant moon shone in the zenith; she inundated the fields of heaven with soft whiteness, she shook her torch over the Rhine and made the crests of its restless waves scintillate; she poured over the tops of the trees a rain of silvery light; she suspended from their branches necklaces of sapphires and azure diamonds, which the breeze in passing sportively dashed together. The great slumbering woods thrilled at the touch of this dew of light which bathed their lofty brows; they felt something divine insinuating itself in the horror of their sombre recesses. From time to time a nightingale gave to the wind a few notes sonorous and sustained; it seemed the voice of the forest, speaking in its sleep,—its soul carried away in ecstasy exhaling its intoxication in a long sigh of love.

Gilbert had been sitting up very late recently since

he had decided to remain but a short time at Geierfels, and he had grown pale over the Byzantines in the hope of advancing in his task so much, that Count Kostia would more easily consent to his departure. Robust as was his constitution, he finished by tiring himself out, and nature claiming its rights, sleep seized him at the moment when he was about leaving the bank to seek his room, and have a little nocturnal chat with Agathias and Procopius.

When he awoke, the moon had already declined towards the horizon, which discovery surprised him greatly, as he thought he had slept but a few moments. He rose and shook his limbs, stiff from the dampness. Fortunately, he was the only one at Geierfels who had free ingress and egress; the turret which he inhabited communicated with the terrace by a private staircase, to the entrance of which he had the key. Fortunately too the bull dogs had learned to know him, and never dreamed of disturbing his movements. He gained the little door without any difficulty, opened it, and having lit a candle which he drew from his pocket, commenced cautiously to ascend the winding staircase, the steps of which were broken in many places. He had just reached the first landing where terminated the spacious corridor which extended along the principal façade parallel with the terrace, and was preparing to cross it, when he heard a long and painful groan, which seemed to come from the other end of the gallery. Starting, he remained motionless some moments, with neck extended and ears alert, peering into the obscurity from whence he expected to see some melancholy phantom emerge; but almost immediately a gust of wind driving through the broken square of a dormer window made it grind upon its hinges and give out a plaintive sound, which reverberated through the corridor. Gilbert then fancied that what he had taken for a sigh was only the moaning of the wind, counterfeiting in its melancholy gambols the voice of human grief. Resuming his ascent, he had already mounted some steps, when a second groan, still more dismal than the first, reached his ears and froze the blood in his veins. He was sure he could not be deceived now; the wind had no such accents—it was a wail, sharp, harsh and heartrending, which seemed as though it might come from the bosom of a spectre.

A thousand sinister suppositions assailed Gilbert's mind, but he gave himself no time to reflect. Agitated, panting, his head on fire, he sprang with one bound down the staircase and reaching the entrance of the gallery, cried out in a trembling voice and scarcely knowing what he said:

"Who's there? Who wants assistance? I, Gilbert, am ready to come to his aid!—"

His voice was swallowed up and lost in the sombre arches of the corridor. No answer; the darkness remained dumb. In the rapidity of his movement, Gilbert had extinguished his candle; he prepared to relight it, when a bat flew by and struck his forehead with his wings. The start which this unforeseen attack gave him, made him drop the candle; he stooped to pick it up, but could not find it. In spite of this accident, he walked on. A feeble ray of moonlight which came in by the dormer window and shed through the entrance of the corridor a long thread of blueish light, seemed to guide him a few steps. Then he groped his way with arms extended and touching the wall. Every few steps he stopped and listened, and repeated in a voice hoarse with excitement:

"Who's there? You who are moaning, can I do anything to help you?"

Nothing answered him except the beating of his heart and the murmur of the wind, which continued to torment the hinges of the dormer window.

The gallery into which Gilbert had entered, was divided half way in its length by two steps, at the bottom of which was a large iron door, always kept open during the day, but closed and double locked as night set in. Approaching this, Gilbert saw a feeble light glimmering beneath the door. He descended the steps, and looking through the key-hole from which the key had been withdrawn, saw what changed the frightful anguish he had just been suffering into surprise and terror.

At twenty paces from him he saw the appalling figure of a phantom standing erect; it was enveloped in a large white cloth wound several times round its body, passing under its left arm, and falling over the right shoulder. In one hand it held a torch and a sword, in the other an oval ebony frame of which Gilbert could only see the back, but which seemed to enclose a portrait. The face of this spectre was emaciated, drawn and of unusual length; its skin, withered and dry, seemed to be incrusted upon its bones, its complexion was sallow; a profuse perspiration trickled from its brows and glued the hair to its temples. Nothing could describe the expression of terror in its face. It seemed to Gilbert that its two burning eyeballs penetrated even through the door, though they saw nothing which surrounded them; their vision seemed turned within, and the invisible object which fastened their gaze, a heart haunted by spectres.

Suddenly the lips of this nocturnal wanderer opened, and another groan more fearful than the first issued from them. It seemed as if his burdened breast wished to shake off by a violent effort a mountain of weariness, the weight of which was crushing it, or rather as though the soul sought to expel itself in this despairing cry. Gilbert was seized with inexpressible agitation, his hair stood on end. He started to fly; but a curiosity stronger than his terror prevented him from leaving the spot and kept him riveted to the door. By the eyebrows and cheek bones, in spite of the distortion of the face, he had recognized Count Kostia.

At length this sinister somnambulist stirred from his motionless position and advanced at a slow pace; he walked like an automaton. After taking a dozen steps he stopped, looked around him and slightly bent forward. His strained features resumed their natural proportions, life re-animated his brow, the deathlike inertia of his face gave place to an expression of sadness and prostration. For a few seconds his lips moved, without saying a word, as if to become flexible and fashioned anew to the use of speech;—then, in a soft voice which Gilbert did not recognize, and with the plaintive accents of a suffering child, he murmured:

"How heavy this portrait is! I can carry it no longer; take it out of my hands, it burns them. In mercy, extinguish this fire. I have a brand in my breast. It must be kept covered with ashes; when I can see it no more, I shall suffer less. It is my eyes that make me suffer, if I were blind I could return to Moscow."

Then in a harsher voice:

"I could easily destroy this likeness, but *the other*, I cannot kill it, curses on me! it is the better portrait of the two. There is her hair, her mouth, her smile. Ah, thank God, I have killed the smile. The smile is no longer there. I have buried the smile. But there is the mole in the corner of the mouth. I have kissed it a thousand times; take away that mole, it hurts me. If that mole were gone I should suffer less. Merciful Heaven! it is always there. But I have buried the smile. The smile is no more. I have buried it deep in a leaden coffin. It can't come . . . .

Then suddenly changing his accent, and in a tragical, but bitter voice, his eyes fixed upon the large rusty sword which he held in his right hand, he muttered:

"The spot will not go away." The iron will not drink it. It was not for this blood it thirsted. I shall find it in the other, it will drink that. Ah! we shall see how it will drink it."

Upon this, he relapsed into silence and appeared to be thinking deeply. Then raising his head, he cried in a voice so strong and vibrating that the iron door trembled upon its hinges:

"Morlof, then it was not thou!" Ah! my dear friend, I was deceived. . . . Go, do not regret life. It is only the dream of a screech-owl. . . . Believe me, friend, I want to die, but I cannot. I must know . . . . I must discover. . . . Ah! Morlof, Morlof, leave thy hands in mine, or I shall think thou hast not forgiven me. . . . God! how cold these hands are . . . . cold . . . cold. . . ."

And at these words he shuddered; his head moved convulsively upon his shoulders, and his teeth chattered; but soon calming himself, he murmured:

"I want to know the name, I must know that name! Is there no one who can tell me that name?"

Thus speaking, he raised the picture to a level with his face, and with bent head and extended neck, appeared to be trying to decipher upon the canvas some microscopic writing or obscure hieroglyphics.

"The name is there!" said he. "It is written somewhere about the heart,—at the bottom of the heart; but I cannot read it, the writing is so fine, it is a female hand; I do not know how to read a woman's writing. They have a cipher of which Satan alone has the key. My sight is failing me. I have flies in my head. There is always one of them that hides this name from me. Oh! in mercy, in pity, take away the fly and bring me a pair of pincers. . . . With good pincers I will seek that name even in the last fibres of this heart which beats no more."

He added with a terrible air:

"The dead do not open their teeth. The one who lives will speak. You shall see how I will make him speak. You shall see how I will make him speak. . . . Tear off his black robe, stretch him on this plank. The iron boots! the iron boots! tighten the boots!"

Then interrupting himself abruptly, he raised his eyes and fixed them upon the door. An expression of fury mingled with terror swept over his face, as if he had suddenly perceived some hideous and alarming object. His features became distorted; his mouth worked convulsively and frothed; his eyes, unnaturally dilated, darted flames; he uttered a hollow moan, took a few steps backward, and suddenly dropping his torch to the ground, where it went out, he cried in a frightful voice:

"There are eyes behind the door! there are eyes! there are eyes!"

Horror-struck, distracted, beside himself, Gilbert turned and took to flight. In spite of the darkness, he found his way as if by a miracle. He crossed the corridor at a run, mounted the staircase in three bounds, dashed into his chamber and bolted the door. Then he hurriedly lighted a candle, and having glanced about to assure himself that the phantom had not followed him into his room, dropped heavily upon a chair, stunned and breathless. In a few moments he had collected his thoughts, and was ashamed of his terror; but in spite of himself his agitation was such that at every noise which struck his ear, he thought he heard the step of Count Kostia ascending the staircase of his turret. It was not until he had bathed his burning head in cold water, that he recovered something like tranquillity; and, determining by a supreme effort to banish the frightful images which haunted him, he seated himself at his work-table and resolutely opened one of the Byzantine folios. As he began to read, his eye fell upon an unsealed letter which had been left on his table during his absence; it ran thus:

"Man of grand phrases, I write to you to inform you of the hatred with which you inspire me. I wish you to understand that from the first day I saw you, your bearing, your face, your manners, your whole person, have been objects of distrust and aversion to me. I thought I recognized an enemy in you, and the result has proved that I was not mistaken. Now I hate you, and I tell you so frankly, for I am not a hypocrite, and I want you to know, that just now in my prayers I supplicated St. George to give me an opportunity of revenging myself upon you. What do you want in this house? What is there between us and you? How long do you intend to torture me with your odious presence, your ironical smiles, and your insulting glances? Before your arrival I was not completely unhappy. God be praised, it has been reserved for you to give me the finishing stroke. Before, I could weep at my ease, with none to busy themselves in counting my tears; the man that makes me shed them does not lower himself to such petty calculations; he has confidence in me, he knows that at the end of the year the account will be there; but you! you watch me, you pry into me, you study me. I see very well that, while you are looking at me, you are indulging in little dialogues with yourself, and these little dialogues are insupportable to me. Mark me now, I forbid you to study me. I forbid you to understand me. It is an affront which you have no right to put upon me, and I have the right to be incomprehensible if it pleases me. Ah! once a little while ago, I felt that you had your eyes fastened on me again. And then I raised my head, and looked at you steadily and forced you to blush. . . . Yes, you did blush; do not attempt to deny it! What a consolation to me! What a triumph! Alas! for all that, I dare not go to my own window any longer for fear of seeing you ogling the sky, and making declarations of love to nature with your sentimental air.

Tell me now in a few words, clever man that you are, how you manage to combine so much sentimentality with such skillful diplomacy? Tender friend of childhood, of virtue and of sunsets, what an adroit courtier you make! From the first day you came here, the master honored you with his confidence and his affection. How he esteems you! how he cherishes you! what attentions! what favors! Will he not order us to-morrow to kiss the dust under your feet? If you want to know what disgusts me the most in you, it is the unalterable placidity of your disposition and your face. You know the faun who admires himself night and day in the basin upon the terrace; he is always laughing and looks at himself laugh. I detest this eternal laughter from the bottom of my soul, as I detest you, as I detest the whole world with the exception of my horse Soliman. But he at least is sincere in his gayety; he shows himself what he really is, life amuses him, great good may it do him! But you envelope your beatific happiness in an intolerable gravity. Your tranquil airs fill me with consternation; your great, contented eyes seem to say: "I am very well, so much the worse for the sick!" One word more. You treat me as a child, —I will prove to you that I am not a child in showing you how well I have divined you. The secret of your being is, that you were born without passions! Confess honestly that you have never in your life felt a sentiment of disgust, of anger or of pity. Is there a single passion, tell me, that you have experienced, or that you are acquainted with, except through your books? Your soul is like your cravat, which is always tied precisely the same way, and has such an air of repose and rationality about it, that it is perfectly insufferable to me. Yes, the bow of that cravat exasperates me; the two ends are always exactly the same length, and have an effect of *inderangeability* which nearly drives me mad. Not that this famous bow is elegant. No, a thousand times no! but it has an exasperating accuracy. And in this, behold the true story of your soul. Every night when you go to bed you put it in its proper folds; every morning you unfold it carefully without rumpling it! And you dare to plume yourself on your wisdom! What does this pretended wisdom prove? Nothing, unless it be that you have poor blood, and that you were fifty years old when you were born. There is, however, one passion which no one will deny that you possess. You understand me,—man of the gilded tongue and the viper's heart,—you have a passion common to many others! But, hold, in commencing this letter, I intended to conceal from you that I had discovered everything. I feared it would give you too much pleasure to learn that I know.—Oh! why can't I make you stand before me now this moment! I should confound you! how I would force you to fall at my feet and cry for pardon!

"Oh, my dear flowers, my Maltese cross, my verbenas, my white starred flox, and you my musk rosebush, and above all my beautiful variegated carnation, which ought to be opening to-day! Was it then for him,—was it to rejoice the eyes of this insolent parasite, that I planted, watered, and tended you with so much care? Beloved flowers, will you not share my hate? Send out from each of your cups, from each of your corollas, some devouring insect, some wasp with pointed sting, some furious horse-fly and let them all together throw themselves upon him, harrass him and persecute him with their threatening buzzing, and pierce his face with their poisoned stings. And you yourselves, my cherished daughters, at his approach, fold up your beautiful petals, refuse him your perfumes, cheat him of his cares and his hopes, let the sap dry up in your fibres, that he may have the mortification of seeing you perish and fall to dust in his hands. And may he, this treacherous man, may he before your blighted petals and drooping stems, pine away himself with ennui, spite, anger and remorse!

CHAPTER IX.

THE domestic corps of M. Leminof consisted of a French cook, a German valet de chambre named Fritz, and the faithful and robust Ivan. He also employed a gardener and a porter; but they did not form a part of his household, and returned every evening to the neighboring village, where they passed the night.

The cook and the valet de chambre had been in the service of Count Kostia but a few months. They both slept in the entre-sol, and during the night all communication between the two stories was cut off by a large oaken door at the foot of the grand staircase, which the Count closed and double-locked himself. As to Ivan, his position was not that of a common servant. In his quality of serf, he was the property, the thing of his master; but his intelligence and devotion to him had won for him the honor of becoming his *man*, an appendage of his person. For more than thirty years he had never quitted him; at Moscow, as well as in his travels, he had served him with irreproachable fidelity, and had mingled in all the great and small adventures of his life; had given to him essential proofs of his attachment and ability; and, what was still more important, without ever having been taken into his confidence, he possessed all his secrets, yet seemed to see nothing. Real treasure for a master, such a servant,—who has the gift of reading his heart, and whose clairvoyance never betrays itself by a word, a smile, or a look. Thus Ivan possessed the full confidence of the Count, and he enjoyed that half liberty which is the portion of responsible agents. Woe to him if at any time he committed the slightest fault! His least negligence, his most excusable forgetfulness exposed him to severe punishment, and he cruelly expiated the honor of his responsibility. Dangerous as was this honor, he was still proud of it, for he had a dignity after his fashion. Not but that he had once desired to be emancipated: in his youth he had dreamed of becoming a peddler and pursuing this vocation on the high-roads; but since his beard had begun to turn grey, he had acquired a taste for sedentary life, and if his master had emancipated him now, he would not have known what to do with his liberty. To feel himself necessary was happiness to him, and his happiness was real. This was the secret of that perpetual smile wh ch surprised Gilbert so much. It must be owned too, that ordinarily, and when he had nothing to reprove him for, M. Leminof treated his serf humanely. If on the preceding day he had chastised him with so much rigor for an offence which was not attributable to him, it was because he had arrears to make up. Six weeks before, as we have seen, the indefatigable watchfulness of Ivan was defeated by his prisoner; and Stephane, for the first time in his life, had coursed the plains without his guardian. This unforeseen escapade had plunged Ivan into such an excess of despair, that Count Kostia had taken pity on him.

"Do not tear thy hair, my son!" he had said to him. "For this once I pardon thee; but I do not pardon second offences, and for the least negligence thou shalt be paid double."

Still, after having beaten him, the Count had dressed his wounds with his own hands, a proof of benevolence by no means common. The next day, when father Alexis had been bitten by the odious Solon, had Count Kostia bathed the poor priest's bloody cheek with his own hands? Had he even dreamed of offering his ointment to him? Ah! it was because, in the scale of his affections, his serf and his chaplain did not weigh the same!

Thus Ivan had reasons for not being too much discontented with his master, and he had better yet for being contented with himself. He possessed a certain natural nobility of character mingled with gentleness, his manners were grave and circumspect, and he was always self-possessed; no free man ever respected himself more. Satisfied with his lot, he was not tempted to seek forgetfulness of it in the excitement of intoxication; he never drank strong liquors, but to make up for it, had a very pronounced taste for tea, which Count Kostia let him drink at discretion, and when he had swallowed five or six cups, he generally found himself in a state of tranquil ecstasy, in which he fully enjoyed life and himself. In these moments he would often sing with a pure and melodious voice, accompanying himself with a guitar, one of those popular songs of his country, whose beauty strikes all travellers. Oh poor sick nerves of Stephane, what grievous disturbance these songs and this guitar caused you! Let us add that Ivan also knew nothing of another kind of intoxication very common in his class: he was never intemperate in his language. Away from his master as in his presence, he had the same quiet manner and was as discreet in his speech as in his conduct. Incredibly strong, handling upon occasion with incomparable skill the hatchet which he always carried suspended from his girdle, capable with its aid of constructing at need a boat, a wagon or a house, he possessed, without the vices of the *moujiks*, all the qualities of body and mind which will perhaps make them, when they shall have shaken off the yoke of servitude and misery, one of the first peoples of the earth. One thing however grieved Ivan. He had a sensitive heart, and he wished that good might come to all who surrounded him. This was another thing which his smile indicated. To be loved by Stephane he would have given much; but this was a problem as difficult to solve as the quadrature of the circle. How could Stephane ever love one whose sight recalled to him unceasingly all the misery of his condition—the agent of the tyrant, the turnkey of his prison? And when I say prison, it is not a figure of speech. Stephane had very nearly the life of a prisoner, and if there were no bars at his window, it was only because it looked out upon a steep roof, which sloped over a precipice; this was enough to render gratings unnecessary. M. Leminof's apartments were in a sort of projection of the building, upon which the two long parallel galleries opened, one leading to Gilbert's turret, and the other to the square tower occupied by Stephane. The gallery upon the left was divided half-way by a large oak door, as was that on the right by an iron one; but this oak door never opened, there was a wicket in it, the key of which Ivan kept. At a few steps from the door, a long and narrow cabinet opened into the wall: it was here that the serf lodged. Forty paces further at the end of the corridor, appeared the winding staircase which led to the apartments of Stephane, which were in the second story of the tower and consisted of three large rooms. This tower had no secret entrance like the one occupied by Gilbert; there was no egress except by the corridor, and from the corridor by the wicket. So the young man was well guarded. And remember that the wicket was never opened to him, except on Sunday morning at the hour of mass, twice a week for his ride, and on other days at the dinner hour, which was towards evening. The rest of the time he lived like a recluse, and for diversion could either stand at his casement and watch the sky, or pace the long vaulted corridor like a young lion caged, stopping in his turns pensively, and standing with folded arms before the enormous oak door to look at its great hinges, the iron bolts, and the thick timbers, which must seem to him to cast a sarcastic defiance upon his feeble arms, and poor, consuming heart. Thus the private domain of Ivan was composed of a door, a gallery, a tower and a child, and no one ever entered upon his grounds except father Alexis, who came two hours every Saturday to explain the Catechism to Stephane. Ivan alone took charge of the prisoner's wants; he washed and mended his linen, cut and even made his clothes; an office in which he acquitted himself wonderfully, having fairy fingers and great natural taste. It is well known that in Russia the common people have innate instincts of elegance which betray themselves in all their handiwork. It might be considered enough to fill the position of *valet de chambre*, tailor and door-keeper; but in addition, Ivan was governor also, for M. Leminof, who troubled himself as little as possible about his son, gave only general instructions, leaving to the serf the task of regulating the details. Ivan was disposed to make the most moderate use of his power, and if he had yielded to his inclinations, the wicket door would have remained open oftener than closed; but he knew by experience that even in the interest of his pupil it was necessary to be strict: too much indulgence would have provoked the severity of the master and aggravated the condition of the victim. During the preceding year, the rides on horseback having become too frequent, the Count spoke one day of selling Soliman. This would have been a terrible blow to Stephane. Soliman, as he wrote Gilbert, was the only being he loved in the world. At another time, at the pressing solicitation of the young man, Ivan had consented to take him several consecutive evenings on the terrace to breathe the fresh air. At the end of a week the Count, whom nothing escaped, said to Ivan:

" My son, your young master's hair is too long, I shall soon give you an order to cut it."

This threat made Ivan shudder, for Stephane, who paid little attention to his person, had been recently seized with a passionate admiration for his magnificent curls; he took great care of them, dressed them, perfumed them, and one day as he gazed at them in the glass with excessive satisfaction, Ivan was forced to smile.

"Do not laugh," cried he turning quickly, "this hair is the only bond which holds me to life!"

Cut Stephane's hair! Ivan's hand would have trembled in executing this barbarous order; but Stephane did not believe in his good intentions. The idea of being governed by a serf was revolting to the pride of this impetuous young man, and his manners betrayed it; for he who trembled before his father, generally treated with imperious arrogance this inferior who held him in his power, and who with the end of his little finger could make him bend like a reed. As, however, in spite of his sixteen years and his sad life, he had remained more of a child than could have been believed, he continually flattered himself that he could get the better of his jailer; and to subdue him, he employed means, whose impotence he had proved a hundred times. Sometimes it would be the most absurd arguments, but more frequently he flew into a passion and lavished upon him the greatest contempt. At times, too, with his cap on one side, he would descend the staircase of the tower with a light step, cross the corridor rapidly, and arriving at the wicket, say in a careless tone:

"Ivan, open the door for me, and go saddle my horse. Go quickly, I'm in a hurry."

Ivan would shrug his shoulders and answer:

"You are dreaming."

"And you, you're asleep! Did you understand me? The weather is fine; I want to go out, I want to stroll, I intend to pass the whole day out of doors."

"You wish!" Ivan would say, shaking his head in a melancholy way. It is certain that these words "I wish" had a strange effect, pronounced by Stephane. Then the young man would become angry; cry, storm, and Ivan would say:

"Don't speak so loud; your father will hear you."

This made him lower his voice; but his efforts were not remitted, but on the contrary became more violent. To end this, the serf would take down his guitar and pretend to tune it, at which Stephane stopping his ears, would fly. These were his good days. There were others, when retired profoundly within himself and yielding to the weariness of his lot, he preserved a gloomy silence and sat for whole hours crouching upon the floor in one of the corners of his room, his head in his hands, contemplating with closed eyes the gray and clouded horizon of his life, and trembling at the idea that hours would succeed hours, days days, and years years, without bringing any change in the dry monotony of his existence.

Gilbert never had any intercourse with Ivan. He sometimes saw him in M. Leminof 's study, but they had not exchanged two words since their first meeting in the forest. The honest serf, who read faces, had vowed to him from the first a respectful affection. His sympathies had become still more lively, as might naturally be supposed, since Gilbert had interceded in his favor, and admiration mingled with them, knowing as he did, better than any one else, how much courage it required to interfere with his terrible master when transported by anger.

Therefore he wished deadly evil to Fritz, the valet de chambre, for the free talk which he indulged in below stairs in regard to the young secretary. This Fritz, who was at least six feet in height, was a clown of the ante-chamber who thought himself quite a personage. Gilbert was but little affected by his disagreeable ways and supercilious tone; but one day this master blockhead took such strange liberties with him, that he lost all patience. It happened the very morning after that exciting night in which Gilbert had experienced so many varied emotions. Fritz chose his time badly. There are moments when even the buzzing of a fly will upset the most amiable man in the world.

CHAPTER X.

THE castle clock had struck eight, when Gilbert sprang from his bed. Shall I confess that in dressing himself, when he came to tie his cravat, he hesitated for a moment? However, after reflection, he adjusted the knot as before, and would you believe it, he tied this famous, this regular knot without concentrating any attention upon it? His toilet finished, he went to the window. A sudden change had taken place in the weather; a cold, drizzly rain was falling noiselessly; very little wind; the horizon was enveloped in a thick fog; a long train of low clouds, looking like gigantic fish, floated slowly through the valley of the Rhine; the sky of a uniform grey, seemed to distill weariness and sadness; land and water were the color of mud. Gilbert cast his eyes upon his dear precipice: it was but a pit of frightful ugliness. He sank into an arm-chair. His thoughts harmonized with the weather; they formed a dismal landscape, over which a long procession of gloomy fancies and sinister apprehensions swept silently, like the trail of low clouds which wandered along the borders of the Rhine.

"No, a thousand times no!" mused he, "I can't stay in this place any longer; I shall lose my strength here, and my spirits and my health too. To be exposed to the blind hatred of an unhappy child, whose sorrows drive him to insanity; to be the table companion of a priest without dignity or moral elevation, who silently swallows the greatest outrages; to become the intimate, the complaisant friend of a great lord, whose past is suspicious, of an unnatural father who hates his son, of a man who at times transforms himself into a spectre, and who, stung by remorse, or thirsting for revenge, fills the corridors of his castle with savage howlings,—such a position is intolerable, and I must leave here at any cost! This castle is an unhealthy place; the walls are odious to me? I will not wait to penetrate into their secrets any further.

And Gilbert ransacked his brain for a pretext to quit Geierfels immediately. While engaged in this research, some one knocked at the door: it was Fritz, with his breakfast.

This morning he had the self-satisfied air of a fool who has worked out a folly by the sweat of his brow, and reached the fortunate moment when he can bring his invention to light. He entered without salutation, placed the tray which he carried upon the table; then turning to Gilbert, who was seated, said to him, winking his eye:

"Good morning, comrade! Comrade, good morning!"

"What do you say?" said Gilbert astonished, and looking at him steadily.

"I say: Good morning, comrade!" replied he, smiling agreeably.

"And to whom are you speaking, if you please?"

"I am speaking to you yourself, my comrade, and I say to you, Good morning, comrade! good morning!"

"Gilbert looked at him attentively, trying to find some explanation of this strange prank, and this excessive and astounding insolence.

"And will you tell me," he continued, after a few moments' silence, "will you be good enough to tell me, who gave you permission to call me comrade?"

"It was . . . . it was . . . ." answered Fritz, hemming and hawing. And he reflected a moment, as though trying to remember his lesson, that he might not stumble in its recital. "Ah! 'resumed he, it was simply his Excellency the Count, and I cannot conceive what you see astonishing in it."

"Have you ever heard the Count," demanded Gilbert, who felt his blood boiling in his veins, "call me your comrade?"

"Ah! certainly!" he answered with a long burst

of laughter. " Every day, when I come from him, M. le Count says to me: 'Well! how is your comrade, Gilbert?' And isn't it very natural? Don't we eat at the same rack? Are we not, both of us, in the service of the same master? And don't you see. . . ."

He was not able to say more, for Gilbert bounded from his chair, and crying:

" Go and tell your master that he is not my master!" He seized the valet de chambre by the collar. He was at least a head shorter than his adversary, but his grasp was like iron; and in spite of appearances, great Fritz proved but a weak and nerveless body, and greatly surprised at this unexpected attack, he could only open his large mouth and utter some inarticulate sounds. Gilbert had already dragged him to the top of the staircase. Then, Fritz recovering from his first flurry, tried to struggle, but he lost his footing, stumbled, and fell headlong down the staircase to the bottom. Gilbert came near following him in his descent, but fortunately saved himself by clinging to the balustrade. As he saw him rolling, he feared that he had been too violent, but felt reassured, when he saw him scramble up, feel himself, rub his back, turn to shake his fist and limp away.

He returned to his chamber and breakfasted peaceably.

" Quite an opportune adventure," thought he. " Now I shall be inflexible, unyielding, and if my trunks are not packed before night, I'm an idiot."

Gathering up under his arm a bundle of papers which were needed for the day's work, he left the room, his head erect and his spirits animated; but he had hardly descended the first flight of steps before his exaltation gave way to very different feelings. He could not look without shuddering at the place where he had stood like one petrified, listening to the horrible groans of the somnambulist. He stopped, and, looking at the packet which he held under his arm, thought to himself that it was with a spectre he was about to discuss Byzantine history. Then resuming his walk, he arrived at M. Leminof's study, where he almost expected tc see the formidable apparition of last night appear before his eyes, and hear a sepulchral voice crying out to him: "Those eyes behind the door were yours!" He remained motionless a few seconds, his hand upon his heart. At last he knocked. A voice cried: "Come in."

He opened the door and entered. Heavens! how far was the reality from his fancy.

M. Leminof was quietly seated in the embrasure of the window, looking at the rain and playing with his monkey. He no sooner perceived his secretary than he uttered an exclamation of joy, and after shutting up Solon in an adjoining room, he approached Gilbert, took both his hands in his and pressed them cordially, saying in an affectionate tone:

"Welcome, my dear Gilbert, I have been looking for you impatiently. I have been thinking a great deal since yesterday on our famous problem of the Sclavonic invasions, and I am far from being convinced by your arguments. Be on your guard, my dear sir, be on your guard! I propose to give you some thrusts that will trouble you to parry."

Gilbert, who had recovered his tranquillity, seated himself, and the discussion commenced. The point in dispute was the question of the degree of importance and influence of the establishment of the Sclavonians in the Byzantine empire during the middle ages. Upon this question, much debated at present, Count Kostia had espoused the opinion most favorable to the ambitions of Muscovite policy. He affected to renounce his country and to censure it without mercy; he had even denationalized himself to the extent of never speaking his mother tongue and of forbidding its use in his house. In fact, the idiom of Voltaire was more familiar to him than that of Karamzin, and he had accustomed himself for a long time even to think in French. In spite of all this, and of what ever he might say, he remained Russian at heart: this is a quality which cannot be lost.

Twelve o'clock sounded while they were at the height of the discussion.

"If you agree, my dear Gilbert," said M. Leminof, we will give ourselves a little relaxation. "Indeed you're truly a terrible fellow; there's no persuading you. Let us breakfast in peace, if you please, like two good friends, afterwards we will renew the fight."

The breakfast was invariably composed of toast *au caviar* and a small glass of Madeira wine; and every day at noon they suspended work for a few moments to partake of this little collation.

"Judge of my presumption," suddenly said M. Leminof, underscoring, so to speak, every word, "I passed *last night* (and he put a wide space between these two words) in pleading against you the cause of my Sclavonians. My arguments seemed to me irresistible. I beat you all hollow. I am like those fencers who are admirable in the training school, but who make a very bad figure in the field. I had prodigious eloquence *last night;* I don't know what has become of it; it seems to have fled like a phantom at the first crowing of the cock."

As he pronounced these words, Count Kostia fixed such piercing eyes on Gilbert, that they seemed to search through to the most remote recesses of his soul. Gilbert sustained the attack with perfect *sang froid.*

"Ah! sir," replied he coolly, "I don't know how you argue at night; but I assure you by day you're the most formidable logician I know."

Gilbert's tranquil air dissipated the suspicion which seemed to weigh upon M. Leminof.

"You act," said he gayly, "like those conquerors who exert themselves to console the generals they have beaten, thereby enhancing their real glory; but bah! arms are fickle, and I shall have my revenge at an early day."

"I venture to suggest that you do not delay it long," answered Gilbert in a grave tone. "Who knows how much longer I may remain at Geierfels?"

These words re-awakened the suspicions of the Count.

"What do you mean?" exclaimed he.

Whereupon Gilbert related in a firm, distinct tone the morning's adventure. As he advanced in the recital, he became warmer and repeated with an indignant air the remark which Fritz had attributed to the Count, and strongly emphasized his answer.

"Go and tell your master that he is not my master."

He flattered himself that he would pique the Count; he saw him already raising his head, and speaking in the clouds. He was destined to be mistaken to-day in all his conjectures. From the first words of his eloquent recital, Count Kostia appeared to be relieved of a pre-occupation which had disturbed him. He had been prepared for something else, and was glad to find himself mistaken. He listened to the rest with an undisturbed air, leaning back in his easy chair with his eyes fixed on the ceiling. When Gilbert had finished—

"And tell me, pray," said he without changing his posture, "how did you finish this rascal?"

"I took him by the collar," replied Gilbert, "and flung him down head first."

"*Peste!*" exclaimed the Count raising himself and looking at him with an air of surprise and admiration. "And tell me," resumed he smiling in his enjoyment, "did this domestic animal perish in his fall?"

"He may perhaps have broken his arms or legs. I didn't take the trouble to inquire."

M. Leminof rose and folded his arms on his breast.

"See now how liable our judgments are to be led astray, and how full of sense that Russian proverb is which says: 'It takes more than one day to compass a man!' Yesterday you had such a sentimental pathetic air, when I permitted myself to administer a little correction to my serf, that I took you in all simplicity for a philanthropist. I retract it now. You are one of those tyrants who are only moved for the victims of another. Pure professional jealousy! But," continued he, "there is one thing which astonishes me still more, and that is, that you Gilbert, you could for an instant believe—"

He checked himself, bent forward towards Gilbert, and looked at him scrutinizingly, making a shade of his two bony hands extended over his enormous eyebrows; then taking him by the arm, he led him to the embrasure of the window, and as if he had made a sudden change in his person which rendered him irrecognizable:

"Nothing could be better than your throwing the scoundrel down stairs," said he, "and if he is not quite dead, I shall drive him from here without pity; but that you should have believed that I, Count Leminof— Oh! it is too much, I dream— No, you are not the Gilbert that I know, the Gilbert I love, though I conceal it from myself—"

And taking him by both hands, he added:

"This man was silly enough to tell you that I was your master, and you replied to him with the Mirabeau tone: 'Go and tell your master—' My dear Gilbert, in the name of reason, I ask you to remember that the true is never the opposite of the false; it is another thing, that is all; but to which I add, that in answering as you did, you have cruelly compromised yourself. We should never contradict a fool; it is running the risk of being like him."

Gilbert blushed. He did not try to amend anything, but readily changing his tactics, he said smiling:

"I implore you, sir, not to drive this man away. I want him to stay to remind me occasionally that I am liable to lose my senses."

But what were his feelings when the Count, having sent for his valet de chambre, said to him:

"You have not done this on your own responsibility—you received orders. Who gave them?"

Fritz answered stammering:

"Do please forgive me, your excellency! It was M. Stephane who, yesterday evening, made me a present of two Russian crowns on condition that every morning for a week I should say to M. Saville 'good morning, comrade.'"

A flash of joy shone in the Count's eyes. He turned towards Gilbert, and pressing his hand, said to him:

"For this once, I thank you cordially for having addressed your complaints to me. The affair is more serious than I had thought. There is a malignant abscess there, which must be lanced once for all."

This surgical comparison made Gilbert shudder; he cursed his hasty passion and his stupidity. Why had he not suspected the real culprit? Why was it necessary for him to justify the hatred which Stephane had avowed towards him?

"And how happens it, sir," resumed Count Kostia, with less of anger in his tone, "that you have an opportunity of holding secret conversations with my son in the evening? When did you enter his service? Do you not know that you are to receive neither orders, messages, nor communications of any kind from him?"

Fritz, who in his heart blessed the admirable invention of lightning rods, explained as well as he could, that the evening before, in going up to his excellency's room, he had met Ivan on the staircase, going down to the grand hall to find a cap which his young master had forgotten. Apparently he had neglected to close the wicket, for Fritz, in going out through the gallery, had found Stephane, who, approaching him steathily, had given him his little lesson in a mysterious tone, and as Ivan returned at this moment without the cap he said:

"Dost thou not see, imbecile, that it's on my head," and he drew the cap from his pocket and proudly put it on his head, while he ran to his rooms laughing.

When he had finished his story, Fritz was profuse in his protestations of repentance, servile and tearful; the Count cut him short, declaring to him, that at the request of Gilbert he consented to pardon him; but that at the first complaint brought against him, he would give him but two hours to pack. When he had gone out, M. Leminof pulled another bell which communicated with the room of Ivan who presently appeared.

"Knowest thou, my son," said the Count to him in German, that thou hast been very negligent for some time? Thy mind fails, thy sight is feeble. Thou art growing old, my poor friend. Thou art like an old bloodhound in his decline, without teeth and without scent, who knows neither how to hunt the prey nor how to catch it. Thou must be on the retired list. I have already thought of the office I shall give thee in exchange. . . . Oh! do not deceive thyself. It is in vain to shrug thy shoulders, my son; thou art wrong in believing thyself necessary. By paying well I shall easily find one who will be worth as much——"

Ivan's eyes flashed.

"I do not believe you," replied he, in Russian; "you know very well that you are not amiable, but that I love you in spite of it, and when you have spent a hundred thousand roubles, you will not have secured one to replace me, whose affection for you will be worth a kopeck."

"Why dost thou speak Russian?" resumed the Count. "Thou knowest well that I have forbidden it. Apparently thou wishest that no one but myself may understand the sweet things which thou sayest to me. Go and cry them upon the roof, if that will give thee pleasure; but I have never asked thee to love me. I exact only faithful service on thy part, and I answer for it that thy substitute, when his young master shall tell him 'go and find my cap, which I have left in the grand hall,' will answer him coolly: 'I am not blind, my little father, your cap is in your pocket.'"

Ivan looked at his master attentively, and the expression of his face appeared to reassure him, for he began to smile.

"Meantime," said the Count, "so long as I keep thee in thy office, study to satisfy me. Go to thy room and reflect, and at the end of a quarter of an hour, bring thy little father here to me; I want to talk with him, and I will permit thee to listen, if that will give thee pleasure."

As soon as Ivan had gone, Gilbert begged M. Leminof not to pursue this miserable business. "I have punished Fritz," said he, "with perhaps undue severity; you yourself have rebuked and threatened him; I am satisfied."

"Pardon me. In all this Fritz was but an instrument. It would not be right to allow the real culprit to go unpunished!"

"It is no trouble to me to pardon that culprit," exclaimed Gilbert, with an animation beyond his control, "he is so unhappy!"

M. Leminof gave Gilbert a haughty and angry look. He strode through the room several times, his hands behind his back; then, with the easy tempered air of an absolute prince, who condescends to some unreasonable fancy of one of his favorites, made Gilbert sit down, and placing himself by his side:

"My dear sir," said he to him, "your last words show a singular forgetfulness on your part of our reciprocal agreements. You had engaged, if you remember, not to take any interest in any one here but yourself and myself. After that, what difference can it make to you, whether my son is happy or unhappy? Since, however, you have raised this question, I consent to an explanation; but let it be fully understood, that you are never, never, to revive the subject again. You can readily perceive, that if your society is agreeable to me, it is because I have the pleasure of forgetting with you the petty annoyances of domestic life. And now speak frankly, and tell me what makes you conclude that my son is unhappy."

Gilbert had a thousand things to reply, but they were difficult to say. So he hesitated to answer for a moment, and the Count anticipated him:

"*Mon Dieu!* I must needs proceed in advance of your accusations, a concession which I dare to hope you will appreciate. Perhaps you reproach me with not showing sufficient affection for my son in daily life. But what can you expect? The Leminofs are not affectionate. I don't remember ever to have received a single caress from my father. I have seen him sometimes pat his hounds, or give sugar to his horse; but I assure you that I never partook of his sweetmeats or his smiles, and at this hour I thank him for it. The education which he gave me hardened the affections, and it is the best service which a father can render his son. Life is a hard stepmother, my dear Gilbert; how many smiles have you seen pass over her brazen lips! Besides, I have particular reasons for not treating Stephane with too much tenderness. He seems to you to be unhappy, he will be so forever if I do not strive to discipline his inclinations and to break his intractable disposition. The child was born under an evil star. At once feeble and violent, he unites with very ardent passions a deplorable puerility of mind; incapable of serious thought, the merest trivialities move him to fever heat, and he talks childish prattle with all the gestures of great passion. And what is worse, interesting himself greatly in himself, he thinks it very natural that this interest should be shared by all the world. Do not imagine that his is a loving heart that feels a necessity of spending itself on others. He likes to make his emotions spectacular, and as his impressions are events for him, he would like to display them, even to the inhabitants of Sirius. His soul is like a lake swept by a gale of wind that would drive a man-of-war at the rate of twenty-five knots an hour; and on this lake Stephane sails his squadrons of nut-shells, and sees them come, go, tack, run aground and capsize. He keeps his log-book very accurately, pompously registers all the shipwrecks, and as these spectacles transport him with admiration, he is indignant to find that he alone is moved by them. This is what makes him unhappy; and you will agree with me that it is not my fault. The *régime* which I prescribe for my invalid may appear to you a little severe, but it's the only way by which I can hope to cure him. Leading a regular, uniform life,—and sad enough I admit—he will gradually become surfeited with his own emotions when the objects of them are never renewed, and he will end, I hope, by demanding the diversions of work and study. May he be able some day to discover that a problem of Euclid is more interesting than the wreck of a nutshell! Upon that day he will enter upon full convalescence, and I shall not be the last to rejoice in it."

M. Leminof spoke in a tone so serious and composed, that for a few moments Gilbert could have imagined him a pedagogue gravely explaining his maxims of education; but he could not forget that expression of ferocious joy which was depicted on his face at the moment when Stephane fled sobbing from the garden, and he remembered also the somnambulist who, on the preceding night, had uttered certain broken phrases in regard to a *living portrait* and *a buried smile.* These mysterious words, terrible in their obscurity, had appeared to him to allude to Stephane, and they accorded badly with the airs of paternal solicitude which M. Leminof had deigned to affect in the past few minutes. He had a show of reason, however, in his argument; and the picture which he drew of his son, if cruelly exaggerated, had still some points of resemblance. Only Gilbert had reason to think that the Count purposely confounded cause and effect, and that Stephane's malady was the work of the physician.

"Will you permit me, sir," answered he, "to tell you all that I have on my heart?"

"Speak, speak, improve the opportunity: I swear to you it won't occur again."

And looking at his watch:

"You have still five minutes to talk with me about my son. Hurry; I will not grant you two seconds more."

"I have heard it said," resumed Gilbert, "that in building bridges and causeways, the best foundations are those which *humor* the waves of the sea. These are foundations with inclined slopes, which, instead of breaking the waves abruptly, check their movement by degrees, and abate their force without violence."

"You favor anodynes, Monsieur disciple of Galen," exclaimed M. Leminof. "Each one according to his temperament. We cannot reconstruct ourselves. I am a very violent, very passionate man, and when, for example, a servant offends me, I throw him headforemost down stairs. This happens to me every day."

"Between your son and your valet de chambre, the difference is great," answered Gilbert a little piqued.

"Did not your famous revolution proclaim absolute equality between all men?"

"In the law it is admirable, but not in tne heart of a father."

"Good God!" cried the Count, "I do not know that I have a father's heart for my son; I know only that I think a great deal about him, and that I strive according to my abilities to correct in him very grave faults, which threaten to compromise his future welfare. I know also for a certainty that this whiner enjoys some pleasures of which many children of his age are deprived, as, for example, a servant for himself, a horse, and as much money as he wants for his petty diversions. You are not ignorant of the use which he makes of this money, neither in regard to the two thalers expended yesterday to corrupt my valet, nor of the seven crowns with which he purchased the delightful pleasure, the other day in your presence, of having his foot kissed by a troop of young rustics. And at this point, I will tell you that Ivan has reported to me that, on this same day, Stephane turned up his sleeve to make you admire a scar which he carried upon one of his wrists. Oblige me by telling me what blue story he related to you on this subject."

This unexpected question troubled Gilbert a little.

"To conceal nothing from you," answered he hesitatingly, "he told me, that for an escapade which he had made, he had been condemned to pass a fortnight in a dungeon in irons."

"And you believed it!" cried the Count, shrugging his shoulders. "The truth is, that, for a fortnight, I compelled my son to pass one hour every evening in an uninhabited wing of this castle; my intention was not so much to punish him for an act of insubordination, as to cure him of the foolish terrors by which he is tormented, for this boy of sixteen, who often shows himself brave even to rashness, believes in ghosts, in apparitions, in vampires. I ought to authorize him to guard himself at night by the best toothed of my bull-dogs. Oh! what a strange compound God has given me for a son!"

At this moment the noise of steps was heard in the corridor.

"In the name of the kind friendship which you

profess for me, sir," exclaimed Gilbert, seizing one of M. Leminof's hands, "I beg of you, do not punish this child for a boyish freak for which I forgive him with all my heart!"

"I can refuse you nothing, my dear Gilbert," answered he with a smiling air. "I spare him from his pretended dungeons. I dare hope that you will give me credit for it."

"I thank you; but one thing more: the flowers you deprived him of."

"*Mon Dieu!* since you wish it, we will have them restored to him, and to please you, I will content myself with having him make his apologies to you in due form."

"Make apologies to me!" cried Gilbert in consternation; "but that will be the most cruel of punishments."

"We will leave him the choice," said the Count, dryly. And as Gilbert insisted: "This time you ask too much!" added he in a tone which admitted of no reply. It is a question of principles, and in such matters I never compromise."

Gilbert perceived that even in Stephane's interest, it was necessary to desist, but he understood also to what extent the pride of the young man would suffer, and cursed himself a thousand times for having spoken.

Some one knocked at the door.

"Come in," cried the Count in a hoarse voice; and Stephane entered followed by Ivan.

CHAPTER XI.

STEPHANE remained standing in the middle of the room. He was paler than usual, and kept his eyes on the floor; but his bearing was good, and he affected a resolute air which he rarely displayed in the presence of his father. The Count remained silent for some time; he gazed with a cold eye on the supple and delicate body of his son, the exquisite elegance of his form, his fine and delicate features, framed in the slightly darkened gold of his hair. Never had the beauty of his child filled the heart of this father with keener bitterness. As for Gilbert, he had eyes only for a little black spot which he noticed for the first time upon the uniformly pale complexion of Stephane: it was like an almost imperceptible fly, under the left corner of his mouth.

"That is the mole," thought he, and he fancied he could hear the voice of the somnambulist cry:

"Take away that mole! it hurts me!"

Shuddering at this recollection, he felt tempted to rush from the room; but a look from the Count recalled him to himself; he made a strong effort to master his emotion, and fixing his eyes upon the window, he looked at the falling rain.

"As a preliminary question," suddenly exclaimed the Count, speaking to his son; "do me the favor, sir, to tell me how much time you have passed in what you call a dungeon, for I do not remember."

Stephane's face colored with a vivid blush. He hesitated a moment and then answered:

"I was there in all fifteen hours, which appeared to me as long as fifteen days."

"You see!" said the Count looking at Gilbert. "And now," resumed he, "let us come to the point; a scene of the greatest impropriety occurred in this house this morning. Fritz, my valet, in presenting himself to my secretary, who is my friend, permitted himself to say three times : 'Good morning, comrade ; comrade, good morning!'"

At these words Stephane's lips contracted slightly, as if about to smile; but the smile was arrested on its way.

"My little story amuses you, apparently," pursued the Count raising his head.

"It is the incredible folly of Fritz which diverts me," answered Stephane.

"His folly seems to me less than his insolence," replied the Count; "but without discussing words, I am delighted to see that you disavow his conduct. I ought not to conceal from you the fact, that this scoundrel wished to make me believe that he acted upon your orders, and I was resolved to punish you severely. I see now that he has lied, and it remains for me but to dismiss him in disgrace. Gilbert trembled lest Stephane's veracity should succumb under this temptation; the young man hesitated but an instant.

"I am the guilty one," answered he in a firm voice, "and it is I who should be punished."

"What," said M. Leminof, "was it then my son, who, availing himself of the only resources of his mind conceived this truly happy idea. The invention was admirable, it does honor to your genius. But if Fritz has been but the instrument to carry out your sublime conceptions, why do you laugh at his stupidity?"

"Oh, poor soul!" replied Stephane with animation, "oh! the donkey, how he spoiled my idea! I didn't order him to call M. Saville his comrade, but to treat him as a comrade, which is a different thing. Unfortunately I had not time to give him minute instructions, and he misunderstood me, but he did what he could conscientiously to earn his fee. The poor fellow must be pardoned. I am the only guilty one, I repeat it. I am the one to be punished."

"And might we know, sir," said the Count, "what

your intention was in causing M. Saville to be insulted by a servant?"

"I wished to humiliate him, to disgust him, and to force him to leave this house."

"And your motive?"

"My motive is that I hate him!" answered he in a hoarse voice.

"Always exaggerations," replied the Count sneeringly. "Can you not, sir, rid yourself of this detestable habit of perpetual exaggeration in the expression of your thoughts? Can I not impress upon your mind the maxims upon this subject which two men of equal genius have given us; M. de Metternich and Pigault Lebrun! The first of these illustrious men used to say that superlatives were the seals of fools, and the second wrote these immortal words:

"'Everything exaggerated is insignificant.'" Then extending his arm:

"To hate! to hate!" exclaimed he, "you say the word glibly. Do you know what it is? Sorrow, anger, jealousy, antipathy, aversion, you may know all these; but hatred, hatred!—you have no right to say this terrible word. Ah! hatred is a rough work! it is ceaseless torture, it is a cross of lead to carry, and to sustain its weight without breaking down requires very different shoulders than yours!"

At this moment Stephane ventured to look his father in the face. He slowly uplifted his eyes, inclining his head backward. His look signified "You are right, I will take your word for it; you are better acquainted with it than I."

But the Count's face was so terrible that Stephane closed his eyes and resumed his former attitude. A slight shudder agitated his whole frame. The Count perceived that he was near forgetting himself, and drove back the bitter wave which came up from his heart to his lips in spite of himself:

"Besides, my young friend here is the least detestable being in the world," pursued he in a tranquil tone. "Judge for yourself; just now he pleaded your cause to me with so much warmth, that he drew from me a promise not to punish you for what he has the kindness to call only a boy's freak. He even stipulates that I shall restore you your flowers, which he pretends give you delight, and within an hour Ivan will have carried them to your room. In short, two words of apology are all he requires of you. You must admit that one could not have a more accommodating disposition, and that you owe him a thousand thanks."

"Apologies! to him!" cried Stephane with a gesture of horror.

"You hesitate! oh! this is too much! Do you then wish to revisit a certain rather gloomy hall?"

Stephane shuddered, his lips trembled.

"In mercy," cried he, "inflict any other punishment upon me you please, but not that one. Oh! no, I cannot go back to that frightful hall. Oh! I entreat you, deprive me of my customary walks for six months; sell Soliman, cut my hair, shave my head,—anything, yes anything rather than put my feet in that horrible dungeon again! I shall die there or go mad. You don't want me to become insane?"

"When one is unfortunate enough to believe in ghosts and apparitions at the age of sixteen," retorted the Count, "he should free himself as soon as possible from the ridiculous weakness."

Stephane's whole body trembled. He staggered a few steps, and falling on his knees before his father, clung to him and cried: "I am only a poor sick child, have pity on me. You are still my father, are you not? and I am still your child? *Mon Dieu! Mon Dieu!* You do not, you cannot, want your child to die!"

"Put an end to this miserable comedy," cried the Count, disengaging himself from Stephane's clasp. "I am your father, and you are my son; no one here doubts it; but your father, sir, has a horror of scenes.

This has lasted too long; end it, I tell you. You are already in a suitable posture. The most difficult part is done, the rest is a trifle!"

"What do you say, sir?" answered the child impetuously, trying to rise. "I am on my knees to you only. Ah! great God! I to kneel before this man! it is impossible! you know very well it is impossible!"

The Count, however, pressing his hand upon his shoulder, constrained him to remain upon his knees, and turning his face to Gilbert:

"I tell you, you are kneeling before the man you have insulted, and we all understand it."

Was it indeed thus that Gilbert understood it? Quiet, impassible, his eyes fixed upon the window, he seemed a perfect stranger to all that passed around him.

A cry of anguish escaped Stephane, a frightful change came over his face. Three times he tried to rise, and three times the hand of his father weighed him down again, and kept him in a kneeling posture. Then, as if annihilated by the thought of his weakness and powerlessness, he yielded, and covering his eyes with both hands, he murmured these words in a stifled and convulsive voice:

"Sir, they do me violence,—I ask pardon for hating you."

And immediately his strength abandoned him, and he fainted; as a lily broken by the storm, his head sank, and he would have fallen backward, if his father had not signed to Ivan, who raised him like a feather in his robust arms, and carried him hastily out of the room.

Gilbert's first care after returning to his turret, was to light a candle and burn Stephane's letter. Then he opened a closet and began to prepare his trunk. While engaged in this task, some one knocked at the door. He had only time to close the closet and the trunk when Ivan appeared with a basket on his arm. The serf came for the flowers, which he had orders to carry to the apartment of his young master. Having placed five or six in his basket, he turned to Gilbert and gave him to understand, in his teutonic gibberish mingled with french, that he had something important to communicate to him. Gilbert answered in a tone of ill humor, that he had not time to listen to him. Ivan shook his head with a pensive air, and left. Gilbert immediately seated himself at the table, and upon the first scrap of paper which came under his hand, hastily wrote the following lines:

"Poor child, do not distress yourself too much for the humiliation to which you have just submitted. As you said yourself, you yielded only to violence, and your apologies are void in my eyes. Believe me, I exact nothing. Why did I not divine this morning that Fritz spoke in your name! I should not have felt offended, for it is not to me that your insults are addressed, it is to some strange Gilbert of your imagination. I am not acquainted with him. But what can it avail you to provoke contests, the result of which is certain in advance. It is a hand of iron which lately weighed upon your shoulder. Do you hope then to free yourself so soon from its grasp. Believe me, submit yourself to your lot, and mitigate its rigors by patience, until the day when your eyes have become strong enough to dare to look him in the face, and your hand manly enough to throw the gage of battle. Poor child! the only consolation I can offer you in your misfortune, I should be a culprit to refuse. I have but one night more to pass here; keep this secret for me for twenty-four hours, and receive the adieus of that Gilbert whom you have never known. One day he passed near you and looked at you, and you read an offensive curiosity in his eyes. I swear to you, they were full of tears."

Gilbert folded this letter, and slid it under the facing of one of his sleeves; then taking the key of the private door in his hand, and posting himself at the head of the staircase, he waited Ivan's return. As soon as he heard the sound of his steps in the corridor, he descended rapidly and met him on the landing at the gallery.

"I do not know what to do," said Ivan to him. "My young master is not himself, and he has broken the first flower-pots I carried to him in a thousand pieces."

"Take the others too," replied Gilbert, taking care to let him see the key which he flourished in his hand. "You can put them in your room for the time being. When he becomes calmer he will be glad to see them again."

"But will it not be better to leave them with you until he asks for them?"

"I don't want to keep them half an hour longer," replied Gilbert quickly, and he descended the first steps of the private staircase.

"As you are going on the terrace, sir," cried the serf to him, "don't forget, I beg of you, to close the door behind you."

Gilbert promised this. "It works well," thought he; "his caution proves to me that the wicket is not closed." He was not mistaken. For the convenience of his transportation, the serf had left it half open, only taking the precaution to close and double lock the door of the grand staircase. Gilbert waited until Ivan had reached the second story, and immediately remounting upon tiptoe, he darted into the corridor, followed its entire length, turned to the right, passed before the Count's study, turned a second time to the right, found himself in the gallery which led to the square tower, sprang through the wicket, and arrived without obstacle at the foot of the tower staircase. He found the steps littered with the *débris* of broken pots and flowers. As he began to descend, loud voices came to his ears; he thought for a moment that M. Leminof was with his son. This did not turn him from his project. He had nothing to conceal. "I will beg the Count himself," thought he, "to read my farewell letter to his son." Having reached the top of the staircase, he crossed a vestibule and found himself in a long, dark alcove, lighted by a solitary glass door, opening into the great room ordinarily occupied by Stephane. This door was ajar, and the strange scene which presented itself to Gilbert, as he approached, held him motionless a few steps from the threshold. Stephane, with his back towards him, stood with his arms crossed upon his breast. He was not speaking to his father, but to two pictures of saints hanging from the wall above a lighted taper. These two paintings on wood, in the style of father Alexis, represented St. George and St. Sergius. The child, looking at them with burning eyes, apostrophized them in a voice trembling with anger, at intervals stamping his foot and running his hands furiously through his long hair and tossing it in wild disorder. Illustrious Saints of the Eastern Church, heard you ever such language before?

"Ah! you know," said he to them, "that I have always loved, cherished, nourished, venerated and adored you. Morning and evening I implored you; extended supplicating arms towards you. The light which burns at your feet has never gone out. I have filled it with perfumed oil, with my own hands. Often have I risen in the night to reanimate the dying flame. I was foolish enough to believe in you, and I cried to you from the depths of my misery: 'Oh! patron saint, protect a poor child who has nobody but you to defend and love him!' 'Wait a little while longer,' you would say, 'we will visit thee in thy desolation, we will keep watch over thee, thou shalt see the brightness of our swords shine over thy head.' We will say to these walls: 'Fall! and at the first movement of our lips, they will sink down appalled.' And now, hypocrites, what have you done for me? Where are your works? where are the indications of your pity? Where are the evidences of your tenderness? Ah! Saint George, where were you then, you great slayer of dragons, when I but just now tremblingly invoked your aid? You know too, I did not ask you to cover me with your sword, to draw me out of the lions' den, or preserve me from the fiery furnace. I said to you: 'Only enable me to go hence with head erect and honor intact.' . . . Why hast thou not heard me, St. George? Was it a miracle beyond thy strength, to infuse into my blood a little calm and courage? But what am I saying? Thou didst hasten to my call, but it was to fight against me! Yes, in the moment of supreme anguish, when prostrate and vainly begging to rise, I felt that thou didst bend down my knees thyself, that thy hand forced my head down to the ground, and that thou didst make me drink the cup of shame and ignominy to the very dregs. Ah! this shame! it is yours! drink it! I throw it back into your faces! Listen to me, perfidious and lying saints, I curse you a hundred, a thousand times! I curse you because your hearts are made of stone! I curse you because you are vain, insolent impostors, who beg for the homage of men, and then repel the little ones who prostrate themselves before you! I curse you because you are like sycophantic and begging dogs, who go from door to door, asking to be tickled and scratched, and then bite the hands that feed and caress them. Inexorable saints, in the great ocean of heavenly pity you could not find one drop of dew to moisten the forehead of a dying child!"

At these words he sprang on a chair, tore the two pictures from the wall, threw them to the ground, and seizing his riding whip, switched them furiously. In this affair, St. George lost half of his head and one of his legs, and St. Sergius was disfigured for the rest of his days. When he had satisfied his fury, Stephane hung them up again on their nails, turning their faces to the wall, and blew out the lamp; then he rolled upon the floor, twisting his arms and tearing his hair—but suddenly sitting up he drew from his bosom a small heart-shaped medalion which he gazed on fixedly, and as he looked the tears began to roll down his cheeks, and in the midst of his sobs, he cried out:

"O my mother! I desire nothing from you! you could do nothing for me; but why did I have time to know you? To remember! to remember—what torment! Yes, I can see you now—— Every morning you gave me a kiss, high up my forehead at the roots of my hair. The mark is there yet—sometimes it burns me. I have often looked in the glass to see if I had not a scar there—— O, my mother! come and heal my wound by renewing it! To be kissed by one's mother, Great God! what happiness! Oh! for a kiss, for a single kiss from you, I would brave a thousand dangers, I would give my blood, my life, my soul. Ah! how sad you look! there are tears in your eyes. You recognize me, do you not? I am much changed, much changed; but I have always your look, your forehead, your mouth, your hair. How I love your dress! I should like to touch it. It is the very same, of which a single fold covered my whole body when I ran to you in my plays for refuge. I crouched at your feet, leaned my head on your knees, and you drew the skirt of your silk dress over me and it hid me from sight; and you said to those looking for me, 'The little pigeon is not here, I don't know what has become of him.' Ah! in mercy, tell them still, I am not there. Tell them in such a way as to make them believe you. I don't want to see or hear them. O, mother! mother! Can you not give me wings to fly to you? Or at least, I beg you, show me the way to your tomb. A mother's ashes will grow warm even after six years, if her child goes to lie there, won't they? I will lie there near you very still, and you will tell them in your sweet voice when they come to look for me: 'The little pigeon is not here; I don't know what has become of him.'"

Then starting up suddenly, Stephane walked around the room with an unsteady step. He held the medallion closely grasped in his right hand and kept his eyes upon it. Again he held it out at arm's length and looked at it steadily with half closed eyes, or drawing it nearer to him, he said to it sweet and tender things, pressing it to his lips, kissing it a thousand times and passing it over his hair and his cheeks wet with tears; it seemed as though he were trying to make some particle of this sacred image penetrate his life and being. At last, placing it on the bed, he knelt before it, and burying his face in his hands, cried out sobbing "Mother, mother, it is long since your daughter died. When will you call your son to you?"

Gilbert retired in silence. A voice from this room said to him: "Thou art out of place here. Take care not to meddle in the secret communion of a son and his mother. Great sorrows have something sacred about them. Even pity profanes them by its presence." He descended the staircase with precaution. When he had reached the last step,—extending his arm in the direction of the Count's room he muttered in a low tone: "You have lied! Under that tunic of black velvet there is a beating heart!" Then advancing with a rapid step through the corridor, he hoped to pass out unseen; but on reaching the wicket, he found himself face to face with Ivan, who was coming out of his room, and who in his surprise dropped the basket he held in his hand.

"You here!" exclaimed he in a severe tone. "Another would have paid dearly for this——"

Then in a soft voice, expressing profound melancholy.

"Brother," said he, "do you want both of us to be killed? I see you do not know the man whose orders you dare to brave." And he added, bowing humbly: "You will pardon me for calling you brother? In my mouth, that does not mean 'comrade.'"

Gilbert gave a sign of assent, and started to leave, but the serf, holding him by the arm, said:

"Fortunately the *barine* has gone out; but take care; two days since he had one of his turns, he has one every year, and while they last, his mind wanders at night, and his anger is terrible during the day. I tell you there is a storm in the air, do not draw the thunderbolt upon your head."

Then placing himself between Gilbert and the door, he added with a grave air:

"Upon your conscience, what have you been doing here? Have you seen my young father? Has he been talking to himself? You could understand what he said, for he always talks in French. He only knows enough Russian to scold me. Tell me, what have you heard? I must know."

"Don't be alarmed," answered Gilbert. "If he has secrets he has not betrayed them. He was engaged in complaining to himself, in scolding the saints and weeping. Neither must you think that I came hither to spy upon him, or to question him. As he had met with sorrow, I wanted to console him by imparting the agreeable news of my near departure; but I had not the courage to show myself to him, and besides, I am not quite certain now what I shall do."

"Yes, you will do well to go," eagerly answered the serf; but go secretly, without warning any one. I will help you, if you wish it. You are too inquisitive to remain here. Certain suspicions have already been excited on your account, which I have combatted. Then, too, you are imprudent!" Thus saying, he drew from his pocket the candle which Gilbert had dropped in the corridor, the preceding night.

"Fortunately," said he, returning it to him, "it was I who found it, and picked it up, and I wish you well, you know why. But before going from here," added he in a solemn tone, "swear to me, that during the time you may yet remain in this house, you will not try to come into this gallery again, and that you will not ramble in the other any more in the night. I tell you your life is in danger if you do."

Gilbert answered him by a gesture of assent, and passing the wicket, regained his room, where alternately standing at the window, or stretched upon an easy chair, he passed two full hours communing with his thoughts. The dinner-bell put an end to these long meditations. There was but little conversation during the repast. M. Leminof was grave and gloomy, and seemed to be laboring under a great nervous excitement which he strove to conceal. Stephane was calmer than would have been expected after the violent emotions he had experienced, but there was something singular in his look. Father Alexis alone wore his everyday face; he found it very good, and did not judge it expedient to change it. Towards the end of the repast, Gilbert was surprised to see Stephane, who was in the habit of drinking only wine and water, fill his glass with Marsala three times, and swallow it almost at a single draught. The young man was not long in feeling the effect of it; his face flushed, and his gaze became vacant. Towards the close of the meal, he looked a great deal at the Apocalyptic frescoes of the vaulted ceiling: then turning suddenly to his father, he ventured to address him a question. It was the first time for nearly two years,—an event which made even father Alexis open his eyes.

"Is it true," asked Stephane, "that living persons, supposed to be dead, have sometimes been buried?"

"Yes, it has sometimes happened," replied the Count.

"But is there no way of establishing the certainty of death?"

"Some say yes, others no. I have been told of a frozen man who was dissected in a hospital. The operator, in opening him, saw his heart beating in his breast: he took flight and is running yet."

"But when one dies a violent death—poisoned for example?"

"My opinion is, that they can still be mistaken. Physiology is a great mystery."

"Oh! that would be horrible," said Stephane in a penetrating voice, "to awaken by bruising one's forehead against the cover of a coffin."

"It would certainly be a very disagreeable experience," answered the Count. And the conversation dropped. Stephane appeared very much affected by his father's answers. He gazed no more at the ceiling, but fixed his eyes on his plate. His face changed color several times, and as if feeling the need of stupefying himself, he filled his glass with wine for the fourth time, but he could not empty it, and had hard ly touched it with his lips before he set it on the table with an air of disgust.

Tea was brought in. M. Leminof served it; and leaving his cup to cool, rose and walked the floor. After making two or three turns, he called Gilbert, and leaning upon his arm continued his walk, talking with him about the political news of the day. Stephane saw them come and go; he was evidently deeply agitated. Suddenly, at the moment when they turned their backs, he drew from his sleeve a small packet, which contained a pinch of yellow powder, and unfolding it quickly, held it over his still full cup; but as he was about emptying it, his hand trembled, and at this moment, his father and Gilbert returning to his side, he had only time to conceal the paper in his hand. In an instant he raised it again; but at the decisive moment his courage again failed him. It was not until the third trial that the yellow powder glided into the cup, where Stephane stirred it with his spoon. This little scene had escaped Gilbert. The Count alone had lost nothing of it; he had eyes at the back of his head. He reseated himself in his place and drank his tea slowly, continuing to talk with Gilbert, and apparently quite unconscious of his son; but not a movement escaped him. Stephane looked at his cup steadily, his agitation increased, he breathed heavily, he shuddered, and his hand trembled with feverish excitement. After waiting several minutes, the Count turned to him and, looking him full in the eyes, said:

"Well! you do not drink? Cold tea is a bad drug."

The child trembled still more; his eyes had a glassy brightness. Turning his head slowly, they wandered over everything about him, the table, the chairs, the plate and the black oak wainscotting. There are moments when the aspect of the most common objects stirs the soul with solemn emotion. When the condemned man is led out to die, the least straw on the floor of his cell seems to say something to his heart. Finally, gathering all his courage, Stephane raised the cup and carried it to his mouth; but before it had touched his lips, the Count took it roughly from his hands. Stephane uttered a piercing cry and fell back in his chair with closed eyes. M. Leminof looked at him for a moment with a sarcastic and scornful smile; then bending over the cup he examined it with care, smelt of it, and dipping his spoon in it, drew out two or three yellow grains which he rubbed and pulverized between his fingers. Then in a tone as tranquil and as indifferent as if speaking of the rain, or of the fine weather, he said:

"It is phosphorus, a sufficiently active poison, and phosphorus matches have been the death of a man more than once. But I saw your little paper some time before. If I am not mistaken the dose was not strong enough." And dipping his finger in the cup, he passed it over his tongue, and curled his lip disdainfully. "I was not mistaken," continued he, "it would only have given you a violent colic. It was very imprudent in you ; you do not like to suffer, and you know we have only fresh-water physicians in this neighborhood. Why didn't you wait a few hours ? Doctor Vladimir Paulitch will be here to-morrow evening." And then he went on in a more phlegmatic tone : "It should be a first principle to do thoroughly whatever you undertake to do at all. Thus, when a man wants to kill himself according to rule, he should not begin by exciting suspicions in talking of the cemetery. And as these affairs require the exercise of coolness, he should not try to get intoxicated. The courage which a person finds at the bottom of a glass of Marsala is not of a good quality, and the approach of death always sobers one. Finally,when a man has seriously resolved to kill himself, he does not do this little thing at the table, in company, but in his room, after having carefully bolted the door. In short, your little scene has failed in every point, and you do not know the first rudiments of this fine art. I advise you not to meddle with it any more."

At these words he pulled the bell for Ivan.

"Your young master wanted to kill himself," said he ; take him to his room and prepare him a composing draught that will put him to sleep. Watch with him to-night, and in future be careful not to leave any phosphorus matches in his rooms. Not that I suspect him of entertaining any intense desire of killing himself,—but who knows ? Wounded vanity might drive him to try it. As his nerves are excited, you will see that for some days he takes a great deal of exercise. If the weather is fine to-morrow, keep him in the open air all day, and in the evening walk him on the terrace ; he must get his blood stirred up."

From the moment that his father had taken the poisoned cup from him, Stephane had remained petrified on his chair, with livid face and arms hanging over his knees, giving no sign of life. When Ivan approached to take him away, he rose with a start, and leaning upon the arm of the serf, he crossed the room without opening his eyes. When he had gone, the Count heaved a long sigh of weariness and dejection.

"What did I tell you?" exclaimed he, throwing upon Gilbert a scrutinizing look; "this boy has a theatrical turn of mind. I would wager my life that he hadn't the faintest desire to kill himself: he only aimed at exciting us; but certainly if it was the sensitive heart of father Alexis which he took for a target, he has lost his trouble." And he directed Gilbert's attention to the worthy priest, who, as soon as he had emptied his cup, had fallen sound asleep on his stool, and smiled at the angels in his dreams. Gilbert gave the Count a lively and agreeable surprise by answering him in the steadiest tone:

"You are entirely right, sir; it was only a very ridiculous affectation. Fortunately, we may consider it pretty certain that our young tragedian will not regale us a second time with his little play. Where courage is required, it is good to have an opportunity of seeing to the bottom of one's sack; nothing is more likely to cure a boaster of the foolish mania for blustering."

"Decidedly my secretary is improving," thought the Count; "he has a tender mouth and feels the curb." And in the joy which this discovery gave him, he felt that he entertained for him sentiments of real friendship, of which he would not have believed himself capable. His surprise and pleasure increased still more when Gilbert resumed:

"But apropos, sir, do you persist in believing that, according to Constantius Porphyrogennatus, all Greece became Sclavonian in the eighteenth century? I have new objections to present to you on that subject. And first this famous Copronymus of whom he speaks. . . ."

They did not rise from the table until eleven o'clock. It was necessary to awaken father Alexis, who slept during the whole time, his right arm extended over his plate, and his head leaning upon his elbow. The Count having shaken him, he rose with a start and exclaimed:

"Don't touch it! The colors are all fresh; Jacob's beard is such a fine gray!"

"Your eternal patriarchs again!" said the Count, assuming a severe expression. "You would have done better to take some interest in the deplorable scene which has just taken place here."

"A scene has just taken place?" answered the priest, opening his eyes.

"What, are you asleep yet, father? I refer to the cup of poisoned tea."

"Holy Virgin! the tea was poisoned! But I drank some of it, I drank a great deal of it!" And he felt of his body, as if to assure himself that he was still alive.

"This is too much," said the Count, affecting to lose patience. "Let us see, are your ideas clearing up? Ah! there you are at last. Well, know, sir, that I hold you responsible for what has just passed, for, after all, of what service have your pastoral instructions been to this child?"

"Ah! great God! has he tried to poison you?" cried father Alexis with a gesture of horror.

"Pshaw! your supposition lacks common sense. Yet what surprises me is, that you should take such an event so coolly. Is such a sin so venial in your eyes? My father, these affairs are within your jurisdiction; think of it, and weigh carefully the most trivial details. I expect from you counsel and remedies. One thing more: never speak to him of this painful affair. You understand me; in your conversations with him avoid any expression which could contain the slightest allusion to what has just happened."

Upon this he turned on his heel, and the good father went his way, moving his head with a pensive air. He was equally embarrassed in having to give counsel upon a matter of which he was entirely ignorant, and in the fear of some day unwittingly alluding to a secret which he knew nothing about.

Before leaving M. Leminof, Gilbert desired to hear some news of Stephane. The Count went himself to inquire, and brought Ivan back with him, and Gilbert learned from the lips of the serf that the young man had taken his potion and was tranquilly sleeping.

The compliant secretary retired humming an aria. M. Leminof followed him with his eyes, and, pointing after him, said to his serf in a confidential tone:

"Thou seest that man there; just fancy! I feel friendship for him. He is at least my most cherished—habit. My suspicions were absurd, thou wert right in combatting them. By way of precaution, however, make a tour of the corridor between midnight and two o'clock. Now come and double lock me in my room, for I feel a paroxysm coming on. To-morrow at five o'clock thou wilt come to open it for me."

"Count Kostia!" murmured Gilbert when he found himself in his room, "fear no longer that I shall think of leaving you. Whatever happens, I remain here. Count Kostia, understand me, you have buried the smile: I take heaven to witness that I will resuscitate it."

CHAPTER XII.

The day following the one on which Gilbert had resolved to remain at Geierfels, father Alexis rose at an early hour and betook himself as usual to his dear chapel; he entered with a slow step, bowed back, and anxious face; but when he had traversed the nave and stood before the main entrance to the choir, the influence of the holy place began to dissipate his melancholy; his thoughts took a more serene turn, and his face brightened. The chapel, which formed part of a little detached building separated from the main one by a court, received the light at sunrise through three great arched windows opening upon a gallery with a colonnade. During the night the weather had cleared, and at this moment a ray of sunlight from one of the casements fell upon the face of one of the evangelists which decorated the choir; this mark of favor with which heaven honored one of his masterpieces gratified the paternal pride of the good priest. As soon as he had said his mass and laid aside his albe of figured silk, he took off his black robe and put on an ugly cassock covered with stains of grease and paint; this was his artist's costume. Then having turned up his sleeves, he solemnly mounted a little ladder which led to a scaffolding fixed against the wall, and encumbered with pieces of straw and pots filled with oil, varnish, diluted plaster and isinglass.

For several days father Alexis had been occupied in painting a group of three figures, Abraham, Isaac, and Jacob, with their posterity on their knees. It was the exact copy of a picture in the Convent of Lavra. These patriarchs were gravely seated upon a grassy bank, separated from each other by little shrubs of a somewhat fantastic shape. Their venerable heads were crowned with aureoles; their abundant hair, combed with the greatest care, fell majestically upon their shoulders, and their thick beards descended to the middle of their breasts. Draped in great mantles with rigid and symmetrical folds, each held in his outstretched arms a white linen cloth containing the heads of eight children ranged in line, an insufficient symbol, perhaps, of that posterity as numerous as the stars of heaven, the promise of which flattered their pride. These heroes of the old covenant had the faces of monks, long, emaciated, and austere ; but in the sadness which they expressed there was nothing dreamy or ecstatic. They seemed to be occupied with some petty calculation, and one could fancy them saying: "Behold the many years that we have fasted and risen at night to sing matins; these are considerable advances."—And they were calculating the reimbursements which would be made to them some day, and were preparing an exact debit and credit account.

Father Alexis worked for nearly an hour, when he heard a step in the court, and turning his head quickly, perceived Gilbert coming towards the chapel. The priest thrilled with joy, as a fisherman might, who after long hours of mortal waiting, sees a fish of good size imprudently approaching his net. Eager for his prey, he threw aside his brush, quickly descended the ladder with the agility of a young man, and ran to place himself in ambuscade near the door, where he waited with bated breath. As soon as Gilbert appeared, he rushed upon him, seized him by the arm and looked upon him with eyes which seemed to say : "You are caught, and you won't escape from me either."

When he had recovered from his first excess of joy, "Ah my son," exclaimed he, "what happy inspiration brings you hither?"

"M. Leminof is not well to-day," answered Gilbert, "and I thought I could make no better use of my leisure than to pay my respects to you."

"Oh! what a charming idea," said the priest, looking at him with ineffable tenderness. "Come, come, my son, I will show you all, yes all."

This word *all* was pronounced with such an energetic accent, that Gilbert was startled. It may be readily believed that it was not exactly about Byzantine pictures that he was curious at this moment. Nevertheless, he entered with great good-nature into a minute examination of the images of the choir and the nave; he praised all which appeared praiseworthy, kept silent upon the prominent defects which offended the delicacy of his taste, and allowed himself to criticize only some of the details; above all, he listened with such concentrated attention to the explanations which the priest heaped upon him, that the former, in a very short time, had conceived the liveliest affection for him, and testified it by his looks, his smiles, and by little caresses quite paternal in their tenderness.

"My son, I have reserved my three patriarchs for the climax!" finally said the good father. "We will see what you say to them." Then conducting him to the foot of the ladder, he exclaimed: "Mount with your eyes closed, you can open them when you reach the top. Close your eyes, close them well; you will run no risk of falling. I will go up behind you."

Gilbert complied with his request. I would not swear that on re-opening his eyes he experienced that dizziness upon which father Alexis had counted; but he smiled with an air of satisfaction. Standing by his side, the priest devoured him with his eyes and murmured between his teeth:

"Although I told you this was reserved for the climax, my dear child," resumed he, after giving him time to recover himself, "don't be afraid of offending me, but tell me frankly which of these three figures you admire most?" It will be noticed that father Alexis possessed the difficult art of putting questions well.

"To be frank with you," replied the indulgent Gilbert, "my preference is for Abraham. He has a certain air of majesty."

"*Peste!* you have fine taste!" cried the priest pinching his arm affectionately. "Yes; this Abraham is the finest jewel in my crown. However, I do not wish to have your admiration for the grandfather render you unjust towards the son and the grandson.

Look at Isaac attentively. Do you not find that he has a something, I hardly know what, in his face?"

"You are right. Well then! father, to treat everybody with consideration, we may say that the head of Abraham is more majestic, and that of Isaac more expressive."

"Eh! eh! my son, you are a consummate judge in such matters, you have an eye for the beautiful—but Jacob? I think really that Jacob—"

"His beard is certainly a superb gray."

"How well you talk! 'Agreeable words are like the honey comb,' is written in the Proverbs. Yes, that beard is fine! But you say nothing about those pretty shrubs!"

"Oh! they are only accessories."

"Speak not lightly of accessories," said the priest in a reproachful tone; "they are more important than you think. What is, for instance, a dinner, if you please, without side dishes? and what again is the finest narrative in the world without details? Happiness itself (worldly happiness of course, you understand) has neither pungency nor flavor, if it is not seasoned with small pleasures. You are still young, my son, and you despise little things. When you are older you will acknowledge the importance of accessories, and find that to live well, you must give a position to sauces. But look at this grass, please; see how fresh, how velvety it is—Holy Virgin! you do not deign to look at it. You have eyes for nothing but Abraham. You are certainly taken with Abraham. It is a weakness which I pardon you. Stop, examine a little more closely this fold of his mantle, there, above the knee." Gilbert shuddered in seeing the conversation work like a shuttle from Abraham to the sward, and from the sward to Abraham—a magic circle in which he ran the risk of being confined until evening. The danger was imminent; he hastened to avoid it by announcing to the priest that he wished to talk with him of a serious matter.

"A serious matter?"

And the face of the good father became grave.

"Have you anything to confess to me? What am I saying? you are not orthodox my child,—would to God you were." Then striking his forehead:

"Now that reminds me that there are certain explanations which I should be very glad of. Let us quit this scaffolding for fear of distraction; but don't bid farewell to my patriarchs, you have not seen all —for example—"

"Let us descend, let us descend," said Gilbert, putting his foot upon the ladder.

They descended and seated themselves upon the end of a white marble step, which extended the entire width of the nave, at the entrance of the choir.

"My son," began the priest timidly, "yesterday evening—"

"That is precisely what I want to talk to you about," said Gilbert.

"Ah! you are a good, generous child. You saw my embarrassment, and you wished,—I confess it, a slight drowsiness,—flesh is weak,—ah, it is good in you. Favors do not turn your head. Speak, speak, I am all attention."

"It is understood that you will keep the secret, father, for you know—"

"I understand! we should be lost if it were known that we talked of certain things together. Oh! you need not be afraid. If Kostia Petrovitch alludes to this matter, I shall appear to know nothing, and I shall accuse myself of having violated the precept of the great Solomon, who said, "When thou sittest down to eat with a prince, consider attentively what is done before thee."

"Speak with confidence, my child, and rest assured that this mouth has an old tongue in it which never says what it does not want to."

When Gilbert had finished his recital, father Alexis burst forth in exclamations accompanied by many signs of the cross.

"Oh! unhappy child!" cried he; "what folly is thine! He has then sworn his own destruction? To wish to die in mortal sin! A spirit of darkness must have taken possession of him. Then he invokes St. George no longer every morning and evening? He prays no more,—he no longer carries on his heart the holy amulet I gave him. Ah! why did I fall asleep yesterday evening? What beautiful things I would have said to him! I would have commenced by representing to him—"

"I do not doubt your eloquence; but it is not remonstrance, nor good counsel that this child wants: a little happiness would answer the purpose far better."

"Happiness! Ah! yes, his life is a little sad. There are certain maxims of education—"

"It is not a question of maxims of education, but of a father who betrays an open hatred to his son."

"Holy Virgin!" exclaimed the priest with a gesture of terror, "you must not say such things, my child. These are words which the good God does not like to hear. Never repeat them, it would be neither prudent nor charitable."

Gilbert persisted; announcing the conjectures which he had formed as certainties, and even exaggerating his suspicions in the hope that the priest, in correcting him, would furnish the explanations which he desired. The success of this little artifice surpassed his expectation.

"I know for a certainty," said he, "that M. Leminof loved his wife,—that she was unfaithful to him, —that he finished by suspecting her, and that he revenged himself—"

"False! false!" cried the priest with deep emotion. "To hear you one would believe that Count Kostia killed his wife. You have heard lying reports. The truth is that the Countess Olga poisoned herself, and then feeling the approach of death, became terrified and implored aid. It was useless : they could not counteract the effects of the poison. She then sent in haste for me. I had but just time to receive her confession. Oh ! what a frightful scene, my child ! Why recall it to me ? And above all, whose calumnious tongue—"

"I have been told, also," pursued the inflexible Gilbert, "that after this deplorable event M. Leminof, holding in abhorrence the localities which witnessed his dishonor, quitted Moscow and Russia, and went to Martinique. Having arrived there, he lost, after some months' residence, one of his two children, a daughter if I am not mistaken, and this death may have been hastened by—"

"A fresh calumny ! " interrupted the priest, looking steadily at Gilbert. The young girl died of yellow fever. Kostia Petrovitch never raised a finger against his children. Ah ! tell me what viper's tongue—"

"It is not a calumny, at least, to state that he has two good reasons for not loving his son. First, because he is the living portrait of his mother, and then because he doubts, perhaps, if this child is really his son."

"An impious doubt, which I have combatted with all my strength. This child was born nine years before his mother committed her first and only fault. I have said it, and I repeat it. It has been objected that he was born after six years of a marriage which seemed condemned by heaven to an eternal sterility : —fatal circumstance, which appeared proof positive to a vindictive and ulcerated heart. But again, who could have told you—"

"One more word : before leaving for Martinique, M. Leminof did everything he could to discover the lover of his wife. His suspicions fell upon one of his intimate friends named Morlof. In his blind fury he killed him, but nevertheless Morlof was innocent."

"Did they tell you that he assassinated him?" said father Alexis, who became more and more agitated. "Another calumny! he killed him in regular duel. Holy Virgin! the sin was grave enough; but the police hushed up the matter, and absolution has been granted him."

"Alas!" resumed Gilbert, "if the church has pardoned, the conscience of the murderer persists in condemning; it curses that rash hand which shed innocent blood, and by a strange aberration it exhorts him to wash out this fatal mistake in the blood of the real offender. This offender, after six years fruitless search, he has not given up the hope of discovering; he will go into the very bowels of the earth to find him, if he must, and if by chance there is some heart upon which the name is written, he will open that heart with the point of his sword to decipher those letters of blood and of fire!"

Gilbert pronounced these last words in a vibrating voice. He had suddenly forgotten where he was and to whom he was speaking. He thought he again saw before him the scene of the corridor, and could again hear those terrible words which had frozen the blood in his veins. The priest was seized with a convulsive trembling; but he soon mastered it. He raised himself slowly and stood up before Gilbert, his arms crossed upon his breast. Within a few moments his face became dignified, and at the same time his language. Now the transformation was complete; Gilbert had no longer before him the timid, easy soul who trembled before a frown, the epicure in quest of agreeable sensations, the vain artist ingeniously begging eulogies. The priest's eyes opened wide and shone like coals of fire; his lips, wreathed in a bitter smile, seemed ready to launch the thunders of excommunication; and a truly sacerdotal majesty diffused itself as if by miracle over his face. Gilbert could scarcely believe his eyes; he looked at him in silence, incapable of recognizing this new father Alexis, who had just been revealed to him.

Then, said the priest, speaking to himself:

"Brother! what simplicity is yours! A few caresses, a few cajoleries, and your satisfied vanity silences your distrust and disarms your good sense! Did you not know that this young man is the intimate friend of your master?"

Then bowing towards Gilbert:

"They thought then that you could make me speak. And you imagined yourself that a coarse artifice and some threatening talk would suffice to tear from me a secret I have guarded for nearly seven years. Presumptuous young man, return to him who sent you, and repeat faithfully what I am about to say to you: One day at Martinique, in a remote house some distance from the outskirts of the town of St. Pierre,—let me speak, my story will be short.—Picture to yourself a great dark hall, with a table in the centre.—They shut me in there near noon; the next day at evening I was there still, and for thirty hours I neither ate nor drank. The night came,—they stretched me upon a table,—bound me and tied me down. Then I saw bending over me a face more terrible than thou wilt ever see, even in thy dreams, and a mouth which sneered as the damned must sneer, approached my ear and said to me: 'Father Alexis, I want your secret—I will have it.' I breathed not a word; they tightened the cords with a jack, and I did not speak; they piled weights on my chest, and I spoke not; they put boots upon me which I hope never to see upon thy feet, and I spake not; my bones cracked, and I spake not; I saw my blood gush out, and I did not speak. At length a supreme anguish seized me, a red cloud passed over my eyes, I felt my heart freezing, and I thought myself dying. Then I spoke and said: 'Count Leminof, thou canst kill me, but thou shalt not tear from me the secrets of the confessional.'" And at these words, the priest stooping, laid bare his right foot and showed Gilbert the bruised and withered flesh, and bones deformed by torture; then covering it again he recoiled, as if from a serpent in his path, and cried in a thundering voice, extending his arms to Heaven:

"God curse the vipers who take the form of doves! O Solomon, hast thou not written in thy Proverbs: 'When he shall speak graciously, do not believe him, for he has seven abominations in his heart?'"

As he listened to the recital of the priest, Gilbert was reminded of some incoherent phrases of the somnambulist, which he had not been able to explain: "*Stretch him on this table! the black robe! Tighten the iron boots!*"

"That black robe then," said he to himself, "was father Alexis."

He rose and looked at the priest in surprise and admiration; he could not take his eyes from that face which he believed he saw for the first time, and he murmured in a low voice:

"My God! how complex is the heart of man! What a discovery I have just made!"

Then he tried to approach him; but the priest, still recoiling and raising his arms threateningly above his head, repeated:

"Cursed be the vipers who come in the form of doves!"

"And I say," cried Gilbert, "blessed forever be the lips which have touched the sacred coal, and keep their secrets even unto death!"

And rushing upon him he took him in his arms and kissed three times the scar which the cruel bite of Solon had left.

Father Alexis was surprised, stupefied, and confounded. He looked at Gilbert, then at Abraham, then at Jacob. He uttered disjointed phrases. He called upon Heaven to witness what had happened to him, gesticulated and wept until, overcome by emotion, he dropped on the marble step, and hid his face, bathed in tears, in his hands.

"Father," said Gilbert respectfully, seating himself near him, "pardon me for the agitation I have caused you. And if by chance some distrust of me remains, listen to what I am about to tell you, for I am going to put myself at your mercy, and by betraying a secret it will depend upon you to have me expelled from this house the day and hour you please."

He then related to him the scene of the corridor. "Judge for yourself what impression the terrible words I heard produced upon me! For some days my mind has been at work. I ceaselessly tried to picture to myself the details of this lamentable affair; but fearing to stray in my suspicions, I wished to make a clean breast of it, and came to find you. I have grieved you sorely, father; once more, will you pardon my rash curiosity?"

Father Alexis raised his head. Farewell to the saint! farewell to the prophet! His face had resumed its habitual expression; the sublime tempest which had transfigured it, had left but a few almost invisible traces of its passage. He looked at Gilbert reproachfully—

"Ah!" said he, "it was only for this that you sought me? my dear child, you do not love the arts then?"

"Believe me," replied Gilbert smiling, "I love them passionately. Just now I admired your patriarchs in earnest; hereafter I shall admire them still more, for in looking at them I shall be reminded of that little house on the outskirts of St. Pierre."

"Permit me to say, my dear child," interrupted father Alexis "that these two subjects have no analogy. Had I revealed the secret of the confessional, I should have merited eternal damnation. I did my duty, that is all, and in my place, any honest and orthodox priest would have done the same; but my patriarchs— But do not forget that the talent of an artist is given by God to only a small number of his favorites; it is a treasure of which he is sparing. One can be caloyer, archimandrite, prototype, bishop or archbishop, and not be able to draw even the end of a patriarch's nose, or one of those little pomegranate leaves which I have painted below them on the wall. Talent, my child, is a gift of divine grace, which should be used in all humility; but I confess it, my heart dances a little in my breast when I reflect that if father Alexis should die, no one could be found perhaps, from Astrakan to Paris, to make a picture in the least resembling the patriarch Abraham and his family. I am vexed," continued he, "that I related that story of the iron boots. I have never before repeated it to any one, and I had nearly forgotten it. I have forgiven it, forgiven everything, and that would not astonish you, if you had been, as I have, a witness of this man's despair. He aged twenty years in a few months. He never slept, and was half mad. There is something of Peter the Great in him. His will is iron, and his passions fire. He was born to be Czar, to govern an empire and to strangle his enemies. For God's sake do not put yourself in his way, he will shiver you like glass. You do not know his passions. They are convulsions. The idea of having been deceived gnaws him like a cancer. It is a wound which will never close, and the sufferings which he endures at times, you can imagine by the groans you heard the other night. He is to be pitied. He loved his wife,—she was marvellously beautiful: you can form an idea of it by her son, who resembles her as a pigeon a dove. And when I say he loved her, it was as the Grand Pacha loves his favorite Sultana, or, it might be more correct to say, she was in his eyes like a jewel of great price, an emerald, a topaz, which he loved to see glisten in the sun. But above all, she was his property, and no proprietor was ever more jealous of his possessions. But answer me frankly; have you truly reported all you heard in the corridor? Yes, you know nothing more? You could swear it? Now then I am tranquil! My dear child, do not wander any more at night,—evil might befall you. Besides, your trouble will be thrown away, for I am much mistaken or Kostia Petrovitch has himself locked in his room as long as the attack lasts. That was his custom last year; for I must tell you, that since we returned to Europe, he has one of these attacks every summer. The first two commenced the fifth of July, the anniversary of his wife's death. This one came sooner, and took him by surprise. God grant that it may be short, for while it lasts his disposition is not amiable. You see a proof of that in the little scratch which I carry on my cheek."

"Father," replied Gilbert after a silence, "suffer me to ask you one more question,—only one. How happens it, that after the frightful scene which you have related to me, you have continued to live with M. Leminof?"

"That is a question," said he artlessly, "that I have never put to myself." He reflected a few moments in silence, and then, having collected his thoughts, he continued:

"It is so long, my child, since I have had the pleasure of conversing with a living soul, and you are a man of such amiable manners, that I cannot resist the desire of unwinding my little skein before you,—assured as I am of your absolute discretion. My wife died three months after the Countess Olga. God grant her peace! A great deliverance for me, you will say? I agree to that; but if in becoming a widower it had been necessary for me, according to custom, to bury myself in a monastery,—what shall I say? Holy Virgin! pardon me, but I have little taste for monastic life. It was at that time that Count Kostia came to see me one day. He announced his intention of seeking distraction from his sorrows in travelling over the world, and asked if I felt disposed to accompany him, assuring me that he would treat me with the greatest consideration. He caressed, wheedled and bewitched me. I was a thousand miles from suspecting his intentions. I consented. The novelty of adventure charmed me. He removed all difficulties and we left. Hardly had we arrived at Martinique, when he unmasked himself. One day wandering with him in the country, Kostia Petrovitch said to me what you repeated just now,—that there was a name, a terrible name, a hated name, that he wished to know at any cost,—that I knew to what a fatal error his first researches had led him, and that henceforth he would not trust to his suppositions, but that he must have evidences, certainties, that he not only wished to know, but that he must know; but however, that he no longer cherished any desire of vengeance. A mere affair of curiosity! But this curiosity consumed his heart and his life, deprived him of appetite, of sleep, and was shortening his days. I had no trouble in believing this. My child, I see him yet standing before me, both of his hands placed on my shoulders, his flaming eyes fixed upon mine. He added that this cursed name I ought to know, I did know. My look, my agitation, my pallor, my silence answered him. That moment commenced for me a long train of suffering and anguish. It was every day, prayers, supplications, importunities. He turned and turned about me, a smile on his lips, a threat in his eyes. He was like a serpent trying to fascinate his prey. 'At what price will you sell your secret,' said he. 'I will not bargain.' He made me promise upon promise,—offered me even half of his fortune. And I, I pointed to the crucifix which hung upon my breast! Then he changed his tactics. I was put upon a regime of terror. My nerves are feeble, my child, and God knows moreover what trials they have endured. One night, awaking suddenly from my sleep, I found him sitting on the side of my bed; in one hand he held a lamp, in the other a pistol, which he pointed at me. But let it pass, let it pass; I have already said that I have forgiven all. After the torture of the boots, I was a long time recovering. When I regained my feet, other trials commenced. Privations, solitude, strict captivity, my brushes thrown into the fire, absolutely forbidden to draw or even to touch a pencil,—such were the means to which he had recourse to conquer me. For a time I began to waste away. He saw it, and feared that I might die, for he did not wish my death. My hollow eyes, my emaciated frame, and my haggard look frightened him; I bore already upon my face a deathly pallor. He had me cared for, raised all his prohibitions, permitted me to satisfy my appetite, to draw and to paint. From that time my life became tolerable. I have still, it is true, some ugly hours to pass; the days follow each other and are unlike; at the moment when I least expect it, the storm breaks—then I bend my head, keep still and await a change. This man's temper is very uneven. He passes whole months absorbed in study. As the Russian proverb says: 'Every baron has his fancy.' His is to love big books to madness. I heard him say one day, that the visible form of happiness was a great folio. And indeed his old books do him good, they give him, for a time at least, quiet and health; but suddenly his memories revive, and his wound begins to bleed afresh. Then the wild boar, which seemed to be tamed, shows his natural ferocity—and then beware of his tusks! I have felt them often, as you can believe, but my skin has become hardened to them. In short, if I live on the *qui vive*, still I live, and that is something. And then one ought not to calumniate this fearful man. He is not incapable of feeling. Would you believe that he has never spoken to Stephane of the fault, nor of the tragic death of his mother? He has kept him in entire ignorance, and he suffers this child to cherish the memory of the poor sinner as a saint. Another trait of magnanimity which I recommend to your admiration: Kostia Petrovitch has never deigned to give a glance at my pictures, which he inaptly calls daubs; but he has never complained of their being too costly, and I do not spare the colors. Look at these golden aureoles, they are at least two feet in diameter. Well! he has never said to me, 'Father Alexis, thy gold foil costs me too dearly; count upon thy fingers all the roubles I have paid for it.' What do you say to that my child? Does it not appear to you that this man has good in him? In short, whatever you think of him, know that I have never dreamed of quitting him, I am accustomed to his face. Kostia Petrovitch made me suffer so much once that I am much obliged to him for not doing so any more. And what is happiness after all, if it is not the art of consoling ourselves? I have become very proficient in this art, and I readily forget all in cultivating the small talents which Heaven in its munificence has bestowed upon me. Besides, if I wanted to go away, is it certain that I could? What this man wants, he wants indeed, and he intends to have me always under his hand; for if he has renounced the idea of extorting my secret by violence, he still cherishes the hope of drawing it from me some day, by some adroit surprise. His method is skilful; he rests six months without saying anything to me, and then suddenly, when he thinks me disarmed, he throws his hook in my soul; but Heaven be praised! whatever bait he puts there, my secret never bites at it. There are angels of God who keep guard day and night over the secrets of the confessional. What more can I say to you, my child? I am at an age when a man does not feel like changing his lot, and when he employs the strength which remains to him in submitting or in forgetting. Look at Ivan, that other greybeard. For fifteen years he begged his master to free him. He wanted to be a travelling peddler, to wander over the high roads, to go away upon his nimble feet from Moscow to Tiflis and from Tiflis to Astrachan. To-day, if his liberty were given him, and he were sent from here, he would be like an eagle with clipped wings, thrown from his nest and told to go where he willed, that all space was his."

During this long recital, the face of the priest was elevated and illuminated again;—but he had scarcely finished, when passing his hand over the pit of his stomach, he said:

"Young man, come with me into the Sacristy. I have some caviar in the closet, some buttered toast and a bottle of muscat wine, which I will regale you with. It is a nectar that has no parallel. You can tell me the news over it. Afterwards we will mount the scaffolding and you shall see me paint. I want to show you how I lay on my colors."

Impatient at these continued changes, Gilbert rose abruptly and said:

"I thank you, father, it is time for me to go. Fortunately I leave reassured in regard to you; but Stephane!"

"You are going already!" exclaimed the priest in a disappointed tone; and pushing in his mouth the forefinger of his right hand, and withdrawing it with a loud noise:

"Think of that Fuencarral muscat!"

"And Stephane!" repeated Gilbert, making his way towards the door."

The priest led him back.

"Ah yes," said he shaking his head and stroking his beard, "ah yes! the wicked child! he wanted to kill himself. It runs in the blood. The evil genius of his mother is in him. There is a taste for poison in this family. One of his maternal grand uncles put an end to himself with arsenic in due form at the age of fifty."

"Does Stephane resemble his mother in character as well as in face?"

"Oh, no! Olga Vassilievna was a sweet soft woman, gentle as a lamb and frail as a flower. She often hummed a song which commenced thus:

"I am a little white rose,
And if the storm wind grazes me with its wings—"

Poor Olga Vassilievna! the storm has passed over her and broken her. Have you watched the pretty white down which floats in the spring breezes? It ascends and descends—falls upon the grass and remains poised on the long stiff blades, until a gust of wind takes it up again and carries it a few steps further. Such was Olga Vassilievna. She was so amiable that Kostia Petrovitch did with her whatever he wished. A falcon became the husband of the dove. She had her caprices of course, her little fancies, but she expressed them so gracefully and gently! When she fluttered through her parlors, she looked like a pretty muslin cloud. And her laces, I assure you, were not lighter than her little heart. In summer she passed long hours coiled in the depths of an easy chair, or lying in a hammock, her fan in her hand, prattling like a magpie with her visitors, or she glided softly through her garden and sometimes fell exhausted at the end of a path. Often has her husband carried her to the house in his arms. It was through weakness that this woman sinned. If Count Kostia had never left her, she would have died pure and stainless; protected by his presence, she would never have thought of putting the tip of her delicate little foot outside of the path of duty. Ah, why had Kostia Petrovitch such a passion for big books? Why did he go away to Paris to bury himself in the dust of libraries? It was the first time they had been separated. She had just recovered from an illness, and it would have been dangerous to expose her to the fatigues of travel, and he could not delay his departure. He published learned dissertations in the "*Contemporain*," and had researches to make in Paris. He was to have remained there eighteen months. Suddenly he received a letter from Russia, which he hardly read before he sped homeward like an arrow. He arrived when no one expected him, and found the Countess Olga seven months advanced in pregnancy, while he had been absent ten. He remained shut up with her for three hours, and at the end of this interview she poisoned herself. But observe, my child, how complicated are events in this world. If Kostia Petrovitch had never made that cursed voyage, I should perhaps have been a monk to-day languishing in the cell of a monastery. And see how causes entwine themselves with effects, for finally—"

"So Stephane resembles his mother but in face."

"And in what else could he resemble her? He is violent, passionate, a smothered volcano. Although of slight figure and thin as a reed, he courses through the woods on horseback for twenty-four hours without fatigue. What frightens me is this inclination for poison, which seems hereditary."

"I do not know," replied Gilbert, stopping at the entrance of the lobby hung in black velvet, into which the door of the chapel opened—"I do not know that it is exactly from inclination that Stephane has attempted to poison himself, and I doubt if he loves phosphorus, as you, for example, love painting. I think I have discovered that he is unhappy, very unhappy."

"After all," said the priest, smiling, "they have never put iron boots on him." And he looked down upon his poor crippled feet with an expression which seemed to say: "You remember it well."

"Ah! my father, there are moral sufferings, which for a noble and proud soul—"

Gilbert did not finish. The face of the old child before him took away his courage.

"I am speaking in Hebrew to him," thought he.

Father Alexis scratched his ear, and said in a grave tone:

"Yes, you have just named his trouble, it is his pride, his fatal pride. This child commits the sin of pride twenty times a day, and I really think his character grows worse. Once he was much more amiable, more patient. Within a year he has become gloomy and irritable; he has fits of insubordination."

"It seems very natural to me," replied Gilbert, "that with the progress of years—"

"Ah! what are you saying?" exclaimed the priest in a magisterial tone. "This child is already sixteen. Has not the time arrived for him to put a little ballast in his hare-brained head? Holy Virgin, he is of an age when he should reflect, reason, and meditate seriously upon the teachings of his spiritual father. It is full time that he should understand that the ways of God are mysterious, and that we are here below in a land of trials."

And as Gilbert put his hand upon the knob of the door he added in a low voice: "Listen to me, I want to confide to you still another secret. These paintings which you see around you are not only a monument of art, of which posterity will speak, they are besides, if I may dare to say so, a pious invention destined to draw down upon our heads the blessings of the Holy Trinity. One day I made a vow to trace upon these walls all the glories of religion, and I supplicated the Holy Virgin, to accomplish some resplendent miracle in return as soon as this great work should be completed,—one which would put an end to all the sufferings of this house. Well! one night she appeared to me. My child, I have a quick hand, and I flatter myself that before two months—"

Gilbert smiled, bowed without answering, and went out.

"This priest is strange," mused he as he crossed the yard.

"That young man is singular," mused father Alexis, as he made his way to the sacristy.

CHAPTER XIII.

THAT day Gilbert passed an entire hour at his window. It was not the Rhine which fixed his attention, nor the precipice, the mountains nor the clouds. The narrow space within which he confined his gaze was bounded on the west by the great square tower, on the south by a gable, on the north by a spout; I mean to say that the object of his contemplations was a very irregular, very undulating roof, or to speak more accurately, two adjacent and parallel roofs, one higher than the other by twelve feet, and both inclining by a steep slope towards a frightful precipice.

As he closed the window, he said to himself:

"After all, it is less difficult than I thought; two rope ladders will do the business, with God's help!"

M. Leminof finding himself too much indisposed to leave his room, Gilbert dined alone in his turret; after which he went out for a walk on the borders of the Rhine. As he left the path for the main road, he saw Stephane and Ivan within twenty paces of him. Perceiving him, the young man made an angry gesture, and turning his face, started his horse off at full speed. Gilbert had scarcely time to leap into the ditch to avoid being run down. As Ivan passed, he looked at him sadly, shook his head and carried his finger to his forehead, as if to say: "You must pardon him; his poor mind is very sick." Gilbert returned to the castle without delay, and as he reached the entrance to the terrace, he saw the serf leaning against one of the doors, where he seemed to be on guard.

"My dear Ivan," said he, "you appear to be waiting for some one."

"I heard you coming," answered he, "and I took you for Vladimir Paulitch. It was the sound of your step which deceived me; you haven't such a measured step generally."

"You are a keen observer," replied Gilbert smiling; "but who, I pray, is this Vladimir Paulitch?"

"He is a physician from my country. He will remain two months with us. The *barine* wrote to him a fortnight since, when he felt that he was going to be ill; Vladimir Paulitch left immediately, and day before yesterday he wrote from Berlin that he would be here this evening. This Vladimir is a physician who hasn't his equal. I am waiting for him to arrive."

"Tell me, good Ivan, is your young master in the garden?"

"He is down there under the weeping ash."

"Very well, you must permit me to speak to him a moment. You will even extend the obligation by saying nothing about it to Kostia Petrovitch. You know he cannot see us, for he keeps his bed now, and even if he should rise, his windows open on the inner court."

Ivan's brow contracted. "Impossible, impossible!" he murmured.

"Impossible? Why? Because you will not."

"And if I should, do you think that Stephane would consent? You don't know, then, how he detests you? The sound of your voice would be enough to put him to flight. He is in a very sad, morose humor to-day. Didn't you see how he urged his horse on you? We left this morning at eight o'clock. He generally gallops like the wind, and amuses himself by making Soliman prance and caracole; to-day he kept him at a walk. He wouldn't open his mouth; not a word, not a syllable! His head down, he heard nothing, saw nothing. At noon we stopped at an inn to breakfast. He didn't want to eat, and I had to force him to. It was not until we were again in the saddle that he broke silence; but it would have been much better if he had held his tongue. Ah! if father Alexis had heard him! He blasphemed against Heaven, and cursed himself a hundred times for not having had the courage to kill himself. Then in a moment afterwards he said: 'After all, I'm glad I'm not dead, for it is possible for me yet to be revenged on my enemies. And even if I don't succeed, mortification will kill me, Ivan. What's the use of poison? I shall be dead within six months any way.'"

"Ivan, my good Ivan, it is absolutely necessary for me to speak to your young master. I have made him submit to a humiliation against my will. He mistakes my sentiments and credits me with the blackest intentions, and it will be torture to him in future to be condemned to sit at the same table with me daily. Let me explain myself to him. In two words I will make him understand who I am, and that I wish him no harm."

The discussion was prolonged some minutes, Ivan finally yielding, but on the condition that Gilbert should not put his good will to the proof a second time. "Otherwise," said Ivan, "if you still attempt to talk with him secretly, I cannot permit him to go out, and of course he could only blame you, and would then have the right to consider you an enemy."

Upon his side, the serf promised that the Count should know nothing of the interview.

"Recollect, brother," continued he, "that this is the last improper favor that you will obtain from me. You are a man of heart, but sometimes I should say that *you had been eating belladonna.*"

Stephane had left the circular bank where he had been sitting, and stood with his back against the parapet of the terrace, his arms hanging dejectedly, and his head sunk upon his breast. His revery was so profound that Gilbert approached within ten steps of him without being perceived; but suddenly rousing himself, he raised his head quickly, and stamped his foot imperiously.

"Go away!" cried he, "go away, or I will set Vorace on you!"

Vorace was the name of the bull-dog that kept him company at night, and was crouching in the grass some paces distant. Of all the watch-dogs of the castle, this one was the strongest and most ferocious.

"You see," said Ivan, retaining Gilbert by the arm, "you have nothing to do here."

Gilbert gently disengaged himself and continued to advance.

"Get out of my sight," screamed Stephane. "Why do you come to trouble my solitude? Who gives you the right to pursue me, to track me? How dare you look me in the face after—"

He could say no more. Excitement and anger choked his voice. For some moments he looked alternately at Gilbert and the dog; then changing his purpose, he moved as if to fly, but Gilbert barred the way.

"Listen to me but a minute," said he in a gentle and penetrating voice, "I bring you good news."

"You!" exclaimed Stephane, and he repeated, "You! you! good news!"

"I!" said Gilbert, "for I come to announce to you my near departure."

Stephane stared with wide open eyes, and recoiled slowly to the wall, where, leaning back again, he exclaimed: "What! you are going? Ah! certainly the news is excellent, as well as unexpected; but you are giving yourself unnecessary trouble, there was no need to forewarn me. Your departure! great God! I should have been notified of it in advance by the clearness of the air, by the more vivid brightness of the sun, by some strange joy diffused through all my being. Oh! I understand, you are not able to digest the outrage done to you by the excellent Fritz at my order. You consider the reparation insufficient. You are right, I swear it by St. George, my heart made no apologies to you. I upon my knees to you! Horror and misery! As I told you yesterday, I yielded only to force. It was the same as if I should make my bull-dog throw you down at my feet now!"

Gilbert made no answer; he contented himself with drawing from his pocket-book the letter which he had written the day before, and presenting it to Stephane.

"What have I to do with this paper?" said Stephane with a gesture of disdain. "You have told me your news, that is sufficient for me. Anything more you could add would spoil my happiness."

"Read!" said Gilbert. "I have granted you such a great favor that you can well afford to grant me a small one."—Stephane hesitated a moment, but the habitual tediousness of his life was so great that the want of diversion overcame his hatred and scorn.

"This letter is not bad!" said he as he read. "Its style is eloquent, the penmanship is admirable too. It involuntarily suggests to me the tie of your cravat. Both are so correct that they are insufferable."

Gilbert smiling, untied his cravat and let the ends hang down upon his vest.

"It is not worth while to incommode yourself," pursued Stephane, "we have so short a time to live together! Pray do not renounce your most cherished habits for me. The bow of your cravat as well as your writing, harmonize wonderfully with your whole person. I do not suppose, however, that to please me you would reconstruct yourself from head to foot. The undertaking would be considerable."

Gilbert let him talk and felt no anger, for he noticed with some satisfaction that having read his letter once he had begun to read it again.

"How charming these last lines are!" resumed the young man after a silence.

"I swear to thee that my eyes were full of tears!"

"Did you count them—those precious tears? However, I will be indulgent, for there is a word in this eloquent note which delights me. I see that you have had wit enough to discover that my pretended apologies were nothing. And then the charming part—My dear sir, at what hour do you go? Oh! tell me the hour! I want to know the hour, I want to assist in person at this moving and delicious scene. Ah! blessed, blessed for ages upon ages, may those be who aid you in packing,—the porter who will carry your luggage on his shoulders; the six horses that will take you away at a gallop; the coachman who will urge them with voice and whip; the carriage that will jolt your dear person over every rut of the road! And above all, a thousand thanks, a thousand blessings, a thousand good things, to the whirlwind of dust which, down there at the first turning of the road, will hide forever from my sight one of the men who has made me suffer more than any one else, and whom I hate from the bottom of my soul!"

"Take breath, I beg of you," answered Gilbert coolly, "and permit me to speak. I have made a little change in my programme: I shall not leave tomorrow. I have granted myself a week's delay."

Stephane's face darkened, and his eyes flashed.

"I swear to you here, upon my honor," continued Gilbert, "that in a week I will leave, never to return, unless you yourself beg me to remain."

"What baseness! and how cleverly this little plot has been contrived; I see it all. By force of threats and violence they hope to compel me a second time to bend my knees to you and cry with clasped hands, 'Sir, in the name of Heaven, continue us the favor of your precious presence!' But this act of cowardice I shall never commit! Rather death! rather death!"

"Do not rave so, I implore you! On my honor your father shall never know a word of what we have just said,—you and I. I do not know how much Ivan has understood; but he has sworn secrecy, and I trust his word. In asking delay, I desire only to give you time to reflect. A week is not a century. In a week you will whisper to me one of these two words: 'Go' or 'Stay,' and I shall conform to your wishes without hesitation. I will also, if you persist in dismissing me, allege reasons for my departure which can in no way implicate you."

While Gilbert spoke, Stephane kept his eyes obstinately fixed upon him. At these last words, he laughed aloud.

"Oh, this is a little too much! If you are not a scoundrel, sir, you are a lunatic. What, is it possible that you imagine—?"

"If I want you to wait a few days before coming to a decision," replied Gilbert calmly, "it is because you do not know me yet. Who knows but there may exist between us a secret congeniality of disposition and inclinations which you do not suspect, and which may ripen in time into perfect friendship?"

Stephane measured him with contemptuous glances.

"It is you who are raving now, sir," answered he in an icy tone. "Spare me your idle fancies, my pride will not allow me to hear more."

And as Gilbert sought to take his hand, he drew off several steps.

"A word only," resumed Gilbert, without being discouraged. "Submit me to some proof. Have you no caprice which it is in my power to satisfy?"

And showing him with his finger a fragment of white quartz four feet below the parapet, at the place where the precipice began—

"See that pretty piece of quartz," said he: "shall I get it for you?"

Stephane did not deign to turn his head, but meanwhile the unexpected turn the conversation had taken, surprised as well as moved him. But he took great care to let no indication of it appear.

"Throw yourself at my feet," cried he impetuously; "drag yourself in the dust, kiss the ground before me, and demand pardon and mercy of me! At this price I will grant you, not my affection certainly, but my indulgence and pity."

"Impossible!" answered Gilbert, shaking his head. "I am like you; I should not know how to kneel, unless some one stronger than myself constrained me by violence. Oh, no! in such a performance I should lose even the hope of being some day esteemed by you. The more so as in the trial to which I wish you would subject me, I should desire to have some danger to brave, some difficulty to surmount."

Stephane could not conceal his astonishment. Never in all his life had he heard language like this. Nevertheless distrust and pride triumphed still over every other feeling.

"Since you wish it!" said he sneering . . . . and he drew a kid glove from one of his pockets, rubbed it between his hands and threw it to the bull-dog, who caught it in his teeth and kept it there. "Vorace," said he to him, "keep your master's glove between your teeth, watch it well; you will answer to me for it."

Then turning to Gilbert,—"Sir, will you please restore my glove to me? I should be infinitely obliged to you for it."

"Ah! this is then the trial to which you will subject me?" answered Gilbert with a smile upon his lips.

Stephane looked him in the face. For the first time, he could not avoid being struck by its noble expression and the clearness and purity of his glance. Gilbert's face had become transparent, and would have revealed to the least clairvoyant of eyes the intrepidity of his character matured by the struggles of life, the purity of a heart predestined to an eternal youth.

Stephane was involuntarily moved, and strove in

vain to conceal it by the jocular tone in which he replied:

"No sir, it is not a test of your sincerity, but a jest which we shall do well not to push further. This animal is not amiable. Should you be unfortunate enough to irritate him, it would be impossible even for me, his master, to calm his fury. Be good enough then to leave my glove where it is, and return peaceably to your study to meditate upon some important problem in Byzantine history. That will be a trial less perilous and better proportioned to your strength. Good-evening, sir, good-night."

"Oh! permit me," replied Gilbert, "I am resolved to carry this adventure to its conclusion!"

And gently repulsing Stephane, who sought to retain him, he walked straight toward the bull-dog.

"Take care," cried the young man shuddering, "do not trifle with that beast, or you are a dead man!"

"Take care," repeated Ivan, who not having understood half of what had been said, hardly suspected Gilbert's intention. "Take care, this dog is a ferocious beast."

Meantime Gilbert, crossing his arms upon his breast, advanced slowly towards the bull-dog, keeping his eyes steadily fixed on those of the animal, and when he thought he had disconcerted him by his undaunted gaze sufficiently to make him relax his grip upon the prize, he suddenly tore the glove from him and waved it in the air with his right hand. At the same moment Vorace, with a howl of rage, bounded up to leap at the throat of his despoiler. Gilbert sprang back, covering himself with his left arm, and the dog's jaws only grazed his shoulder. Yet when he touched the ground again, he held between his teeth a long strip of cloth, a scrap of linen and a morsel of bloody flesh. Mad with fury the bull-dog rolled over on the grass with this prize which he could hardly devour, and then suddenly, as if seized with a paroxysm of frenzy, he moved towards the castle doubling upon himself; but reaching the foot of the turret, he looked for his enemy and returned like an arrow to pounce upon him again.

"Throw down the glove," cried Ivan, "and climb the ash."

"I will surrender the glove only to him who asked me for it!" answered Gilbert.

And hiding it in his bosom, he drew a knife from his pocket. He had not time to open it. The dog, with bristling hair and foaming jaws was already within three steps of him, gathering himself to spring upon him; but he had scarcely raised himself from the ground when he fell back with his head shattered. The hatchet which Ivan carried at his girdle had come down upon him like a flash. The terrible animal vainly attempted to rise, rolled writhing in the dust, and breathed out his life with a hoarse and fearful howl.

"Thanks, my good Ivan," said Gilbert pressing the serf's hand.

Then approaching Stephane, who stood immovable, trembling in every limb, and his head buried in his hands:

"Here is your glove," said he, in a caressing voice. "Compose yourself, I am still alive. Unfortunately I seem condemned always to make you unhappy; your dog is dead, and it was for me that Ivan killed him. Can you forgive me?"

Stephane removed his hands from his face and took the glove; but at the sight of Gilbert's mutilated and bloody arm, he cried:

"Oh! the horrible wound!" and pointed at it with his finger, then suddenly fainted, and would have fallen to the ground if Ivan had not caught him.

"Brother," said the serf to Gilbert, "you have done a fine piece of work here! Wasn't I right in saying that you eat belladonna sometimes? See, the child has nearly fainted. I must carry him to his tower quickly. Your wound bleeds a great deal; bind your handkerchief around your arm. That's right! Now come quickly and open the door of the private staircase for us, and Heaven grant we meet nobody in the corridor. Make haste! and as soon as my young father comes to, I will come to you and take off your clothes and dress your wound."

Gilbert made his way rapidly to the little door, and opened it. Ivan passed in before him, mounted the staircase in three leaps, and darted into the corridor with his previous burden. When Gilbert reached his own room, he attempted to examine his wound; but had lost so much blood and, in trying to detach the handkerchief which adhered to the wound, the pain was so great that he felt himself growing faint, too. A mist came over his eyes, and he had only time to throw himself on a chair, which stood near the bed, when his head dropped on the pillow and he lost consciousness.

CHAPTER XIV.

DOCTOR VLADIMIR PAULITCH arrived at the castle just in time to take care of Gilbert. The wound was wide and deep, and in consequence of the great heat which prevailed, it might easily have proved serious; fortunately, Doctor Vladimir was a skilful man, and under his care the wound was soon healed. He employed certain specifics, the uses of which were known only to himself, and which he took care to keep a secret from his patient. His medicine was as mysterious as his person.

Vladimir Paulitch was forty years of age; his face was striking but unattractive. His eyes had the color and the hard brightness of steel; his keen glances, subject to his will, often questioned, but never allowed themselves to be interrogated. Well made, slender, a slight and graceful figure, he had in his gait and movements a feline suppleness and stealthiness. He was slow, but easy of speech, and never animated; the tone of his voice was cold and veiled, and whatever the subject of conversation might be, he neither raised nor lowered it; no modulations; every one of his sentences terminated in a little minor cadence, which fell sadly on the ear. He sometimes smiled in speaking, it is true, but it was a pale smile which did not light up his face. This smile signified simply: "I do not give you my best reason, and I defy you to divine it."

Endowed with that admirable quickness of perception which is frequently met among the Sclavonians, Vladimir had glanced at everything, formed impressions of everything. He spoke with ease five or six languages; he knew all the literatures of Europe; and there was no science of which he had not acquired some smattering; but he had examined nothing thoroughly, investigated nothing profoundly: in all the books which he had skimmed over he had studied but little more than the preface, so that with the exception of the medical art, where instinct served him better than study, he had in his mind commencements only, and his thoughts were but sketches of errors or truths. He prided himself on having examined all systems of philosophy and on despising them all. He had taken no lessons nor counsel from any of the illustrious thinkers who have been the teachers of the human race, and he flattered himself that he was indebted to no one; he made up of all sorts of shreds and patches his own *credo* and philosophy; he was one of those minds which have neither father, mother, family nor country: veritable foundlings of intelligence, *keimathloses* of the kingdom of thought, for whom there is no place of which they can say: "This is my country! This is the old homestead. There is the cradle where I dreamed my first dreams.

There is the school where my tongue was first unloosed."

Vladimir believed himself to be one of the "emancipated minds," and yet the supreme servitude of thought is to be dependent upon fortuitous things. Woe to the intellects which draw all their light from the accidents and vicissitudes of life, and which have frequented no other school than that of chance. Doubtless it is good to profit by the lessons of experience, and Casanova was right in pitying men whose reflective faculties have never been awakened by some extraordinary event in opposition to their daily habits. They are not the less to be pitied, however, who never reason, but from their personal experience, and who, drifting with the current of events, take the fortunes and misfortunes of their lives for their oracles. Vladimir's youth had been heaped with the favors of Heaven; and prosperity expanding his soul had given to its aims a noble and lofty direction; but at thirty he had been smitten with a great misfortune which had shattered all the energies of his being and laid waste at the same time his intellect and his heart. One night's frost had sufficed to destroy all the hopes of his spring. From that moment he looked at men and facts only through his own misfortune; and God not having wrought a miracle in his favor, he was persuaded that the world is governed by a blind and implacable fatality. Thus infatuated, and as if idolatrous of his unhappiness, he replied to all arguments of philosophy or religion, "I know what to depend upon; destiny has revealed its secret to me."

One morning when Ivan had come by order of the doctor to dress Gilbert's wound, our friend questioned him as to the character and life of Vladimir Paulitch. Of the man, Ivan knew nothing, and confined himself to extolling the genius of the physician; he expressed himself in regard to him in a mysterious tone. The imposing face of this impenetrable personage, the extraordinary power of his glance, his impassible gravity, the miraculous cures which he had wrought, it needed no more to convince the honest serf that Vladimir Paulitch dealt in magic and held communications with spirits; and he felt for his person a profound veneration mingled with superstitious terror. He told Gilbert that since the age of twenty-five, Vladimir had been directing a hospital and private asylum which Count Kostia had founded upon his estates, and that thanks to him these two establishments had not their equals in all Russia.

"Last year," added the serf, "he came to attend the *barine*, and told him that his malady would return this year, but more feebly, and that this would be the last. You will see that all will come to pass as he has said. Kostia Petrovitch is already much better, and I wager that next summer will come and go without his feeling his nerves."

As Ivan prepared to go, Gilbert detained him to ask news of Stephane. The serf had been very discreet, and had related the adventure upon the terrace to his master without compromising any one. The only trouble he had had was in persuading him that it was not on a sign from Stephane that the dog had attacked Gilbert.

"But, sir," demanded he, in his familiar language, "what did you mean by tearing my young father's glove from poor Vorace?"

"He had defied me, and I thought myself bound in honor. It was a great piece of folly; you can readily believe I have no desire to try it again."

"You will do wisely," replied Ivan, in a slightly ironical tone, "especially as you are very much mistaken if you flatter yourself that you have won his heart by it. For several days he has refused to set foot on the terrace for fear of meeting you there."

This unpleasant news rendered Gilbert uneasy, but he carefully concealed his sadness.

"From what motive," said he to himself, "does Stephane seek to avoid me? Is it a ruse, intended to lull the distrust of his jailer? or is it false shame which makes him apprehensive of seeing me again? or have I but succeeded in stirring up the hatred which he had vowed against me?"

The next day Gilbert dined in the great hall of the castle with M. Leminof and father Alexis.

"Do not disturb yourself because Stephane does not dine with us," said the Count to him. "He is not sick; but he has a new grievance against you; you have caused the death of his dog. I ask your pardon, my dear Gilbert, for the irrational conduct of my son. I have given him three days for the sulks. When that time has passed, I intend that he shall put on his good looks for you, and that he shall take his place at the table opposite you without frowning."

"And how is it that Doctor Vladimir is not with us?"

"He has begged me to excuse him for a time. He finds himself much fatigued with the care he has given me. A magnetic treatment, you understand. I should inform you that every year, some time during the summer, I am subject to attacks of neuralgia from which I suffer intensely. By the way, you have seen our admirable doctor several times. What do you think of him?"

"I don't know whether he is a great savant, but I am inclined to think he is a first-class artist."

"You cannot pay him a finer compliment; medicine is an art rather than a science. He is also a man capable of the greatest devotion. I am indebted to him for my life, and it was not as physician that he saved me either. A pair of stallions ran away with me within twenty paces of a precipice; the doctor appearing from behind a thicket darted to the heads of the horses and hung on to them by their nostrils which he held in an iron grip. You have the whole scene from these windows. What was amusing in it was, that having thanked him, with what warmth you can imagine, he answered, in a tranquil tone, and wiping his knees—for the horses in falling had laid him full length in the dust—'It is I who am obliged to you; for the first time I have been suspended between life and death, and it is a singular sensation. But for you I should not have known it.' This will give you an idea of the man and his *sang froid!*"

"I am not surprised at his having the agility of a wild cat," replied Gilbert; but I suspect the *sang froid* is feigned, and that his placidity of face is a mask which hides a very passionate soul."

"Passionate is not the word, or at least the doctor knows only the passions of the head. There was a time when he thought himself desperately in love; an unpardonable weakness in such a distinguished man; but he was not long in undeceiving himself, and he has not fallen into such a fatal error since."

"So curiosity and medicine are the only passions of Vladimir Paulitch!"

"You are right. He has consecrated all his time and all his thoughts to the study and practice of his art. A more austere life cannot be conceived; he has indulged in no pleasures, granted nothing to his senses, and certainly this great restriction of all common enjoyments does not proceed from religious scruples. The doctor believes in nothing but atoms, but he is ascetic by taste. You know the admirable definition which Voltaire gave of love, 'a fabric of nature, which imagination has embroidered!' Vladimir Paulitch is unprovided with this imagination which embellishes with embroidery, and on the other hand, the plain fabric excites his contempt. I mean to say that he disdains voluptuousness from intellectual pride. So this fearful infidel, who holds morality to be a chimera and lives in abstinence, you can consider either a libertine without vices or a saint without principles. Ah, he's a singular character."

"According to what you say," remarked Gilbert, "his virtue is but an accident."

"Are you quite sure that virtue is ever anything else?" retorted M. Leminof.

The night having come, Gilbert, who had inquiries to make, crossed the yard of which the chapel formed one side, and gaining the rear by a private door, went in search of father Alexis. It was not long before he discovered him, for the priest had left his shutters open, and he was seated in the embrasure of the window, peaceably smoking his pipe, when he perceived Gilbert.

"Oh, the good boy!" cried he, "let him come in quickly! My room and my heart are open to him."

Gilbert showed him his arm in the sling on account of which he could not climb the window.

"Is that all, my child?" said father Alexis. "I will hoist you up here."

Gilbert raised himself by his right arm, and father Alexis drawing him up, they soon found themselves seated face to face uniting to their heart's content the blue smoke of their chibouques.

"Have you not noticed," said father Alexis, "that Kostia Petrovitch has been in a charming humor today? I told you that he had his pleasant moments! Vladimir Paulitch has already done him much good. What a physician this Vladimir is! It is a great pity that he does not believe in God; but some day, perhaps, grace will touch his heart, and then he will be a complete man.

"If I were in your place, father, I should be afraid of this Vladimir," said Gilbert. "Ivan pretends that he is something of a sorcerer. Aren't you afraid that some fine day he may rob you of your secret?"

Father Alexis shrugged his shoulders.

"Ivan talks foolishly," said he. "If Vladimir Paulitch were a sorcerer, would he not have long since penetrated the mystery which he burns to fathom? for he does more than love Count Kostia; he is devoted to him even to fanaticism. It is certain that having discovered that the Countess Olga was enceinte, he had the barbarity to become her denouncer; and that letter which announced to Count Kostia his dishonor, that letter which made him return from Paris like a thunder-clap, that letter in short which caused the death of Olga Vassilievna, was written by him—Vladimir Paulitch."

"And Morlof," said Gilbert, "was it this Vladimir who denounced him to the unjust fury of the Count?"

"On the contrary, Vladimir pleaded his cause; but his eloquence failed against the blind prejudices of Kostia Petrovitch. This Morlof was, unfortunately for himself, a fashionable gentleman well known for his gallantries. A man of honor, however, incapable of betraying a friend; this reputation for gallant success, of which he boasted, was his destruction. When Count Kostia interrogated his wife, and she refused to denounce her seducer, it occurred to him to name Morlof, and the energy with which she defended him, confirmed the Count's suspicions. To disabuse him, it needed but that tragic meeting of which I was informed too late. In breathing his last sigh, Morlof extended his hand to his murderer and gasped 'I die innocent!' And in these last words of a dying man, there was such an accent of truth that Count Kostia could not resist it: light broke in upon his soul."

As the darkness increased, father Alexis closed the shutters and lit a candle.

"My child," said he, refilling and lighting his pipe, "I must tell you something I learned to-day, a few moments before dinner, which appeared to me very strange. Listen attentively, and I am sure you will share in my astonishment."

Gilbert opened his ears, for he had a presentiment that father Alexis was about to speak of Stephane.

"It is a singular fact," resumed the priest, "and one that I should not wish to relate to the first-comer, but I am very glad to impart it to you, because you have a serious and reflective mind, though unfortunately you are not orthodox; would to God you were. Know then, my child, that to-day, Saturday, I went according to my custom to Stephane to catechize him, and for reasons which you know, I redoubled my efforts to impress his unruly head with the holy truths of our faith. Now it appears that without intending it, you have caused him sorrow; and you can believe that such a character, far from having pardoned you, has taken the greatest pains to get me to espouse his side in the difficulty. However, he who will usually fly into a passion and talk fiercely if a fly tickles him, recited his griefs to me with an air of moderation and a tranquility of tone which astonished me to the last degree. As I endeavored to discover a reason for this, I happened to raise my eyes to the images of St. George and St. Sergius which decorate one of the corners of his room, and before which he was in the habit of saying his prayers every morning. What was my surprise, my grief, when I perceived that the two saints had suffered shameful outrages. One had no legs, the other was disfigured by a horrible scar. 'Holy Virgin!' cried I with a trembling voice, 'who has had the audacity to lift a profane hand to these venerated images?' But he answered, smiling: 'The culprit is here, father. It was I who the other day, in a paroxysm of righteous anger, switched these two saints unmercifully to punish them for not coming to my aid.' How can I describe to you my astonishment? My arms dropped, a cold sweat came on my forehead, and my tongue failed me. I knew not what to say—what to think. When I recovered from the shock, burning with indignation, I could not find words strong enough to show to this impious youth the enormity of his crime. Whip St. George! whip St. Sergius! What a sacrilege! what a crime! Ah! my child, these were two of my finest works. But can you believe it, Stephane did not appear to manifest the slightest contrition? His impassible coolness exasperated me. With hands raised to Heaven, I threatened him with the thunder of God. Without being excited, without changing countenance, he left his chair, came to me and placed his hand on my mouth. 'Father,' said he, with an air of assurance which awed me, 'listen to me. I have been wrong, if you wish it so, and still, under the same circumstances, I should do it again, for since I have chastised them, the two saints have decided to come to my aid, and the very day after their punishment, without any change in my life, all at once I felt my heart become lighter; for the first time, I swear to you, a ray of celestial hope penetrated my soul. What do you say to that, my child? I had often heard similar things related, but I did not believe them. Little boys may be whipped, but as for saints!—Ah! my dear child, the ways of God are very strange, and there are many great mysteries in this world."

Father Alexis had such an impressive air in speaking of this great mystery, that Gilbert was tempted to laugh; but he controlled himself; he was too grateful for his obliging narrative, and could have embraced him with all his heart.

"Good news!" said he to himself. "That heart has become lighter; that 'ray of celestial hope.' Ah! God be praised, my effort has not been thrown away. St. George, St. Sergius, you rob me of my glory, but what matters it? I am content!"

"And what reply did you make to Stephane?" said he to the priest. "Did you reprimand him? Did you congratulate him?"

"The case was delicate," said the good father, with the air of a philosopher meditating on the most abstruse subject; "but I am not wanting in judgment, and I drew out of the affair with honor."

"You managed admirably," cried I, looking at him with admiration; then immediately putting on a serious face, "but the sin is enormous."

The third day after, Gilbert didn't wait for the bell

to ring for dinner before going down to the great hall. He was not very much surprised to find Stephane there. Leaning with his back against the sideboard, the young man, on seeing him appear, lost his composure, blushed, and turned his head towards the wall. Gilbert stopped a few steps from him. Then in an agitated manner, and with a voice at once gentle and abrupt, he said:

"And your arm?"

"It is nearly well. To-morrow I shall take off my sling."

Stephane was silent for a moment. Then in a still lower voice:

"What do you mean to do?" murmured he; "what are your plans?"

"I wait to know your good pleasure," replied Gilbert.

The young man covered his eyes with both hands, and, as Gilbert said no more, he seemed to feel a thrill of impatience and vexation.

"His pride demands some mercy," thought Gilbert. "I will spare him the mortification of making the first advances."

"I should like very much to have a conversation with you," said he gently. "This cannot be upon the terrace, Ivan will not leave you alone there. Does he keep you company in your room in the evening?"

"Are you jesting?" answered Stephane, raising his head. "After nine o'clock Ivan never comes near my room."

"And his room, if I am not mistaken," answered Gilbert, "is separated from you by a corridor and a staircase. So we shall run no risk of being overheard."

Stephane turned towards him and looked him in the face.

"You think of everything," said he, with a smile sad and ironical. "Apparently, to reach me, you will be obliged to mount a swallow. Have you made your arrangements with one?"

"I shall come over the roofs," said Gilbert quietly.

"Impossible!" cried Stephane. "In the first place, I do not wish you to risk your life for me again. And then—"

"And then you do not care for my visit?"

Stephane only answered him by a look.

At this moment steps sounded in the vestibule. When the Count entered, Gilbert was pacing the further end of the hall, and Stephane, with his back turned, was attentively observing one of the carved figures upon the wainscoting. M. Leminof, stopping at the threshold of the door, looked at them both with a quizzical air.

"It was time for me to arrive," said he laughing. "This is an embarrassing *tête-à-tête*."

The following day Gilbert left for Frankfort. A bookseller of that city had just sent to M. Leminof a catalogue of old books, among which they found the glossary of the *Grécité Byzantine*, by Du Cange, a standard work of which the Count possessed but a blemished and incomplete copy. Gilbert persuaded him to send him at once to secure this prize. He arrived at Frankfort that evening. The next day his first task was to find a rope-maker, of whom he ordered two rope ladders, giving him the measures. The rest of the day was devoted to the purchase of books. He not only secured the glossary, but as he was a great *connoisseur* in curious literature, in rummaging the shop of an antiquary, he found treasures with which he was delighted. He was not less pleased when, in the evening, they sent him the two ladders he had ordered. He hid them in the bottom of his trunk, and the next day renewed the search for old books. During the hunt, he saw in front of a shoemaker's shop a pair of shoes with felt soles—admirable contrivances to avoid slipping! The shoes fitted him, and he bought them without hesitation. He purchased also a girdle, a soft, broad-brimmed hat, a pair of thick pantaloons, and a red woollen shirt.

The following Saturday, towards noon, he returned to Geierfels. He hoped to be able to exchange a few words with Stephane before dinner; but the Count came into the hall before his son. Fortunately, at the end of the dinner, he rose from the table to fetch a bottle of Tokay from a closet to drink to the return of his secretary. While his back was turned, and he was occupied in searching for the bottle and uncorking it, Gilbert made a sign which attracted Stephane's attention, and immediately traced some letters upon the table-cloth with the handle of his knife. These letters were: "*This evening.*"

During the remainder of the meal Stephane's manner was excited. He changed color every moment, and was the first to leave the table, giving, as he turned, a look at Gilbert which betrayed the tumult of his thoughts. Then he disappeared.

"He still regrets his big dog," said the Count sneeringly. "The passions of Monsieur my son are decidedly very interesting."

CHAPTER XV.

At about ten o'clock Gilbert began to make preparations for his expedition. He had no fear of being surprised; his evenings were his own—that was a point agreed upon between the Count and himself. He had also just heard the great door of the corridor roll upon its hinges. On the side of the terrace the thick branches of the trees concealed him from the watch dogs who, had they suspected the adventure, could have given the alarm. There was nothing to fear from the hillock below the precipice; it was frequented only by the young girl who tended the goats and who was not in the habit of allowing them to roam so late among the rocks. Besides, the night, serene and without a moon, was propitious; no other light than the discreet glistening of the stars, which would help to guide him, without being bright enough to betray or disturb him; the air was calm, a scarcely perceptible breeze stirred at intervals the leaves of the trees without agitating the branches. Thanks to this combination of favorable circumstances, Gilbert's enterprise was not desperate; but he did not dream of deceiving himself in regard to its dangers.

The castle clock had just struck ten when he extinguished his lamp and opened the window. There he remained a long time leaning upon his elbows: his eyes at last familiarized themselves with the darkness, and favored by the glimmering of the stars, he began to recognize with but little effort the actual shape of the surrounding objects. The window was divided in two equal parts by a stone mullion, and had in front a wide shelf of basalt, surrounded by a balustrade. Gilbert fastened one of his rope ladders securely to the mullion and one of the balusters on the left side; then he crept upon the ledge of basalt and stood there for a few moments contemplating the precipice in silence. In the gloomy and vaporous gulf which his eyes explored, he distinguished a wall of whitish rocks, which seemed to draw him towards them, and to provoke him to an aërial voyage. He took care not to abandon himself to this fatal attraction, and the uneasiness which it caused him disappearing gradually, he stretched out his head and was able to hang over the abyss with impunity. Proud at having subdued the monster, he gave himself up for a moment to the pleasure of gazing at a feeble light which appeared at a distance of sixty paces, and some thirty feet beneath him. This light came from Stephane's room; he had opened his window and closed the white curtains in such a way that his lamp, placed behind this transparent screen, could serve as a beacon to Gilbert without danger of dazzling him.

"I am expected." said Gilbert to himself.

And immediately, bestriding the balustrade, he descended the trembling ladder with a step as light and firm as if he had never done any thing else in his life.

He was now upon the roof. There he met with more difficulty. Partly covered with zinc and partly with slate, this roof—the whole length of which he must traverse—was so steep and slippery that no one could stand erect on it. Gilbert seated himself and remained motionless for a moment to recover himself, and the better to decide upon his course. A few steps from this point, a huge dormer window rose, with triangular panes of glass, and reached to within two feet of the spout. Gilbert resolved to make his way by this narrow pass, and from tile to tile he pushed himself in that direction. It will readily be believed that he advanced but slowly, much more so on account of his left arm, which, as it still pained him, required to be carefully managed; but by dint of patience and perseverance he passed beyond the dormer window, and at length arrived safely at the extremity of the roof, just in front of Stephane's window.

"God be praised, the most difficult part is over," he said to himself, breathing freely.

But he was far from correct in his supposition. It is true he had now only to descend upon the little roof, cross it, and climb to the window, which was but breast high; but before descending it was necessary to find some support—stone, wood or iron, to which he could fasten the second rope ladder, which he had brought wound about his neck, shoulders and waist. Unfortunately he discovered nothing. At last, in leaning over, he perceived at the outer angle of the wall a large iron corbel, which seemed to sustain the projecting roof; but to his great chagrin, he ascertained at the same time, that the great roof passed three feet beyond the line of the small one, and that if even he should succeed in attaching his ladder to the corbel, the last rounds would float in empty space. This reflection made him shudder; and turning his eyes from the precipice, he examined the ridge-pole, where he thought he saw a piece of iron projecting. He was not mistaken: it was a kind of ornamental moulding, which formed the pediment of the ridge. It was not without great effort that he raised himself even there, and when he found himself seated astride the beam, he rested a few moments to breathe, and to study the strange spectacle before him. His view embraced an immense extent of abrupt, irregular roofing, from every part of which rose turrets of every kind, in the shape of extinguishers, pointed gables, corners, retreating or salient angles, bell-towers, open to the daylight, profound depths where the gloom thickened, grinning chimneys, heavy weathercocks cutting the milky way with their iron rods and feathered arrows; from the top of the chapel steeple a great cross of stone, seeming to stretch out its arms; here and there the whitish zinc, cutting the dark blue of the slates; in spots an indistinct glittering and flashes of pale light enveloped in opaque shadows, and then the tops of three or four large trees which extended beyond the eaves, as if prying into the secrets of the attic. By the glittering light of the stars, the slightest peculiarity in the architecture assumed singular contours, fantastic figures were profiled upon the horizon like Chinese shadows; everywhere an air of mystery, of curiosity, of wild surprise. All these shadows leaned towards Gilbert, examined him and interrogated him by their looks.

Some said, "Who is this person? Assuredly he is not one of us. What is he doing here? It can only be a bold thief who is about to pick the window fastenings and break open a secretary."

"Let him alone," said the others. "Don't you see it is a lover who is in luck? His mistress expects him, and if he don't break his neck first, the propitious hour will strike for him."

"I am nothing of the kind," replied Gilbert. "I am only a poor bookworm who has suddenly conceived the idea of scrambling over the roof to reanimate a child dying of sadness and isolation. Besides, take my word for it, I'm more astonished at my adventure than you are."

After this dumb colloquy, he looked back to the precipice, enjoyed the pleasure of contemplating the dull white waters of the Rhine, glimpses of which he caught here and there winding through the plain in undulating circles like an enormous serpent with glistening scales; for a moment he listened to its noisy, dull rumbling, which seemed to reproach the watch-dogs, the owls, the winds and the sleepy weathercocks for their silence.

When he had recovered breath, Gilbert approached the projecting ornament from which he proposed to suspend his ladder; he had been greatly deceived; he found that this *ovolo* of sheet iron, for a long time roughly used by the elements, held only by a wretched nail, and that it would inevitably yield to the least strain."

"It is decided," said he. "I must go by the iron corbel!" And although it cost him an effort, his mind was soon resolutely fixed. Impatient at the loss of so many steps and at the waste of so much precious time in vain efforts, he redescended the roof much more actively than he had mounted it. Arriving below, and by the power of his will conquering a new attack of vertigo with which he felt himself threatened, he lay down upon his face parallel with the spout, and advancing his head and arm beyond the roof he succeeded, not without much trouble, in tying the cord firmly to the iron corbel. This done, he launched the ladder into space, and without loitering to see it float, he swung himself slowly round, by degrees turning his head from the side of the roof and his feet to the side of the ladder; when he was completely turned, he let himself glide outside of the roof up to the armpits, thus resting suspended by the elbows. Critical moment! If but a lath, but a nail should break— He had no time to make this alarming reflection; he was too much occupied in drawing towards him with his feet the ladder which kept slipping away, and when at length he succeeded in planting them upon one of the upper rounds, detaching his left arm from the roof, he seized the corbel firmly, and soon after, his right hand removing itself in its turn, grasped one of the upright cords of the ladder.

"That's not bad for a beginner," thought he.

He then began to descend, giving careful attention to every movement. But at the moment when his feet had reached the level of the small roof, having had the imprudence to look down into the space beneath him, he was suddenly seized with a dizziness a thousand times more terrible than he had already experienced. The whole valley began to be agitated, and rolled and pitched terribly. By turns it seemed to rise to the sky or sink into the bowels of the earth. Presently the motion was accelerated, trees and stones, mountains and plains were all confounded in one black whirlwind, which struggled with increasing fury, and from which came forth flashes of lightning and balls of fire. Suddenly it seemed to him that his breath failed him. He closed his eyes, a stifled cry escaped from his panting breast. It was all over, the whirlwind had struck him and was carrying him into space. He lost consciousness for a few seconds; what was his surprise upon reopening his eyes, to find himself still upon his ladder. He had clung to it with such strength that his nails were buried deeply in the rope, and he had seized one of the upper rounds between his teeth, which were so fastened in it that he withdrew them with difficulty. He looked down upon the valley; it had become motionless. He raised his eyes to the firmament, from which the stars looked at him encouragingly. He passed his tongue over his feverish lips, breathing with free lungs the night air, which seemed to be perfumed. Tears of joy escaped from his eyes, and in artless rapture, he tenderly kissed the ladder which he had just attacked with his teeth. Restored to himself, to dispel the emotion which the remembrance of his frightful nightmare caused him, he had recourse to old Homer, and recited in one breath that passage of the Iliad where the divine bard describes the joy of a herdsman contemplating the stars from a craggy height. Gilbert never, in after life, read these verses without recalling the sweet but terrible moment when he recited them suspended in mid-air; above his head the infinite smile of starry fields, and under his feet the horrors of a precipice. As soon as he felt more calm, he commenced the task of effecting his descent upon the small roof, less steep than the other, and covered with hollow tiles which left deep grooves between them. To crown his good fortune, the spout was surmounted from place to place by iron ornaments imbedded in the wall and rolled up in the form of scrolls. Gilbert imparted an oscillating motion to the ladder, and when it had become strong enough to make this improvised swing graze the gutter, choosing his time well, he disengaged his right foot and planted it firmly in one of the grooves, loosening at the same time his right hand from the ladder and quickly seizing one of the scrolls. A moment after, the ladder left to itself, returned to its place. Midnight sounded, and Gilbert was astonished to find that he had spent two hours upon his adventurous excursion. To mount the roof halfway, cross it, and climb into the window was but a slight affair, after which, turning the curtains aside with his hand, he called in a soft voice: "Am I expected?" and leaped with a bound into the room.

With his chin upon his knees and his head buried in his hands, Stephane was crouching at the feet of the holy images. Hearing and perceiving Gilbert, he started, raised himself quickly and remained motionless, his hands crossed above his head, his neck extended, his lips quivering and opening with a smile, lightnings and tears in his eyes. How paint the strangeness of his countenance? A thousand diverse emotions betrayed themselves there. Surprise, gratitude, shame, anxiety, long expectation at last satisfied; a remnant of haughtiness which felt its defeat certain; an obstinate incredulity forced to surrender; the disorder of an imagination, enchanted, rapt, distracted, the delights of hope and the bitterness of memory; all these appeared upon his face, and formed a mélange so confused that to see him thus laughing and crying at once, it seemed as if it was his joy which wept and his sadness which smiled. His first agitation dispelled, the predominating expression of his face was a dreamy and startled sweetness. He moved backwards from Gilbert and fell upon a chair at the end of the room.

"Do I intrude? Must I go away?" asked Gilbert, still standing. Stephane made no answer.

"Evidently my face does not please you," continued Gilbert, half turning towards the window.

Stephane contracted his brows.

"Do not trifle, I beg of you," said he, in a hollow voice. "We have serious matters between us to discuss."

"The seriousness which I prefer, is that of joy."

Stephane passed his thin and taper hands nervously through his hair.

"Joy?" said he. "It will come, perhaps, in its time, through speaking to me about it, who knows? Now I seem to be dreaming. The disorder of my thoughts frightens me. Ask me no questions, for I should not know how to answer you. And then the sound of my voice mortifies me, irritates me. It is like a discord in music. Let me be silent and look at you."

And approaching a long table which stood in the middle of the room, he signalled to Gilbert to place himself at one side of it and seated himself at the other.

After a long silence, he began to express his thoughts audibly, as if he had become reconciled to the sound of his voice:

"This bold, resolute air, so much pride in the look, so much goodness in the smile. It is another man. Ah! into what contempt have I fallen. I have seen nothing, divined nothing. I despised him, I hated him,—this one whom God has sent to save me from despair. See what was concealed under this simple unaffected air; this serene face, whose calmness irritated me; this gentleness which seemed servile, this wisdom which I thought pedantry; this pliancy of disposition which I took for the meanness of a crouching dog. All this! can it really be the same man? He was silent for a moment and then continued in a more assured voice:

"How did you manage to reach here? Ah! my God! that great roof is so steep! Only to think of it makes me shudder and sets my head to whirling. While waiting I prayed to the saints for you. Did you feel their aid? I should like to know whether they stood by me in this. They have so often broken faith."

Silence again, during which Stephane looked at Gilbert with a steadiness sufficient to disconcert him.

"So you have risked your life for me!" continued the young man; "but are you quite sure that I am worth the trouble? Come now, be frank. Has any one spoken to you of me? Or have you, by studying my character, made some interesting discovery. Answer, and be careful not to lie. My eyes are upon you, they will readily discover if you are sincere."

"Really you astonish me," answered Gilbert, tranquilly; "and what can I have to conceal from you? All I know resolves itself into two points. In the first place, I know that you belong to the race, to the brotherhood of noble souls; I know, besides, that you are very unhappy.—Pardon me, I know another thing still. I know beyond a doubt that I have conceived a lively and tender friendship for you, and that I should be very unhappy too if I could not expect any return from you."

"You feel friendship for me? How can that be?"

"Ah! a strange question! Who has ever been able to answer it? It is the mystery of mysteries. I love you, because I love you: I know of no other explanation. You have certainly never made any very flattering advances to me, I think I have sometimes even had cause to complain of you.

"Ah, well! in spite of your scorn, of your haughtiness, of your injustice, I loved you. Ask the secret of this anomaly of Him who created man, and who planted in his heart that mysterious power which is called sympathy."

"Why," said Stephane, "was not this sympathy reciprocal? As for me, from the first day I saw you I hated you. I do not know with what eyes I looked at you, but I thought that I recognized an enemy. Alas! suspicion and distrust invaded my heart long ago. And mark, even at this moment I still doubt, I fear I may be the dupe of some illusion: I believe and I do not believe, and I am tempted to exclaim with one of the Holy Evangelists, 'My patron, my brother, my friend, I believe, help thou mine unbelief!'"

"Your incredulity will cure itself, and be sure, a day will come when you will say with confidence: there is in this world a soul, sister of my own, into which I can fearlessly pour all my cares, all my thoughts, all my sorrows and all my hopes. There is one who occupies himself unceasingly about me, to whom my happiness is of great moment, of supreme interest, a being to whom I can say all, confess all; a being who loves me because he knows me, and who knows me because he loves me; a being who sees with me, who sees in me, and who would not hesitate, if necessary, to sacrifice everything, even his life, upon the holy altar of friendship. And then would you not cry out in the joy of your heart: God be praised! I possess a friend! By the blessing of God I have learned what it is to love and to be loved."

Stephane began to weep:

"To be loved!" said he. "It is a great word and I hardly dare to pronounce it. To be loved! I have never been. I believe though, that my mother loved me,—what do I say? I am sure of it, but it was a long time ago. My mother,—it is like a legend to me. It seems to me I was not born when I knew her. I remember that she often took me upon her knees and covered me with kisses. Such joys are not of this world; I must have tasted them in some distant star, where hearts are less hard than here, and where I lived some time, a sojourn of peace and innocence. But one day my mother dropped me from her arms, and I was thrown upon this earth where hatred expected me and received me in her bosom. Oh! hatred, I know her! This second mother cradled me in her arms, nourished me with her milk, lavished upon me her careful lessons and watched over me night and day. Ah! hatred is a marvellous providence. It sees everything, thinks of everything, notices everything, is omnipresent, always on the alert, unconscious of fatigue, ennui or sleep. Hatred! she is the mistress of this castle, she governs it; these great corridors are full her. I cannot take a step without meeting her; even here in this solitary room I see her image floating upon the panelling, upon the tapestry, about the curtains of this bed, and often at night, in my sleep, she comes and sits upon my breast and peoples my dreams with spectres and terrors. To be hated without knowing wherefore,—what torment! And remember too, that in my early infancy, this father who hates me was then a father to me. He rarely caressed me and I feared him; he was imperious and severe; but he was a father after all, and occasionally he took the trouble to tell us so. Often in our presence his gravity relaxed, and I recollect that he sometimes smiled upon me. But one day, a cursed day,—I was then ten years old; my mother had been dead a month.—He was shut up in his room while a week passed, during which I did not see him. I said to my governess: 'I want to see my father.' I knocked at his door, entered and ran to him. He repelled me with such violence that I fell and struck my head against the leg of a chair. I got up bleeding, and he looked at me with scorn, laughed and left the room. My mind wandered, all my ideas were thrown into confusion; I thought the sun had gone out and that the world had come to an end. A father who could laugh at the sight of the blood gushing from his child! And what a laugh! He has made me hear it often since, but I have not been able to accustom myself to it yet. A fever attacked me, and I became delirious. They put me to bed, and I cried to those who took care of me: 'I am cold, I am cold, make me warm.' And in that icy body I felt a heart that seemed on fire, which consumed itself. I could have sworn that a red-hot iron had been passed into it."

Stephane dried his tears with a curl of his hair, and then leaning with his elbows upon the table, he resumed in a feeble voice: "I do not want you to be deceived. You entertain friendship for me and you ask a return; that is very simple, friendship lives by exchange. If I had nothing to give you, you would soon cease to love me. Listen to me then. Yesterday, for the first time in my life, I went into myself,—

a singular fancy, which you alone have been able to inspire in me; for the first time I examined myself seriously, I laid hold of my heart with both hands, and examined it as a physician does his patient; I carried my researches even to the very bottom, and I recognized there a strange barrenness and blight, which frightened me. It has been suffering a long time,—this poor heart; but within a year a fearful crisis has passed within me, which has killed it. And now there is nothing in this breast but a handful of cold ashes, good for nothing but to be thrown out of the window and scattered in the air."

"What! you are orthodox," said Gilbert, in a tone of authority; "you believe in the saints after your own fashion, and nevertheless you have yet to learn that death is but a word, or better, a respite, a pause in life, a fallow time followed by fresh harvests. You are ignorant of the fact, or you forget, that there are no ashes so cold but that when the wind of the spirit breathes upon them, they will be seen to start, rise up and walk. You have left to me the care of teaching you that your soul is capable of rejuvenescence, of unexpected regeneration; that upon the sole condition that you wish and desire it, you will feel unknown powers awakened in your breast, and that without changing your nature, but by transforming yourself from day to day, you will become to yourself an eternal novelty!"

Stephane looked at him smiling.

"So you have crossed the roofs to come and preach conversion to me, like father Alexis!"

"Conversion! I don't know. I don't undertake to work miracles; but the metamorphosis—"

"Oh! yes, the metamorphosis of plants," exclaimed Stephane in a tone of caressing irony; "perhaps you have even brought the book."

"It is really a question of books— One day I bought of a seed merchant, a poor root of sorry appearance, a yellowish bulb, covered with overlapping scales, which rustled under my fingers like dead leaves. On reaching home, I took this bulb in my hands and said to it: 'Thou shalt be a lily,' and it replied: 'What folly! All in me is withered, dried up. Look at me well, thou wilt see that I am dead.'—'Leave it to me' cried I; 'I will implore the aid of the elementary powers. I will say to Heaven, give it to drink; to the earth, nourish it with thy juices. I will say to the sun, warm it with thy rays.' And so this poor plant, which believes itself dead, shall be resuscitated, shall pierce the stone of its tomb, shall live, shall grow, and the glory of its efflorescence shall dazzle my eyes. . . . I said truly. This dull root, buried by me in the bosom of the earth, felt itself moved with a pang of non-existence, with a confused desire to live; and this desire, this pang became a soul; this soul took life and this life entered into the divine cycle of its metamorphoses. At the same time unchangeable and diverse, gathering itself within itself, or expanding itself at the will of the throbbings of a mysterious fever, it comes to light in the shape of long, quivering leaves, then darts towards the sky a thin, delicate stem; and this stem expanding at the top, crowns itself with a silver diadem, displaying to view a dazzling flower, whose perfume the breezes inhale with delight. Listen to me then, oh! my beautiful, pure lily! Believe in the nourishing juices of the earth, in the refreshing dews of heaven; above all, believe in the splendors of the sun. In this breast, in this heart which loves you, I bring you a ray of this all powerful sunlight. Oh! drink in long draughts of the light and heat, and some day you also will bloom, I swear it to you, under the eyes of eternal goodness."

Stephane began to weep again.

"I do not know if you speak truth," murmured he; "but your manner, your voice, your looks,—your looks above all!"

Then repressing his tears:

"You speak to me much of my soul; but my life, my destiny, will you also find the secret of transforming them?"

"That secret we will seek together. I have already some light upon it. Only let us not press it. Before undertaking that great work, it is essential that your heart should recover its health and strength."

"Ingrate that I am!" cried Stephane. "My destiny! it has changed from to-day. Yes, from this moment I am no longer alone in the world. Frightful void in which I consumed myself, despair who with your frightful wings made it night for an abandoned child, it is all over now, I am delivered from you; the instrument of torture is broken. Henceforth, I believe, I hope, I breathe! But think of it my friend, for me to live, will be to see you, to hear you, to speak to you. Could you come here often?"

"As often as prudence will permit,—two or three times a week. We will choose our days well; we will consult the sky, the wind, the stars. On other days, at propitious hours, we will place ourselves at our windows, and communicate by signs which we will agree upon, for it seems that you, like me, are long sighted. And besides, I know the sign language. I will teach it to you, and if you ever send me such a message as this upon your fingers: 'I am sad, I am sick, come this evening at any risk'—Well, whatever the winds and stars may say—"

"Great God! interrupted Stephane," to expose your life foolishly! I will rather die. Curses upon me if ever by a caprice— But away with such a thought! And how long, if you please, will this happiness, which you promise me, last? Some day, alas! retaking your liberty—"

"I have two, perhaps three years to pass here; it will even depend upon me whether I stay longer or not. Whatever happens, be assured, that before I leave this house, your destiny will have changed. I have told you to believe in the sun; believe also in the unforeseen."

"The unforeseen!" exclaimed Stephane, "I believe in him, since I have seen him enter here by the window."

And suddenly carrying his hand to his heart, he closed his eyes, became pale and uttered a piteous moan. Gilbert sprang towards him; but repulsing him gently:

"Fear nothing," said he; "joy has come, I feel it there, it burns me. Let me enjoy a suffering so new and so sweet." He remained some minutes with his eyes closed; then re-opening them, and shaking his beautiful head with its long curls, he said sportively:

"Sit down there quick, and teach me the deaf mute language."

"Impossible," replied Gilbert; "the hour for going has already struck."

Stephane impatiently stamped his foot.

"Teach me at least the first two letters; if I don't know *a* and *b*, I shall not be able to close my eyes to-night."

Gilbert taking him by the arm, led him to the window, where, drawing aside the curtain, he pointed out to him the stars already paling, and a vague whiteness which appeared at the horizon. Then suddenly changing his tone, but still carried away by his impetuous nature, which stamped upon all the movements of his mind the character of passion, Stephane became much excited at the idea of the dangers which his friend was about to brave.

"I will go with you," said he, "I want to know what risks you run in coming here. To descend from the large roof to the small one, you must have had a ladder. I want to see this ladder, I want to assure myself that it is strong."

"Do not be afraid, I have attended to that."

"When I tell you that I wish to see it! I will believe only my own eyes and hands. Where is this ladder? I positively must see it."

"And I forbid you to climb this window. Take my word, my rope ladder is entirely new and very strong."

"Ah!" exclaimed Stephane, struck with a sudden idea. I will bet that you have fastened it to that great iron corbel, which stretches its frightful beak up there at the angle of the wall. And just now you were suspended in space on this treacherous floating cord. Monstrous fool that I was not to understand it."

And to Gilbert's great astonishment, he added:

"You do not yet love me enough to have the right to run such risks."

"Do be a little calmer," said Gilbert. "You displayed just now a gentleness and wisdom which enchanted me. Take care; Ivan might wake and come up."

"These walls are deafened, the flagging is thick; between this room and the staircase there is an alcove, a vestibule and two large closed doors; and between the rail of this staircase and the cage of my jailer, there is a long corridor. Besides, he is capable of everything but rambling at night round my apartment; but what matters it?—Let him come to surprise us, this hateful Ivan! I will resign myself to everything rather than see you put your feet upon that horrible ladder again. And take my word for it, if you violate my injunction,—at that very moment before your eyes, I will throw myself headlong down the precipice."

"You are extremely unreasonable," replied Gilbert, in a severe tone; "I must leave here at any cost. Since my ladder displeases you, instead of uttering a thousand follies, try rather to discover—"

Stephane struck his forehead.

"Here is my discovery," interrupted he; "opposite this window, on the other side of the roof, there is another, which, if you can only open it, will certainly let you into some empty lofts. Where these lofts will take you I don't exactly know, for Ivan told me once when he wanted to store some broken furniture there, that he had not been able to find the entrance; but you will no doubt discover some window near, by which you can get out upon the great roof, half-way from your turret, and so you will be spared a great deal of trouble and danger. Ah! if this proves so, how proud I shall be of finding it out."

"Now you are as I like to see you," said Gilbert; "instead of prancing like a badly bitted horse, you are calm, and you reason."

"So to reward me you will permit me to accompany you."

"God forbid! and if you presume to go without my permission, I swear to you that I will never come here again."

And as Stephane resisted and chafed, Gilbert took his head between his hands, and drawing him to his breast, pressed a paternal kiss on his forehead, just at the roots of his hair. This kiss produced an extraordinary effect, which alarmed him; Stephane shuddered from head to foot, and a cry escaped him.

"Awkward fellow that I am," said Gilbert, in an uneasy tone; "I have wounded you without intending it."

"No," murmured he, "it is of no consequence; but that was the place where my mother used to kiss me. May the saints be with you. I love you. Good-bye!"

And thus speaking he covered his face which was on fire, with both hands.

Ah! if Gilbert had understood! But he divined nothing; he descended to the roof, crossed it, and discovered, as he groped about, a window all the panes of which were broken; which saved him the trouble of opening it. When he found himself in the lofts, he lighted the candle which he had taken the precaution to bring in his pocket. The place which he had just entered was a wretched garret, three or four feet wide. In front of him he noticed four or five steps, ascended them, and opened an old door without any fastening. This let him into a vast corridor, which had no visible place of exit at the other end; it was infested by spiders and rats, and encumbered with dilapidated old furniture. Gilbert discovered on raising his eyes that he was in the mansard, lighted by the great dormer window. The bolt which held the shutter was so high up that he could not reach it with his hand. An old rickety table stood in a corner buried under a triple coating of dust. Having reached the window by its aid, Gilbert drew the bolt; he mounted upon the roof and, supporting himself by one of the projecting timbers of the pediment, restored the shutter to its embrasure and fastened it as well as he could; after which he made his way once more towards the small roof; for, before returning to his lodging, it was necessary at any cost to detach and draw up the ladder, an unimpeachable witness which would have testified against him. While Gilbert was extended at length fully occupied in this delicate operation, Stephane, standing at his window and trembling like a leaf, was tearing his handkerchief with his beautiful teeth. The ladder withdrawn, Gilbert cried out to him:

"Your lofts are admirable. Hereafter, coming to see you will only be a pleasure trip."

When he found himself again upon his balcony, dawn began to break, and a screech owl returning from his hunt after field mice, passed before him and regained his hole. Gilbert waved his hand to this nocturnal adventurer whose *confrère* he felt himself, and leaping lightly into his room was sleeping profoundly in five minutes. At the same moment Stephane, raising his eyes to the holy images to which he had given such terrible blows, exclaimed with a passionate gesture: "Oh! St. George, St. Sergius, help me to keep my secret."

CHAPTER XVI.

YESTERDAY evening I returned to Stephane by the dormer window and the lofts; the journey took me but twenty minutes. There was a slight wind, and I was glad to have nothing to do with the iron corbel. Arriving at ten o'clock I returned half an hour after midnight. On leaving the young man, I felt terrified and overjoyed at the same time,—frightened at the impulsive ardor of his temperament and at the efforts it will cost me to moderate his impetuosity; but overjoyed, astonished at the quickness and grasp of his mind, at his vivid imagination, and the truly Sclavonian flexibility of his naturally happy disposition. It is certain that the sad and barren existence he has led for years would have shattered the energies of a soul less finely tempered than his; the vigor and elasticity of his temperament have saved him. But I arrived just in time, for he confessed to me that the idea of suicide had taken possession of him since that unlucky escapade punished by fifteen hours' imprisonment.

"My first attempt was unfortunate," said he, "but I was resolved to try again; I had sounded the ford; another time I should have crossed the stream."

I hastened to turn the conversation, especially as he was not in the humor to weary himself with such a gloomy subject. How happy he appeared to see me again; how his joy expressed itself upon his ingenuous face, and how speaking were his looks! We occupied ourselves at first with the language of signs,

Nothing escaped his eager intellect: he complained only of my slow explanations.

"I understand, I understand," he would cry; "something else, my dear sir, something else, I'm not a fool."

I certainly had no idea of such quickness of apprehension. "The Sclavonians learn quickly," said I, "and forget quickly too."

To prove the contrary, he answered me by signs: "You are an impertinent fellow."

I was confounded. Then all at once:

"Extraordinary man," said he, with a gravity which made me smile, "tell me a little of your life."

"Extraordinary I am not at all," said I.

"And I affirm," answered he, "that humanity is composed of tyrants, valets and a single and only Gilbert."

"Nonsense! Gilberts are abundant."

"There is but one, there is but one," cried he, with a fire and energy that enchanted me.

I must own I am not sorry that for the time being he looks upon me as an exceptional being; for it is well to keep him a little in awe of me. To satisfy him I gave him the history of my youth. This time he reproached me for being too brief, and not going enough into detail.

As his questions were inexhaustible, I said: "After to-day do not let us waste our time upon this subject. Besides, the top of the basket shows the best that's in it."

"There may perhaps be something to hide from me?"

"No; but I will confess that I do not like to talk about myself too much. I get tired of it very soon."

"What?" said he in a tone of reproach, "are we not here to talk endlessly about you, me, us?"

"Certainly, and our favorite occupation will be to entertain ourselves with ourselves; but to render this pastime more delightful, it will be well for us to occupy ourselves sometimes with something else."

"With something else? With what?"

"With that which is not ourselves."

"And what do I care for anything which is neither you nor me?"

"This is the point: he who has the wisdom to go out of himself often ends by finding himself again in objects which appear the most foreign to his being; he observes that man is allied to the whole universe, and that even the stars are of the same family; he discovers secret relations between his soul and nature, between the laws of his thoughts and the laws of the plants, the elements and all the forms of universal life; he discovers that the world and he were made for each other, and fashioned by the same hand; and at the same time, while studying it he learns to know himself better and he repeats with joy the words of the philosopher: "The spirit of man is the spirit of the universe."

"Such a fine discourse passes far beyond my intelligence: but what I do know is, that this mysterious essay accords badly with that admirable programme of friendship which you sketched for me the other day. A true friend, you said, occupies himself unceasingly about his friend; he sees with him, in him, for him."

"Far from curtailing my programme, I complete it. 'To love in God' is an expression which you must have heard often from father Alexis; I translate it thus: 'To think together, to enjoy the universe together, to worship the same ideal together!"

"According to this, I shall never be the friend you dream of, for I do not think I enjoy the universe much; and as for the ideal, I don't know what it is, nor do I care to know either."

"Bah! you must not swear to anything. When the lily shall have blossomed .... Meanwhile, don't you think that one of the greatest pleasures two friends can taste, is to travel together? And what are journeys on foot or horseback compared with those which can be made on the wing by two souls strictly united, and floating together in the kingdom of ideas!"

He remained silent some moments, and then said:

"The master of this house is right in treating you as an idealist.—Ideas! ideas! I have never meddled with them, and I forewarn you that I have a head as empty as a nutshell nibbled by a mouse."

"But at all events you sometimes work, you read, you study?"

"At Martinique, father Alexis gave me two or three hours of lessons every day. He taught me history, geography, and among other stuff of the same kind, the inconceivable merits, and the superhuman perfections of his eternal Panselinos. The dissertations of this spiritual schoolmaster diverted me very little, as you may well suppose, and I was furious that in spite of myself his tiresome verbiage rooted itself in my memory, which is the most tenacious in the world."

"And did he continue his instructions to you?"

"After our return to Europe, my father ordered him to teach me nothing more but the catechism. He said it was the only study my silly brain was fit for."

"So for three years you have passed your days in absolute idleness."

"Not at all; I have always been occupied from morning till night."

"And how?"

"In sitting down, in getting up, in sitting down again, in pacing the length and breadth of my room, in gaping at the crows, in counting the squares of these flagstones, and the tiles of the little roof, in looking at the iron corbel and the water-spout on top of it, in watching the clouds sailing through the empty air, and then in lying down there in that recess of the wall, to rest quiet, with my eyes closed, ruminating over the problem of my destiny, asking myself what I could have done to God, that he chastised me so cruelly, recalling my past sufferings, enjoying in advance my sufferings to come, weeping and dreaming, dreaming and weeping, until overcome with lassitude and exhaustion I ended by falling asleep; or else, driven to desperation by weariness, I ran down to Ivan's lodging, and there gave vent to my scorn, fury and despair, at the top of my lungs."

These words, pronounced in a tone breathing all the bitterness of his soul, troubled me deeply. I trembled to think of this desolate child, whose griefs were incessantly augmented by solitude and idleness, of that soul defencelessly abandoned to its gloomy reveries, of that poor heart maddened, and pouncing upon itself as upon a prey; self-devouring, constantly reopening his wounds and inflaming them, without work or study to divert him a single instant from his monotonous torment. Oh! Count Kostia, how refined is your hatred!

"I'm astonished," said I, "that you didn't go mad, living in this way."

"Henceforth," continued he without answering me, "I shall have sweeter occupations. I shall think of you, I shall believe that I see you, I shall think over all your words, all your gestures; I shall watch the state of the sky and I shall say to the clouds: 'Go, far away and pour out the showers which would make the roofs slippery here;' and to the winds:—'Rage until night; but as soon as the sun sets, cease your blowing, that my friend may be able to come to me;' and to the stars: 'Shine to-night with your brightest fires to light his steps.' And I shall often look at my watch and cry: 'In ten hours,—in five hours,—in two hours he will be here. To beguile the weariness of my long waitings, I will stand at the window, and, whether I see you or not, I will make my fingers tell you all the follies that may cross my mind."

I took his hands and said to him:

"My child, listen to me, and believe in my experience. A life of sentiment will not suffice for a man, and it is a fated delusion to flatter one's self that the void of time can be filled with the heart. Whatever joys the tender and faithful friendship I have vowed to you may be able to procure, they will never be capable of satisfying your whole nature. Do not speak, I know what I am saying. This friendship has the charm of novelty for you and a touch of adventure, which exalts and inflames your imagination. You are a poor doubter suddenly smitten with faith, but you must distrust the lures and deceptions of enthusiasm. Converted unbelievers easily become superstitious. Do not feed on air and chimeras, nor dream of impossible bliss. Falling back from yon clouds upon yourself, you will charge your delusions upon me. You will say to me, is it thus you keep your engagements? False prophet, where is the happiness which you promised me? Alas! I burn with a thirst which you cannot quench, and I see that with all your zeal you know no remedy for the barrenness of my life and soul. Now I ask you, should you ever address such language to me, would not your complaints, your demands, your recriminations, and my inability to satisfy you, be enough to fill our friendship with bitterness, and make it a torture to us, a burden, a source of torment and disgust? My child, I implore you not to imitate the savage, who, prostrated before his divinity, expands his soul in idolatries and senseless hopes, and the next day whips the idol outrageously, reproaching him with lies and impostures. The poor fool's blind fury mistakes its object, for the impostor is himself. He imagined that to be God whose sole crime is not being God."

When I had spoken these words, he cast a furtive look upon the images of the saints, then lowered his head sighing. I resumed:

"Sooner or later the moment will come when you

ought to gather all your energies to conquer or disarm your destiny. Then, standing at your side, I will fight for you; but without you I can do nothing, and upon your wisdom and courage the victory will depend. Prepare yourself then from this day for the great contest, and when the hour strikes, may you find yourself in the possession of health of body and soul. Stephane, Stephane, think of it: strength is health, health is tranquillity, and tranquillity is the precious gift which reason, ripened by reflection and study, bestows upon a well regulated heart. Exercise and nourish your mind then, and one day you will feel your loins strengthened, and the weakness of your faltering heart suddenly reanimated by a life-giving breath. If you refuse to your intellect the nourishment it requires to keep it from perishing or being extinguished; if you scorn my counsels, and insist upon living only through the heart; if in only loving and hating you forget to reason and reflect,—then I fear you will be forever condemned to sterile excitements, to those fevers which consume the soul, and to hopeless impotence of will."

His face was very sad, and I thought I saw tears glistening in his eyes.

"Ah!" said he, "how much better you spoke the other day. 'In this breast, in this heart,' you said, 'I bring you a ray of the sun; drink of the light and the heat, and I swear to you my beautiful lily, you will end by blossoming under the eye of eternal goodness.' You see I was right in boasting of my memory; it is faithful and tenacious, an embarrassing circumstance for those fine talkers who contradict themselves shamelessly from one day to another."

"Permit me to say," replied I, "that I retract nothing; but since your memory is so exact, do you not recollect that I spoke to you not only of the light of the sun, but of the nourishing juices of the earth? Doubtless it is heat which animates and causes the seed to germinate, but plants are not nourished by the sun; the celestial rays are stimulants which awaken in them a secret desire to live, and immediately their roots, attaching themselves like hungry nurselings to the breasts of the earth, draw up the quickening essence, and the sap rises and rises, and the divine mystery is accomplished."

I am much mistaken, or the truth of my words struck him; but he kept it carefully to himself. He walked about the room with a careless and mutinous air; then stopping before me and crossing his arms, he said: "I now see that the night rambler and the *other* are inseparable."

"And aren't you reconciled to the *other* yet?"

"I don't insult him any more, that ought to satisfy him. All my affection is for the hero; the pedant has no claim except upon my tolerance."

"Very well! since you tolerate the pedant, tolerate also his impertinent questions and answer this one if you please. Are there no books in this room?"

"Ah! there I recognize him clearly enough!" cried he. "Books! books! Certainly yes, we have the pleasure of possessing them. Stay, there is a large closet full; but I forewarn you that I have not read a single one of them."

I opened the closet which he pointed out to me. Heavens! what a strange library. I fancy the Count had thrown all his worthless books there, with others of more importance, but for which he had no use. From the midst of the frightful disorder of this dusty collection, I drew out a Universal History in Dutch, four enormous folios; the complete works of Paracelsus, a Persian grammar, an imperfect volume of the *Bibliothèque historique de la France*, by Father Lelong, the *Bibliotheca mediæ et infimæ latinitatis* of Fabricius, and the works of Muret, and I don't know what else. However, I noticed also some works of history in French and a manual of botany. I began to make a selection when Stephane approached me with flushed face and flashing eyes.

" Physician of my soul," said he, "prescribe all the regulations for me you please, but don't speak to me of reading, for I will die rather than obey you."

"Then you hate books?" said I in a grieved tone."

" In my childhood," replied he, " I was an indefatigable reader. At Martinique too, I eagerly devoured many picturesque books of travel, some French classics, and all the tragedies in the world, and some scraps of all of them remain in my head; but for three years, that is to say, from the day when I commenced to think, I have held books in abhorrence."

And with increasing warmth:

" Oh! yes, believe me, I hate them and I shall always hate them from the bottom of my soul."

" But why?"

" Ah! you wish to know why!"

And then, giving way to his fury, he continued in a voice stifled with emotion, "I hate them! I hate them because they are the delight of the father who hates me, and because they have always supplanted me in his heart. Will you do me the favor to understand me? He is not marble; he is not bronze; he is made of flesh and bone, as we are. And at certain hours perhaps, feeling himself sad and weary, he looks about him to find something to love, to caress, to fold in his arms; and perhaps he recollects that he has a child and that a child is one of those objects which a father takes delight in loving, caressing and pressing to his heart, for that might happen, might it not? It is not entirely contrary to nature, or if it is a miracle, this miracle is sometimes wrought? But at the moment when such thoughts come to him, and he feels his heart soften and throb in his breast, he sees his books, his beloved books, his adored books; he opens one of them and becomes absorbed. Good-bye fatigue, good-bye sadness, good-bye the recollection of his child! He is contented, and nothing is wanting to his happiness; and his hands moving with pride over the vellum, forget that just now they were groping to find a blonde head, whose curls they could wreathe about their fingers. That is not all! He has moments too, I call Heaven to witness, when he is seized with a secret trouble in thinking that he has near him, in his own house, a being that his coldness, his harshness, his scorn, his icy smiles, his cruelties, his injustice drive to rebellion and desperation—a being who suffers, who grieves, who gnaws his heart out. . . . And then he hears something like a sigh, or a sob, which reaches him even through the thickness of the walls, and in spite of himself he trembles, he feels in the depths of his soul a something which resembles a pang of remorse. But all at once he sees his book. . . . Farewell to his trouble, farewell repentance! Let the victim sob at his ease, he will hear it no more. He is far from him, he travels, he is at Rome, at Byzantium he is beyond the ocean, beyond the clouds! Can the cries of a child reach him there?—And you ask me why I do not like books! Ah! upon my soul, I hate them as I hate death! I hate them because he loves them to distraction; I hate them because they are his malady; because they dry up and harden his heart; because they are his supreme pleasure, and that in this pleasure he drowns the happiness of his child and his father's heart and feels no shame!"

At these words, beside himself, he seized some of the volumes which I had just selected, and throwing them on the floor, stamped upon them with fury. I entreated him to calm himself; he finished by listening to reason, and picking up the defaced and torn volumes threw them into the closet, shut the door and put the key in his pocket.

"Since this is the case," said I, reseating myself, "I won't speak to you any more of reading; but tell me, haven't you some tastes, some special talent, some favorite pastime?"

"I used to love drawing to distraction. At that time father Alexis gave me lessons in it. I drew from fancy or from nature. He had also begun to teach me to paint. I worked in water colors. I still have my pencils, my brushes and my palette, my paint boxes too; but I never touch them now. For a long time I have had no taste for anything."

Upon that, he drew from a drawer a large portfolio filled with drawings, which he opened before me. I could not repress a cry of surprise and delight. These drawings were principally sketches, but I recognized at the first glance, a skilful and ready pencil, delicate taste, a knowledge of order and proportions, artistic instincts, the marks of a true and happy talent.

"We are saved!" I inwardly exclaimed.

I stopped to examine a woman's face in crayon.

"It is the likeness of my mother," said he, and his eyes filled. "I have drawn it thousands of times from a medallion which I always carry next my heart, and which is a masterpiece."

He drew from his bosom the gold medallion and laid it before me. I could not repress an exclamation at the resemblance between mother and son—resemblance in feature I mean—for the character of the faces differ as much as black and white. The placid, melancholy face of the Countess Olga seemed to say, "Take the trouble to will, I shall not object to anything you do." Yes, there was irresponsibility in that face. I also noticed in the portfolio some water colors, touched by a light but firm hand, and a little further on an indescribably grotesque composition of devils, intertwined with death's heads. I passed over this quickly and came upon a long paper all covered with pen caricatures. I recognized father Alexis and Ivan, taken in all sorts of attitudes and playing the most grotesque pranks. I experienced a feeling of lively relief in observing that his father was not represented there at all. Upon the reverse of the leaf I read this inscription in capital letters: "The most stupid of Holland rats in his cheese." The cheese was a heavy folio and the rat,—well! the rat had a human head, and this head strongly resembled one of my most intimate friends.

"Yes, it is I, it is surely I," I said laughing.

He leaned over my shoulder and blushed.

"What are you looking at there?" he said. And tearing the paper from my hands, he lighted it at the lamp and threw it in the air all ablaze, at the risk of setting fire to the curtains. Then, clapping his hands, he exclaimed: "I have an idea!". Since you want me to work, I'll begin by taking your portrait. I will represent you as I have seen you since you operated on my cataract: it is with the hero that my pencil shall busy itself: the night rambler, the man of the woollen shirt. As for the pedant, let who pleases take care of him!"

"We will see about that by and by, there is ample time." And after having reflected, I added:

"I have an idea too. You love flowers and painting. Paint an herbarium."

"What's that?"

"See this large paper. You will paint in it, in water colors, a collection of all the flowers of this region, of all those, at least, that you may find in your walks. If you don't know their names, I will teach them to you, or we will seek for them together."

"Provided that books take no part in it."

"We will dispense with them as much as possible. I will muster up all my knowledge to tell you the history of these pretty painted flowers; I will tell you of their families, I will teach you how to classify them; in short, will give you little by little, all I know of botany."

He made a hundred absurd objections,—among

others, that he found in all the flowers of the fields and the woods in this country a creeping and servile air; then this, and then that, expressing himself in a sharp but sportive tone.

"I shall teach you botany, my wild young colt," I said to myself, "and not let you break loose."

I have not been able, however, to draw from him any positive promise.

—July 14th.

Victory! By persistent hammering I have succeeded in beating the idea of the painted herbarium into this naughty, unruly head.

But he has imposed his conditions. He consents to paint only the flowers that I will gather myself, and bring to him. After some discussion I yielded the point.

"Ah!" said I, "take care to gather some yourself, for otherwise Ivan . . . ."

Sunday, July 15th.

This afternoon I took a long walk in the woods. I had succeeded in gathering some labiates, the dead nettle, the pyramidal bell-flower and the wild thyme, when in the midst of my occupation, I heard the trot of a horse. It was he, a bunch of herbs and flowers in his hand. Ivan, who according to his custom, followed him at a distance of ten paces, regarded me some way off with an uneasy air; he evidently feared that I would accost them; but having arrived within a few steps of me, Stephane, turning his head, started his horse at full gallop, and Ivan, as he passed, smiled upon me with an expression of triumphant pity. Poor, simple Ivan, did you not hear our souls speak to each other?

July 16th.

Yesterday I carried my labiates to him. After some desultory talk, I endeavored to describe as best I could, the characters of this interesting family. He listened to me out of complaisance. In time, he will listen to me out of curiosity, inasmuch as, to tell the truth, I am not a tiresome master; but I dare not yet interrogate him in a Socratic way. The *short little questions* would make our hot-headed young man angry. The lesson finished, he wished to commence his herbarium under my eyes. The honor of precedence has been awarded to the wild thyme; its little white, finely cut labias and the delicate appearance of the stem pleased him, whilst he found the dead nettle and the bell flower extremely common, and pronounced by him, the word 'extremely' is most expressive. While he made pencil sketches, I told him three stories, a fairy tale, an anecdote of Plutarch and some sketches of the life of Saint Francis of Assisi. He listened to the fairy tale without uttering a word, and without a frown; but the other two stories made him shake his head several times.

"Is what you are telling me really true?" said he. "Would you wager your life upon it?" And when I came to speak of St. Francis embracing the lepers—

"Oh! now you're exaggerating." Then speaking to St. George: "Upon your conscience now, would you have done as much?"

He ended by becoming sportive and frolicsome. As he begged me to sing him a little song, I hummed *Cadet Roussel*, which he did not know; the "three hairs" made him laugh till the tears ran down his cheeks, but he paid dearly for this excess of gayety. When I rose to leave he was seized with a paroxysm of weeping, and I had much trouble in consoling him. I repent having excited him so much. I must humor his nerves, and never put him in that state of mind which contrasts too strongly with the realities of his life. At any cost I must present certain *awakings*.

July 17th.

Day before yesterday, while he was drawing, I looked at him at my leisure. What delicacy of feature, what purity in the lines, I should like to be a painter; what studies I should have in that face! I can find no fault in it, unless perhaps the mouth may be a little too small: when he is in a bad humor it gives him a hard and pinched look; but when he is in a happy mood, the smiles crowd and push upon each other, not finding room to make their way out; the corners of the lips are raised and curved slightly, with a piquant and singular grace. As for his eyes, they are those of his country; iron grey and with but little brightness of their own; but when excited by passion, they sparkle or flame. It is a singular fact that notwithstanding his life, his face remains so young. He has a child's contour of cheek and chin. Where suffering betrays itself, is in his pallor, in the network of bluish veins on both temples, and in the slight emaciation of his hands which is unnatural to his age. And then there is habitually something like a veil over his face; like those semi-transparent autumnal vapors which envelope and drown the outlines of the hills in their floating gauze. When, from the effect of some sudden emotion, the veil falls, one is astonished, dazzled. A charming peculiarity is that his hair is a light chestnut color, his eyebrows nearly brown, and his long curved eyelashes a jet black. This gives a unique character to his perfectly regular face; one cannot get used to it, it is always new.

July, 19th.

I admire his conduct at the table. Seated opposite to me, he never appears to see me, whilst you, grave Gilbert, do not know at times what to do with your eyes; but the other day he crossed the great hall with such a quick and elastic step, that the Count's attention was drawn to him. I must caution him to be more discreet. I am also uneasy because in our nocturnal *tête à têtes* he often raises his voice, moves the furniture and storms round the room; but he assures me there is nothing to fear. The walls are thick and the foot of the staircase is separated from the corridor by a projection of masonry which would intercept the sound. Then the alcove, the vestibule, the two solid oak doors! These two doors are never locked. Ivan, he told me, is far from suspecting anything, and the only thing which could excite his distrust, would be excessive precaution.

"And besides," added he, "by the mercy of God he is beginning to grow old, his mind is getting dull, and he is more credulous than formerly. So I have easily persuaded him that I will never forgive you, as long as I live, for the death of my dog. Then again, he is growing hard of hearing, and sleeps like a top. Sometimes to disturb his sleep, I amuse myself by imitating the bark of Vorace: but I have the trouble for my pains. The only sound which he never fails to hear, is the ringing of my father's bell. I admit, however, that if any one presumed to touch his great ugly oak door, he would wake up with a start. This is because this door is his property, his object, his fixed idea: he has a way of looking at it, which seems to say: "you see this door? it is mine." I believe, that in his eyes there is nothing lovelier in the world than a closed door. So he cherishes this horrible, this infamous door: he smiles on it benignly, he counts its nails and covers them with kisses.

"And you say that after nine o'clock he never comes up here?"

"Never, never. I should like to see him attempt it!" cried he raising his head with an indignant air.

"You see then, that he is a jailer capable of behaving handsomely. I imagine that you do not like him much; but after all, in keeping you under lock and key he is only obeying orders."

"And I tell you he is happy in making me suffer. The wicked man has done but one good action in his whole life,—that was in saving you from the fury of *Vorace*. In consideration of this good action, I no longer tell him what I think of him, but I think it none the less, and it seems to me very singular that you should ask me to love him."

"Excuse me, I do not ask you to love him, but to believe that at heart, he loves you."

At these words he became so furious, that I hastened to change the subject.

"Don't you sometimes regret Vorace?"

"It was his duty to guard me against bugaboos, but I have had no fear of them, since one of them has become my friend."

To which he added in a more serious tone:

"I am superstitious, I believe in ghosts; but I defy them to approach my bed, hereafter. It is only necessary for me to invoke the image of the man of the woollen shirt."

He blushed and did not finish the sentence. Poor child! the painful mystery of his destiny, far from quenching his imagination, has excited it to intoxication, and I am not surprised that he shapes friendship to the romantic turn of his thoughts.

"You're mistaken," I said to him, "it is not my image, it is botany which guards you against spirits. There is no better remedy for foolish terrors than the study of nature."

"Always the pedant," he exclaimed, throwing his cap in my face.

July 22d.

Sometimes he pours out words in torrents. This does not surprise me; he has kept silence for so many years. How has he been able to endure such a life so long? His flexibility has saved him. However passionate he may be his soul is of elastic stuff.

July 23rd.

Vladimir Paulitch appeared yesterday at the end of dinner. The presence of this man occasions me an indefinable uneasiness. His coldness freezes me, and then his dogmatic tone; his smile of mocking politeness. He always knows in advance what you are going to say to him, and listens to you out of politeness. This Vladimir has the ironical intolerance characteristic of materialists. However, he may be a very honest man; but for what reason did he become the denouncer of poor Olga? I do not believe him capable of fanaticism in friendship. As to his professional ability there can be no doubt. The Count has entirely recovered; he is better than I have ever seen him. What vigor, what activity of mind! What confounds me is, that in our discussions, I come to see in him in, about the course of an hour, only the historian, the superior mind, the scholar; I forget entirely the man of the iron boots, the somnambulist, the persecutor of my Stephane, and I yield myself unreservedly to the charm of his conversation. Oh, men of letters! men of letters!

July 26th.

Stephane said to me yesterday: "I am encouraged at times to hope for happiness in the future. since I find that there is a kind of connection in everything which has happened to me for the last three months. One day I had the good luck and the folly to elude Ivan's vigilance; I ran down to the stable, saddled my horse myself, and scoured the country alone. I hardly felt myself at liberty before I conceived the idea of flying, never to return; but to propose is nothing, it is necessary to desire. I wished and did not wish; I hesitated between fear and desire, and alternately spurred my horse and rudely checked him. At length I was obliged to confess that however much I wanted to escape, I should never have the courage to do it, and I returned with hanging head to the route leading to my prison, my soul a prey to the most poignant sorrow. On my way I met a young peasant who looked at me grinning; and out of humor as I was, I cut him across the face with my whip. A little further on, wishing to give my horse a drink, I observed a certain person seated near the spring where I intended to halt, and you know how I discharged my bile and spite upon this unlucky individual. I do not attempt to deny that I was unjust, brutal, treacherous; but I do not regret it, for in fact, if the first time I saw you I had not knocked your hat into the ditch, you would not have been irritated with me; if you had not been irritated, you would not have thought any more about me, you would not have divined my situation, you would not have pitied me and you would not have saved my beautiful tuft of pinks from the hands of the Philistines. If by a silly mistake, I had not suspected you of wishing to appropriate the aforesaid carnation to yourself, I should not have insulted you through the booby Fritz, and then I should not have been forced to apologize to you; without the humiliation which I suffered, I should not have resolved so soon to kill myself; if I had not attempted to kill myself before your eyes, you would not have conceived the project of saving me from despair; you would not have sought me on the terrace, you would not have torn my glove from *Vorace*, and *Vorace* would not have been killed. Then if *Vorace* still lived, you could not come here; we should not be engaged at this moment in looking at each other, in talking, in discoursing of plants, of heroes, of saints, of you, of me; and to finish my reasoning, I should not yet have known the meaning of happiness."

"That is reasoning," said I, "after the fashion of father Alexis."

This he strongly denied, and administered to me three little raps.

July 27th.

He said to me:

"I do not possess happiness yet; but it seems to me, at moments, that I see it, that I touch it."

July 28th.

To-day, Doctor Vladimir appeared again at dessert. He aimed a few sarcasms at me, I suspect that

I do not please him much. Will his affection for the Count go so far as to make him jealous of the esteem which he evinces for me? We talked philosophy. He exerted himself to prove that everything is matter. I stung him to the quick in representing to him that all his arguments were to be found in d'Holbach. I endeavored to show him that matter itself is spiritual, that even the stones believe in spirit. Instead of answering, he beat about the bush. Otherwise, he spoke well, that is to say, he expressed his gross ideas with ingenuity. What he lacks most, is humor. He has something of the saturnine in his mind; his ideas have a leaden tint. The Count, prompted by good taste, saw that he held out too obstinately, without taking into account that Kostia Petrovich himself detests the absolute as much in the negative as in the affirmative. He thanked me with a smile when I said to the doctor, in order to put an end to the discussion:

"Sir, no one could display more mind in denying its existence;" and the Count added, alluding to the doctor's meagerness of person:

"My dear Vladimir, if you deny the mind what will be left of you?"

July 30th.

Yesterday, to my great chagrin, I found him in tears.

"This evening, my friend," said he, "with your permission, we will give up the thyme, the sage and the lavender, for it is impossible for me to talk to you of anything but myself."

The preceding night he had had a dream which moved him deeply. He crossed the corridor; suddenly he felt a hand place itself upon his shoulder, and draw him gently by one of his curls. He turned and recognized his father, who looked smilingly upon him. He woke himself in uttering a cry. Alas! it was but a dream.

"Ah, if you had seen him smile," said he; "it seemed as if the corridor was illuminated."

No more botany! He talked about nothing but his vision and the reflections which it suggested to him. This long, sad conversation has been productive of good in convincing me that he does not return his father hatred for hatred. He cordially detests Ivan; he despises father Alexis, of whose noble and glorious sufferings he is ignorant, and whom he harshly considers a parasite. And as Ivan and father Alexis represent in his eyes two-thirds of humanity, he has little mercy for the *humanum pecus*. As for his tyrant, he neither hates nor despises him; but he feels in his presenee that terror mingled with surprise and horror which great discords of nature inspire. Thus, if to-morrow this father should open his arms to him, he would throw himself into them, crying:

"Unnatural father, you have been mad for eight years. Ah! great God do not let your reason become obscured again."

"Let this inexorable father beat me," said he, "provided he tells me his secret. I prefer bad treatment to his silence. When we were at Martinique he had attacks of such violence that they made my hair stand on end. I would gladly have sunk into the earth; I trembled lest he should tear me in pieces; but he at least thought about me. He looked at me; I existed for him, and in spite of my terrors I felt less unhappy than now. Do not think it is my captivity which grieves me most. At my age it is certainly very hard and very humiliating to be kept out of sight and under lock and key; but I should be very easily resigned to that if it were my father who opened and closed the door. But alas! I am of so little consequence in his eyes that he deputes the task of tyrannizing over me to a serf. And then, during the brief moments when he constrains himself to submit to my presence—what a severe aspect, what threatening brows, what grim silence! Consider, too, the fact that he has never entered this tower; no, has never had the curiosity to know how my prison was made. Yet he cannot be ignorant of the fact that I lodge above a precipice. He knows, too, that once the idea of suicide took possession of me, and he has not even thought of having this window barred."

"That is because he did not consider your attempt a serious one."

"Then how he despises me!"

I represented to him that his father was sick, that he was the victim of a nervous disorder which deranges the most robust organizations, that doctor Vladimir guaranteed his cure, that once recovered, his temper would change, and that then would be the moment to besiege this citadel thus rendered more vulnerable."

"We must not, however, be precipitate," said I, "let us have courage and patience."

I reasoned so well that he finally overcame his despondency. When I see him yield to my reasoning, I have a strong impulse to embrace him; but it is a pleasure I deny myself, as I know by experience what it costs him. A moment afterwards, I don't know why, he spoke to me of his sister who died at Martinique.

"Why did God take her from me?"

"Alas!" said I, "she could not have supported the life to which you have been condemned."

"And why not, pray?"

"Because she would have suffered ten times as much as you. Think of it,—the nerves and heart of a woman!"

He looked at me with a singular expression; apparently he could not understand how any one could suffer more than he. After this he talked a long time about women, who are to him, from what he said, an impenetrable mystery, and he repeated eagerly:

"You do not despise them, as *he* does?"

"That would be impossible, I remember my mother."

"Is that your only reason?"

"Some day I will tell you the others."

As I left and was already nearly out of the window, he seized me impetuously by the arm, saying to me:

"Could you swear to me that you would be less happy if you did not know me?"

"I swear it."

His face brightened, and his eyes flashed.

August 7th.

The sap rises, rises— Blessed be heaven and earth!

August 8th.

And you too are transformed my old Gilbert; you have visibly rejuvenated. A new spirit has taken possession of you. Your blood circulates more quickly; you carry your head more proudly, your step is more elastic, there is more light in your eyes, more breath in your lungs, and you feel a celestial leaven fermenting in your heart. My old friend, you have emerged from your long uselessness to give birth to a soul! oh! glorious task! God bless mother and daughter!

August 9th.

Stephane is painfully astonished at the friendship which his father displays towards me.

"He has the power of loving then, and does not love me? It is because I am detestable!"

Poor innocent! It is certain that in spite of himself, the Count has begun to like me. Good father Alexis said to me the other evening:

"You are a clever man, my son; you have cast a spell upon Kostia Petrovitch, and he entertains an affection for you, which he has never before manifested for any one."

After all, it can be explained, and there are good reasons why he should like me a little. In the first place I am very useful to him ; in the second, he finds me easy to live with, inasmuch as he does not know, and I hope never will know—; thirdly, I have judgment and ability to criticise, and for these reasons he overlooks my idealism, " my puppets," and what he calls my " nonsense ; " fourthly, I have a Spinozian turn of mind which suits him : *non flere, non indignari, sed intelligere :* fifthly, sixthly and seventhly, we both carry Byzantium in our hearts—enough to unite two men for life and death !

" My beloved Stephane, my child, my nurseling, do not be vexed at this friendship, which astonishes you so ; it will some day be our anchor of safety."

August 11.

The book closet is always locked ; he even pretends that he has thrown the key out of the window ; but what need have we of books ? Plants take their place. His painted herbarium is enriched every day. He already enumerates twenty species and five families. Yesterday Stephane so far forgot himself as to look at it with an air of satisfied pride. How happy I was ! I kept my joy to myself, however. He further delighted me by deciding to write from memory at the bottom of each page the French and Latin names for each plant. " It is a concession I have made to the pedant," said he ; but this did not prevent him from being proud of having written these forty names without a mistake. Last time I carried to him some crowsfeet and anemones. He took the little celandine in his hand, crying:

" Let me have it ; I am going to tell you the history of this little yellow fellow."

And he then gave me all the characteristics with marvellous accuracy. What a quick and luminous intellect, and what overflowing humor ! His hands trembled so much that I said to him :

"Keep cool, keep cool. It requires a firm and steady hand to raise the veil of Isis."

I contented myself with explaining in a few words who Isis was, which interested him but moderately. His masterpiece, as a faithful reproduction of nature, is his marsh ranunculus which I had introduced to him under the Latin name of *ranuncula scelerata*. He has so exquisitely represented these insignificant little yellow flowers that it is impossible not to fall in love with them."

"This little poisoner has inspired me," said he. "By dint of practising father Alexis, I begin to wish good to the rascals."

I rebuked him sharply, but he was not much affected by my rating.

August 13.

The Count's conduct is atrocious, and yet I understand it. His pride, his whole character, despotic; the horror of having been deceived. . . . And besides, is he really Stephane's father? . . . These two children born after six years of marriage, and a few years later to discover. . . . Suspicions often have less foundation. And then this fatal resemblance which keeps the image of the faithless one constantly before his eyes! The more decided the resemblance, the greater must be the hatred. Even his smile, that strange smile which belongs to him alone, Stephane according to father Alexis, must have inherited from his mother. "*I have buried the smile!*" Frightful cry which I can hear still! Finally, I believe that in the barbarous hatred of this father there is more of instinct than of system. It lives from day to day. I am sure that Count Kostia has never asked himself: 'What shall I do with my son when he is twenty?'

August, 14th.

Ivan, of whom I asked news of Stephane said to me:

"Do not be uneasy about him any more. He

has become much better within the past month, and he grows more gentle from day to day; this is the result of seeing death so near."

August, 15th.

M. Leminof greatly astonished me this morning.

"My dear Gilbert," said he unreservedly, "I do not claim that I am a perfect man; but I am certainly what might be called a good sort of fellow, and I possess, in the bargain, a certain delicacy of conscience which sometimes inconveniences me. Without flattery, you are, my dear Gilbert, a man of great merit. Very well! I am using you unjustly, for you are at an age, when a man makes a name and a career for himself; and these decisive years you are spending in working for me, in collecting, like a journeyman, the materials of a great work which will bring neither glory nor profit to you. I have a proposition to make to you. Be my coadjutor; we will compose this monumental work together; it shall appear under our two names, and I give you my head upon it, shall make you famous. We agree upon nearly all questions of fact, and as to our difference in ideas. . . . *Mon Dieu!* we are neither of us born quibblers; we shall end in agreeing, and even supposing we do not agree, I will give you *carte blanche;* for, to speak frankly, an idea is not just the thing I should be ready to die for. What say you to it my dear Gilbert? We will not part until the task is finished, and I fancy that we shall lead a happy life together."

In spite of his persuasions, I have not consented; he has only drawn from me a promise that I will give him an answer within a month. Stephane, Stephane, how awkward I shall be, if I do not make this happy incident instrumental in accomplishing your deliverance! The day will come when I can say to your father: For the sake of your health, for the sake of your repose, of your studies, of the work we have undertaken together, send this child away from your house; his presence troubles and irritates you. Send him to some school or college. By a single act you will make two persons happy. Gracious heaven, the stronghold will be hard to take! But by dint of patience, skill and vigilance .... have I not already carried a fortress by storm—Stephane's heart? No, I do not despair of success. But it will cost me dear, this success that I hope for! To see him leave this house, to be separated from him forever! At the very thought my heart bleeds.

August, 16th.

Doctor Vladimir will leave us during the early part of next month. I shall not be sorry. Decidedly this man does not please me. The other day at the table, he looked at Stephane in a way that alarmed me.

August, 17th.

What is working in Stephane's heart? I am satisfied with him in all respects.

In the first place, he loves me much; then he works, he becomes more interested in his herbarium every day, in that which is not "ourselves." His intellect strengthens and expands visibly; its blooming is enchanting to me; but it is disturbed occasionally by a secret anxiety, the cause of which he conceals from me. The other day I said:

"What's the matter with you?"

He answered me, while passing his hands over his forehead:

"It is nothing. Let us talk of ranunculuses gentians and anemones."

August 18.

The sky is propitious for my nocturnal excursions. Not a drop of rain has fallen for six weeks. The north wind which sometimes blows violently in the day time, abates regularly in the evening. As to the vertigo, no return of it. Oh! the power of habit!

August 19.

What a misfortune! Day before yesterday Stephane, in crossing the vestibule in front of the great hall, impelled by some odd motive, gave vent to a loud burst of laughter. The Count started from his chair and his face became livid. To-day Soliman was sold. A horse dealer is coming directly to take him away. Ivan, whom I just met, had great tears in his eyes. Poor Stephane, what will he say?

August 20.

It is very singular! Yesterday I expected to find him in a state of despair. He was gay, smiling.

"I was sure," said he, "that I should pay dearly for that unlucky burst of laughter."

My father is mistaken; it was not a burst of gaiety, but a purely nervous spasm which seized me while thinking of certain things, and at a moment when I was not at all merry. However, besides life, there were but two things left to take from me, my horse and my hair, and thank God, he was not happily inspired in his choice, and has not struck me in the most sensitive place."

"What! between Soliman and your hair."

"Isn't it beautiful?" said he quickly.

"Magnificent without any doubt!" I answered, smiling.

"I've always been a little vain of it," continued he, waving his curls upon his shoulders; "but I value it more since I know it pleases you."

"Oh! for that matter," I replied, "if you had your head shaved, I should not love you any the less."

This answer, I don't know why, seemed to affect him deeply. During the rest of the evening he was thoughtful and gloomy.

August 23.

But what has come over him? He seems more resigned to his lot; he complains no more of Ivan nor of his father; he pretends not to regret those long rides which he used to take twice a week through the woods; in short, he affects an astonishing indifference for everything which moved and warmed his heart. And meantime, he is a prey to some perplexity which alarms me. I think I can sometimes divine that his eyes are addressing mute reproaches to me. He seems to say: "Now my sadness comes from you, my friend, my consoler." Pshaw! it is some caprice, some fancy. I shall succeed in making him confess it.

August 24.

I thought it glorious to be able to communicate to him the overtures which his father has made me, and the project they suggested to me. I said to him:

"What a joy it would be to me to release you from this prison, and yet with what bitter sadness this joy would be mingled! But wherever you go, we will find some means of writing and of seeing each other. The friendship between us is one of those bonds which destiny cannot break."

"Oh, yes!" replied he in a sarcastic tone, "you will come to see me once a year, upon my birth-day, and will be careful to bring me a bouquet."

He burst into a fit of laughter which much resembled that of the other day.

August 30.

How he made me suffer yesterday! I have not recovered from it yet. What! was it he—was it to me? God! what bitterness of language; what keen irony! Count Kostia, you make a mistake—this child is really yours. He may have the features and smile of his mother, but there is a little of your soul in his. What grievances can he have against me? I can imagine but two. Sunday last, near three o clock, we were both at the window. He commenced a very animated speech by signs, and prolonged it far beyond the prudential limits which I have prescribed to him. He spoke, I believe, about Soliman, and of a walk which he had refused to take with Ivan. I did not pay close attention, for I was occupied in looking round to see that no one was watching us. Suddenly I saw on the slope of the hill, big Fritz and the little goat girl, to whom he is paying court, seated on a rock. At the moment I was about to answer Stephane, they raised their eyes to me. I began then to look at the landscape, and presently quitted the spot. Stephane could not see them from his window, and of course did not understand the cause of my retreat. The other grievance is, that for the first time three days have passed without my paying him a visit; but day before yesterday the wind was so violent that it overthrew a chimney near by, . . . and it was to punish me for such a grave offence that he allowed himself to say that I was no doubt an excellent botanist, an unparalleled philanthropist, but that I understood nothing of the refinements of sentiment.

"You are one of those men," said he, "who carry the whole world in their hearts. It is useless for you to deny it. I am sure you have at least a hundred intimate friends."

"You are right," I replied; "it is even for the hundredth one that I have risked my life."

After this came his eternal tirade on suicide. I begged of him a hundred times to leave that odious subject; but how persistently he returned to it! He spoke of nothing but laudanum, of morphine, of arsenic; he pretended to consult me with eager curiosity in regard to the properties of all kinds of poisons.

"When one desires to make way with himself in good shape," he said, "poison is the best method, and I know some one who will depend upon it."

Then picking up a flower of henbane which lay on the table:

"How lovely your ugliness seems to me!" he said: "I like your broad scalloped leaves like shameless hands which never loosen their grip; I like your ugly, hairy stem; I like your acrid and repulsive odor, too; but if you care to know what I like in you above everything, it is that your heart swells with poison, and that your face is livid and hideous like death."

I snatched the unlucky plant from his hands, and having thrown it out of the window, I left him without saying good-bye. To tell the truth, I have always suspected him of being more passionate than sensible;. but if he were simply passionate?—perhaps, although he conceals it from me, the loss of his dear Chestnut——

August, 31.

I was unjust to him. His heart is restless, stormy, subject to grievous returns of distrust and incredulity; but it is still a heart. Yesterday evening, in spite of the storm, in spite of the firm resolution I had formed of remaining away from him several days, I could not keep away. The journey was not an easy one; the rain and the wind plastered my hair to my face; the air was full of melancholy noises, and the rafters of the roof trembled and cracked under me. At last I arrived. What a cry of joy and of horror he uttered on seeing me! With what warmth of affection he pressed my hands in his! How repentance depicted itself upon his face, and with what effusion he poured out his heart at my feet! I asked no explanations—I have a horror of them, and this is one of those cases where silence is the best interpreter between souls. I allowed him to sit on the floor, with his head resting on my knees. He remained in this posture nearly an hour, not saying a word, with his eyes closed, while the rain beat violently against the panes, and the howling winds vented their fury in the gloomy night. When he arose—

"These," said he, "are the happiest moments I have yet passed in this world."

But his happiness was singularly disturbed, when at midnight, as I prepared to depart, the storm had redoubled its violence. The poor child became pale with anguish.

"You see you are well punished," I said to him; "this will teach you not to spoil, by your naughty freaks of temper, that beautiful and holy thing we call friendship."

At the moment when I had just ascended my floating ladder, which shook in the wind, and was standing upon my narrow balcony, trying to draw it in, the heavens opened; I felt as if lashed by a whirlwind of flame, and within thirty paces of me the lightning struck the top of a great tree with a terrible noise. How it happened that I did not fall I cannot tell; but what I know is, that I reëntered my room, drenched to the skin, but with a contented heart.

September 7th.

During the last week, I have seen him three times. He has given me no cause for complaint; he works, he reflects; his judgment is forming; not a moment of ill-humor; he is calm, docile, and gentle as a lamb. Yes, but it is this excess of gentleness which disturbs me. There is something unnatural to me, in his condition, and I am forced to regret the absence of those transports, and the childishness of which I have endeavored to cure him. "Stephane, you have become too unlike yourself. But a short time since, your feet hardly touched the ground; lively, impetuous, and violent, there came from your lips by turns flashes of merriment or of anger, and in an instant you passed from enthusiasm to despair; but in our recent interviews I could scarcely recognize you. No more freaks of the rebellious child; no more of those familiarities which I loved! Your glances, even, as they meet mine, seem less assured; sometimes they wander over me doubtfully, and from the surprise they express, I am inclined to believe that my figure must have grown some cubits, and you can no longer take it in at a glance. And then those sighs which escape you! Besides, you no longer complain of anything; your existence seems to have become a stranger to you. It must be that without my knowledge—— Ah! unhappy child, I will know. You shall speak; you shall tell me. . . .

September, 10th.

Heavens! what a flood of light! Father Alexis, you did not tell me all! The more I think of it . . . . Ah! Gilbert, what scales covered your eyes! Yesterday I carried him that copy of the poem of the *Metamorphoses*, which I had promised him. A few fragments that I had repeated to him, had inspired him with the desire of reading the whole piece, not from the book, but copied in my hand. We read it together, distich by distich. I translated, explained and commented. When we arrived at these verses: "May you only remember how the tie which first united our souls was a germ from which grew in time a sweet and charming intimacy, and soon friendship revealed its power in our hearts, until love coming last, crowned it with flowers and with fruit—" At these words he became agitated and trembled violently.

"Do not let us go any further," said he, pushing the paper away. "That is poetry enough for this evening."

Then leaning upon the table, he opened and turned the leaves of his herbarium; but his eyes and his thoughts were elsewhere. Suddenly he rose, took a few steps in the room, and then returning to me:

"Do you think that friendship can change into love?"

"Goethe says so; we must believe it."

He took a flower from the table, looked at it a moment and dropping it on the floor, he murmured, lowering his eyes:

"I am an ignoramus; tell me what is this love?"

"It is the folly of friendship."

"Have you ever been foolish?"

"No, and I do not imagine I ever shall be."

He remained motionless for a moment, his arms hanging listlessly; at length, raising them slowly, he crossed his hands over his head, one of his favorite attitudes, raised his eyes from the ground, and looked steadily at me. Oh! what a strange expression! His wild look, a sad and mysterious smile wandering over his lips, his mouth which tried to speak, but to which speech refused to come! That face has been constantly before me since last night; it pursues me, possesses me, and even at this moment its image is stamped in the paper I am writing on. This black velvet tunic, then, may be a forced disguise? Yes, the character of Stephane, his mind, the singularity of his conduct,—all these things which astonished and frightened me are now explained. Gilbert, Gilbert! what have you done? into what abyss . . . . And yet, perhaps I am mistaken, for how can I believe—— There is the dinner bell . . . . I shall see *him* again! I tremble, I feel within me . . . . Oh my poor tormented heart, hide your emotion at least from their eyes!

CHAPTER XVII.

Some hours later, Gilbert entered Stephane's room, and struck by his pallor and with the troubled expression of his voice, inquired about him anxiously.

"I assure you I am very well," Stephane replied, mastering his emotion. "Have you brought me any flowers?"

"No, I have had no time to go for them."

"That is to say, you have not had time to think of me."

"Oh! I beg your pardon! I can think of you while working, while reading Greek, even while sleeping. And last night I saw you in my dreams: you treated me as the pedant, and threw your cap in my face."

"That was a very extravagant dream."

"I am not so sure about that. It seems to me that one day—"

"Yes, one day, two centuries ago."

"Is it then so long since our acquaintance commenced?"

"Perhaps not two centuries, but nearly. As for me, I have already lived three lives: my first I passsed with my mother. The second—let us not speak of that. The third began upon the night when, for the first time, you climbed into this window. And that must have been a long time ago, if I can judge of it by all which has passed since then, in my soul, in my imagination, and in my mind. Is it possible that these two centuries have only been two months? How can it be that such great changes have been wrought in me, in so short a time, for they are so marvellous that I can hardly recognize myself?"

"One of these changes, of which I am proud, is that you no longer throw your cap at my head."

"That was a liberty I took only with the pedant."

"And are you at last reconciled to him?"

"I have discovered that the pedant does not exist. There is a hero and a philosopher in you."

"That is a discovery I did not expect from you, and one that astonishes as much as it flatters me."

"When I tell you that I am changed throughout, and that I no longer recognize myself——"

"And I, in spite of your transformation, recognize you very easily. My dear Stephane has preserved his habit of exaggerating all his impressions.

Once I was a man who ought to be smothered; now I am an extraordinary being who passes his life in executing heroic projects. No, my poet, I am neither a scoundrel nor a knight errant, and the best that can be said of me is that I am not a blockhead, that I do not lack heart, and that I run over the roofs with remarkable agility. Upon this last point, I am ready to maintain against all, that in pirouetting on rafters I have no equal; but this is not all, for to exhaust the catalogue of my perfections, it is proper to add that I have eyes of periwinkle color, that I tie the bow of my cravat marvellously, and that I know how to distinguish between a labiate and a papilionaceous plant."

"Silence!" cried Stephane, with the impetuosity of former times. "Silence! I forbid you to speak in this tone of my patron saint, my guardian angel; of the incomparable friend who has saved me from despair, folly and death." Then, in a more gentle tone:

"No, I exaggerate nothing. I speak of things as they are, and the proof that you are an extraordinary man is, that in all you do, you appear perfectly simple and natural."

And as Gilbert shrugged his shoulders and smiled:

"Ah! you need not laugh?" he continued: "Feel my pulse, you will see I have no fever. And have you not noticed how calm I have been for several days?"

"I confess that your quietness surprises me; but is it really a calm? I suspect that you have only covered the brazier, and that the fire smoulders under the ashes."

"And you stir up the ashes to draw out sparks. As you please, but I forewarn you, that you will not succeed, and that I shall remain insensible to all your efforts."

"So, for a week, you have really felt more tranquil in heart and mind?"

"Yes, and I have a good reason for it. There

was a great fomentor of seditions in me, a great stirrer up of rebellion. It was my pride. Very well! you know the pretty scene I enacted for you ten days ago; that fine discourse upon the henbane—that was the despairing blow of my pride, which plays its pranks even to the last, and feeling itself wounded unto death, wished to sell its life dearly."

"All that is very mysterious to me."

"Yes, it is a great mystery which it is full time I unfolded to you."

"Speak then, I will listen to you with religious attention," said Gilbert, who was almost breathless.

Stephane hid his face in his hands; then after a long silence:

"No," said he, "I have not the courage to speak yet. Besides, before making my revelation, which you will perhaps consider extravagant, I want to prove to you more thoroughly that my senses have been restored, and that I have become wise in your school. Know, then, that before I became acquainted with you, religion was in my eyes but a coarse magic in which I believed with passionate irrationality. I considered prayer as a kind of sorcery, and attributed to it the power of compelling the divine will; every day I called upon Heaven to perform a miracle in my favor, and, finding myself refused, my ungranted prayers fell back like lead upon my heart. Then I rebelled against the celestial intelligences which refused to yield to my enchantments, or else I sought in anguish to ascertain to what error in form, to what neglected precaution, to what sin of omission I could attribute the impotence of my operations in magic and my formulas. Ah! Saint George, Saint Sergius, if you could speak, what strange revelations you might make to him! You could tell of the extravagant questions heaped upon you, the absurd prodigies I implored from your swords, the importunities with which I wearied your patience, and by turns my kneelings, my prostrations, my sobs, the torrents of tears which I shed at your feet, my head beating the walls or sweeping the flagging with its dishevelled hair: then suddenly my indignation, my eyes flashing fury, cries of rage, transports, abuse; my hands in delirium threatening heaven, and my feet grinding your golden aureoles under their senseless stamping. Ah! my friend, that I have become absolutely incapable of such follies, I should not like to swear; but what I do know is, that one evening . . . that evening, my Gilbert, when your eloquence at once so tranquil and so passionate, had taken a sublime flight, and by means of a poor camomile flower with its pale face, you tried to reveal to me some of the grand laws of nature. I had listened to you with an inattentive ear; but after your departure, as is often the case with me, all that you had said returned vividly to my mind; and forgetting the past, the present—forgetting even my existence, I darted away from this castle and flew into space away to that sapphire star which I see from my window sparkling in the horizon; and from the height of that aerial belvedere, I began to converse with that supreme reason which manifests itself equally in the little wild flowers, and in the splendors of the night. Then, suddenly feeling a strange sweetness pervading to the very depths of my being, I asked myself: Is this religion? And I answered: Yes, religion; and that is to feel content in the truth. My Gilbert, what I felt that day I may not feel again for a long time; but is it not enough that I have tasted, once in my life, of such holy delights, to be no longer treated by you as an irrational child that one would be ashamed to talk to seriously?"

Gilbert answered only by a pressure of the hand.

"Alas!" said he to himself, "when he has revealed his secret, I shall no longer have the right to tell him that he is foolish."

"You have become more tractable," continued Stephane, "which gives me courage to proceed. It was once my habit, I will tell you further, after having prayed, to seat myself there upon the floor beneath the night-lamp, and closing my eyes, abandon myself to long hours of insane revery. These were veritable visions, I assure you, so well did I succeed in presenting to myself the chimeras with which I soothed my mind. I saw the heavens open and the Eternal Father holding council in his palace. 'Celestial spirits,' said he, pressing his hand over his white beard, it is full time to come to the aid of this child.' And immediately he gave orders to his messengers and servants. St. George clothed himself in his shining armor and descended through the air with the voice of thunder; with one blow of his formidable sword he clove this gloomy castle in twain; the walls fell in; I felt myself raised in space; angels bore me upon their wings of fire, and proceeded to deposit me in some flowery isle, where my mother and happiness awaited me. Sometimes I contented myself with tasting the bitter pleasures of vengeance. By the order of God, devils penetrated here, armed with their flaming forks; they seized Ivan by the throat, put him upon the wheel, upon the gridiron. . . . vain and hideous imaginations, which served but to aggravate my pain and to redouble my terrors.

"Well, my Gilbert, the other evening you spoke to me here of a joy which owes nothing to fortune, and on which it has no influence; a divine joy which man can taste even in the midst of suffering, and which beguiles away his most gloomy weariness. You had hardly gone when I seated myself at the feet of the saints, and having recited my orisons, gave myself up to revery; but this time I no longer imagined the Eternal Father forgetting the universe but to occupy himself with my fate; I saw no more devils torturing my jailer. It was Christ who appeared before me, clothed in a black mantle. He stood upright in mid heaven, and suns pressed in a crowd about him, the better to see his face, as curious children make a row to see the king pass in a street. The silent earth contemplated him also; the trembling ocean threw off its crests of foam; the palm trees waved gently upon their rocks, and great eagles, with extended wings, whirled slowly, tracing in the empty air a long train of fire. Then he turned aside the folds of his robe, and displayed a large wound, from which flowed the red blood, at sight of which, a smile so sweet flitted over his lips, that one would have supposed a new dawn was rising over the universe. And still his blood flowed constantly, and the stars, the ocean, the palm trees of the desert, the eagles of heaven, all distracted, cried out, 'Lord, who then are you?' Then a voice, sweet as the sigh of an organ, answered them,'I am joy in suffering.'"

At these words Stephane's eyes kindled and looked steadily at Gilbert.

"And now am I nothing but a charmed dreamer, a half crazy child, a sick brain feeding on crotchets, an incorrigible, wrong-headed follow? No, you admit that I have profited by your lessons; that a grain of wisdom has fallen into my brain, and that without having seen the bottom of things, I have at least lucid intervals. If this be so, my Gilbert, believe what I am going to say as you would the Holy Bible. You have worked with all your strength to cure my soul, and there is not a more skillful physician in the world than you. But all of your trouble would have been lost, if you had not had by your side an all-powerful ally, whom you don't know, and whom I am about to reveal to you. Ah! tell me, when you came in this room the first time, did you not feel that a celestial spirit followed in your track and entered with with you? You went, he remained, and has not left me, and never will. Look, do not these walls speak of him? Do not these saints move their lips to murmur his name to you? And the air we breathe here, is it not full of those delicious perfumes which these envoys of Heaven scatter in their earthward journeys? How strange this spirit appeared to me at first! His face was all unknown to me, it had never appeared to me in my dreams. Startled and bewildered, I said to him: Who then art thou? What is thy name? And one day, Gilbert, one day, it was through your mouth that he answered me. Gilbert, Gilbert, oh! what a singular company you have introduced to me in his person. Sometimes he seated himself near me, pale, melancholy, clothed in mourning, and breathed into my heart a venomous bitterness, such as I had never dreamed of. And feeling myself seized with an inexpressible desire to die; I cried out 'I know you, you must be the brother of death?' But all at once transforming himself, he appeared to me holding a fool's cap in his hand. He shook the bells and sang to me songs which filled my ears with feverish murmurings. My head turned, smoke floated before me, my dazzled eyes were intoxicated with visions, and it seemed to me, poor child, nourished with gall and tears, that life was an eternal *fête*, upon which Heaven looked down smiling. Then I said to the spirit: 'Now I know you better, you are the brother of folly.' But he changed himself again, and suddenly I saw him standing erect before me folded in the long white wings of the seraphim; at once serious and gentle, divine reason shone in his deep eyes and the serenity on his brow announced an inhabitant of heaven. In these moments, my Gilbert, his voice was more penetrating and more persuasive than yours; he repeated your words and gave me strength to believe in them; he engraved your lessons on my mind; he instilled your wisdom into my folly, your soul in my soul; and know that if the lily has drunk the juices of the earth, if the lily has grown, if the lily should blossom one day, it shall not be from the impotent sun rays which you brought to me in your breast, to which thanks must be rendered; but to him, the celestial spirit, to him who lighted in my heart a divine flame with which, may it please God that yours too may be illuminated!" And rising at these words, he almost gasped: "Have I said enough?" Do you understand me at last?"

"No!" answered Gilbert, resolutely, "I do not know this celestial spirit at all."

Stephane writhed his arms.

"Cruel! you do not wish then to divine anything!" murmured he, distractedly. And going to the window, he stood some moments leaning against it. When he turned towards Gilbert, his eyes were wet with tears; but by one of those rapid changes which were familiar to him, he had a smile upon his lips, "What I dare not say to you, I have just now written," resumed he, drawing a letter from his bosom.

"It was a last resort which I hoped you would not force me to call to my aid. Oh hard heart! to what humiliations have you not abased my pride!" He presented the letter,—but changing his mind, he said:

"I wish to add a few words to it."

And ran and seated himself at the table. His pen had fallen on the floor, and not being able to find it, he quickly sharpened a pencil with a keen edged poniard which he drew from the depths of a drawer.

"What a singular penknife you have there," said Gilbert approaching him.

"It is a Russian stiletto of Toula manufacture. It belongs to Ivan, he lent it to me day before yesterday, when we were out walking, to uproot a plant with. He has forgotten to take it back."

"You will oblige me by returning it to him," answered Gilbert, "it is a plaything I don't like to see in your hands."

Stephane gave a sign of assent, and bent over the paper. The letter which he had written was as follows:

"My Gilbert, listen to a story. I was eleven

16

years old when *my brother Stephane* died. Scarcely was he buried when my father called me to him. He held in his hand a suit of clothes like these I wear now, and he said to me: 'Stephane, understand me clearly. It was my daughter that just died, my son lives still.' And as I persisted in not understanding him, he had a coffin brought in, placed on a table and he laid me in it; and closing the cover by degrees, he said, 'My daughter, are you dead?' When it was entirely closed, I decided to speak, and I cried out, 'Father, your daughter is dead. It shall be as you desire.' Then he drew me out of the coffin half dead with fear and horror, and exclaimed, 'Stephane, remember that my daughter is dead. Should you ever happen to forget it.... He said no more, but his eyes finished the sentence. Gilbert, at this moment the daughter of my father comes back to life to tell you that she loves you with an unconquerable love which she can no longer conceal. In my simplicity, I thought at first that I loved you as you loved me; but you yourself have taken care to undeceive me. One day you spoke of our approaching separation, and you said to me: 'We shall see each other sometimes!' And you did not hear the cry of my heart which answered you; to pass a day without seeing you! What a hell!

"When I had fairly comprehended that your friendship was a devotion, a virtue, a wisdom, and that mine was a folly, then the daughter of my father thought of dying, so bitter were the torments which her rebellious pride inflicted upon her. Ah! what would I not have given, my Gilbert, if, divining who I was, you had fallen at my feet crying: 'I too know how to love madly!'

"But no; you have understood nothing, suspected nothing. My hair, the resemblance to my mother imprinted on my face, the smile, which they tell me, passed from her lips to mine.... Oh! blindest of men! how I have hated you at moments! But does it not really seem that a fatality pursues me? That hand with its iron grip fastened on my shoulder, and forcing me to prostrate myself before you, I feel no longer, with its nails pressing into my flesh; and yet my knees, trembling, powerless, bend under me, and again you see me fall at your feet. Yes, my poor pride is dead indeed. The thunder growled when it gave up its last breath. You remember that stormy night. Glued to the window pane, I tried to pierce the darkness with my eyes, to discern you in the midst of the tempest. All at once the heavens were ablaze, and I saw you standing upon the ledge of your window, bending proudly over the abyss, at which you seemed to hurl defiance. Enveloped in flashing light, you appeared to me like a blissful spirit, and I exclaimed to myself: 'This is one of the elect of God! I can ask of him without shame for indulgence and mercy!' And now, my Gilbert, do not presume to tell me that my love is a malady, which needs only careful attention. Oh God! all that would be useless; the saints themselves have refused to cure me. Do not try to terrify me, either, or speak to me of insurmountable obstacles to our union; of dangers which threaten us. The future! We will talk of that hereafter. Now, I want to know but one thing; that is, if you are capable of loving me as I love you? Friend, if hatred can change into love, would it be impossible for friendship? . . . Gilbert, Gilbert, forget what the refined barbarity of my father has made of me; forget my gusts of passion, my violence, the unruliness of a badly educated child; forget the vehemence of my language, the rudeness of my actions; forget the fountain; my whip raised to you; forget those young villagers I compelled to kiss my feet; forget even the cap which I threw in your face, for, Heaven is my witness, I feel a woman's heart awakened in my bosom; it shakes off its long sleep, it stirs, it sighs, it speaks, and the first name it utters, the only one it ever wants to know, is yours! . . .

"What more shall I say? I would like to appear to you in your dreams decked as if for a *fête*: clothed in white, a smile upon my lips, pearls about my neck, around my head the flowers you love—white anemones and blue gentians. Only take care, some of the henbane flowers have slipped into my crown. Tear them from my hair yourself, lest their perfume instill a deadly poison into my heart. But no, I do not wish to frighten you. Stephane is wise; she is reasonable; she does not ask the impossible; she gives you time to breathe; to recover yourself. Wait, if you wish it, a week, a fortnight, a month, before coming here again; until that blessed day dawns when you can say with your adored poet: 'In its turn, friendship revealed its power to my heart, and at length love, coming last, crowned it with flowers and fruit.'"

To this letter Stephane added these words: "And if that day, Gilbert, if that day should never come—"

But here she hesitated; her hand trembled; she looked alternately at Gilbert and the knife; then rising—

"I do not know how to finish my letter," she said. "You can easily supply what is lacking. But you must not read it here; carry it to your turret; you will meditate upon it there more at leisure."

And at these words, having returned the paper to him, she burst into a fit of laughter.

"Again that same laugh, which I detest," said Gilbert, trying to hide the anguish which was consuming him.

"Do you want to know what it means?" said the young girl, looking him in the face. "When we were at Baden-Baden, three years ago, Father Alexis had a fancy to take me to a gambling house, and in entering I heard a burst of laughter much resembling those which shock you so. 'Who is laughing in that way?' said I to the good father. He found on inquiring that it was a man who had just gained enormous sums, and who was preparing to play double or quits.

"Double or quits!" added she; "to play double or quits! If I should lose—"

All at once her eyes dilated, and shot fire; she turned her head backward, and raising her arm towards Gilbert, she exclaimed:

"You know who I am, and you have condemned me in your heart. Ah! think twice; you have my life in your hands." And recoiling a few steps she suddenly turned, fled across the room, threw open a small side-door and disappeared.

How did Gilbert manage to reach his turret?

All he knows himself is, that on coming out of the dormer window, beside himself, forgetting all idea of danger, he committed, for the first time, the signal imprudence of walking erectly over the roof, which ordinarily he found difficult to cross even in crawling; seeing and hearing nothing, entirely absorbed in a single thought, he started forward at a quick pace. From his gait and carriage, the moon, which shone brightly in the sky, must have taken him for a madman, or a somnambulist. He reached the end of the roof, when a broken slate slipped under his feet. He lost his balance, fell heavily, and it would have been all over with him, if, in falling, his hand had not by a miracle encountered the trailing end of his ladder, by which he had strength enough to hold himself. Slates are brittle, and when hurled against a hard substance break in a thousand pieces. The one which Gilbert had just precipitated into space met a point of rock which scattered it into fragments, one of which struck, without wounding, the hand of a man who happened to be rambling an hour on the border of the ravine.

As fate would have it, this evening M. Leminof had an important letter to forward by the mail; and near nine o'clock, contrary to all the usages and customs of his house, he had sent Fritz to a large town about a league distant, where the courier passed during the night. Unluckily, upon his return, Fritz saw a light shining in the cottage of his Dulcinea. Appetite, the opportunity, some devil also urging him, he left the road, walked straight to the cabin, opened the door, which was only closed by a latch, entered with stealthy tread, and surprised his beauty seated upon a stool and mending her linen. He drew near her, said gallant things to her, and soon began to take liberties. The damsel, frolicsome and forward, instead of awakening her father, who slept in the neighboring room, rushed to the door, darted out and gained upon a run the serpentine path which ran along the edge of the ravine. A hundred times more active than Fritz, she kept in advance of him; then halted, called him, and the moment when he thought he was going to seize her, she escaped and ran on faster. She continued this game until becoming weary she hid herself behind a bush, and laughing in her sleeve, saw the amorous giant pass her, continue to ascend, reeking with sweat, slipping frequently and constantly fearing he would fall down the precipice. At length, by dint of scrambling, he arrived at the place where the path ended at the perpendicular fall of the precipice, a height of forty feet. By what means had his fantastic princess scaled this wall? All at once he heard a silvery voice which called him from below. In his rage he struck his forehead with his fist; but at the moment he was about to descend, a singular noise struck his ear—a piece of slate grazed his hand and drew from him an exclamation of surprise. Raising his head quickly, and favored by the light of the moon, he saw upon his right a shadow suspended in the air. It mounted, stopped upon the ledge of a window, stooped down and soon disappeared.

"Oh! oh!" said he, much astonished, "here's

something odd! Monsieur secretary goes out at night, then, to make the rounds of the roofs? And for this we have provided ourselves with rope ladders. I am much mistaken if his Excellency, the Count, will relish this little amusement. Peste, the jolly fellow has a good foot and a good eye. There must be a great deal to gain to risk his skin this way. Faith! these demure faces are not to be trusted."

The great Fritz was so stupefied with his discovery that he seated himself a moment upon a stone to collect his thoughts. The fine idea which his thick skull brought forth was that the secretary belonged to the illustrious brotherhood of ambidexters, and that his nocturnal circuits had for their object the search for a hidden treasure. Proud of his sagacity, and delighted with the opportunity to satisfy his resentment, he descended the path, not without trouble, and deaf to the voice and the laughter of his enchantress, who challenged him to new trials, he regained the road and strode on to the castle.

"Oh! then, Mr. Secretary," said the knave to himself with a wicked smile, "you threw me down a staircase, and thought you'd get me turned out of doors. What will you say if I make you go out by the window?"

CHAPTER XVIII.

The next day—it was the second Sunday of September—Gilbert went out at about ten o'clock in the morning and directed his steps to a wild and solitary retreat. It was a narrow glade upon the borders of a little pond dried up by the summer heat, near which he had often gathered plants for Stephane. Among groups of trees which straggled up on all sides, under a patch of blue sky, a ground of blackish clay, cracked and creviced, herbage, dried rushes; here and there some patches of stagnant water, the surface of which was rippled by the gambols of the aquatic spider; further on a large tuft of long-plumed reeds, which shivered at the least breath and rocked upon their trembling stems drowsy red butterflies and pensive dragon flies; upon the steep banks of the pond, sad flowers, pond weed, the marsh clover, the sand plantain; in a corner, a willow with roots laid bare, which hung over the exhausted pool as if looking for its lost reflection; around about, nettles, briars, dry heather, furze stripped of its blossoms; that damp and heavy atmosphere which is natural to humid places; the light of day thinly veiled by the exhalations from the earth; an odor of decaying plants, long silence interrupted by dull sounds; an air of abandonment, of idleness, of lassitude, the melancholy languor of a life departing regretfully; the recollection of something which was, and will never reappear, never! Such was the word which this wild solitude murmured to Gilbert's ear. Never! repeated he to himself, and his heart was oppressed by a sense of the irretrievable. He seated himself upon the sward, a few steps from the willow, his elbows upon his knees and his head in his hands, and lost himself in long and painful meditation. I shall tell all; he felt at intervals in the depths of his being, in the very depths, the agitation of a secret joy which he dared not confess to himself; but it was a passing movement of his soul which he did not succeed in defining in the midst of the whirlwind which shook him. And then in such a moment, he thought but little of asking himself what he could or could not feel. His mind was elsewhere. Sometimes he sought to picture to himself all the successive phases of this unhappy existence, of which, henceforth, he held the key; sometimes he felt a tender admiration for the energy and elasticity of this young soul which unparalleled misfortunes had not been able to crush. And now to abandon him, to break such close and sweet ties, was it not to condemn him to despair, to deliver him up a a victim to the violence of his passions rendered more violent by unhappiness? Ought he not at least to attempt to draw from this impulsive heart this fatal arrow, this baleful love which to his eyes was a danger, an extravagance, a calamity? And from reflection to reflection, from anxiety to anxiety, he always returned to deplore his own blindness. The eccentricities of Stephane's conduct, certain salient points in his character, the passionate *abandon* of his language; his face, his hair, his glançes, the charm of his smile; how was it that so many indications had escaped him? And this want of penetration which resulted from the rather unromantic character of his mind, he attributed to bluntness of sensibility and charged himself with it as a crime. He was profoundly absorbed in his revery when the cry of a raven aroused him. He opened his eyes, and when he had lost sight of the croaking bird, which crossed the glade in rapid flight, he looked for a moment at a handsome, variegated butterfly which fluttered about the willow; then noticing in the grass, within reach of his hand, a pretty little marsh flower, he drew it carefully from the soil with its root and set about its examination with an attentive eye. He admired the purple tint of its pistil and the gold of its stamens, which contracted charmingly with the brilliant whiteness of the petals, and said unconsciously: "There is a lovely flower which I have not yet shown to my Stephane: I must carry it to him."

But instantly recollecting himself, and throwing away the innocent flower spitefully, he exclaimed:

"Oh, fortune, what singular games you play!"

"Yes, fortune is singular!" answered a voice which was not unknown to him; and before he had time to turn, Dr. Vladimir was seated beside him.

Vladimir Paulitch had employed his morning well. Scarcely out of bed, he had given a private audience to Fritz, who, not daring to address his master directly, for his frowns always made him tremble, had come to ask the doctor to receive his revelations and obligingly transmit them to his Excellency. When in an excited and mysterious tone he had disclosed his important secret:

"There is nothing astonishing in that," replied Vladimir coldly. "This young man is a somnambulist, and the conclusion of your little story is, that his window must be barred. I will speak to Count Kostia about it."

Upon which Fritz slunk away discomfited and much confused at the turn the adventure had taken.

After his departure Vladimir Paulitch concluded to take a walk upon the grassy hillock, and on his way said to himself: "Have my suspicions, then, been well founded?"

He had passed an hour among the rocks, studying the spot, examining the aspect of the castle from this side, and particularly the irregularities of the roof. As his eyes rested on the square tower which Stephane occupied, he saw him appear at the window, and remain there some moments, his eyes fixed upon Gilbert's turret.

"Aha! Now we see how matters stand!" said he, "but to risk his head in this way, our idealist must be desperately in love. And he'll carry it through! We must find him and have a little chat."

In reascending to the castle, Vladimir had seen Gilbert turn into the woods, and without being perceived, had followed him at a distance.

"Yes, fortune is singular!" repeated he, "and we must resist it boldly and brave it resolutely, or submit humbly to its caprices and die. This is but reasonable; half measures are the expedients of fools. As for me, I have always been the partisan of *sequere Deum*, which I interpret thus: 'Take luck for your guide, and walk on blindly.'"

And as Gilbert made no answer, he continued: "May I presume to ask you what caused you to say, just now, that fortune plays us odd tricks?"

"I was thinking," replied Gilbert, tranquilly, "of the emperor Constantine the Great, who you know—"

"Ah! that is too much," interrupted Vladimir. "What! on a beautiful morning, in the midst of the woods, before a little dried-up pond, which is not without its poetry, seated in the grass with a pretty white flower in your hand—the emperor Constantine the subject of your meditations? As for me, I have not such a well-balanced head, and I will confess to you that just now, in rambling among the thickets, I was entirely occupied with the singular games of my own destiny, and what is more singular still, I felt the necessity of relating them to some one."

"You surprise me," replied Gilbert; I did not think you so communicative."

"And who of us," resumed Vladimir, "never contradicts his own character? In Russia the duties of my position oblige me to be reserved, secret, enveloped in mystery from head to foot, a great pontiff of science, speaking but in brief sentences and in an oracular tone; but here I am not obliged to play my rôle, and by a natural reaction, finding myself alone in the woods with a man of se nse and of heart, my tongue unloosens like a magpie's. Let us see; if I tell you my history do you promise to be discreet?"

"Undoubtedly. But if you must have a confidant, how happens it that intimate as you are with Count Kostia—"

"Ah! precisely, when you know my history you will understand for what reason in my interviews with Kostia Petrovitch I speak often of him, but rarely of myself."

And at these words Vladimir Paulitch turned up his sleeves, and showing his wrists to Gilbert; "Look!" he said. "Do you see any mark, any scar?"

"No, I cannot detect any."

"That is strange. For forty years, however, I have worn handcuffs, for such as you see me—I, Vladimir Paulitch; I, one of the first physicians of Russia; I, the learned physiologist, I am the refuse of the earth, I am Ivan's equal; in a word, I am a serf!"

"You a serf!" exclaimed Gilbert stupefied.

"You should not be so greatly astonished; such things are common in Russia," said Vladimir Paulitch, with a faint smile. "Yes, sir," he resumed, I am one of Count Kostia's serfs, and you may imagine whether or not I am grateful to him for having had the goodness to fashion from the humble clay of which nature had formed one of his *moujiks*, the glorious statue of doctor Vladimir Paulitch. However, of all the favors he has heaped upon me the one which troubles me most is, that, thanks to his discretion, there were but two men in the world, himself and myself, who knew me for what I am. Now there are three.

"My parents," continued he, "were Ukraine peasants, and my first profession was taking care of sheep; but I was a born physician. The sick, whether men or sheep, were to my mind the most interesting of spectacles. I procured some books, acquired a slight knowledge of anatomy and chemistry, and by turns I dissected, and hunted for simples, the virtues of which I tried with indefatigable ardor. Poor, lacking all resources, brought up from infancy in foolish superstitions, from which I had trouble in emancipating myself; living in the midst of coarse, ignorant men degraded by slavery, nothing could repulse me or discourage me. I felt myself born to decipher the great book of nature, and to wring from it her secrets. I had the good fortune to discover some specifics against the rot and tag sore. That rendered me famous within a circuit of three leagues. After quadrupeds, I tried my hand on bipeds. I effected several happy cures, and people came from all parts to consult me. Proud as Artaban, the little shepherd, seated beneath the shade of a tree, uttered his infallible oracles, and they were believed all the more implicitly, as nature had given to his eyes that veiled and impenetrable expression calculated to impose upon fools. The land to which I belonged was owned by a venerable relative of Count Kostia. At her death she left her property to him. He came to see his new domain; heard of me, had me brought into his presence, questioned me, and was struck with my natural gifts and precocious genius. He had already proposed to found a hospital in one of his villages where he resided during the summer, and it occurred to him that he could some day make me useful there. I went with him to Moscow. Concealing my position from every one, he had me instructed with the greatest care. Masters, books, money, I had in profusion. So great was my happiness that I hardly dared to believe in it, and I was sometimes obliged to bite my finger to assure myself that I was not in a dream. When I reached the age of twenty, Kostia Petrovitch made me enter the school of medicine, and some years later I directed his hospital and a private asylum which he founded by my advice. My talents and success soon made me known. I was spoken of at Moscow and was called there upon consultations. Thus I was in a fair way to make a fortune, and what gratified me still more, I was sought after, fêted, courted, fawned upon. The little shepherd, the *moujik*, had become King and more than King, for a successful physician is adored as a god by his patients; and I do not believe that a pretty woman gratifies her lovers with half the smiles which she lavishes freely upon the magician upon whom depends her life and her youth. At this time, sir, I was still religious. Imagine the place Count Kostia held in my prayers, and with what fervor I implored for him the intercession of the saints and of the blessed Mary. Prosperity, nevertheless, has this much of evil in it; it makes a man forget his former self.

"Intoxicated with my glory and success, I forgot too soon my youth and my sheep, and this forgetfulness ruined me. I was called to attend a cavalry officer retired from service. He had a daughter named Pauline; she was beautiful and charming. I thought myself insensible to love, but I had hardly seen her before I conceived a violent passion for her. Bear in mind that I had lived until that time as pure as an ascetic monk; science had been my adored and lofty mistress. When passion fires a chaste heart, it becomes a fury there. I loved Pauline with frenzy, with idolatry. One day she gave me to understand that my folly did not displease her. I declared myself to her father, obtained his consent, and felt as if I should die of happiness. The next day I sought Count Kostia, and telling him my story, supplicated him to emancipate me. He laughed, and declared such an extravagant idea was unworthy of me. Marriage was not what I required. A wife, children, useless encumbrances in my life! Petty delights and domestic cares would extinguish the fire of my genius, would kill in me the spirit of research and vigor of thought. Besides, was my passion serious? From what he knew of my disposition, I was incapable of loving. It was a fantastic trick which my imagination had played me. Only remain a week without seeing Pauline, and I would be cured. My only answer was to throw myself at his feet. I glued my mouth to his hands, watered his knees with my tears, and kissed the ground before him. He laughed throughout, and asked me with a sneer, if to possess Pauline it were necessary to marry her. My love was an adoration. At these insulting words anger took possession of me. I poured forth imprecations and threats. Presently, however, recovering myself, I begged him to forgive my transports, and resuming the language of servile humility, I endeavored to soften that heart of bronze with my tears. Trouble lost; he remained inflexible. I rolled upon the floor and tore my hair; and he still laughed— That must have been a curious scene. Recollect that at this epoch I was quite *recherché* in my costume. I had an embroidered frill and very fine ruffles of *point d'Alençon.* I wore rings on every finger, and my coat was of the latest style and of elegant cut. Fancy, also, that my deportment, my gait, my air breathed of pride and arrogance. Parvenues try it in vain, they always betray themselves. I had a high tone, an overbearing manner. I enveloped myself in mysterious darkness, which obscured at times the brightness of my genius, and as I had accomplished several extraordinary cures, strongly resembling miracles, or tricks of sorcery, my airs of an inspired priest did not seem out of place, and I had devotees who encouraged these licenses of my pride by the excess of their humility. And then, behold, suddenly, this man of importance, this miraculous personage, flat upon his face, imploring the mercy of an inexorable master, writhing like a worm of the earth under the foot which crushed his heart! At last Kostia Petrovitch lost patience, seized me in his powerful hands, set me upon my feet, and pushing me violently against the wall, cried in a voice of thunder, 'Vladimir Paulitch, spare me your effeminate contortions, and remember who I am and who you are. One day I saw an ugly piece of charcoal in the road. I picked it up at the risk of soiling my fingers, and, as I am something of a chemist, I put it in my crucible and converted it into a diamond. But just as I have set my jewel, and am about to wear it on my finger, you ask me to give it up! Ah! my son, I do not know what keeps me from sending you back to your sheep. Go, make an effort to conquer your passion; be reasonable, be yourself again. Wait until my death, my will shall emancipate you; but until then, even at the risk of your displeasure, you shall be my *thing*, my *property*. Take care you do not forget it, or I will shatter you in pieces like this glass;' and, seizing a phial from the table, he threw it against the wall, where it broke in fragments.

"Sir, Count Kostia displayed a little too much energy at the time, but at bottom he was right. Was it just that he should lose all the fruits of his trouble? Think what a gratification it was to his pride, to be able to say to himself: the great doctor, so fêted, so admired, is my thing and my property. His words were true; he wore me as a ring upon his finger. And then he foresaw the future. For two consecutive years it has only been necessary for him to move the end of his forefinger, to make me run from the heart of Russia to soothe his poor tormented nerves. You know how the heart of man is made. If he had had the imprudence to emancipate me, I should have come last year out of gratitude; but this time—"

While Vladimir spoke, Gilbert thought to himself, "this man is truly the compatriot of Count Leminof."

And then recalling the amiable and generous Muscovite with whom he had once been intimate, he justly concluded that Russia is large, and that nature, taking pleasure in contrasts, produces in that great country alternately the hardest and the most tender souls in the world.

"One word more," continued Vladimir, "Count Kostia was right; but unfortunately passion will not listen to reason. I left him with death in my heart, but firmly resolved to cope with him and to carry my point. You see that upon this occasion I observed but poorly the great maxim, *Sequere fatum*. I flattered myself I should be able to stem the current. Vain illusion!—but without it would one be in love?

Pauline lived in a small town at about two leagues from our village. Whenever I had leisure, I mounted a horse and flew to her. The third day after the terrible scene, I took a drive with this amiable girl and her father. As we were about to leave the village, I was seized with a sudden trembling at the sight of Count Kostia on the footpath, holding his gold-headed cane under his arm and making his way quietly towards us. He recognized us, smiled agreeably and signed to the coachman to stop and to me to descend.

"Plague upon the thoughtless fellow! whip up, coachman!" cried Pauline gayly.

But I had already opened the door.

"Excuse me," said I, "I will be with you in a moment."

And while saying these words I was so pale, that she became pale too, as if assailed by a dark presentiment. Kostia Petrovitch did not detain me long. After saluting me with ceremonious politeness, he said in a bantering tone:

"Vladimir, faith she is really charming. But I am sorry to say that if your engagement is not broken off before this evening, to-morrow this pretty girl will learn from me who you are."

After which, saluting me again, he walked away humming an aria.

"Money, sir, had always appeared to me so small a thing compared with science and glory; and besides, my love for Pauline was so free from alloy, that I had never conceived the idea of informing myself in regard to her fortune, or the dowry which she might bring to me. That evening, as we took tea together in the parlor of my expected father-in-law, I contrived to bring up this important question for consideration, and expressed views of such a selfish character, and displayed such a sordid cupidity, that the old officer at last became indignant. Pauline had a proud soul; she listened to us some time in silence, and then, rising, she crushed me with a look of scorn, and, extending her arm, pointed me the door. That devil of a look, sir, I have not forgotten; it has long pursued me, and now I often see it in my dreams.

"Returning home, I tried to kill myself; but so awkwardly that I failed. There are some things in which we never succeed the first time. I was prevented from renewing the attempt by the *Sequere fatum*, which returned to my memory. I said to the floods which beat against my exhausted breast: 'Carry me where you please, you are my masters, I am your slave.'

"And believe me, sir, this unhappy adventure benefited me. It led me to salutary reflection. For the first time I ventured to think, I eradicated from my mind every prejudice which remained there, I took leave of all chimeras, I saw life and the world as they are, and decided that heaven is a myth. My manners soon betrayed the effect of the enlightenment of my mind. No more arrogance, no more boasting. I did not divest myself of pride, but it became more tractable and more convenient; it renounced ostentation and vain display; the peacock changed into a man of good breeding. This, sir, is what experience has done for me, assisted by *Sequere fatum*. It has made me wise, an honest man and an atheist. So I said a little while afterwards to Count Kostia:

"'Of all the benefits I have received from you, the most precious was that of delivering me from Pauline. That woman would have ruined me. Ah! Count Kostia, how I laugh to myself when I recall the ridiculous litanies with which I once regaled your ears. You knew me well. A passing fancy—a fire of straw. Thanks to you, Kostia Petrovitch, my mind has acquired a perspicuity for which I shall be eternally grateful to you.'

"This declaration touched him; he loved me the more for it. He has always had a weakness for men who listen to reason. Until then, notwithstanding the marks of affection which he lavished upon me, he had always made me feel the distance between us. But from that day I became intimate with him; I participated in his secrets, and, what cemented our friendship still more, was that one day I had an opportunity of saving his life at the risk of my own."

"And Pauline?" said the inquisitive and sympathetic Gilbert.

"Ah! Pauline interests you! Comfort yourself. Six months after our rupture she made a rich marriage. She still lives in her little town; she is happy, and has lost none of her beauty. I meet her sometimes in the street with her husband and children, and I have the pleasure of seeing her turn her head always from me. And I, too, sir, have children; they are my pupils. They are called in Moscow *the little Vladimirs*, and one of them will become some of these days a great Vladimir. I have revealed all my secrets to him, for I do not want them to die with me, and my end may be near. I have yet an important work to accomplish; and when my task is finished, let death take me. The life of the little shepherd of Ukraine has been too exciting to last long. 'Short and sweet,' is my motto."

And at these words, leaning suddenly towards Gilbert, and looking him in the eye:

"Apropos," said he, "were you really thinking of Constantine, the emperor, when you exclaimed: 'Oh, fortune! what strange tricks you play?'"

Gilbert was nearly disconcerted by this sudden attack, but promptly recovered himself.

"Ah! ah!" thought he, "it was not for nothing, then, that you told me your history; you had a purpose! Who knows but that Count Leminof has sent you to get my confidence?"

Vladimir employed all the skill he possessed to make Gilbert speak; his insidious questions were inexhaustible: Gilbert was impenetrable. From time to time they looked steadily at each other, each seeking to embarrass his adversary, and to surprise his secret, but in vain; they fenced with glances, but they were both so sure in the parries, that not a thrust succeeded. At last Vladimir lost patience.

"My dear sir," exclaimed he, "I have the weakness to put faith in dreams, and I had one the other night which troubled me very much. I dreamed that Count Kostia had a daughter, and that he made her very unhappy, because she had the twofold misfortune of not being his daughter and of resembling in a striking manner a woman whose remembrance he did not cherish. You see that dreams are as singular as the tricks of fortune. But the most serious matter was, that the unhappiness and beauty of this child had strongly touched your heart and that you had conceived an ardent passion for her.

"What must I do," you said to me one day.

"Then I related my story to you, and said: 'You know the character of Kostia Petrovitch. Do not hope to move him, it would be an amusement for him to break your heart. If I had been as much in love as you are, I should have carried off Pauline and fled with her to the ends of the world. An elopement!—that is your only resource. And mark (it was in my dream that I spoke thus), and mark—if you perform this bold stroke successfully, the count, at first furious to see his victim escape him, will at last be reconciled to it. The sight of this child is a horror to him; even the tyranny which he exercises over her, excites him and disorders his nerves. After she has left him, he will breathe more freely, will enjoy better health, and will pardon the ravisher, who will have relieved his life of the ferment of hatred which torments him. Then you can treat with him, and I shall be much mistaken if it is long before your dear mistress becomes your wife.' It was thus I repeat, that I spoke to you in my dream, and I added: 'Do not lose an instant; there is danger in remaining here. Kostia Petrovitch has suspicions; to-morrow perhaps it will be too late!'"

"And then you awoke," interrupted Gilbert laughing.

Then rising he continued:

"Your dreams have no common sense, my dear doctor; for without taking into consideration that M. Leminof has no daughter, the faculty of loving has been denied to me by nature, and the only abduction of which I am capable is that of ink spots from a folio. With a little chlorine you see—"

He took a few steps to pick up the little flower which he had thrown away, and continued as he retraced with Vladimir the path which led to the castle. "Let us speak of more serious things. Do you know the family of this pretty flower?"

Thus walking on they conversed exclusively upon botany, and having arrived at the terrace, separated amicably. Vladimir saw Gilbert move away, and then muttered between his teeth:

"Ha! you won't speak, you refuse me your confidence, and you only take off spots of ink! Then let your fate work itself out!"

Shall I describe the feelings which agitated Gilbert's heart? They will readily be divined. In addition to the anxiety which preyed upon him, a further and greater source of uneasiness was the fear that all had been discovered. "In spite of my precautions," thought he, "some spy stationed by the Count may have seen me running over the roof, but it is very improbable."

"I am inclined to believe rather, that the lynx eyes of Vladimir Paulitch have read Stephane's face. At the table he has watched her narrowly. Perhaps, too, my glances have betrayed me. This mind, coarse in its subtilty, has taken for a common love, the tender and generous pity with which a great misfortune has inspired me. Doubtless he has informed the Count, and it was by his order that he attempted to force my confidence, and to draw out my intentions. Stephane, Stephane, all my efforts then will have but resulted in heaping upon your head new misfortunes!" He was calmed a little, however, by the reflection that she had authorized him of her own accord to remain away from her for at least two weeks. "Before that time expires," thought he, "I shall have devised some expedient. It is, first of all, important to throw this terrier, who is upon our track, off the scent. Fortunately he will not be here long. His departure will be a great relief to me, for he is a dangerous person. If only Stephane will be prudent!"

Dinner passed off well! Vladimir did not make his appearance. The Count was amiable and gay. Stephane, although very pale, was as calm as on the preceding days, and his eyes did not try to meet those of Gilbert, who felt his alarm subsiding; but when they had risen from the table, Kostia Petrovitch having left the room first, his daughter had time, before following him, to turn quickly, draw from her sleeve a little roll of paper, and throw it at Gilbert's feet; he picked it up, and what was his chagrin when, after having locked himself in his room, he read the following lines: "The spirit of darkness has returned to me! I could not close my eyes last night. My head is on fire. I fear, I doubt, I despair. My Gilbert, I must, at any cost, see you this evening, for I feel myself capable of anything. Oh! my friend, come at least to console me—come and take from my sight the knife which remains open on my table."

Gilbert passed two hours in indescribable anguish. Whilst day lasted, he stood leaning upon his window sill, hoping all the time that Stephane would appear at hers, and that he could communicate to her by signs; but he waited in vain, and already night began to fall. He deliberated, wavered, hesitated. At last, in this internal struggle, one thought prevailed over all others. He imagined he could see Stephane, pale, dishevelled, despair in her eyes; he thought he could also see a knife in her hands, the slender blade flashing in the darkness of the night. Terrified by these horrible fancies, he turned a deaf ear to prudential counsels, suspended his ladder, descended, crossed the roofs, clambered up the window and sprang into the room. Stephane awaited him, crouching at the feet of the saints. She rose, bounded forward and seized the knife laying upon the table with a convulsive motion, turned the point towards her heart, and cried in a vibrating voice:

"Gilbert, for the first and the last time, do you love me?"

Terrified, trembling, beside himself, Gilbert opened his arms to her. She threw the poniard away, uttered a cry of joy, of delirium, leaped with a bound to her friend, threw her arms about him, and hanging upon his lips she cried:

"He loves me! he loves! I am saved."

Gilbert, while returning her caresses, sought to calm her excitement; but all at once he turned pale. From the neighboring alcove came a sigh like that he had heard in one of the corridors of the castle.

"We are lost!" gasped he in a stifled voice. "They have surprised us."

But she, clinging to him, her face illuminated by delirious joy, answered:

"You love me! I am happy. What matters the rest?"

At this moment the door of the alcove opened and Count Kostia appeared upon the threshold, terrible, threatening, his lips curling with a sinister smile. At this sight his daughter slowly raised her head, then took a few steps towards him, and for the first time dared to look that father in the face who for so many years had held her bowed and shuddering under his iron hand. Then like a young lion with bristling mane, her hair floating in disorder upon her shoulders, her body quivering, her brows contracted, with flashing eyes and in a thrilling voice, she cried:

"Ah! it really is you then, sir!"

"You are welcome. You here, great God! Truly these walls ought to be surprised to see you. Yes, hear me, deaf old walls, the man you see there upon the threshold is my father! Ah, tell me, would you not have divined it by the tenderness in his face, by that smile full of goodness playing about his lips?" And then she added: "Unnatural father, do you remember yet that you once had a daughter? Search well, you will find her, perhaps, at the bottom of your memory. Very well! this daughter whom you killed, has just left her coffin, and he who resuscitated her is the man before you." Then, more excitedly still: "Oh, how I love him, this divine man! and in loving him, obedient daughter that I am, what have I done but execute your will? for was it not you yourself who one day threw me at his feet? I have remained there."

At these words, exhausted by the excess of her emotion, her strength deserted her. She uttered a cry, closed her eyes, and sank down. Gilbert, however, had already sprang towards her; he raised her in his arms and laid her inanimate form in an arm chair; then placing himself before her, made a rampart of his body. When he turned his eyes upon the Count again, he could not repress a shudder, for he fancied he saw the somnambulist. The features of Kostia Petrovitch were distorted, his eyes bloodshot, and his fixed and burning pupils seemed almost starting from their sockets. He bent down slowly and picked up the knife, after which he remained some time motionless without giving any signs of life except by passing his tongue several times over his lips as if to assuage the thirst for blood which consumed him. At last he advanced, his head erect, his arm holding the knife suspended in the air ready to strike. As he drew near, Gilbert recovered all his composure, and in a clear, strong voice, cried out:

"Count Leminof, control yourself, or you will lose your reason."

And as the frightful phantom still advanced, he quickly uncovered his breast, and exclaimed in a still louder voice:

"Count Kostia, strike, here is my heart, but your blows will not reach me,—the spectre of Morlof is between us."

At these words the Count uttered a cry like a fallow deer, followed by a long and plaintive sigh. A terrible internal struggle followed; his brow contracted; the convulsive movements which agitated his body, and the flakes of foam which stood upon his lips, testified to the violence of the effort he was making. Reason at length returned; his arms fell and the knife dropped, the muscles of his face relaxed and his features by degrees resumed their natural expression. Then turning in the direction of the alcove, he called out:

"Ivan, come and take care of your young mistress, she has fainted."

Ivan appeared. Who could describe the look which he threw upon Gilbert? Meanwhile the Count had reëntered the alcove; but returned immediately with a candle, which he lighted quietly, and then with an easy gesture, said to Gilbert:

"My dear sir, it seems to me we are in the way here. Be good enough to leave with me by the staircase; for please God, you do not return by the roof. If an accident should happen to you, the Byzantines and I would be inconsolable!"

Gilbert was so constituted, that at this moment M. Leminof inspired him more with pity than anger. He obeyed, and preceding him a few steps, crossed the alcove and the vestibule and descended the stairs. When at the entrance of the corridor, he turned, and placing his back against the wall, said sadly:

"I have a few words to say to you!"

The Count stopping upon the last step, leaned nonchalantly over the balustrade and answered smiling:

"Speak, I am ready to hear you; you know it always gives me pleasure to talk with you."

"I beg you, sir," said Gilbert, "to pardon your daughter the bitterness of her language. She spoke in delirium. I swear to you that at the bottom of her heart, she respects you, and that you have only to wish it to have her love you as a father."

M. Leminof answered only by a shrug of the shoulders, which signified—"What matters it to me?"

"I am bound to say further," resumed Gilbert, "that your anger ought to fall upon me alone. It was I who sought this child, who hated me; and I constrained her to receive me. I pressed my attentions upon her and had no peace or rest until I had gained her affection."

The count shrugged his shoulders again, as much as to say: "I believe you, but how does that change the situation?"

"As for me," continued Gilbert, "I assure you upon my honor, that it was only yesterday I drew from your daughter her secret."

The Count answered:

"I believe you readily; but tell me, if you please, is it true that you now love this little girl as she loves you?"

Gilbert reflected a moment; then considering only the dignity and interests of Stephane, he replied:

"Yes, I love her with a pure, deep love."

A sarcastic joy appeared upon the Count's face.

"Admirable!" said he; "that is all I wish to know. We have nothing more to say."

Gilbert raised his head: "One word more, sir!" he exclaimed. "I do not leave you until you have sworn to me that you will not touch a hair of your daughter's head, and that you will not revenge yourself upon her for my well-meant imprudence."

"Peste!" said the Count laughing, "you are taking great airs; but I owe you some gratitude, inasmuch as your coolness has saved me from committing a crime which would have been a great folly, for only fools avenge themselves with the knife. So I shall grant you even more than you ask. Hereafter, my daughter shall have no cause to complain of me, and I will interest myself paternally in her happiness. It displeases her to be under Ivan's charge; he shall be only her humble servant. I intend that she shall be as free as air, and all of her caprices will be sacred to me. I will begin by restoring her horse, if he is not already sold. I will do more: I will permit her to resume the garments of her sex. But for these favors I exact two conditions: first, that you shall remain here at least six months; second, that you will try neither to see, speak, nor write to my doll, without my consent."

Gilbert breathed a deep sigh.

"I swear it, on my honor!" replied he.

"Enough! enough!" resumed M. Leminof, "I have your promise, and I believe in it as I do in the gospels."

When the Count reëntered his study, Doctor Vladimir, who was impatiently awaiting him, examined him from head to foot, as if seeking to discover upon his garments or his hands some stain of blood, then controlling his emotion:

"Well," said he coolly, "how did the affair terminate?"

"Very well," said the Count, throwing himself in a chair. "I have not killed any one. This young man's reason restored mine."

Vladimir Paulitch turned pale.

"So," said he with a forced smile, "this audacious seducer gets off with a rating."

"You haven't common sense, Vladimir Paulitch! What are you saying about seduction? The Gilberts are an enigma to you. They are not born under the same planets as the Doctors Vladimir and the Counts Leminof. There is a mixture in them of the humanitarian, the knight-errant, the gray sister and the St. Vincent de Paul, added to all which, our philanthropist has a passion for puppets, and from the time of his arrival he has forewarned me that he intended to make them play. He must have wanted, I think, to give himself a representation of some sacramental act, of some mystery play of the middle ages. The piece began well. The principal personages were faith, hope and charity. Unfortunately, love got into the party, and the mystery was transformed into a drama of cloak and sword. I am sorry for him; these things always end badly."

"You are mistaken, Count Kostia!" replied Vladimir ironically; "they often end with a wedding."

"Vladimir Paulitch!" exclaimed the Count, stamping his foot, "you have the faculty of exasperating me. To-day you spent an hour in kindling the fire of vengeance in my soul. You hate this young man. I believe, on my honor, that you are jealous of him. You are afraid, perhaps, that I may put him in my will in place of the little shepherd of the Ukraine? Think of it as you please, my dear doctor; it is certain that if I had had the awkwardness to kill this admirable companion of my studies, I should lament him now in tears of blood, for I know not why, but he is dear to me in spite of all. But who loves well, chastises well, and I cannot help pitying him in thinking of all the sufferings which I shall make him undergo. Now go to bed, doctor. To-morrow morning you will go on your nimble feet, three leagues from here, on the other side of the mountain, to a little inn, which I will direct you how to find. I will follow on horseback. I need exercise and diversion. We will meet there and dine together. At dessert we will talk physiology, and you will exert yourself to entertain me."

"But what are you thinking of?" exclaimed Vladimir surprised to the last degree. "Will you permit these two lovers—"

Oh! you have but a dull mind, in spite of your wisdom," interrupted the Count. "In matters of vengeance, you only know the calicoes and cottons. Mine I prefer to weave of silk and threads of gold."

On returning to his room, Vladimir Paulitch said to himself:

"These two men are too rational. The piece moves too slowly. I must hasten the denouement."

CHAPTER XIX.

EARLY in the morning Ivan entered Gilbert's room. The face of the poor serf was distressing to see. His eyes were red and swollen, and his features bloated. The bloody marks of his nails were visible on his face; forehead and cheeks were furrowed with them. He informed Gilbert that towards noon Count Kostia would go out with Vladimir Paulitch and would be absent the rest of the day.

"He left me here to watch you and to render an account to him upon his return of all I should see and hear. I am not ugly;—but after what has passed, you would be foolish to expect the least favor from me. My eyes, ears and tongue will do their duty. You must know, too, that the *barine* is in a very gloomy mood to-day. His lips are white, and he frequently passes his left hand over his forehead, a sure sign that a storm is raging within."

"My dear Ivan," answered Gilbert, "I also shall be absent all day; so you see your task of watching will be easy."

Ivan breathed a sigh of relief. It seemed as if a mountain had been taken from his breast.

"I see with pleasure," said he, "that you repent of your sin, and that you promise to be wiser in the future; ah! if my young master would listen to reason, like you."

"Your young master, as you call him, will be as rational as myself. But do me the favor to tell me—"

"Oh! don't be alarmed; his fainting fit was not long. I had hardly got to him, when he opened his eyes and asked me if you were still alive. On hearing my answer he exclaimed: 'Ah! my God! how happy I am! He lives and loves me!' Then he tried to rise, but was so weak that he fell back. I carried him to his bed and he said to me: 'Ivan, for four nights I have not closed my eyes,' and at these words he smiled and fell asleep smiling, and he is asleep yet."

"In order to be wise, Stephane must be occupied. She must work with her mind and her hands. Here, take this little white flower," added he, handing him the one he had plucked the day before; "ask her, for me, to paint it in her herbarium to-day."

And as Ivan examined the plant with an air of distrust, he added:

"Go, and fear nothing. I've not hidden a note in it. I am a man of honor, my dear Ivan, and never break my word."

Ivan hid the flower in one of his sleeves and went out muttering to himself:

"How is all this going to end? Ah! may the Holy Trinity look down in pity upon this house. We are all lost!"

Gilbert went out. Leaving upon his right the plateau and its close thickets, he gained the main road and followed the bank of the Rhine for a long distance. A thousand thoughts crowded in confusion through his mind; but he always came to the same conclusion:

"I will save this child, or lose my life in the attempt."

As the sun began to sink towards the horizon, he returned to the castle. He went in search of father Alexis and found him in the chapel. The good father had learned from Ivan what had happened the night before. He reproached Gilbert severely, but nevertheless, after hearing his explanations, softened considerably, and in a tone of grumbling indulgence, repeated the old proverb, "every one to his trade." "Oxen," added he, "are born to draw the plough, birds to fly, bees to make honey, Gilberts to read and make great books, and father Alexis to edify and console his fellow-creatures. You have encroached upon my prerogatives. You wanted to walk in my shoes. And what has been the result of your efforts? The spoiling of my task! Have you not observed how much better this child has been for the last two months, how much more tranquil, gentle and resigned? I had preached so well to her, that she at last listened to reason. And you must come to put in her head a silly love which will cost both of you many tears."

Upon which, seizing him rudely by the arm, he continued:

"And what need had we of your assistance, the good God and I? Have you forgotten? Open your eyes and look! To-day, my child, even to-day I have put the finishing touch to my great work."

Then he pointed his finger to two long rows of sallow faces, surmounted by golden halos, which two lamps suspended from the ceiling illuminated with a mysterious light. Like a general enumerating his troops, he said:

"Look at these three graybeards. That is Isaac, this Jeremiah, and this Ezekiel. On the other side are the holy warrior martyrs. Then St. Procopius, there St. Theodore, who burnt the temple of Cybele. His torch may yet be relighted. And these archangels, do you think their arms will be forever nerveless and their swords always asleep in their scabbards?"

Then falling upon his knees he prayed aloud:

"And thou, holy mother of God, suffer thy unworthy servant to summon thee to keep thy promise. Let thy august power at last be made manifest. At the sight of thy frowning brows let there be accomplished a mystery of terror and tears in hardened hearts. Let the neck of the proud be broken, and let his haughty head, bent down by the breath of thy lips, as by the wind of a tempest, bow to the very earth and its hair sweep the dust of this pavement."

Just then they heard a voice calling:

"Father Alexis, father Alexis, where are you?"

The priest turned pale and trembled. He tried in vain to rise, his knees seemed nailed to the ground.

"Ah! my child, did you not hear a divine voice answer me?"

But helping him to his feet, Gilbert said with a sad smile:

"There is nothing divine in that voice. It has a strongly marked Provençal accent, and if I am not mistaken, it belongs to Jasmin the cook, who is there in the court with a lantern in his hand, and is calling you."

"Perhaps you are right," answered the good father, shaking his head and passing his hand over his forehead, which was bathed in perspiration. "Let us see what this good Jasmin wants. Perhaps he brings my dinner. I had notified him, however, that I proposed to fast to-day."

Jasmin no sooner saw them come out of the chapel than he ran towards them and said to the priest:

"I don't know, father, what has happened to Ivan, but when I went into his room to carry him his dinner, I found him stretched on his bed. I called him and shook him, but couldn't wake him up."

A shudder ran through Gilbert's whole body. Seizing the lantern from Jasmin he darted off on a run; in two seconds he was with Ivan. Jasmin had told the truth; the serf slept heavily and profoundly. By dint of pulling him by the arm, Gilbert succeeded in making him open his eyes; but he soon closed them again, turned towards the wall and slept on.

"Some one must have given him a narcotic," said Gilbert, whispering to father Alexis who had just joined him.

And addressing Jasmin, who had followed the priest,

"Has any one been here this afternoon?"

"I ask your pardon," said the cook. "Doctor Vladimir returned from his walk at about five o'clock. This surprised me very much, as Count Kostia told me before he left, that M. Stephane would dine here alone to-day."

"The Doctor is at the table then, now."

"Pardon, pardon! He didn't wish any dinner. He told me in a joking way, that he would shortly go to a grand dinner in the other world."

"But where is he then? In his study?"

"Two hours afterwards, he went out with M. Stephane."

"Which way did they go?" cried Gilbert, shaking him violently by the arm.

"Ah! pardon, sir, take care, you'll put my arm out of joint," answered the huge Provençal.

"Jasmin, my good Jasmin, answer me: which way did they go?"

"Ah! I remember now, they took the road to the woods."

Gilbert darted off instantly. Father Alexis cried after him in vain:

"Wait for me, my child, I will accompany you. I am a man of good judgment." As if carried by the wind, Gilbert was already in the woods. His head bare, pale, out of breath, he ran at the top of his speed. Night had come, and the moon began to silver over the foliage which quivered at every breath of wind. Gilbert was blind to the moon's brightness, deaf to the sighing of the wind. He heard nothing but the diminishing sound of steps in the distance, he saw nothing but a cloud of blood which floated before his eyes and indicated the path; the sole thought which shed any light upon his mind, filled with gloomiest apprehensions, was this:

"I did not understand this man! It was an offensive alliance which he proposed to me yesterday. I refused to avenge him: he is going to revenge himself, and a Russian serf seeking vengeance is capable of anything."

On he ran with unabated speed, and would have run to the end of the world if, in an elbow of the road, some steps before him, he had not suddenly perceived Stephane. Standing in the moonlight erect and motionless, Gilbert stopped, held out his arms, and uttered a cry. She trembled, turned, and running to him, cried:

"Gilbert, do you love me?"

He answered only by pressing her to his heart; and then perceiving Doctor Vladimir, who was sitting on the edge of a ditch, his head in his hands, he stammered:

"This man here with you!"

"I do not know," said she in a trembling voice, "whether he is a madman or a villain; but it is certain that he is going to die, for he has poisoned himself."

"What have you to say?" said Gilbert, looking wildly at the dejected face of the doctor, upon which the moon was shining full. "Explain, I beg of you."

"What do I know?" said she; "I think I have been dreaming since yesterday evening. It seems to me, however, that this man came to my room for me. He had taken the precaution to drug Ivan. I was dying with melancholy. He persuaded me that you, my Gilbert, were waiting for me in one of the paths of this forest, to fly with me to a distant country.' 'Let us go, let us go,' I cried; but on the way I began to think, I grew suspicious, and at this turning of the road I said to my gloomy companion: 'Bring my Gilbert to me here; I will go no further.' Then he looked at me with frightful eyes, and I be-ieve said to me: 'What is your Gilbert to me? Follow me or you die;' and then he fumbled in his bosom as if to find a concealed weapon; but if I am not mistaken, I looked at him steadily, and crossing my arms, said to him: 'Kill me, but you shall not make me take another step.'"

Vladimir raised his head.

"How deceptive resemblances are," said he in a hollow voice. "I once knew a woman who had the same contour of face, and one evening, by the sole power of my eye, I compelled her to fall at my feet, crying: 'Vladimir Paulitch, do with me what you will.' But your young friend has a soul made of different stuff. You can believe me if you wish, sir; but the fact is that her charming face suddenly struck me with an involuntary respect. It seemed to me that her head was adorned with a royal diadem. Her eyes glowed with a noble pride; anger dilated her nostrils, and while a scornful smile flitted over her lips, her whole face expressed the innocence of a soul as pure as the rays of the moon shining upon us. At this sight I thought of the woman of whom I spoke to you yesterday, and I felt a sensation of horror at the crime I had premeditated, and I, Doctor Vladimir, I prostrated myself at the feet of this child, saying to her: 'Forgive me, I am a wretch;' after which I swallowed a strong dose of a poison of my own composition, whose antidote I do not know, and in two hours I shall be no more."

Gilbert looked steadily at him.

"Ah! great God," thought he, "it was not the life but the honor of Stephane which was in danger!

But the promised miracle has been wrought, only this is not the one which father Alexis expected, since it has been the work of the God of nature."

Stephane approached him, and taking his hands murmured:

"Gilbert, Gilbert, let us fly—let us fly together! There is yet time!"

But he only muttered:

"I see through it all!" Then turning to Vladimir he said in a tone of authority, "Follow me, sir! It is right that Count Kostia should receive your last breath."

"Vladimir reflected for a moment, then rising, said:

"You are right. I must see him again before I die; but give me your arm, for the poison begins to work and my legs are very weak."

They began to walk, Stephane preceding them a few steps. At intervals, Vladimir would exclaim:

"To die—to breathe no more—no more to see the sun—no more to remember—to forget all!" And then he added, "One thing disturbs my happiness. I am not sufficiently revenged!"

At last his voice died upon his lips and his legs failed him. Gilbert was obliged to carry him on his shoulders, and was nearly giving out under the burden when he saw father Alexis coming towards them breathless. He gave him no time to recover breath, but cried:

"Take this man by the feet. I will support his shoulders. Forward! my good father, forward! We have no time to lose."

Father Alexis hastened to comply with Gilbert's request, and they continued on their way with bowed heads and in gloomy silence, Stephane alone, with her cap drawn over her eyes occasionally uttered disconnected words and alternately cast a furtive glance at Gilbert, or gazed sadly at the moon. Arriving at the castle, they crossed the court and ascended the stairs without meeting any one; but entering the vestibule of the first story, in which all the lamps were lighted, they heard a noise of steps in the corridor which led to the square tower.

"M. Leminof has returned," said Gilbert trembling. "Father Alexis, carry this man to his room. I will go and speak to the Count, and will bring him to you in a moment."

Then taking Stephane by the arm, he whispered to her:

"In the name of Heaven, keep out of the way. Go down on the terrace and conceal yourself. Your father must not see you until he has heard me."

"Do you think I am afraid, then?" she replied, and escaping from him, darted off in the direction of the corridor.

Meanwhile father Alexis had entered the room of Vladimir Paulitch, whom he sustained with difficulty in his trembling arms. At the moment he laid him upon his bed, a voice which reached even to them, uttered these terrible words:

"Ah! this is braving me too much! Let her die!" Then a sharp cry pierced the air, followed by the dull noise of a body falling heavily upon the floor.

Father Alexis looked at Vladimir with horror. "The mother was not enough," cried he, "thou hast just killed the daughter!"

And he sprang out of the room distracted.

Vladimir sat up. An atrocious joy gleamed in his face; and recovering the use of his speech: he murmured, "my vengeance is complete!"

But at these words a groan escaped him—the poison began to burn his vitals. Nevertheless he forgot his sufferings when he saw the Count appear, followed by the priest, and holding in his hand a sword, which he threw in the corner.

"Count Kostia," cried the dying man, "what have you done with your daughter?"

"I have killed her," answered he sternly, questioning him with his eyes.

Vladimir remained silent a moment.

"My good master," resumed he, "do you remember that Pauline whom I loved? do you also remember having seen me crouched at your feet crying, 'Mercy! Mercy! for her and for me?' My good master, have you forgotten that corner of the street where you said to me one day: 'This woman is charming; but if your marriage is not broken off before this evening, to-morrow she will learn from me who you are?' That day, Count Kostia Petrovitch, you had a happy and smiling air. Say, Kostia Petrovitch, do you recollect it?"

The Count answered only by a disdainful smile.

"Oh! most simple and most credulous of men, continued Vladimir, how could you think that I would empty the cup of sorrow and of shame to the very dregs, and not revenge myself upon him who smiled as he made me drink it?"

"Six months later, you saved my life," said the Count, slightly shrugging his shoulders.

"Because your days were dear to me. You do not know then the tenderness of hatred! I wished you to live, and that your life should be a hell."

And then he added, panting:

"The lover of the Countess Olga, . . . was I."

The Count staggered as if struck by lightning. He supported himself by the back of a chair, to avoid falling; then springing to the table he seized a carafe full of water and emptied it in a single draught. Then in a convulsed voice, he exclaimed:

"You lie! The Countess Olga could never have given herself to a serf!"

"Refer to your memory once more, Kostia Petrovitch. You forget that in her eyes, I was not a serf, but an illustrious physician, a sort of great man. However, I will console you. The Countess Olga loved me no more than I loved her. My magnetic eyes, my threats had, as it were, bewitched her poor head; in my arms she was dying with fear, and when at the end of one of these sweet interviews, she heard me cry out, 'Olga Vassilievna, your lover is a serf,' she nearly perished of shame and horror."

The Count cast upon his serf a look of indescribable disgust, and, making a superhuman effort to speak, once more exclaimed: "Impossible! That letter which you addressed to me at Paris—"

"I feared that your dishonor might be concealed from you, and what would life have been to me then?"

M. Leminof turned to the priest, who remained standing at the other end of the room. "Father Alexis, is what this man says true?"

The priest silently bowed.

"And was it for this, foolish priest, that you have endured death and martyrdom—to prolong the days of a worm of the earth?"

"I cared little for his life," answered the priest, with dignity, "but much for my conscience, and for the inviolable secrecy of the confessional."

"And for two years in succession you have suffered my mortal enemy to lodge under my roof without warning me?"

"I was ignorant of his history and of the fact that he had reasons for hating you. I fancied that a mad passion had made him a traitor to friendship, and that in repentance he sought to expiate his fault, by the assiduous attentions which he lavished upon you."

"Poor fellow!" said the Count, crushing him with a look of pity.

Then Vladimir resumed in a voice growing more and more feeble:

"Since that cursed hour, when I crawled at your feet, without being able to soften your stony heart with my tears, I became disgusted with life. To feel that I belonged to you was every instant a torment. But if you ask me why I have deferred my death so long, I answer that while you had a daughter living my vengeance was not complete. I let this child grow up; but when the clock of fate struck the hour I waited for, courage suddenly failed me, and I was seized with scruples, which still astonish me. But what am I saying? I bless my weakness, since I brought home a victim pure and without stain, and since her virginal innocence adds to the horror of your crime. Ah! tell me, was the steel which pierced her heart the same that silenced Morlof's? Oh, sword, thou art predestinated!"

Count Kostia's eyes brightened. He had something like a presentiment that he was about to be delivered from that fatal doubt which for so many years had poisoned his life, and he fixed his vulture-like eyes upon Vladimir.

"That child," said he, "was not my daughter."

Vladimir opened his vest, tore the lining with his nails and drew out a folded paper, which he threw at the Count's feet:

"Pick up that letter!" cried he, "the writing is known to you. I meant to have sent it to you by your dishonored daughter. Go and read it near your dead child."

M. Leminof picked up the letter, unfolded it, and read it to the end with bearing calm and firm. The first lines ran thus: "Vile *Moujik.* Thou hast made me a mother. Be happy and proud. Thou hast revealed to me that maternity can be a torture. In my ignorant simplicity, I did not know until now it could be aught else than an intoxication, a pride, a virtue, which God and the church regard with favor, and the angels shelter with their white wings. When for the first time I felt my Stephan and my Stephane stir within me, my heart leaped for joy, and I could not find words enough to bless Heaven which at last rewarded six years of expectation; but now it is not a child I carry in my bosom, it is a crime. . . ."

This letter of four pages shed light, and carried conviction into the mind of Count Kostia.

"She was really my daughter," said he, coolly. . . "Fortunately I have not killed her."

He left the room, and an instant after, re-appeared, accompanied by Gilbert, and carrying in his arms his daughter, pale and dishevelled, but living. He advanced into the middle of the room. There, as if speaking to himself, he said:

"This young man is my good genius. He tore my sword from me. God be praised! he has saved her and me. This dear child was frightened, she fell, but she is unhurt. You see her, she is alive, her eyes are open, she hears, she breathes. To-morrow she shall smile, to-morrow we shall all be happy."

Then drawing her to the head of the bed and calling Gilbert to him, he placed their hands together, and standing behind them, embracing their shoulders in his powerful arms, and thrusting his head between theirs, he forced them, in spite of themselves, to bend with him over the dying man.

Gilbert and Stephane closed their eyes.

The Count's and Vladimir's were wide open devouring each other. The master's flamed like torches; the serf's were sunken, glassy, and filled with the fear and horror of death. He seemed almost petrified, and murmured in a failing voice:

"I am lost. I have undone my own work. To-morrow, to-morrow, they will be happy."

One last look, full of hatred, flashed from his eyes, over which the eternal shadow was creeping, his features contracted, his mouth became distorted, and, uttering a frightful cry, he rendered up his soul.

Then the Count slowly raised himself. His arms in which he held the two young people as in a living vice, relaxed, and Stephane fell upon Gilbert's breast. Confused, colorless, wild-eyed, intoxicated with joy and terror at the same time, clinging to her friend as the sailor to his plank of safety, she said in an indistinct voice:

"In the life to which you condemn me, my father, the joys are as terrible as the sorrows."

The Count said to Gilbert:

"Console her, calm her emotion. She is yours. I have given her to you. Do not fear that I shall take her back again." Then turning again to the bed he exclaimed: "What a terrible thorn death has just drawn from my heart!"

In the midst of so many tragic sensations, who was happy? Father Alexis was, and he had no desire to hide it. He went and came, moved the furniture, passed his hand over his beard, struck his chest with all his might, and presently in his excess of joy threw himself upon Stephane and then upon Gilbert, caressing and embracing them. At last, kneeling down by the bed of death, under the eyes of the Count, he took the head of the dead man between his hands and kissed him upon the mouth and cheeks, saying:

"My poor brother, thou hast perhaps been more unfortunate than guilty. May God, in the unfathomable mystery of his infinite mercy, give thee one day, as I have, the kiss of peace! Then raising his clasped hands, he said: "Holy mother of God: blessed be thy name. Thou hast done more than I dared to ask."

At that moment Ivan, roused at last from his long lethargy, appeared at the threshold of the door. For some minutes he remained paralyzed by astonishment, and looked around distractedly; then, throwing himself at his master's feet and tearing his hair, he cried:

"*Seigneur Père*, I am not a traitor! That man mixed some drug in my tea which put me to sleep. *Seigneur Père*, kill me, but do not say that I am a traitor."

"Rise," returned the Count gayly, "rise, I say. I shall not kill thee. I am not going to kill anybody. My son, thou'rt a rusty old tool. Dost know what I shall do with thee? I shall slip thee in among the wedding presents of Madame Gilbert Saville."

EPILOGUE.

EPILOGUE.

CHAPTER I.

STEPHANE passed the following day shut up in her tower. An hour before dinner M. Leminof paid her a visit. When he entered she was busy painting. She rose and went to meet him. The Count took her hand, pressed it gallantly to his lips, and offering his arm, led her to the sofa, where he seated himself beside her. For a few moments she looked at him in silence; then suddenly began to tremble.

"The man who is seated there is my father, thought she, and, but for Gilbert, would have been my assassin."

The Count frowned slightly. He anticipated a scene of tears, stormy explanations, sentimental effusions, and he held tears, explanations and sentiment in horror.

"My dear child," he said in an off-hand manner; "for six years past you have had but little cause to praise my affection; but what would it avail if we talked about it until to-morrow? Let it suffice you to know that, deceived by false evidences, I did not consider you my daughter. Yesterday evening a happy accident revealed to me my dreadful error, and there is no fear of my ever falling into it again. Let us forget the past, then, and occupy ourselves entirely with the future."

Stephane quickly recovered from her agitation, and replied to her father in a playful tone:

"Please believe that I am the greatest forgetter in the world if I only have a little aid."

M. Leminof was so charmed with her answer and

her sportiveness that he gave her three friendly little taps upon the right cheek.

"Besides," continued she, "you have surprised me in a moment of very good humor. I made a discovery to-day which delighted me. I am convinced that I have a strong mind, and to save words, a great character."

"Did you doubt it?" asked the Count smiling.

"I knew that I was violent, very violent; but that's not the same thing. A few weeks since, permit me to omit the precise date, I lived in such a whirlwind of excitement, that I had no time to study myself; my heart beat too fast, I was in a fever. Yesterday evening, in settling my fate, you restored tranquillity to my soul, and that night no more spectres came to sit at the head of my bed, but a grave and quiet personage whose face was entirely new to me, and who, to my question as to her name, answered: 'I am your Reason.' Upon which we embraced, and quickly became very good friends."

"You are charming, my dear," said the Count. "Report to me faithfully, I beg of you, what your Reason said to you."

"'Where did you come from?' I asked her first."

"'From a corner of this room,'" she replied.

"'How did you enter?'"

"'By the window in the footsteps of your great friend.' I must tell you sir—"

"Call me father."

"I must tell you, father, that when my great friend came for the first time to visit Stephane, he was escorted by a troop of celestial spirits, of whom one was called Hope, another Health, another Joy ...."

"Another Love," interrupted the Count.

"Thank you for naming him for me. Reason formed the rear guard, and at first, as she told me, she was so frightened by the noise which Love made, and the imperious airs which he put on, that she ran and hid herself in a little corner, to bide her time."

"She is patient, because she is eternal," said M. Leminof. "But tell me, to reinstate herself she certainly made you a long and rather severe speech?"

"Short, but good. She represented to me, that in violation of my dignity and intelligence, I had not feared to say to my great friend, 'If you do not love me, I shall kill myself,' and that in answering 'I love you,' he had treated me as a furious lunatic, whose caprices must be humored to calm him. In short, she spoke so well, and what she said accorded so admirably with her whole person, with her manner, her compassionate looks, her tender melancholy, that I became convinced, and I passed judgment upon myself. I slept badly, and was sad when I awoke; but my reason gave me strength to avail myself of the admirable remedy which my great friend has often recommended to me. I gave occupation to my mind, I set about painting, so earnestly that, touched by my docility, this good personage wished to keep me company, and she came and installed herself at the bottom of the pretty white corolla, whose shape and tint my brush is trying to imitate. She is crouching there with her legs crossed under her, and her hands clasped behind her head, as the little Russian girls sit when they are thinking—those at least whom I have the opportunity of knowing. It is certain that in this posture I thought I saw her, and I said to her, 'Well, speak to me.' But she had discoursed so much during the night, that she gave speech to the little swamp flower, who related to me her story at length. 'I have gained my suit,' said she, 'for I have blossomed, as you see; but nevertheless, like all plaintiffs, what weary waiting have I not endured!"

"She showed me also that these great and rapid acquisitions of happiness which sometimes dazzle men and little Russian girls, are deceptive; that *chi va piano va sano*, and that durable happiness grows little by little, and day by day, as the plants of the woods and the suns themselves. When she had said all this, another voice came from the bottom of the corolla and murmured: 'Gilbert does not love thee yet, but I swear to thee that one day he will love thee.' "

" 'Oh! my dear Reason,' I cried, 'I take you at your word.' "

" And at this moment I felt so tranquil that I was seized with a delightful fit of enthusiasm for your daughter."

" 'You have a strong mind,' said I to myself. 'You have a great character!' And I ran to embrace myself in my mirror."

M. Leminof was charmed, transported, astounded. "I, who had so much dreaded this interview," thought he. "I expected tears, fainting fits, with scratches by way of interlude. She is certainly charming, and Gilbert is a sorcerer."

"You do well to trust in your reason," said he. "Your great friend is a great original; I believe, however, that he is not blind; and you are beautiful, my dear child. To tell the truth, your eyes perhaps are a little heavy, and your cheeks a little thin and pale. Be patient; happiness . . ."

"It is a kind of pallor which does not wear off," interrupted she. "My heart will forget all, but I fear that my face will always remember. After all, what matters it?" added she gayly; "if he finds me too pale, I will put on a little rouge."

"I forbid you," exclaimed the Count, resuming his despotic tone. "Your mother had an insupportable mania for daubing. No rouge pots in my house! for if I must tell you all, my dear, what I like best in you is that very pallor. It will be your stamp; I am not sorry that you have one. . . ."

Stephane made no answer, but rising and clapping her hands, exclaimed:

"Well, then, send me right off to a boarding-school, where I can finish my education. I will learn to walk, to sit, to dress my hair, to move my head gracefully, to handle a fan without breaking it . . . At first I shall appear like a boy in disguise ; but I shall soon change, and in a year I shall no longer be the little man in the black tunic, and he will love me." . . .

"Although in the way of grace you have nothing to learn," replied her father, who had become a model of paternal gallantry, "I will do everything to please you. Then, too, you are very young ; you are but seventeen. That is not winter nor its ice. Besides, you need a change of air, and to put some distance between yourself and this dungeon, these corridors, and the gloomy face of your father."

"I am no longer afraid of you," answered she ; "still I think with you that it will be well for us to remain some time without seeing each other. . . ."

"I am delighted that we agree," said he. "I have always thought that in life, as in writing, it is important to arrange the transitions well."

He rose in his turn, and approached the table upon which the herbarium lay open. He was enchanted to find his daughter so rational, for he appreciated reason in others ; but the good will which he felt that he bore her already, became mingled with respect and admiration when he had cast his eyes over the herbarium. He knew how to appreciate and enjoy talent of all kinds.

"What a discovery I have just made ! " exclaimed he. "What ! my dear child, did you paint these charming pictures ? What delicate tracery, what truthful coloring ! You have the eye and the hand of an artist. Where did you get your talent ? Your mother, whose face yours so strongly resembles, had not a shadow of it. I am much mistaken if she ever painted anything but her face. There is a ranunculus which is a masterpiece. It is nature itself."

He looked at his daughter with almost affectionate eyes. I say almost, for the story which I am relating does not belong to the golden legends ;

then covering the name of the plant at the bottom of the page with his hand, he asked:

"What do you call this brownish flower?"

Stephane laughed.

"My dear sir," said she, "that is the *guaphalium sylvaticum.* That word is derived from the Greek; *guapto* (I card), *guapheus* (carder), *guaphalon* (floss and down). The products of the *guaphals* are cottony. And now would you like to know the family name, its history? You have but to speak. I am ready to satisfy you."

"You carry me from surprise to surprise. Just fancy, I thought you incapable of connecting two ideas! What a monstrous injustice I did you! Ah, then, tell me, was botany one of the celestial spirits that your great friend—"

"It was the first which Gilbert presented to me. I received him at first badly enough; but little by little I discovered that he was delightful society. Gilbert's idea was, that to become well, Stephane should occupy himself with something besides Stephane, and singularly enough, Stephane decided to believe in it."

"He was entirely right. It is a very stupid person who is willing to pass his time in angling in the shallow waters of his own being, and I admire you both infinitely; him for inculcating such wise principles, and you for suffering him to teach them. And God knows how many books he has made you read."

"Ah!" exclaimed she, "let him ask my life, I will give it to him; but to make me read anything but his scrawls, I defy him."

"How is that?" said the Count, astonished. "It seems to me that in your childhood you were a great reader?"

"Learn, then, that for nearly three years I have had an aversion to everything printed."

"And why so?"

"I will tell you frankly; because you liked it too much."

"What ingratitude!" said he. "Just reflect. If I had not adored books, your great friend would have remained in his great Paris, and you, my dear—"

"And I should not be in this world!" interrupted she with a bitter smile.

Then recovering her gayety immediately, she continued: "Yes, that's true, and I'm much obliged to the folios. So the better to testify my respectful gratitude, I will take care not to touch them for fear of wearing them out, and I will extend my tender solicitude to twelvemo's and even down to the thirty-two's.

"I know very well," said the Count, "who has disgusted you with reading; it is father Alexis. That poor father—"

But she interrupted him, exclaiming, as she drew herself up, "say nothing more against the good father. He did a grand thing last evening. He kissed before your eyes the corpse of your enemy, which you were guilty of insulting."

The Count bit the end of his mustache; but in the humor in which she had put him, he could not be offended with the freedom of her language.

"With your queenly attitudes," said he to himself, "with your grand airs, your grand manners, your grand gestures and your home thrusts, you are my own blood—my soul recognizes you."

"Let us go to dinner," said he, offering his arm.

"Will you do me a favor?" she answered, in a caressing tone. "Send me up the wing of a chicken. I do not wish to see my great friend again, until I take leave of him. You can say that I have a headache; but do not speak to him, I beg of you, of my reflections, nor of my projects! I am curious to see what he will say. And besides, if, possibly, he should suddenly begin to love me—"

"I saw him this morning, and I ought not to conceal from you the fact, that he was as calm as a statue."

Stephane breathed a sigh.

"Oh! my dear Reason," said she, "come to my aid!"

"Adieu, my dear child," said her father. "Upon my honor, there is a little Russian girl whose passionate admirer I have become within a quarter of an hour."

"A little affection would suit me better," replied she.

And as he bowed to kiss her hand, she anticipated him, and threw herself in his arms. Luckily her head was bent, and she did not see the air of hesitation, anguish and ferocious repugnance, which suddenly distorted the Count's face. He covered it hastily with his hands, and, seeing nothing but the top of her head and her hair, he murmured:

"It is of a darker shade," and twice touched it with his lips.

As he descended the staircase, he said to himself: "My daughter is very remarkable. Yesterday she made the wretch who threatened her honor cower in the dust by a single glance; to-day she is calm and sensible; does not whine and makes no scenes; she jests, converses rationally and paints. And what a delicate and firm stroke! She has wit, courage, flashing eyes. How we must distrust appearances! That poor Olga had neither talent, good sense, nor character. She was a pretty paroquet, who passed her days in brightening her plumage. And then the hair of the other is decidedly darker."

The next day in the forenoon, Vladimir Paulitch was buried. The Count and Gilbert accompanied the body to its last resting place. When the first shoveful of earth fell upon the coffin, with that dull and hollow sound, which is like the cry of eternity swallowing its prey, the eyes of Count Kostia lighted up and flashed; but he hastily dropped his eyelids over the burning balls, and under an air of gravity and meditation concealed the delirious excitement which throbbed in his breast. The ceremony ended, and having reached the last houses of the village, he begged Gilbert to wait for him and retraced his steps to the cemetery, which the grave diggers were just quitting, and standing motionless on the mound under which Vladimir slept, he remained several moments in contemplation, with crossed arms and a smile on his lips; then he spat upon the earth, and cried in the terrible language of Job:

"The sepulchre is thy house. Make thy bed in darkness. Murderer of Morlof, cry to the grave: 'Thou art my father!' cry to the worms: 'ye are my mother and my sisters!' Thy hopes have descended with thee into the depths of the tomb, and ye will repose together in the dust."

Then slowly leaving the cemetery he rejoined Gilbert, and as they mounted the paved road which led to the castle, he said with good-natured brusqueness, "My dear Gilbert, I hope that you have no prejudices, and that you will see no objection in having some day a few thousands of crowns income. Observe that in giving you my daughter, the obligation is all on my side; I have a very considerable debt to pay her; you alone can discharge it for me. Besides, I thus secure you for myself too. You will never leave me. We will pass our days reading Greek together. That is the only serious thing in life."

"Will you be kind enough," replied Gilbert, "to ask your daughter to come to you? I will answer you in her presence."

When they had entered the Count's study, and Stephane had joined them, Gilbert resumed:

"Count Kostia, reciprocal love is the only valid excuse for a disproportionate union. Now, if I am sure that I love your daughter passionately, shall I dare to say in her presence that I am equally certain of her sentiments for me? Living in solitude and in strict seclusion, she has not chosen me—has not preferred me to any one else. A happy fatality, which I shall always bless, whatever the result may be, has made me her consoler, and if I may be permitted to say it, the instrument of her salvation. Does she not mistake for love the gratitude which my devotion has inspired in her noble heart? Is it certain that when she is restored to liberty, she will not run the risk of meeting some object in the world more worthy of her affection? And ought I not to fear that some day, drawing comparisons terrible for me—Ah! sir, let her consent to make this trial which I dread for myself before plighting her faith to me. Give her opportunities of frequenting and observing society, and let her decide if, among those who will be attracted by her beauty, there may not be one whom she may prefer to her devoted Gilbert. If in a year I shall have gained my suit, and her heart still belongs to me, I will abandon myself without any scruples to the love which I have vowed to her, and my proud happiness will only be equalled by my gratitude."

While Gilbert was speaking, Stephane had exchanged more than one glance with her father.

"Have I not read him well?" said she, rising. "He does not yet love me. I am still to him the little man in the velvet tunic."

Then, as Gilbert attempted to disclaim it:

"Oh, do not be afraid that I shall kill myself," said she; "the time of poisoning and daggers has passed. You man of little faith, who fear to walk upon the waters, I will cure you of your incredulity; but if the physician makes you suffer, blame no one but yourself. You have been rash. You have just offered me a superfluous affront. If, as propriety demands, you had permitted me to speak first, you would have heard me myself ask my father for the postponement of my happiness. I have reflected a great deal within the last twenty-four hours, and I have concluded that before marrying, a girl who respects herself should learn to dance and to courtesy. Gilbert, Gilbert! your precipitation might have been fatal to you. Think of it, you have just offended me, and think, too, that some day you will love me. That is written on high. What would you think if within that time I should write in my turn: 'I am not sure of his affection, let us put it to the proof.' Gilbert, women are vindictive, and you cannot doubt, I think, that the daughter of my father knows what vengeance is. But you need not fear; I am generous. Wait for the next 14th of September in confidence; that day I swear to you there will be celebrated in two hearts a *fête* of which even the angels will be jealous."

At these words she extended her hand to him; but as he attempted to carry it to his lips, she withdrew it quickly, and raising her head proudly, said:

"Don't be in such haste. The day will come, believe me, when you shall kiss it upon your knees and in tears."

Then smiling him an adieu, she darted from the room.

The Count pressed Gilbert's hand.

"You are the most gallant man in the world," said he; "but women are women. You are playing a hazardous game, I forewarn you. Be it at your own risk and peril!"

EPILOGUE, CHAPTER II.

Fragments from Gilbert's Journal.

Paris, September 20th.

Little fountain, little fountain, it was at the entrance of your rustic grotto, it was by the sound of your foaming waters, that destiny traced the first lines of the most remarkable chapter of my life. What do I say? A chapter? Is it not rather a question of an entire life?

September 27.

On arriving in hell, Ulysses sacrificed some sheep and a black ram, and having dug a ditch with his sword, filled it with the flowing blood of his victims. Then from the depths of Erebus, the pale swarm of empty shades gathered and surrounded the hero, vague and floating like dreams, without voice, color, face, memory, as if dispossessed of themselves and deprived of their souls; but when Ulysses had permitted them to lean over the ditch and drink therefrom, life returned to them and words of truth came from their lips.

God has with his own hands placed in the breasts of great men a bloody chalice, and like a good shepherd tending his flocks, he leads the long train of heaven's daughters, ideas invisible, impalpable and immortal, to this divine watering-place. As soon as these phantoms have drunk a few drops of this miraculous blood, they take face and form, and men see with astonishment radiant forms passing among them, who, with fingers pointing to heaven, tell them the secrets of the future.

But if to accomplish such prodigies the heart of a great man is necessary, a virtue less powerful, but similar, is inherent in all noble and sincere hearts. Do we not feel, we, the little ones of this world, at certain times, sighing shades flitting mysteriously about us, demanding to live? Let us hold to their lips this enchanted cup, which we carry in our bosoms; for though but a vase of clay, it is not the less the work of the Supreme artist. After having quenched their thirst, these august mendicants which Heaven sends us will not dazzle the world with their glory, but they will reveal it to the soul of him who has ministered to their wants. . . .

Daughters of heaven, Oh my adored phantoms, you whom once I called by a familiar name which I shall give you no more, one day, pure doves, one day you came flocking around the still full cup of my heart, and drank long draughts of life. And now when I am alone, and talking to myself, there are voices which answer me. . . .

October 1st.

Upon leaving father Alexis, I said to him: "Father, to my knowledge you have worked two miracles which I admire infinitely. Once they put you to the torture to make you speak, but you did not speak. At another time, under the eyes of a man whose anger you had reason to fear, you embraced his most bitter enemy, who had just expired in convulsions. At that moment the unhappy man had still a breath of life; he felt your lips press his, and a mysterious serenity suddenly spread itself over his face. My father, these are two well authenticated miracles. As to the others . . ."

October 30th.

She is at Munich, not in a boarding-school, but with a friend of her father's, the Baroness de N——. She is living, she says, in a whirlwind to which she finds it difficult to become accustomed.

November 3d.

I work a great deal, but am not without diversion. Oh! how often it happens that I forget Byzantium, my scribblings and my ink! The vision always before me, is an old castle built upon a rock, great sombre woods, a precipice, a little fountain, steep roofs, gables, chimneys, weather-cocks, and a flood of silvery waves sparkling in the light of the stars. And in the midst of all this, there passes and repasses before me a little black tunic which plays various parts in my dreams. Sometimes it is a little boy in a wild wood, with a cold and haughty eye, galloping upon a chestnut horse, and cutting the air with his whip; then all at once I see a poor child, pale with grief, who sits at my feet and rests his head upon my knees. Presently the child, raising himself, changes into an impetuous young girl, with flaming eyes, flashing a knife in the air. And finally I see her, as she appeared to me a few moments before my departure. "Ah, you see!" she said to her father, "he does not love me yet."—No, it was no longer *he*, it was a woman who spoke.

January 3d.

In her last letter, she informed me that she had already broken three fans. The other day she had an attack of ill humor. "Ah! if I had had that switch which you are acquainted with in my hand."

January 15.

She has attended a Court ball, and was much amused. "I felt that I was pretty, and compliments were not lacking." Gilbert, to-day you know what jealousy is.

April 16th.

Love! love! I have never known it until this morning! At eleven o'clock a package was brought to me. My hands trembled in opening it. The package enclosed a medallion, the medallion enclosed a portrait. At the bottom of the portrait were written these words: "*New episode in the metamorphosis of a lily.*" What a sudden emotion shook my heart! Yes, it is she, it is really she! her hair, her eyes, her mouth, I recognize everything but the white satin dress. But I should never have imagined her so beautiful! Happiness has put the last touch to her charms, and the veil which shadowed her face has fallen forever. Thou art mine, thou belongest to me, thou art my property, thou art my jewel, my crown! And it is right, for thou art my work, my creation. It was I who breathed into thy heart the fire of life; it was I who resuscitated the dead smile; it was I who opened thine eyes to see heaven; but in spite of my rights, am I worthy to possess thee? I passed three hours wandering in the least frequented paths of the woods. Nearly overcome with my happiness, I stumbled along with a tottering step, as one sick with joy; a golden mist floated before my eyes, and my thoughts lost themselves in the vague kingdom of folly.

July 30.

It is nearly a month since she has written to me. My God! what has happened?

August 9.

I have just received this note: "Gilbert, swear to me, whatever may happen, that I can rely upon your friendship. If you do not assure me of this, I shall be the most unhappy of women." I answered, "Yes, I swear it to you in tears."

August 17.

Here is her answer: "I thank you for your promise; I thank you also for your tears; but time will dry them. Wait a few days and you shall know all."

August 21.

Of what can I accuse her? Did I not myself release her from the pledge she had given me? Was I playing a comedy? Alas! I foresaw what has happened, and it was for that I insisted on proving her heart. The result condemns our love; but where is her crime, her perfidy?

September 10.

I am a prey to weakness, to dejection so profound, that it seems as though life were leaving me.

September 13.

Yesterday I found among the rubbish a plant of the deadly nightshade. It is my turn, thought I, to regard this sad flower with complacency, and to wish that its poison were distilled into my blood. But no, I shall live, I shall bear my sorrow with fortitude; I will preserve my dignity and consummate the work of my devotion. When I see her again, I will cover my face so carefully with the mask of friendship, that it will be impossible for her to penetrate it. I will hide my tears, and see her happiness with a smile upon my lips; not a complaint, not a murmur, not a sigh shall escape from my breast to trouble the serenity of my conscience.

September 14—Morning.

I fear that I shall not have the strength to live. Gilbert, recall thy reason which is deserting thee.

Same day—Midnight.

Oh! cruel one! it was a trial then, a vengeance! When the door opened and I saw her, I fell upon my knees. She approached me slowly. "I swore to make you a little crazy;" and still advancing, she extended a little white hand, which I moistened with my tears. "Upon your knees and weeping," said she, in a low voice, adding in a still lower tone: "I upon my knees, you standing, then the world was upside down; that had to be changed." And I felt her lips press my forehead. At this moment, the Count entered. "My dear Gilbert, said he, I congratulate you: upon my word you're a lucky fellow!"

EPILOGUE, CHAPTER III.

After spending a winter at Geierfels, they all left for Constantinople. The history of the Byzantine Empire should be written on the spot. This year they passed the fine season at Menemen, upon the borders of the Hermus, a few leagues from Smyrna, at a charming house which a Greek banker of their acquaintance had put at their disposal. At the time I write, they had just returned from Pera; next year they intend to visit Persia. Stephane is of the opinion that they will move on even to Cabul. Why not to Thibet? We shall see if we live!

Ivan has been emancipated, and he has taken what God has sent him; but he has firmly decided to end his days with his former *bârine*. Father Alexis still preserves all of his teeth and makes good use of them. Is it necessary to add that he still paints with all his might? Lately he decorated the modest Greek church of Menemen with apocalyptic figures. His happiness is not unclouded however; he fears that the immortal frescoes at Geierfels will be injured by the dampness and frost; so he proposes to go there and restore them, before long. Count Kostia is better, but is obliged to keep himself constantly occupied. In his mania for work he sometimes wearies his son-in-law. The history of the Byzantine Empire is well under way; the first volume is in press; a hint to the critics! Kostia Petrovitch also takes a great deal of bodily exercise. As soon as he feels his dark moods approaching, he averts them by excessive fatigue. He invariably treats his daughter with irreproachable courtesy; but all his affection is bestowed upon the little Kostia who made his entrance into the world about ten months since, and whose Mentor he flatters himself he shall some day be. Meanwhile he fondles and coddles him, and spoils him with indulgence. By a freak of nature the child is the image of his grandfather. He was born with prominent cheek bones, and a heavy pair of eyebrows, which grow thicker day by day. This is a certificate of great value to him.

Stephane still holds printed matter in holy horror; it is a malady of which she will not be cured. In recompense, she tenderly loves her beautiful herbarium which wins the admiration of connoisseurs, and which she proposes to enrich with all the plants of Cabul. Gilbert often makes his puppets play before his wife. One evening when this exhibition had filled her with delight, she repeated to him with fervor, the last verse of the poem of the *Metamorphosis:*

"Let this day be dear to us! To the flower succeeds the fruit: Sacred love begets in us such unity of sentiments and thoughts, that blended in harmonious contemplation, our two souls together discover the celestial country!"

However plants blossom and fructify in vain, they do not renounce their leaves and their roots. Last spring, Count Kostia and his son-in-law made an excursion to Pergamos, and on leaving promised to return to Menemen the fourth day, during the forenoon; but in a country where there are no roads, it is difficult to be prompt in keeping engagements and the travellers were delayed. Stephane became anxious, tormented herself, dreamed of brigands and precipices; she spoke harshly to father Alexis who tried to console her, and threatened to box poor Ivan for repeating a Russian proverb on patience. Finally, beside herself, she ordered her horse, and when Gilbert arrived towards noon, he found that she had left upon a full gallop to seek him, and that she had gone into lonely and suspected regions, with no protector save an ugly pocket pistol. He scolded her for her folly, as was natural. She became angry, went off in a transport of rage, stamped her foot and ran away to her room where she locked herself in; but after twenty minutes she came out again with a serene face, and it was all over.

Some hours later, a little before sunset, she might have been seen sitting on the veranda which extended across the front of the house. She wore a flowing oriental dress, of a pistachio color, ornamented with gold embroidery and laces. Her waist, slender and supple as a reed, was girdled by a scarf of amaranth crape, with floating ends and long fringe. Her delicate feet were encased in Turkish slippers. A necklace of pearls encircled her snow white throat. She changed the arrangement of her hair every day. This evening it was raised like a crown above the forehead. In one hand she held a fan, in the other a switch. In this world one cannot take too many precautions. Thus see her reclining in the corner of a sofa with the fantastic grace of a pretty Angora cat. At her feet, two little goats were lying, one of a reddish brown color, and the other silver grey; goats such as are seen only in sunny climes. At the right a cradle and a sleeping infant. Before her eyes a beautiful flower garden. Beyond the garden a Turkish cemetery planted with cypress and cedars, from which came the soft cooing of turtle doves. The sky was bright blue in the zenith, and nearly green at the horizon.

Stephane called Ivan, who was raking a path.

"Give him a glass of rakie to console him! Fill it to the brim!" said she to father Alexis. I was a little hasty this morning. Alas! my poor Ivan, perhaps not for the last time."

At this moment perceiving Gilbert:

"Come here, quick!" cried she to him. "Sit down by me. I have a story to tell you. It will be as new as it is interesting."

And then, when he seated himself, she continued, fluttering her fan:

"Imagine, that once upon a time, in one of the turrets of an old castle, there lived a poor child who was persecuted by a barbarous tyrant. He was very sad, so sad that he was in danger of dying or going mad. Luckily an amiable and valiant chevalier arrived at the castle; one of those polished chevaliers who know botany, Greek, and the language of puppets. This chevalier was compassionate, and took pity on the child. He was brave, and risked his life to penetrate into the dungeon where the little captive languished. He was wise, and made him partake of a little of his wisdom. He had coolness and address, and twice saved his life. Thus it came to pass that the poor child did not die, and that I am to-day the happiest woman in the universe. What do you say? Isn't my story a pretty one?"

"Oh, how badly reasoned!" exclaimed father

Alexis, who sat a few steps off peaceably smoking his narghilé and sipping a glass of excellent wine. "You have a superficial mind, my dear daughter, and only discern secondary causes. You should say that in that castle where this poor child vegetated, there was a good soul of a priest who knew how to paint; and who, in this barbarous age, was the only one to represent the sound traditions of his great art. And this fine old priest made a contract with the mother of God, and when he had painted in fresco the great white walls of a chapel, he took the liberty of saying to her:

"'I have kept my word. Will you not keep yours?'"

And immediately a miracle was wrought, and the chains of the poor child were broken. This was not all: it happened that this child was a young girl, and she was loved by a young man whom she was to marry after a year's separation. The old priest, who had lived long enough to sorely distrust women, took a notion to send our young girl a little picture which he had painted, two hearts pierced by an arrow, and said to her:

"My daughter, wear this medallion about your neck, look at it every morning and evening. It is an amulet which will keep you faithful to your first love." She took the medallion, and thus it is, that we are to-day the most fortunate mortals on earth; smoking excellent tobacco, drinking Cyprus wine—without cares, without sorrows, and chatting cosily in a pretty garden and under a beautiful sky, which is blue above and green below."

Meantime Count Kostia made his appearance with a pruning-hook in his hand, and hearing father Alexis' peroration:

"That is very well said, Signor Pangloss," he exclaimed, pulling him by the beard; "but we must cultivate the garden."

"And painting," replied the good father, without stirring.

"And our reason," murmured Gilbert, gazing in the eyes of his wife.

"I agree to it," replied she, "upon one condition, "that is, that we shall always believe in the folly of friendship."

And springing with a bound from the sofa, she cried with the tragic air of old times:

"Oh, my dear folly. I shall kill myself the day I cease to hear your charming bells!"

Saying which, she made a little pirouette, poised upon the tip of her right foot. The little startled goats answered her by shaking their little bells, and in the shadow of the cradle two great eyes opened in fright.

Friendly reader, I have reason to believe that she never killed herself, and I delight in the conviction. I have never relished the proverb which says that "the shortest follies are the best." Some are divine; the point is to choose.

THE END.

www.ingramcontent.com/pod-product-compliance
Lightning Source LLC
LaVergne TN
LVHW020232110826
845151LV00003B/901

* 9 7 8 1 4 2 5 5 3 0 6 7 9 *